THE PACT

Carol Coffey

POOLBEG
CRIMSON

This book is a work of fiction. The names, characters, places, businesses, organisations and incidents portrayed in it are either the product of the author's imagination or are used fictitiously. Any resemblance to actual persons, living or dead, events or locales is entirely coincidental.

Published 2018 by Crimson
an imprint of Poolbeg Press Ltd
123 Grange Hill, Baldoyle
Dublin 13, Ireland
www.poolbeg.com

© Carol Coffey 2018

Copyright for editing, typesetting, layout, design, ebook
© Poolbeg Press Ltd

The moral right of the author has been asserted.

A catalogue record for this book is available from the British Library.

ISBN 978-1-78199-8199

All rights reserved. No part of this publication may be reproduced or transmitted in any form or by any means, electronic or mechanical, including photography, recording, or any information storage or retrieval system, without permission in writing from the publisher. The book is sold subject to the condition that it shall not, by way of trade or otherwise, be lent, resold or otherwise circulated without the publisher's prior consent in any form of binding or cover other than that in which it is published and without a similar condition, including this condition, being imposed on the subsequent purchaser.

www.facebook.com/poolbegpress
@PoolbegBooks

Printed and bound by CPI Group (UK) Ltd, Croydon, CR0 4YY

www.poolbeg.com

About the author

Carol was born in Dublin but now lives in Wicklow. A teacher by profession, she has worked in the area of special education for over thirty years.

Carol has used her extensive background in disabilities to bring the world of special needs to the wider population through her writing.

She has written four acclaimed previous novels. Her debut, *The Butterfly State*, centres around a young girl whose communication difficulties caused by autism result in her incarceration in a psychiatric institution for disturbed children. *The Penance Room* is set in Australia where the author lived for over ten years, and provides an insight into the impact of deafness and its resultant isolation on the emotional well-being of a child. *Winter Flowers* explores the impact of generational dysfunction on the development of children, and *The Incredible Life of Jonathan Doe*, set in America, delves into our perception of identity, about finding out who we are and where we truly belong.

The Pact introduces her readers to a new character, Sergeant Locklear, a Native American cop whose battle with his own demons is matched by the strange and complex cases he faces working for the Richmond P.D.

**Also by Carol Coffey
published by Poolbeg**

The Butterfly State
The Penance Room
The Incredible Life of Jonathan Doe
Winter Flowers

Acknowledgements

Thanks to all of the staff of Poolbeg Press for their support for my writing over the years. Particular thanks to Paula Campbell for her ongoing commitment and encouragement. Thanks also to David Prendergast and Caroline Maloney. Finally, a very special thank you to Gaye Shortland for her very hard work, patience and good humour during the editing process!

For my grandmother
Cecilia Coffey

Chapter 1

The 5 a.m. call from Lieutenant Alex Kowalski had woken Locklear from a fitful night's rest. For two weeks since his enforced vacation, the kind of sleep he was accustomed to had eluded him, nights of deep exhaustion when he would sleep soundly and escape the horrors of his waking hours. For it was by day that visions of the murdered – faces of men, women and children – haunted him until the perpetrators were caught and he sentenced the victims to the watery grey grave of his tormented mind. He was known in the department as a detective without a life, who spent what time remained to him trying to solve why others lost theirs and who had taken it from them. It was a life that even now, only a few years from retirement, he knew he did not consciously choose. In his drinking days, when his thoughts were ironically clearer, he believed that this life had chosen him. This life of structure, routine, of method – things he had not known in his youth spent travelling the country with his Native American, mentally fragile mother and her array of badly chosen boyfriends.

As he lay there he went over the information his boss had given him. He had worked under Alex Kowalski for almost thirty years and considered the man as near to a friend as he would ever want, or need. A Mennonite youth named Andrew Fehr had been found hanging in a disused barn on an abandoned farm, barely hanging on to life, Kowalski had said, apologising quickly for the pun that Locklear did not get. The small, tightly knit religious community would not comply with the local police, not even the local pastor who had miraculously found the young man struggling on a rope. The rafters were too high to climb without a ladder so a suicide attempt had been ruled out. There were fresh tyre tracks in the barn and on the dry dirt road leading to town so the boy had not been alone, at least not until he was strung up and left to die. The trooper, a man named Carter who would link up with him when he arrived, said the boy had some kind of mental disability and that the paramedics had said it would be a miracle if he survived, but if he did it was likely that the damage to his brain would mean he would be unable to say what had happened. Locklear felt that this was why Kowalski had chosen him for the case. He usually only dealt with homicides and the young man, at least for now, was still alive, but Kowalski had a good nose and knew this would suit him. He didn't relish the idea of seeing or speaking to a living victim but the boy's brain, he figured, was as good as mush so he was no better than a corpse. He preferred his cases cold, preferred to follow his own leads, preferred when there were no emotions to deal with and he could work on the hard facts.

Locklear lifted himself off his bed and took a cold shower. The July sun was already blazing through the windows of his apartment. He had lived in the tiny one-bed almost as long as he had worked for the Richmond P.D. It suited his needs in this life which were few.

After a brief tour of duty in the army, he had joined the police in South Dakota where he had been born and where his mother, in the throes of dementia despite her middle age, was seeing out the last of her days in a haze of confusion. He stayed to be near to her but found himself unable to visit, unable to see her in that condition. She did not know him and he had never known her. When she died he could find no reason to remain in South Dakota – he had no other family, least none that he knew of, so he wandered around from state to state, much like his mother and he had done together, until his money ran out, forcing him to take a post in New York in narcotics. The work of the division frustrated him – hours spent investigating small-time drug-addicted mules, while their bosses who hid behind legitimate businesses in uptown addresses, walked free. As each year passed, Locklear felt that he was dying inside, a slow death caused by inexplicable rage against an enemy he could not see. It was during these years that his heavy drinking began – initially as a way of finding sleep from the tormented thoughts that filled his every waking moment. Soon, his days were lost in a haze of legal bureaucracy and his long nights in drunken stupors. Four torturous years later, a chance opportunity to work on the murder of a narcotic crime lord had whet his appetite for homicide and he finally found his passion, his home. So, with an ease he did not think possible, he put the bottle away and bided his time.

When a job in homicide came up in Virginia, he did not even think about the upset of relocating on his life. He didn't have very much to move.

It was almost seven by the time he took to the road for the three-hour drive to Dayton, a tiny farming village of Mennonites. Irene, his station's secretary, had booked him into a hotel in the nearby town of Harrisonburg where he would pick up local trooper Carter and take a look at the site. His most recent trooper had thrown in the towel and had asked for an assignment as far away from his fractious superior as possible. The trooper had lasted five months – a record as far as Locklear was concerned.

As he drove along Route 64 he went over the details he knew so far. He knew from previous cases that it took no more than six minutes for a person to die from hanging so the chance arrival of the local pastor was suspicious and not miraculous. He reasoned that the pastor must have been present when the crime was taking place – but why string the boy up and then save him? And if he wasn't in the actual barn, if he was watching from nearby, why let the person commit the crime? Why not stop it? At the junction on 64, he took a right onto the 81 and thought about the victim. Why would someone harm a mentally deficient youth, especially in a religious community? The idea that the perpetrator was unknown to the youth, that the crime was committed by a stranger, was out of the question. Someone had put time and thought into the crime – and emotion – possibly hate – but why? Why not shoot the youth? It was quicker so there was less chance of getting caught. Unless the killer, or would-be killer knew that even if he – or she – was seen, no one in the community would tell.

As he pulled up in front of the large police station, he already knew that this was going to be a frustrating case where nothing made sense and clues led nowhere ... for now. As he pulled back the door into the reception area, he knew immediately that the trooper sitting at the desk farthest from the door was Trooper Carter. Even from a sitting position, Locklear could see that the trooper was tall and lean – an ex local-team baseball hero, now retired and no doubt teaching junior league on Saturday mornings to a brood of kids.

Locklear waited while Carter, who had his back to him, threw a small ball back and forth against the wall while he talked on the phone.

"Sure did ... poor kid was almost dead ..."

Locklear flashed his ID at the man on the desk and then stood silently as Carter revelled in what was probably the most exciting thing to happen around there in a hundred years.

"Yeah ... I did an examination of the scene myself ... got the big boys coming down from the city to tell us how it's done and do what we did all over again."

Locklear coughed.

"Yes ... sir ... can I help you?" Carter spluttered, standing to attention.

Locklear had seen hundreds like Carter over the years. Not-too-bright troopers good at the local police stuff but useless as shit when it came down to serious crime.

"Hope so ... I'm one of the big boys come down to tell you how it's done."

Carter blushed. "Ah, I was just kidding – that was my wife Virginia – she's chuffed I'm working on this – telling her friends and that – so I was just ..."

Locklear took a better look at the man who would be his partner in this investigation. He guessed Carter to be around thirty years of age, yet there was more innocence to his bright blue eyes and thick fair hair than a man of his years had a right to. Despite his height, Carter looked like a boy in a police uniform.

"Your wife's name is Virginia? Seriously?"

Carter blushed some more. "Yeah, her folks are immigrants. Loved the place when they got here and I guess they wanted to show their appreciation of this fine state, you know?"

Locklear nodded at his genial partner, although he didn't know. He rarely understood what ordinary people did in ordinary circumstances.

Carter looked the tough-looking plainclothes detective up and down, trying to make out where he was from. He hadn't said enough to place an accent but he wasn't from around here, that was for sure, so he already knew there'd be trouble. People here didn't take too kindly to strangers poking their noses into things they didn't rightly understand. But the face told a lot. The criss-cross of fine broken veins across his bulbous nose told a story of drinking, past behaviour by the look of things. His dark-brown eyes did not match the pale colouring of his face. He could tell Locklear had once been a handsome man before the ravages of drink set in. The detective had high, hollow cheekbones and a strong jaw line. A furrowed brow told of a man who had spent many years outdoors but his hair was the most interesting, thick and straight, a little on the long side for a police officer and still jet-black for a man of advancing years, suggesting some mixed blood – Native American he would have guessed but mixed up with enough white people to have given him skin no darker than what came naturally from too many years in the sun.

"Well, trooper, are you going to stare at me all day or are we going to Dayton?"

"Guess we're going to Dayton, sir." Carter had seen enough. For the next few weeks, or months, depending on how drawn-out the investigation was, he would be second fiddle to a possibly half-Indian ex-alcoholic who already had him pegged as an idiot country bumpkin cop.

The town of Dayton, which lay just over five miles away, had clearly become an extension of Harrisonburg as the larger town sprawled towards the pretty village. Only a small green belt divided the two towns but the change in landscape during the twelve-minute journey was obvious. Large, middle-class houses gave way to worn-down clapboards. Fast-food joints and express coffee houses disappeared and were replaced by fields dotted with cattle and sheep, milking parlours and an air of poverty. Carter had insisted, albeit politely, that the pair travel in his police car which the locals of Dayton would recognise.

After a brief ride along the John Wayland Highway, Carter turned right onto Mason Street and right again into the parking lot of an impressive faux-Georgian building which seemed at odds with the dilapidated houses that surrounded it. The two-storey building of bright brick was adorned with five marble pillars and large-paned windows that gave a stately, almost regal look to the rural police station.

"What are we doing here?"

Carter shrugged. "This is where your incident room will be."

"I know that! I meant what are we doing here *now*? I've got to take a look at the goddamn site! *Now!*"

Carter did not move. He stared hard at the sergeant as the broad smile slowly drained from his face. "Sir, you ought not to take the Lord's name in vain – especially around here." He sat a while longer, unease rising through his lean body. His fingers twitched around the bulk of keys hanging from the ignition but he did not turn the key.

Locklear watched as each muscle in the trooper's jaw jumped.

"What is it?" he asked, almost shouting without meaning to.

"You'll see," Carter replied quietly, turning the patrol car slowly right onto Mason Street and out of town.

As they neared the site, Locklear sat bolt upright in his seat. "Jesus!"

Carter stopped the car and lowered his head as though he was looking for something on his lap.

The barn and the entrance leading to it, which was the scene of the crime and Locklear's only real hope of figuring out what had happened, was occupied by about fifty people, each stomping over the evidence that he needed to see. The police tape which cordoned off the area had been torn down and two small Mennonite boys were using it as a tug-of-war rope.

Locklear opened the door of the car and was greeted by singing, the soft hum of the voices of Mennonite women spread through the small group. The men stood silently, nodding, their heads bowed and their lips moving without sound. The crowd did not look entirely as Locklear had expected them to. Some of the women were, as he knew was customary, dressed in long, plain grey dresses and white lace bonnets and the men were dressed in black waist-coated suits and white shirts, but most of the people present were dressed in plain clothing, ordinary clothes which were no different to what would be worn in any farming community.

At the entrance to the barn an old Mennonite man of around eighty, in traditional dress, sat in his horse-drawn black carriage, the only buggy to be seen among the pickups and station wagons parked haphazardly around the lot. Locklear noted the body language of the man. He was the only one who did not appear to be praying and his stone-like facial expression gave him the air of a man who did not want to be there.

Locklear moved his gaze to the centre of the crowd, none of whom had taken notice of his arrival. The man holding the Bible looked like just about every preacher he had seen on television, clean cut and freshly shaven with the bright clear eyes of a clean-living man. Dressed in modern clothes, the middle-aged preacher stood around six five with a shock of thick, blond hair. He looked up briefly from the tome and smiled broadly at the visiting policeman before returning to his prayers which Locklear noted were in what sounded like German. Low German it was called, he remembered.

Locklear, aware that he was being ignored, suddenly exploded. *"God dammit!"*

Carter rushed from the car, grabbing him by the arm.

"Sir, be careful not to upset sensibilities here. They mean no harm. Praying is all they're doing."

"Praying all over my goddamn crime scene!" Locklear spat as he marched closer to the crowd.

"They don't see it that way. They answer to no one but the Lord."

Locklear swung round and glared at Carter. "Are you one of them? Are you?"

Carter looked to the ground. "No, sir. I'm Baptist but ..."

"Well, then do your fucking job and help me get these people off my crime scene."

Locklear's language finally roused the attention of the congregation. He looked towards the now hushed crowd which parted without fuss, freeing the path of the preacher.

Locklear could feel himself tense a little. He had no experience interviewing so-called holy men and did not know what the correct protocol should be.

The preacher threw out his right hand.

"*Willkamen*," he said.

Locklear searched for insincerity in that one word but found none. He didn't take the outstretched hand.

"*Snackst de Platt*?" the pastor asked.

Carter moved forward and shook his head. "English, Pastor Plett."

"I'm Pastor Plett – Henry – and this is my wife, Rachel."

Locklear watched as a small dumpy woman, dressed in a long grey dress and a white bonnet covering her blonde hair, moved forward, smiling as she walked through the crowd of worried faces.

"Welcome," she echoed. "You've come from Richmond. We've heard of your arrival. Please come to our house after prayers for sustenance."

Locklear thought for a moment. "Heard of my arrival. From whom?"

Rachel Plett now looked as worried as her husband's small congregation. She glanced nervously over Locklear's shoulder at Carter who had not taken his eyes from the dusty ground, now trampled by fifty pairs of uninvited feet.

"Pastor," Locklear began as gently as his angry mood would allow, "this is a crime scene. None of these people should be here. I need everyone gone *right now* so I can find out what happened here."

Henry Plett's face darkened. "Your name, sir?"

"Sergeant Locklear."

The pastor seemed to hesitate, then said, "Your Christian name?"

Locklear grimaced. He never told anyone his first name. It resulted in too many questions. Only Kowalski knew it and he was not likely to repeat it.

"I am not a Christian," Locklear replied defiantly, hoping to put an end to the probing.

Quiet murmurs grew up from the crowd but the sound he heard loudest was the groan emitted from Carter's mouth.

"Mr Locklear, we are here to pray for young Andrew. He is much loved in our community."

"Then let me do my job. Let me find out who tried to kill him and get off this godd–" He stopped before using his favourite curse word. "Please leave so I can do my job."

Pastor Plett looked at his congregation and beckoned for them to leave. Slowly, men, women and children, even the very young ones, filed silently past him, most with eyes fixed on the ground. An occasional woman glanced at Locklear nervously.

When the last of the crowd had driven off the dusty lot, Locklear surveyed the ground. Scores of tyre tracks crisscrossed the ground around the barn and on the roadway that led into the farmyard, making it impossible for him to figure out the type of car that was present when Andrew Fehr was hanged.

He hunkered down and spread his fingers across the dry earth. Lifting a small piece of soil, he smelt it and held it in his hands. He was never sure why he did this. It was instinctive. It was in his blood. Each time he did this something stirred in him. He loved the earth, the soil, and if his work didn't keep him in cities it would be here, in nature, that he would live and breathe. But there weren't enough murders in the countryside to keep him alive and so he lived among tall buildings and concreted ground where soil was absent and the only trees he saw were plastic offerings in the entrances of foyers.

He stood and walked towards the barn and through its open, weathered wooden doors. Inside, bales of mouldering hay lined its sides. He could hear the quiet footsteps of a nervous Carter behind him. He looked up at the long beam that ran across the middle of the large barn. There was nothing that the boy could have used to climb on, not even the hay which was little more than dust, obviously forgotten by whoever had packed it there.

"I took photos of the tyre tracks and of the rope," Carter said. "They're with forensics in Harrisonburg."

Locklear did not reply. It didn't look like he was going to be able to trust Carter and he had already decided to ask Kowalski to send another outsider to help with the investigation.

"You think that boy climbed up here and tried to hang himself?"

"No, sir," Carter replied quietly.

"Then ... what *do* you think happened?"

Carter stared blankly at Locklear. "I don't rightly know, sir."

"Yep, I was afraid you were going to say that, Carter."

"Why?"

Locklear ignored the question and made his way out of the barn to take in the vista. The abandoned farm was more rundown than he had imagined it would be. A small, dilapidated farmhouse faced the barn, its back to the road, giving the area a sense of old-world isolation. There was no glass in any of the windows and the front door was missing. A torn fly-screen screeched eerily in the wind as it moved backward and forward on its rusted hinges. The farm was situated on a high hill and as far as the eye could see the soil was parched and lifeless, sheltering only a few tufts of dry patchy grass. Locklear scanned further and noticed a small holding set on lower land adjacent to the farm. Its grass was a deep green and fat milking cows grazed in the lush pasture. A tiny house could just about be seen as the land dipped steeply away. It was a simple scene but even in the distance the neighbour's farm appeared to be well kept compared to the wasteland on which he stood. What, he wondered, could make two adjoining farms look so very different?

"Who owns this farm?"

"It belongs to the Fehrs."

"Why aren't they farming it?"

Carter shrugged.

Locklear grunted. For a man who was teamed up with him to supply local knowledge, Carter seemed, or pretended, to know very little. Locklear threw down the soil he was still holding and, as he moved back towards the car, he noticed a tall man standing in the dried-out scrub at the entrance to the farm. A brown-felt cowboy-type hat was pulled down, shielding his eyes. From the clothes he wore Locklear could tell the man was young – light-brown boots over dark-blue jeans and blue-check shirt. As they passed he made no attempt to move and even Carter, who seemed so at ease with the unusual community, visibly tensed.

"Who was that?"

"Luke Fehr," he answered quietly.

"A relative?"

"The victim's older brother."

"Gotta talk to him," Locklear said, looking back into the scrub for the man but he had already disappeared from view.

"Oh, he won't talk to you, sir. Luke Fehr doesn't talk to anyone."

Chapter 2

The short ride back to Harrisonburg was an uncomfortable one as Locklear had anticipated it would be. Lee Carter sulked silently, annoyed obviously that Locklear would not follow his lead in how to engage with the religious group. Locklear categorised the questions he needed answers to before they reached Harrisonburg's hospital where Andrew Fehr had not yet regained consciousness.

"The old guy, the one who sat in his buggy. Who was he?"

Carter sniffed a little, anxious to show some sign that he was displeased with earlier events.

"That's Samuel Shank – he's an elder at the church."

"Why didn't he join in with the praying?"

Carter shrugged. "His wife's a distant cousin of the Fehrs – I think there's no love lost between the two families but I guess he had to show his face for his wife's sake. Ellie Shank is a sweet lady. And ..."

Locklear tensed at the pause. Carter was probably one of the most unusual men he'd been partnered with and was definitely the most annoying, which was saying something given the cretins he'd worked with during his years in New York.

"The Fehrs are shunned. He probably didn't feel they deserved prayers as they're no longer members of the congregation."

"Shunned? Jesus, this is the 21st century!"

Carter grimaced again at Locklear's language but said nothing.

"It's rare to hear of shunning now. It happened generations ago. My dad said it was just after the Civil War. I don't know the whys of it. These people keep things like that private."

Locklear tried to absorb this. "So, then, the Fehrs are *not* Mennonites?"

Carter seemed to need time to respond to this.

"I guess they still are but if they choose to attend church they're not allowed to receive communion. Congregations tend to adhere to the rules in various levels of strictness. In some cases, shunned people can't eat with other Mennonites or do business with them."

"So ... it's permanent, this shunning? There's no way a new pastor can overrule it? Let a person rejoin?"

"I don't know. I don't suppose it upsets Luke Fehr too much – and the other Fehr kids will just follow his lead anyway."

"So, they're outcasts who still live in a place they are not welcome?"

"I guess."

"Then why not leave?"

"And go where? This is the only life they understand. They're poor people without trades or any qualifications. What would they do outside of here?"

Locklear nodded. "Well, why the prayers then? Why the pastor?"

"Pastor Plett is a good man and the people here, they're good people."

"So you don't think that was an attempt to ruin my crime scene?"

"No way, sarge. It wouldn't occur to these people to do that – even if they had something to hide. They lead good, innocent lives. Though people don't like Luke much, everyone here feels sorry for the Fehrs. They've had real hard times and tragedy. Not one person feels any badness towards them –"

"Except the person who tried to hang Andrew," Locklear retorted.

Locklear thought about the crowd he witnessed earlier. The people did look genuinely sorry but they also looked afraid. Everyone, that is, except Samuel Shank.

"Tell me more about Shank. Why was he in traditional dress while most of the others weren't?"

Carter smiled again, his sulk slowly thawing at the prospect of his local knowledge being used in this investigation as he felt it had been intended.

"He's Old Order, most of the Shank family are."

"As opposed to?"

"Well ... new order, I guess, but they don't call themselves that. They're just known as Mennonites mostly."

"What's the difference? The Old can't drive cars, use computers, that sort of stuff?"

Carter shook his head. "No, you're thinking of the Amish community. A few hundred years back they were all one but the Amish came into being when a small group broke away because they didn't feel the followers were adhering strictly enough to the religion. Some Old Order Mennonites still live a strict life but most of these folk drive cars, use technology and have careers. Most stick to farming, though, to keep their families working together and away from people who don't share their beliefs."

"Which are?"

"Well, lots of things. They get baptized as adults for a start – something I personally think is a good thing. They believe it is up to a person to decide if they want to follow a life devoted to God when they're old enough to make that choice. And, they are pacifists, another thing I admire about them."

"You serve in the army, son?"

"No, sir."

"Well, if you had, you'd know that sometimes wars need to be fought to make peace."

"Or maybe I'd return from war thinking the opposite?" Carter retorted, bringing back the unease again to the stifling hot car.

Rockingham Memorial Hospital in Harrisonburg was no different from any other hospital Locklear had ever been to, except on a smaller scale. The four-storey redbrick building looked modern enough and had the air of generalised chaos he'd experienced in any US hospital.

In the main foyer they waited patiently for a Dr Bosch to take them to see the victim. The doctor, when he finally arrived, looked exhausted and couldn't hide his irritation at being called off his rounds to talk to more policemen. When he finally brought them to the foot of Andrew Fehr's bed, Locklear felt an immediate and inexplicable surge of pity for the boy who lay in front of him.

Andrew Fehr was small and skinny for his age. He had mousy-brown, thin hair and a face as pale as the sheet which lay over him. A large red-raw mark was visible on his thin neck and his eyelids were covered in small red dots. Locklear remembered the name of the Tardieu's markings common on the skin of survivors of hangings. The boy was intubated which Locklear knew was not a good sign.

"He's not breathing on his own?"

Bosch lifted the chart hanging on the end of the bed and studied the latest notes.

"He has pneumonia. We'll remove the tube in a couple of days and see how he does."

"Will he survive?" Locklear asked.

"It's too soon to tell." Bosch yawned.

"But your guess is?"

Bosch pursed his lips in disgust. "Doctors do not guess, sergeant. But for a boy who is very underweight he's putting up a fight. Imaging shows he has no spinal-cord injury but there's extensive soft-tissue injury as well as damage to his larynx. His speech might be affected. He was deprived of oxygen as is the case with many survivors of attempted suicide by hanging."

"It wasn't suicide," Locklear interjected swiftly.

The doctor's eyes widened in surprise.

Locklear noticed Carter remained completely silent and, apart from a brief initial look at the boy, had fixed his eyes on the window which looked out onto the hospital's parking lot.

Bosch excused himself and closed the door, leaving Carter and Locklear alone with the almost lifeless body of Andrew Fehr.

Locklear moved closer to the bed and thought a while.

"You examined the body – I mean, this boy?"

"I only got a few minutes with him before the ambulance arrived."

"Was he conscious?"

"No. Harrisonburg's police took a look at him when he was stabilised. There's a report on the system."

"Did you read it?"

"No ... not yet."

Locklear thought he heard a slight gulp in Carter's voice, a whimper of emotion.

"Did you know him well?"

Carter nodded. "He's a good kid, harmless. Lived over the garage where he worked on the outskirts of Harrisonburg."

"There are no parents?"

"Not for many years. Not since he was a small boy."

"Why couldn't he live with the brother we saw earlier?"

"Luke? No, Luke lives a ... well, he's a feral sort of man."

"There's no one else?"

Carter finally took his eyes from the window but still did not look at Andrew Fehr. He rested his eyes on the light over the bed and kept them there. Locklear knew he was stalling for time and wondered what the trooper was trying to keep from him.

"There's an old man named Fehr living alone in the hills – Aaron Fehr. I guess he'd be a grand-uncle of sorts. He wants nothing to do with them. He's a – he's a little – well – nuts, sir – so best keep away from him. There are five of them Fehr kids. Luke's the eldest and his twin, Sara. She had an automobile accident seven years ago. She's been in a vegetative state in hospital ever since. Esther lives in a small unit on the grounds of Pastor Plett's home. Andrew is next and then Abigail. She's fostered by the Wyss family. They've got the farm next to what was once the Fehr farm."

Locklear pulled the sheet back further from Andrew's neck and took a closer look at the markings there. Tiny scratch-marks were visible along the scar – fingernail scratches from where the boy tried desperately to loosen the rope. Again he felt a surge of emotion for the boy. Even in his sleeping state Andrew Fehr seemed like a vulnerable and helpless person.

"You say he's mentally deficient?"

"Well, not exactly ... just a little slow with learning, you know?"

"And you can't think of a reason why anyone in this peace-loving community would want to hurt him?"

Carter shook his head and diverted his eyes away from Locklear again. It was his tell. He did it every time he was lying. He'd make a crap poker-player, Locklear thought.

He raised Andrew's arm up from underneath the sheet which had been tucked tightly around him, revealing a deep bruise on the boy's left wrist. Locklear reached over the body and gently moved the boy's right arm from under the sheet, revealing similar bruising on the wrist – deep thumbmarks caused by someone holding down the boy as he struggled.

Carter's eyes and mouth opened in unison. Locklear felt that the reaction was genuine.

"Well, Carter, what does your peace-loving community say about torturing a dim-witted boy whom everyone seemed to like?"

Chapter 3

The phone conversation with Kowalski went better than Locklear expected. His boss would send Joe Mendoza, a smart young cop, to help with the investigation. Locklear had worked with Mendoza Senior. He had been a good cop. Sharp.

"I thought Mendoza's kid was a homo artist?" Locklear joked.

"You're a real piece of work, Locklear, do you know that? It's his other kid."

Locklear didn't know the kid but knew he would be smart. The only snag was Kowalski insisted that Carter stayed on too, that the chief himself had insisted on it. What Locklear couldn't figure out was why. He didn't like it but knew by the tone of Kowalski's voice that it was non-negotiable. When he thanked his boss for sending a man he could depend on, Kowalski laughed heartily and Locklear hung up. He didn't have time for Kowalski's strange sense of humour.

The drive to Pastor Plett's house on the outskirts of the village was a short one but even in the few minutes it took to get there from the station, Locklear could sense the tension in Carter. Whether that tension was because Carter had heard about the reinforcements Locklear requested or because he was worried about how his superior would behave in the pastor's house to which they had not been invited, he didn't know.

The house was old but looked smarter and more affluent than Locklear had expected. He rang the doorbell and was surprised when the door opened almost immediately. He could already tell that the woman in front of him was Andrew Fehr's sister, Esther. She had the same mousy-brown hair and pale skin. Her eyes were dark grey with shards of amber like the sun trying to cut through the clouds on a dark winter's day.

She stared at him for the longest time, glancing only occasionally at Carter who stood back, until she finally spoke.

"*Kann ick di hulpen?*"

"This is Sergeant Locklear, Esther. He's here because of Andrew," Carter offered nervously.

Esther, on the other hand, showed no signs of nervousness. She threw a sharp glance at Locklear.

"*Laat mi in Roh!*" she spat before closing the door firmly on them.

"She said –"

"I know what she said," Locklear replied, "or I can guess. You speak the language fluently, Carter?"

"No, but I understand a good bit. I went to high school with some of the community. 'Leave me alone' is something I heard a lot from the girls," he said with a grin.

"But they all speak English?"

"Yeah, but they won't. Not 'less they have to."

Locklear reached forward and pressed the bell hard until the door swung open again. This time the surprised face of Pastor Plett greeted him. Without a word, the pastor stood to one side and beckoned for them to come in.

Locklear heard Carter whisper "Sorry" as he passed the preacher in the hallway.

As they were led down a narrow hallway, Locklear noticed that despite the fancy facade, the house was not luxurious on the inside. As he passed several rooms along the dark hallway he noticed they were surprisingly sparse of furniture and dimly lit.

The pastor led the visitors to the kitchen at the back of the house. Inside there was only a large wooden table, four wooden chairs and a tall oak kitchen dresser with rows of old-fashioned crockery on it. A ceramic sink on top of two tiny cupboards was the only other item in the room. He could see no refrigerator or other electric appliances. He looked up and was relieved to see electric lights on the ceiling.

Pastor Plett seemed to read his mind. "We do have electricity. Rachel prefers to have the appliances in the adjoining room. The buzzing from them gives her migraines."

Plett pointed at the table and both men dutifully took a seat on the hard, uncomfortable-looking chairs.

"I assume you are here to talk about young Andrew?"

As if on cue, Esther appeared in the kitchen, still scowling.

Pastor Plett, who had taken a seat opposite the men, stood and placed his hands on her shoulders. Locklear could almost see the tension leave her.

"We have welcome guests for dinner, Esther. Please tell my wife," he said in English.

Esther did what almost passed for a curtsy and left the room, leaving the door open behind her.

"She's a spirited girl," Plett said, grinning.

"You adopted her?" Locklear asked.

"No, Esther came to us six years ago. She was fostered by the Wyss family until she turned eighteen. She works for us now."

"Are you permitted to have a shunned person in your home?" Locklear asked.

Plett's shoulders rose up in defence. He cut a look at Carter as though the trooper had possibly told more to an outsider than he should.

"I'm breaking no rules. Shunning is rarely practised in our faith, Mr Locklear. What happened to the Fehrs happened a long time ago and is outside of my control. My wife and I care deeply for Esther. Our own children are raised. It has done us both good, especially Esther, to keep her here."

Locklear noticed his use of words. It would have, he felt, been more appropriate to say *have* her here, than *keep* her here.

"Tell me about how you came to find Andrew Fehr."

Plett stood and quietly closed the kitchen door. He returned to his seat and took a deep breath. Locklear reckoned he was about to listen to a very tall, well-rehearsed tale. He listened as Plett told of a visit to the Wyss family towards dusk and how he noticed car lights on the dirt road leading up to the Fehrs' farm. Worried that the farm was being robbed by outsiders, he left the Wyss house quickly and took a shortcut up to it on a dirt track through the fields. When he arrived, he could hear a car on the main road. He noticed the barn door open and went inside where he found Andrew hanging. He drove his car under the boy and stood on the roof of the car and propped him up until help came.

"How did you summon help?" Locklear asked suspiciously.

Plett reached into his trouser pocket and took out a cell phone.

"With this."

Locklear thought for a moment. Not lost on him was the fact that his trooper asked not one question.

"Were the lights of the car going towards the farmhouse or away from it?"

Plett moved his tongue around the inside of his mouth – obviously unprepared for that particular question.

"Away from the farm."

"That's quite a steep hill and most of the dirt road veers left, away from your field of view."

Plett said nothing.

"How many minutes did it take you to reach the barn?"

Plett made an attempt to pretend he was recalling the evening, as though his entire story was not practised to perfection.

"Around four minutes."

"Pastor Plett, let's say you hadn't noticed that car until it was a good deal down the roadway and that the murderer had stood and watched Andrew Fehr hanging for two or three minutes – in that case, by the time you reached him he would be dead. So ... either you are lying about the time you noticed the car or you were a lot nearer to the boy when someone tried to hang him."

Plett said nothing but Locklear could see the veins pulsating above his white shirt collar.

The kitchen door opened and Rachel Plett gushed in. Locklear wondered at her precise timing and felt she had been listening at the door. She thrust out her hand.

"*Willkamen.*"

Carter stood and shook her hand warmly and did not seem to notice the steely gaze she gave his partner before beginning to set the table for dinner.

"Pastor, thank you for your kind offer of dinner but we must go. We have a lot of work to do." It was Carter who spoke, taking Locklear by surprise.

"I understand," Plett said.

They stood and moved towards the front door where Plett pretended to take an interest in Carter's conversation about the local baseball team.

Locklear realised Carter was creating the diversion for his benefit. He walked outside, leaving the two in conversation, and wandered around to the back of the house. There he saw Esther Fehr walking towards the small shed-like home she presumably lived in with a plate of food in her hands. He pictured her sitting there alone, day after day, unable to share a meal with anyone except maybe her siblings – though he had no idea if she saw them and if she did what their relationship was. Knowing it was useless to try to talk to her, he walked back to the front of the house where Carter was giving an amused Plett a re-enactment of his swing the previous Saturday.

There was one more question Locklear needed to ask. For now.

"Mr Plett? Were you alone when you visited the Wyss farm that night?"

Plett looked to the ground but his facial expression remained unchanged. He raised his eyes again to meet Locklear's.

"Yes. I was alone."

The motel Irene had organised for Locklear in Harrisonburg did exactly what it said it would do on the roadside sign. Basic accommodation at a good price. He rested the key on the TV stand and sat for a moment on a plastic chair in the hot room. He knew not to even look for the air conditioner. A fan above the bed looked like the only respite he would get from the murderous heat and sleep would probably evade him for however long it took to close the case.

He opened the fridge to find it empty. After all these years he still thought about alcohol, still thought about opening the fridge on a hot day and reaching for a cold beer or opening a bottle of Jameson on a cold winter night. He went outside and bought as many sodas from the vending machine as his change would allow and downed two before getting into the shower. He had at least made some headway with Carter who had seen through Plett's story and knew the pastor was lying. What they didn't agree on was why, Carter being of the opinion that Plett may have seen something he wished he hadn't while Locklear felt the preacher was knee-deep in whatever was going on around here.

It was only nine hours since his arrival yet he felt like he'd been in the town for weeks. He went over what he now knew which wasn't much. Pastor Plett was lying and his wife knew why – maybe she was even a part of it. Luke Fehr wasn't going to talk to him – not unless he made life very uncomfortable for him and even then he guessed the man Carter said lived like a hermit would not speak. Esther would be no better.

He wondered what their relationship with their youngest brother was. In any other case he would been fending off family wanting to point fingers at whoever they felt was responsible for the attack on their loved one, but Esther hadn't even asked how her brother was. He went over Esther's expression when she opened the door. She wasn't afraid of him and she didn't look guilty. Carter had said that the Pletts came under a lot of pressure from church elders including Shank when they took Esther in, which didn't match up with what he knew so far about the pastor who seemed completely devoted to the faith. Nothing added up in this place and it seemed like everyone, including his trooper, was lying.

Locklear dressed and took a walk through the town which looked like hundreds of towns he'd been through. Harrisonburg could, he supposed, be described as a pretty town. It was laid out in neat grids, save the downtown section where the town was first established in the early 1700s.

He turned left onto Main Street past a pretty white steepled church on the corner, reminiscent of bygone days. He stopped to admire the redbrick colonial-style houses along the street and stopped again at the impressive Baptist church. He wondered briefly if this was where Carter came to worship. He could imagine him there each Sunday, dressed in his Sunday best with his wife and brood of baseball-playing kids. Locklear was not affiliated to any church – he didn't even know what beliefs his mother had had – if indeed she'd had any at all.

The town's colonial history was evident in the fine buildings, once homes to rich industrial families and now relegated to government offices and museums. He passed more churches –

Methodist, Mennonite, Catholic, Presbyterian – there was something for everyone in this multi-denominational community. As he reached the main square, he saw that an impressive stone courthouse stood there, its red roof and shining green dome standing out among the fine homes on either side.

Locklear continued up Main Street in the heat until he found himself in the seedier part of town. Soon, redbrick houses gave way to closed-up shops and discount food stores. He passed two pawn shops side by side and knew he was in the part of town he'd feel comfortable in, so he continued on until he found what he was looking for – a diner that looked like a hundred diners he had been to before. He had grown up sitting in the corner of diners, doing his homework in the back booth of whatever sweat-hole his mother found work in and he found them oddly comforting, like a home away from a home he had never truly known. A sign on the window said: "**Waitresses Wanted – Movie Star Lookalikes Welcome.**" He ordered his usual from an ageing busty blonde waitress trying her best to look like Marilyn Monroe. A fake mole had slid down her cheek in the heat and was resting on the corner of her chin. Locklear reasoned that not too many Marilyn lookalikes must have applied. He remembered another sign on a different diner in a different state over fifty years ago when he was just a boy. His mother and he had been driving through Arizona for days, stopping only to eat or rest which involved sleeping in the back of the pickup she had "borrowed" from a boyfriend they were running from. On their last ten dollars, they stopped at a diner in the middle of nowhere. A sign in the window said "**Help Wanted – No Indians No Blacks**" so they kept driving.

By the time he'd finished his meal, the fatigue he'd felt on leaving Carter had evaporated and he made his way back to Dayton to the incident room he had not yet used. He signed in and introduced himself to an overweight officer with an unfriendly manner who pointed to the room at the end of a long corridor.

The Pact

The door to the supposedly secure room was open and surveying the large noticeboard Carter had set up was a tiny Hispanic woman in an oversized police uniform.

She didn't seem to hear him as he stepped up behind her.

"Are you lost?" he asked.

The woman, jolted from her thoughts, swung around to greet him, bumping her large breasts into him.

"No," she said. "I'm Josefina Mendoza."

"Mendoza?"

"Yes," she said with a smile. "Your help. Call me Jo."

"You're a woman?"

Mendoza looked down at her expansive bosom. "Last time I checked."

Locklear ignored the sarcasm. "I was expecting a man," he retorted.

"Well, you got me," she replied, unperturbed.

Locklear was stumped. To say anything further would make him seem sexist which he wasn't – least not as far as he was concerned.

He walked back to reception and lifted the phone. The fat officer ignored him as he shoved a hot dog into his fleshy mouth. The number rang three times before Kowalski answered.

"Kowalski, are you shitting me?"

Kowalski laughed. "Mendoza arrived, huh?"

"Alex – I asked for some goddamn help. Instead you team me up with a Baptist bible-thumping boy afraid of his own shadow and now – what – goddamn it – does she even weigh a hundred pounds?"

"You need her to lift something?"

"Funny. That's real funny, Alex."

"Listen, Locklear – she's sharp, she's got no allegiances, she's tough, she's committed, she's got balls. If you need all that and a penis, I got no one for you right now. So, keep her or send her back. I could sure use her here." He hung up.

Locklear kicked the bin at his feet.

"*Goddamn fucking damn it!*" he shouted.

He turned to find Mendoza standing at the door, listening.

"You ready to get to work now?" she asked.

Locklear breathed a heavy sigh.

"Sure."

Chapter 4

Locklear rose before dawn with a clearer plan than he'd had the day before. At breakfast he sat separate to Mendoza whom Irene had booked into the same motel, knowing that this would irritate him. He was useless with small talk and when a case was on his mind all he wanted to do was think on it, reason it out, see the flaws in alibis and interrogate accordingly. It was why, he supposed, he had loved jigsaw puzzles as a boy. He spent many happy hours alone as a boy piecing the bits together, working out the patterns and colours and shapes in front of him until a picture began to emerge from the jumble of oddly cut shapes. Each time his mother found a new lover she would buy her only child a new puzzle to keep him busy and would buy him another one when the man left, which they all did eventually. By the time he reached adolescence he had about fifty puzzles in the top of the wardrobe of wherever they happened to be living. He was never sure if that reflected badly on his mother's relationship skills or on the characters of the men that she chose. Probably both.

Locklear knew that he had to break Plett's alibi but he needed more to go on. Plett had said he was visiting the Wyss farm on the night someone tried to kill Andrew Fehr, so a visit to the woman who had fostered at least three of the Fehr children was his first port of call. He stopped first at Dayton station to collect Carter who seemed immediately at ease with Mendoza. The trooper slid his tall frame into the back seat which symbolised his new position on the case. Locklear checked to see if Carter was sulking but his genial trooper launched into a friendly conversation with Mendoza and did not seem to notice her monosyllabic responses. Neither did he sulk when she curtly told him she preferred quiet when working on a case so she could think. She turned quickly to Locklear when she said this and had a glint in her eye. He glanced at her questioningly.

"My father worked with you, remember? He told me all about you and your ... ways" – which resulted in a loud guffaw from the backseat passenger.

When they reached the entrance to the Wyss farm, Locklear sent Carter and Mendoza to walk the crime scene again and asked Carter to update Mendoza on where the investigation was at – in as few words as he could manage. He wanted to speak to the family alone.

As he approached the front door, he saw a thin young girl standing at the side of the house. She was looking up towards the Fehr farm. He did not know if the Wysses had any biological children but knew instinctively that this was Abigail Fehr. She had the same colour hair as her siblings and the same deathly pale face. He walked around to face her.

The same stormy-grey eyes as Esther's greeted him with the same bright flecks of amber. He had never seen eyes like those shared by the Fehrs. He said hello but she did not answer him and stood transfixed to the spot, staring at what he did not know.

He rang the bell and was greeted by a plainly dressed woman in her mid-fifties. He could see that Helena Wyss had once been a beautiful woman but that hard work on the farm had worn her down. She was painfully thin and her faded pastel cotton dress hung awkwardly on her emaciated frame.

"Come in," she said quietly, without even asking who he was.

Word had got around, he reasoned.

Locklear sat on a hard wooden chair and glanced around at the meagre furniture in Helena Wyss's kitchen.

"My husband Peter works in Harrisonburg – the farm doesn't pay enough – so, it's just me here ... and Abigail," she said.

"She always like that?" he asked.

"She's upset at the moment. Lost her rag doll. Red, she calls it, because of the colour. Too old for it anyhow. She'll be fine in a while. She has these things – absences – she comes in and out of them. When she comes out of them she says the strangest things and then she's fine again."

"Does she spend a lot of time staring up at her farm?"

Helena Wyss looked upwards as though she could see the pinnacle of the Fehr farm from her kitchen table.

"Yes, but only the Lord knows why. She's been with me a long time now. Seems like she does that every time her brother's been to visit."

"Andrew?"

"No, not Andrew. I meant Luke."

The mention of Luke Fehr caught Locklear's attention. He hadn't yet figured out where the eldest Fehr sibling fit into the picture.

"Would you tell me about Luke ... please? I know you ... people ... don't like talking outside of ..."

"We are not Mennonite, sir. My family were shunned a long time ago – my husband's too."

Locklear automatically licked his lips. It was an odd quirk he had developed and a show of when he knew he was about to make progress. He'd found someone outside of the community who might talk to him, someone other than Carter who was as almost as secretive as the Mennonites themselves.

"So, just like the Fehrs?"

"Yes."

"Could you tell me about it?"

"It was such a long time ago – why is it important?"

Locklear didn't know why it was important but he trusted his instincts. He knew that if he was to understand what was happening in this community now, he needed to understand what happened to the Fehrs in the past.

Helena Wyss ran her lined hands over her equally lined face.

"It was just after the Civil War that the community shunned my family. My great-great-grandfather, Isaac Falk, joined the Union Army to fight against slavery. The Fehrs too."

"And Virginia was a Confederate state?"

"Yes, but that wasn't why we were shunned. Mennonites are against slavery but also against war. Mennonites are not allowed to join the army, to fight. Isaac died in battle only a few weeks after he joined the army and his wife and son received a medal of honour from Abraham Lincoln himself – but it caused a rift in our family that exists to this day. The story of how grief-stricken she was has been passed down through the generations. She carved his initials deep into an old tree in the woods behind this farm the year he fell. With no body to bury, it was the best she could do to honour a husband that she had chosen herself."

She stood and took a small wooden box from a drawer. Inside was a discoloured medal hanging from a faded, threadbare ribbon. She held it out proudly for Locklear to see.

"When Isaac went to war, his wife Hannah suffered terribly. She was shamed and her father cut off all ties with her. He was the pastor here."

"What was his name?" Locklear asked for no real reason.

"Shank. Abe Shank."

"So, you're related to Samuel Shank?"

Wyss pursed her lips. "A distant cousin ... but Samuel

Shank passes my husband and me by in the street. He owns the creamery here and much of the land around it. He won't buy milk from our farm, wouldn't buy it from the Fehr farm back then either, so the land is worthless for us. We only keep what cows we need for ourselves and grow what food we need. That's why my husband is working in an office in Harrisonburg. It was not the life he wanted."

Locklear looked out the kitchen window at Abigail Fehr who had not moved from the spot he had found her in.

"When did you foster the Fehr kids?"

"Seven years ago. We had no children of our own. Luke was too old, a man, and poor Sara – she was so beautiful. Did your trooper ever tell you he was sweet on her?"

Locklear shook his head.

"Well, he was. He was very much in love with Sara Fehr. Of course, Luke would have none of it. Warned young Carter off. Beat him up bad. They had been friends at high school. It was a real shame it went that way. Poor Lee went to pieces when Sara was hurt in the accident and Luke wouldn't even let him visit. Eventually he met someone else and got married but I don't think he ever got over losing Sara, as young as he was."

Locklear thought back to how scared Carter was when they saw Luke Fehr the day before. It made sense now.

"What a loss she was to the family. She looked after those children so well, and she was really only a child herself. When she had her ... *accident* ..."

Locklear locked on to the tone she used when she said 'accident'. She had deliberately accentuated the word, as though it meant something.

"Esther was seventeen so she only stayed with me a year before going to Pastor Plett and his wife. Andrew was fourteen. He was with me until he turned eighteen. And Abigail, I think she'll be with me always. She's sixteen now but she's like a child."

"Sixteen?" he asked, surprised.

"Yes, I know – she looks so much younger."

"What happened to Sara?" he asked abruptly in the hope of getting a straight direct answer.

Helena Wyss looked out the window and her gaze rested on her foster child.

"Her car went over the bridge and into the water. She wasn't even fully licensed to drive and it wasn't even her car. It was her late father's. She was turning twenty-one – she should have been celebrating, looking forward to her future. It's sorrowful to see her tied to all those tubes in that bed. I can hardly bring myself to visit. I do, sometimes, for Abigail's sake, but it would have been better if she'd died. I really do think so."

She turned her head and Locklear saw tears welling up in her eyes.

"The night of Andrew's ... attack ..." he said.

Helena Wyss looked away again and fixed her eyes on the cupboard.

"Pastor Plett said he was here. Is that correct?"

"Yes."

"Why did he come here if you are no longer part of the church?"

Helena Wyss straightened her spine as though Locklear had hit a nerve. "Pastor Plett is a good man. He buys eggs from me and bread. He knows we need the money."

"He's allowed to do business with you?"

"No, he shouldn't come here at all. But the pastor has changed things around here. He's made things better."

"What time was he here?"

"Around dusk. Why?"

Locklear thought for a moment. Carter also felt that Plett was a decent human being but Locklear had a sense that he was hiding something.

"Were you expecting him?"

"No."

"Would that be a normal time for him to call?"

Helena Wyss looked at her folded hands on her worn wooden kitchen table. Locklear could sense that the shunned woman was becoming nervous – afraid perhaps of losing the only Mennonite who would grace her table. She stalled and Locklear could see her inner turmoil. She opted for the truth.

"No."

"Was he alone?"

"Mrs Plett was with him."

Locklear had caught Plett, who had said he was alone that night, in a lie but the reason why he'd lie about the presence of his wife that night was puzzling.

He stood and made his way to the door. Helena followed.

On a small table by the door sat a present wrapped in green tissue paper. A card tucked underneath the ribbon said, "*With Love to Our Andrew.*"

Helena lifted it and smoothed her hands over the tissue paper.

"He was supposed to come here that night. I'd made a cake for his birthday and bought him a book I knew he'd love."

A book? So he liked to read? Wasn't he supposed to have some kind of learning disability? Locklear would have asked but didn't want to distract her from the main issue.

"Who would want to hurt your son, Helena?" Locklear used the word *son* in the hope of unleashing the maternal instinct in the woman, the overwhelming need to protect her young from danger.

She shook her head and Locklear could see a genuine look of confusion on her weary face.

"Everyone loved Andrew," was her only response as she opened the door.

"Did anyone else know Andrew was coming here that night? Would anyone else know he'd be walking along the road?"

Helena Wyss thought for a moment. "Just my husband, Abigail and Pastor Plett."

Locklear moved outside, still absorbing the information.

"Do you miss it? Being part of the church?" he asked.

"No man can take God from you, even if you aren't allowed to worship with your neighbours. We still live a good life, a simple life. What I miss is being part of something."

As he passed Abigail he bent down to meet her eyes. She blinked.

"It's a good year to put things right," she said.

He looked back at Helena Wyss who shrugged.

"She's back," she said.

Locklear walked up the steep hill towards the Fehr farm. He deliberately took the dirt track to see how long it took to walk the distance that Plett said he drove in four minutes flat and discovered a second lie from the preacher. The walk had taken Locklear ten minutes of uphill climbing on foot so it would not have taken Plett four minutes to drive to the spot. The discovery of this second lie did not tell Locklear anything – yet.

When he reached his troopers he found Carter was practising his swing against the side of the Fehr barn with a ball he always seemed to have in his possession while Mendoza, who was sitting on the dusty ground, wrote up her notes.

"Carter, confine your baseball activities to teaching little league to your sons, will you?"

Carter swung around and the look of hurt on his face jolted Locklear.

"What?" Locklear asked.

Carter did not answer. He stuck the ball into his pocket.

"Forensics called," he said quietly. "The tyres in the driveway and barn match the type used in dozens of vehicles around there – it's a dead end."

"And the rope?"

"The only prints they found belonged to Andrew. It was clean."

Mendoza stood and dusted the earth from her bottom.

"This place gives me the creeps, sarge. I feel like I'm being watched."

Locklear knew what she meant. He felt it too.

"You notice the holes around here?" Mendoza asked.

Locklear had noticed signs of digging around the yard the day before when he'd evicted Plett and his congregation off the lot. It was hard to believe that that was only yesterday. He felt weary.

Mendoza beckoned for him to follow her further uphill. She stood at a spot until Locklear arrived, panting from the heat. Carter followed with a furrowed brow, still sore from whatever insult Locklear had unknowingly thrown at him. Beneath their feet were the remnants of several large holes. Someone had made an effort to fill them in but their scars on the dry earth were still visible. They walked further uphill and found more and more holes.

"There must be a hundred of them – more," Carter offered.

"Some of the land disturbance looks old, perhaps years old, decades even," Mendoza said. "The ground has hardened over it but you can see it was disturbed. Other holes are fresh – I'd go as far as to say only days old. What do you suppose someone was – is digging for? Wells?"

Carter shook his head. "The land around here is irrigated and the rainfall is pretty high. The house is on a mains supply. Government did a huge project here back in the fifties."

"How d'you know all this, Carter?" Locklear asked.

Carter looked away and swung his arm around – in mock preparation for the throw of his life.

"I majored in local history, anthropology ... and sport at college," he replied.

Carter's skills were an opportunity Locklear had been

looking for. Now that he knew about the trooper and Sara Fehr, he didn't like to ask Carter to accompany him to the hospital to see her but he now knew exactly what he'd have him do. Something even more useful.

"Someone was looking for something that was buried," he said, more to himself than his troopers.

"Treasure?" Mendoza laughed.

"Something like that," Locklear replied. "Carter, I want you to go to the local library and research the involvement of the Fehrs in the Civil War – what they did then and what happened after it."

"What?"

"Just do it. Mendoza, you're coming with me."

"Where?"

"I'll tell you when we get there."

Chapter 5

After dropping Carter off at the Massanutten Regional Library in Harrisonburg, Locklear swung the car back towards Dayton and the Kindred Spirit Hospital on South Edwin where Sara Fehr had remained for seven years.

Locklear was surprised by the expensive-looking facility and had expected Sara Fehr to be cared for in less salubrious surroundings.

At the entrance to the plush foyer he waited for a consultant to speak with them. Mendoza whistled at the grand design of the open-plan area which looked more like the entrance to an upmarket hotel than a hospital. The back wall was staffed by three women behind an expensive oak desk that ran the width of the reception area. Deep-pile carpet covered the huge area and porters stood on hand to carry the luggage of wealthy patients coming and going from the flamboyant facility.

"How are the family paying for this?" Mendoza asked.

"I doubt they are," Locklear whispered.

Mendoza smiled when a young, pretty, female doctor approached.

"This'll be good," she muttered to Locklear.

"What?"

"Oh, I'm just wondering how you'll cope talking to another intelligent, assertive female. Don't piss her off!"

"Maybe I'll turn on my charm?"

"If you've got some of that I'd like to be introduced to it," Mendoza said.

Locklear showed Doctor Laura Miller his identification and explained the purpose of his visit.

Mendoza took a quick glance at his name: O *Locklear*. She wondered what the O stood for.

The doctor smirked. "Sergeant Locklear, are you really expecting to ask Sara Fehr questions about her brother?"

"Of course not."

"Then why do you want to see her?"

"I just do. It's important," he lied.

The doctor led Locklear and Mendoza down a series of less impressive corridors and into what appeared to be an older, shabbier wing of the facility.

She opened a door at the end of a corridor and led them into a tiled room with only one bed in the far corner under an open window. There was no air conditioning in this part of the building and the heat in the room was stifling. An open doorway gave some reprieve from the heat and led to a small patio area at the back of the hospital. There was a chair beside the bed which was occupied by a young nursing assistant. Apart from the bed and a couple of chairs, the room held only hospital machinery, all beeping and buzzing, recording the signs that Sara Fehr was still alive. Locklear noticed the absence of photos, of colour, of anything personal that would make the sparse room look homely.

He looked the woman over. She was not intubated but a feeding tube ran from her nostril and was taped onto her ghostly pale face. In the dimly lit room, a monitor stuck under the loosely tied hospital gown recorded the rhythm of her heart which appeared steady and strong.

"Can she hear us?" Locklear asked.

"Most unlikely."

Locklear noticed a quick arm jerk from the assistant, as though the young woman had something to say.

"How long have you been caring for her?" he asked the doctor.

"I've only been here about a year but her presentation has not changed in that time. In fact, her condition hasn't changed in the whole time she has been here."

"But people can come out of a coma even after all that time, right?" Mendoza asked.

"Sara's in what's known as a vegetative state – not a coma. She sustained a brain injury during her accident. She was a while under water by the time she was rescued so she was oxygen-deprived. Approximately fifty per cent of people in her situation recover consciousness. Sara is not one of them."

"Will she live?" Locklear asked. "I mean, a normal life span?"

"Do you call this living? She's strong but eventually ... in most of these cases, pneumonia, severe infection, kills them. Maria here has been looking after Sara for most of the seven years she's been here. She can tell you anything you need to know. If you need anything else I'll be in my office on the third floor."

She smiled and left, wiping her brow as she left the heat of the room.

Maria Whieler stood and shyly offered her hand. She wore no make-up or jewellery and the shoes beneath her long nursing outfit were old-fashioned and comfortable.

"I normally work nights – someone called in sick though."

"You've been here since last night?" Mendoza asked.

"I don't mind. I ... I love being with her ... and Dr Miller is wrong. Sara can hear us. I talk to her and I know she hears me."

"Did you know her before the accident?" Locklear asked.

"Yes, we were at school together. We were best friends."

Locklear suppressed an overwhelming urge to ask a ridiculous question about the colour of Sara Fehr's eyes.

"So you are a Mennonite?"

Maria Whieler bit down on her lip. "My father was but not my mother. When he died, we left. I was about twelve. Mama was never happy living in the community. She died seven years ago and so I came back. I hadn't anywhere else to go and Samuel Shank, the old pastor, got me this job and somewhere to live. He's even paying for me to go to nursing school by day."

"Does Sara get any visitors?" Mendoza asked.

Maria locked her eyes on Locklear. "Why do you ask?"

Locklear could hear the apprehension in her voice. "No reason."

"Am I in trouble?"

"No, why would you say that?"

"I do almost everything Mr Shank asks of me. Just sometimes ..."

"Just what? We won't tell him, we promise, don't we, sarge?" Mendoza flashed her white smile at the nervous woman.

"Some nights Luke arrives and he just wants to sit here, with her. He loves her so much. So I leave the swing door unlatched and go for my break. I always know when he's been here. I can smell him. Like the sweet smell of the sea without the sea. And, you know, I swear on those nights there's a smile on Sara's face. I've listened to him sometimes from the doorway, talking to her. Sometimes he brushes her hair and she's calmer. No one knows Luke like me and Sara do. He's sweet, and gentle. I tell Pastor Shank about Mrs Wyss visiting and Abigail and Andrew, Esther on Sunday afternoons, but I never tell him about Luke. You promise you won't tell?"

"Why would Mr Shank not like to see Luke around?"

"No one really likes to see Luke. He's in trouble in the community ... but they're wrong. He's a good man. He has to do the things he does because the land is cursed. Nothing will grow there."

Locklear and Mendoza exchanged a quick glance at each other and returned their gaze to the unusual woman.

"We promise," Mendoza said.

On the way out of the hospital Locklear knocked at Laura Miller's air-conditioned room and opened the door without waiting for a reply.

"Dr Miller, who pays for Sara Fehr's care here?"

Miller frowned but there was a faint smile to her lips, a slight thaw in her earlier frosty demeanour.

"The government covers some of her care."

"Who pays the balance?"

"That's confidential."

"If it's Samuel Shank, don't answer," he said with a smile.

Miller said nothing so he closed the door quietly and made his way to the foyer where Mendoza was helping herself to free coffee.

She handed him a cup and waited.

"What did you think of Sara Fehr's carer?" he asked.

"Apart from the fact that she's a little nuts, she's vulnerable, she's alone in the world and she's in love with Luke Fehr?"

Locklear laughed. Kowalski was right. Mendoza was sharp.

"Mendoza, I want you to find out why Samuel Shank is paying thousands of dollars for the care of an ex-communicated girl whose family he doesn't even like. Now let's go see if Carter has broken his swinging arm lugging history books around the library."

Locklear had decided that the back booth of the large diner on North Liberty Street would become the lunch hangout-point for the team during what he felt would be a long, drawn-out investigation. That first time the three sat in the red leathered booth and Carter recounted what he'd found in the local Civil War records. Not one but two Fehr brothers, Joshua and Daniel, fought on the Union side. They returned from the Civil War changed from the children they were when they left their farm in 1861. Daniel, the younger of the two, aged just fourteen, was awarded a silver medal for his bravery on the battlefield. He did not fight, the record showed, but played the drum continuously while his comrades fell around him. Joshua, aged just sixteen, lost a foot through gunshot but returned home with Daniel to their father's farm on the outskirts of Dayton in August 1866. The record showed that it took the boys nine weeks to get home after they were released from the prison where they were to be shot as traitors for fighting against the Confederates. Of note was the reference to their friendship along the road with a black Union solider named John Grant whom they helped hide on their farm for weeks until his capture by Confederate troops.

"Sir," Carter said, "the Fehrs wouldn't want this getting out in the public domain. Shunned or not, it's shameful for a Mennonite to fight – but to fight with the Union? This town has a long history of tolerance but it never went down well that they wouldn't fight during the war. Hearing that local Mennonites not only fought but fought with the Northerners wouldn't be appreciated."

"I think the Fehrs already know, Carter. That's why they and the Wyss family were shunned. What happened to them when they got back?"

Carter scanned his notes. "Joshua died from a wound infection almost three months after his return and Adam, who had remained on the farm, also died. Daniel survived and remained on the family farm until his death."

"What did Adam die of?"

Carter shrugged.

"Well, find out, Carter and find out about this black soldier Grant. I want to know what happened to him. This is important. I can feel it. I want to know everything there is to know about that family. Tomorrow we'll start on Samuel Shank and I want to interview Andrew's employer and see where the boy lived. We've got a lot of work to do."

"Sir?" Carter said meekly.

"What?"

"Tomorrow's Sunday."

"So?"

"It's family day. My wife and my son, we go to church and then to visit my father. I already missed time with them today."

"OK, Carter. Mendoza?"

Mendoza shook her head. Her son was waiting for her and Sunday would be the only day she'd see him while the investigation was live.

Locklear ran his hand through his black mane. "OK, well, I guess it's just me till Monday."

Chapter 6

Locklear was happy to eat alone in the motel's diner on Saturday evening and spent the rest of the evening in his room where he went over the case until the early hours of Sunday morning. When he eventually slept, he imagined Luke Fehr falling down a dark hole on the land. Locklear saw himself at the bottom, arms outstretched, trying to break the young man's fall. The whole time Luke was falling Locklear could see the face of Samuel Shank laughing as he pulled a sheet over Andrew Fehr's dead body. When he woke he tried to work out what the dream meant but gave up over a cold coffee in his room. He felt agitated. Something was troubling his mind but he did not know what. He phoned the hospital where Dr Bosch's understudy assured him that Andrew was still alive. Twice he lifted the phone to check on Sara Fehr but put it down again, unsure what to say if anyone answered. Sara Fehr had been in the same sorry state for seven years and the only change anyone could expect to hear was that she had died.

He decided to go to Dayton station and go over the facts once again. He didn't really need to see the investigation laid out before him on Carter's tidy noticeboard. It was all in his mind, albeit less tidily than in Carter's arrangement. In neat rows, Carter had the names of the five Fehr children with Andrew at the centre. A red arrow, in what he assumed was Mendoza's scrawl, linked Samuel Shank to Sara Fehr, denoting the exorbitant fees he was paying for Sara Fehr with a question mark. Why? The addresses of each of the Fehr children were written in blue beneath their names – Abigail with the Wysses, Esther with the Pletts, Sara in Dayton's Kindred Hospital and Luke of no fixed abode. Locklear wondered where exactly Luke's no fixed abode was. The man did not look homeless to him. He was cleanly dressed and did not have the look of a man sleeping outdoors. Besides, there was a house on the farm which he could live in. It was another question he needed to ask: why and when the house and farm were abandoned.

It was Andrew Fehr's address that caught his eye: Nick Lombardi's Car Yard, Harrisonburg. It couldn't be. Locklear walked swiftly down to the reception desk where a female cop was on duty. He barked an order for her to type the business name into the internet. He hated computers, didn't know how to use them, and with only a few short years to retirement, he had no intention of becoming familiar with them. A huge photo of Nick Lombardi shot up onto the screen, an online advert of him standing in front of a huge car yard, smiling.

"Do you know who he is?" he asked the cop.

She looked at the screen. "Yes, we got word from Harlem that he was setting up here. We've been keeping an eye on him. He's clean. Business is legit."

Locklear looked at the face of Nick Lombardi. It was more than thirty years since he saw that face. Lombardi looked older. He was smaller and thinner and his hair was slightly greying but he still had that smug look plastered all over his face. The son of a small-time hoodlum who worked as a mechanic as a cover for his stolen-car business, Lombardi was born into a life of crime. He married Rosa Nardoni, a local beauty whose own family had no association with crime, and took the innocent girl down with him. Word was she was pregnant so a quick Catholic marriage was arranged and the seventeen-year-old couple found themselves living in the back room of his parents' house with a young son and no money. It wasn't long before Lombardi found a way of making money. Three times Locklear tried to send him down for running narcotics in New York and three times he walked free with the help of expensive, Mafia-funded lawyers. It was no consolation that Lombardi's son, who ran the business at grass-roots level, started to taste the merchandise and ended up hooked on heroin. Lombardi paid for his son to enter every posh rehab clinic there was but each time he got out he was back on the streets, scoring a fix – a life ruined like hundreds or thousands of unfortunate Lombardi victims. The saying *"if you live by the sword"* came to mind but it was his son, who people in the know said wasn't the brightest light in the harbour, whose future was sacrificed on his father's sword. Locklear wondered what became of the boy. Lombardi was a dangerous, ruthless man. It wasn't beyond the realms of possibility that he got Andrew mixed up in something that resulted in the young man's hanging.

"Legit, my ass," he said to the cop who had lost interest in his search and had begun filing records at the back of the room.

Locklear left the station and drove back to Harrisonburg where he pulled up across the street from Lombardi's garage, which was located in the less salubrious part of town. It was exactly the type of place Lombardi would choose – among the vulnerable and destitute – easy victims to do his dirty work. As he walked across the street he saw the unshirted Lombardi, smoking a cigar and resting his bare arms on the white faux picket fence that ran around the front of the car yard.

"I was wondering when you'd get to me. Heard you was here," he grinned. "Long time no see, my friend."

"I'm not your friend, Lombardi," Locklear spat. "What are you doing in this town?"

Lombardi threw the half-smoked cigar on the pavement and let it smoulder. He straightened and walked to the opening in the fence. He pointed to the rows of expensive pickups.

"Don't you remember how I loved cars? They remind me of my old man."

"I mean – *this* town? Why here?"

The smile slowly faded from Lombardi's face. "To get away from it all," he replied.

Locklear noticed how faint his nemesis's voice suddenly had become.

"You want to come in? I've got a good bottle of Jameson. Your favourite, if I remember."

Locklear moved past Lombardi and took a closer look at the lot.

"I don't drink."

"Ah, a reformed man!"

Locklear swung around. "Are *you* reformed, Nick? What are you *really* doing here?"

A swing door opened. Rosa Lombardi hobbled out of her back door carrying two empty wine bottles and placed them in a garbage bin in the lot. Locklear was shocked by the former beauty's appearance. She was painfully thin and her long black hair was now cut short and bobbed around her yellowed face in small waves. Her upper abdomen was swollen and she walked with the awkward gait of a woman in physical pain.

Locklear turned to look at Lombardi.

"Rosa's sick," Lombardi said.

"I'm sorry," Locklear replied and he meant it. Rosa was as much a victim of Lombardi as the people he sold drugs to. He had poisoned her life in much the same way.

"Your son?"

"My son died – a long time ago. In a back alley in Manhattan with a needle in his arm. Coroner said he was about three days under a cardboard box before anyone noticed. Rosa's never been the same. She started drinking. We never had no more kids. He was everything to her ... and to me."

Locklear did not answer. He knew he should say he was sorry – but he couldn't.

"Anyway, Rosa couldn't take that life no more so we split. Couple years we moved around but we drove through here one day and this yard was for sale so we bought it. Been here about sixteen years."

"I want to see where Andrew Fehr slept."

Lombardi escorted Locklear into the garage showroom and down a small, windowless corridor. A narrow metal staircase at the end of the corridor led up to a second level and housed the small apartment Lombardi provided for Andrew in exchange for a cut in his wages. It struck Locklear how most of the Fehr children lived at the back of somewhere: Esther at the back of the Pletts, Sara at the back of the hospital and Andrew at the back of a car yard which was probably a cover-up business for criminal activity. It was as though the world had no purpose for the motherless children so had stuffed them into the back rooms of other people's lives.

There was only one window in the small room which faced out onto the lot. The room held everything the boy owned and it wasn't much. A single bed was shoved up against a windowless wall to make room for a two-cupboard unit at its foot. On the unit sat a two-ringed camping cooker, a kettle and one mug. Beside the bed was a small wooden locker on which stood three books on geology. Books again. Odd. And geology? Locklear lifted one and wondered why a boy like Andrew would be interested in the subject. A small fridge hummed beside the cupboard. There was no table in the room and a single chair parked against the far wall looked lost, as though it knew it should have a partner. An airless, bulbless bathroom to the right was only lighted by a skylight that did not appear to open.

"Jesus!" Locklear said.

"Hey, these Mennonites don't want much – they like the simple life."

"Ex-Mennonite. His family were shunned."

"Him and me both!" Lombardi quipped.

"Except you deserved it, Lombardi."

"Father Sheehan in Queens … if he's still alive … I made sure he won't never forget me."

Locklear sat down on the neatly made bed. "Remind me how that went again?" He remembered well enough but wanted to keep Lombardi in confessional mode.

Lombardi shrugged, lowered himself onto the single chair and began to talk.

Rosa was pregnant with what would have been their second child. Like with her first pregnancy, his wife's emotions fluctuated between bouts of uncontrolled rage and inconsolable weeping, and so he strayed from her and found comfort with other women in other bedrooms of other homes, leaving his wife and son alone, often for weeks on end. He always intended to come back. He thought she knew that but Rosa, after a particularly prolonged absence, terminated the pregnancy in a back-street clinic where no one would know her. He found her in New Jersey with relatives, a shell of the beautiful girl he knew, and took her back to New York where he tended to her day and night, trying to bring her back to the woman he had known her to be. Tortured by what she'd done, Rosa sought forgiveness in confession but was denied this from their priest, Father Sheehan, and so she took to her bed and spent her days under a cloud of drink-induced sleep. Lombardi did the only thing he knew how and went to the church, gun in hand. The only thing his plan achieved was a chalice full of lead. Sheehan called in the cops but eventually didn't press charges. However, he did report to his boss, resulting in the ex-communication of both Lombardi and Rosa. That was thirty-five years ago and, as far as Lombardi knew, the Church no longer ostracised people. He didn't care but Rosa did. Rosa still cared. Rosa cared, Rosa worried, Rosa fretted and got sick and everything that happened was a result of his, and not his wife's actions.

When Lombardi's tale finally ground to a halt, Locklear stayed silent for a few beats and then asked, "What does Andrew Fehr do here?"

"He cleans up, helps with repairs, drives the cars into the lot at night."

"Drives? I thought he was slow?"

"Slow, my ass. I thought that myself when I hired him but, about two years ago, I had a break-in. I know what you're thinking. Who'd have the nerve to rob from me? People around here – they don't know who I am but they do know I keep a loaded gun under my bed and I ain't scared to use it."

"Thought you'd be shooting your mouth off about your Mafioso links?" Locklear said sarcastically.

"Rosa, she prefers that people don't know nothing and I gotta do what's right by her. I gotta do what I can for her while there's time."

Lombardi fell silent and Locklear waited.

"Anyway, the cops come," he went on. "They're crawling all over my yard. First time in my life I got cops here for the right reasons. I'm spitting chips in the lot. Four cars missing and the till empty. Must have put two hundred bucks in the float that morning and it was a busy day – I had a sale on – sold around six second-hand cars and trucks ... mostly cash."

Locklear laughed. "Cash, huh?"

"You can laugh. You got good reason but I'm legit, my friend. I'm a changed man. That's why me and Rosa is here. We just want peace."

"What do the family say about your new-found life?" Locklear was referring to Lombardi's three brothers who were

The Pact

all involved in a family business that you just don't leave.

Lombardi's smile drifted away. "We don't got no more contact with the family. We never even says where we was going. It broke my heart but it's for Rosa."

Locklear almost believed him.

"Anyways the cops come and they question me and they question the boy. They asks me how much dough was in the till. Course I don't know. It's broken – doesn't add up right. A lot, is all I can say. Then they ask Andrew and he says straight out – $46,845.16c. Most was stuffed into a bag when the till wouldn't shut no more but the jokers got it all. I went through the sales receipts later and he was only a couple of dollars out. I couldn't believe it."

"You didn't put it in a safe at night?"

"I was still thinking I was in New York – thinking, like I said, who's going to be crazy enough to fuck with me?"

"Did you get the money and cars back?"

"Those beautiful cars were found burned out halfway to Richmond. I cried when the police towed them back here. Beautiful cars. The cash, they never got that – but they got the gang, the four kids that did it. Wouldn't say where the money was. Says they knew nothing about it. They're behind bars – safer there if I ever get my hands on them."

Locklear thought about Andrew Fehr and his apparent math skills.

"What does Andrew do here when he's not working?"

"Mostly he sits in his room. Polite kid, old-fashioned. Wouldn't come into the main house unless I was home. Don't reckon he'll ever be the same. Rosa loved having the boy around. Gave her a purpose again. It'll kill her if anything happens to him, or kill her sooner."

"Any idea who'd have done this? Maybe someone with a grudge against you?"

Lombardi's eyes opened wide. It was obvious he hadn't considered this. "No one knows we're here."

"You've got a big online advert with your name all over it."

"Yeah – but, the family, they wouldn't cause me no trouble."

"It's not your family I'm thinking of. It's your victims – their families."

"After all this time? Jesus!"

Locklear sat back and surveyed the room again. He picked up another book from the top of Andrew's locker. *Soil Erosion and Conservation*.

"Where'd he get these books?" he asked, opening the cover. There were no library markings on the sleeve of the well-worn book. He leafed through the pages which were slightly yellowed and the book cover itself was stained and dirty.

"That crazy-ass brother of his brings them. Andrew looks up to him like he's a god."

"Luke Fehr visits here?"

"Well, visits ain't exactly the right phrase. He sneaks up here in the dark like a goddamn bobcat, throwing stones up the window to get the boy's attention. He don't never come in – not once. Andrew comes down and them two disappear in that wreck of a truck the brother drives, shovels in the back like they'll be digging in the dark. Something I'm familiar with."

Locklear looked at Lombardi and wondered how he could joke about murder. There was no telling how many bodies the man buried in the dark or threw off a New York bridge. No doubt Lombardi could justify the killing of every "family" member who had muscled in on his business but he wondered, especially knowing how Joey died, if the faces of overdosed drug-users darkened the man's twilight years.

Locklear stood, took a deep breath in the airless room and put the book back on the locker. He pictured Carter's noticeboard like a jigsaw but still could find no connecting pieces.

"Where do ya suppose they're digging?" Lombardi asked.

"Their farm."

"What for?"

Locklear took in another deep breath in the putrid room. "That's something I don't know. Not yet."

On his way through the yard, he noticed Rosa Lombardi peering at him through an opening in the lace curtains. He turned to face her and nodded but she quickly dropped the curtain and shrank back from the window. In the distance he could hear church bells ringing, worshippers pouring out of the town's many churches, their one-hour lecture over. He imagined Mendoza, with her son and mantilla-wearing widowed mother, leaving the Catholic Church in Richmond and Carter smiling like a fool on the steps of his church. It seemed like everyone belonged to or wanted to belong to something except himself and the thought caused him no hardship.

A new puzzle ran around in his head. When did Andrew Fehr start pretending to be slow and for what reason?

He took a chance and drove towards the Baptist church and parked on the other side of the street, waiting to see if his trooper was among the worshippers. Scores of church-goers filed down the steps of the church as Locklear waited in the heat of his car, watching. He eventually saw Carter pushing a small, crooked-spined boy down the steps of the church in a wheelchair. The strong sun reflected off the shiny wheel-spokes as it moved. There was something so moving, so beautiful and yet so heart-wrenchingly sad about it that Locklear turned away, unable to look at the scene before him. He understood now the look of hurt on the trooper's face when he quipped about junior league lessons.

Carter's wife, a smiling, tiny Asian woman shook hands with the vicar and, heavily pregnant, followed her husband and child, her pretty floral dress blowing in the hot summer wind. The Carters looked happy, despite their misfortune.

Locklear looked away as the trooper tickled and hugged the laughing child. He wondered how Carter could be so gentle when this is what the world threw at him, how he could believe in a God while his first love endured a slow death and his son faced a life of hardship. He felt ashamed at the way he had treated the trooper and resolved to be kinder to him the following morning.

He turned the car and headed back to Dayton towards the Fehr farm in the hope of solving the mystery of the one hundred holes.

The highest point on the Fehr farm gave Locklear a fine view over the Dayton hinterland. Lush green pastures of fat milking cows and tilled fields of crops could be seen for miles. Occasionally a farm bell clanged gently in the breeze, once used to call great hordes of Mennonite men from the fields to eat and pray. On the other side of the steep hill Locklear could see the faint outline of a wood cabin. He could see no electricity poles near the property and he wondered if anyone actually lived there. He reasoned that apart from the population decline, not much had changed in this part of the state for hundreds of years and the thought of that filled him with a sense of both reassurance and of agitation. He knew that he was a man of contradictions and that, while the craving for stability he had as a boy had remained with him, all he had succeeded in doing was to confine his body in one place while his thoughts remained as frantic as a tethered wild horse.

It was a tranquil scene and he remained there for as long as he could before he reluctantly dragged himself down to the lower section of the farm which had unnerved the tough Mendoza. As he descended the steep hill Locklear noticed the soil change. The thick green grass, abundant on one side of the hill, was absent on its northern face. As he descended, the grass became sparser and soon gave way to barren, lifeless land.

The Pact

Locklear knelt down and took a piece of brightly coloured soil in his hand. He smelt it and allowed the material to fall slowly from his hands onto the earth. It suddenly came to him why Maria Whieler had said Luke Fehr smelt like the sea. It was sand she could smell. The lower section of the hill face was nothing but sand. Locklear walked on and as he descended the sand became deeper and the grass sparser. What, he wondered, had caused the grass to disappear and the soil to erode on this scale? Even allowing for the altitude of the farm, run-off and erosion could not account for the extent of soil loss. He knelt down and pulled some weakly held grass from its roots. A sharp crack behind him alerted him to company. Locklear did not turn around. He had been aware of being watched since he walked onto the farm. He was not afraid. He was alone and whoever was watching him could have shot him ten times over as he climbed the hill with the summer sun in his eyes.

"I know it's you who has been digging these holes. What I don't know is why. But ... I'll wager that it has something to do with something that happened here a long time ago."

Locklear's words were met with silence.

"What I do know is that you care very much for this farm and for your brother and sisters."

Locklear waited for a response but all he heard was the wind and the slow steady screech of the farmhouse's rusty swing door.

"I don't know why you don't live on this farm and I don't know who hurt your brother here except that it wasn't you. But what I can tell you is I will find out – so, you can either help me or hide in bushes. Either way is fine with me."

Locklear stood and dusted the sand from his jeans. He walked to the entrance of the farm. He turned and looked back. Luke Fehr was nowhere to be seen.

Chapter 7

It was after midnight when Mendoza's wreck of a car spluttered its way into the motel's car park. Locklear was awake but did not get up to greet her. Instead he lay fully clothed on the hard bed, anxious not to dream of Samuel Shank again. When he rose at seven he realised he had slept well and could not remember his dreams.

Mendoza seemed surprised when he slid into the red plastic booth to face her in the motel's diner for breakfast. She said nothing and continued eating a breakfast of huevos rancheros.

"That stuff will kill you," he said. "All that fat."

"What does O stand for?"

"What?"

"Your initials, O Locklear. I've been thinking about it. What does it stand for?"

Locklear ignored her question and ordered porridge and coffee.

"How do you keep your weight down when you eat that crap?" he asked, looking briefly down at the pounds he'd put on despite not eating anywhere near as much as he should.

"Try running around after a small child and work full time."

"Doesn't your husband help?"

"Don't got one," she replied, smiling.

Locklear stared at the woman. He had noticed how pretty she was but, despite being in her late twenties, Mendoza had dark lines under her eyes, too early for a woman of her years. A small white scar ran horizontally between her chin and lower lip and was matched by a scar of similar vintage over her right eye.

"You get those scars in the line of duty?"

"You could say that."

"What does that mean?"

Mendoza let out a long puff of air. It was too early for that kind of conversation.

"I'll tell you over a beer sometime."

In the incident room of Dayton police station, Carter appeared happy yet surprised by the friendly manner in which his boss greeted him. He glanced at Mendoza who shrugged.

"Guess he missed us!"

"Sir, it's my son's birthday today. I need to be home by five ... if that's OK?" Carter asked, taking advantage of his boss's seeming good mood.

Locklear did not answer. Instead he told the pair what he'd learnt while they were "off enjoying themselves", and he set a plan for the day.

Carter was to return to the library and find historical documents on the Fehr family, especially newspaper articles. Mendoza was to try find out why Shank was paying Sara's medical fees and to check the local cemetery for Fehr graves and take note of their dates of passing.

"Jesus!" she said. "Couldn't you give me anything creepier to do?"

"You want to walk the Fehr farm alone?"

"Think I'm safer in the graveyard."

"What are *you* going to do?" Carter asked meekly.

"I'm going to have a little word with Pastor Plett."

Carter's mouth opened in protest.

"On my own!" Locklear growled.

Esther Fehr was nowhere to be seen when Locklear walked into the Pletts' home for the second time in days.

Rachel Plett seated herself facing him in the front room and apologised that both Esther and her husband had gone to see Andrew, who had not woken up but was now breathing on his own.

"It's OK for me to be here without your husband present?"

Rachel Plett smiled pleasantly. "Yes."

He wondered if she was waiting on her husband to return before discussing the reason for his visit or if her monosyllabic response was designed to make him nervous. If so, it was working.

Rachel Plett reminded Locklear of a doll. Despite her frumpy figure, she had those bright blue eyes and long dark eyelashes he'd seen on dolls on his occasional visits to K Mart. Her hair was thick and was so blonde it appeared white and her skin was flawless save for a small dark mole underneath her left eye.

"How long have you lived in Dayton?"

"Seven years."

Locklear noted the time – the Pletts had arrived at the same time as Sara Fehr's accident and when the Fehr children went into the care of the Wyss family.

"Who was the pastor before that?"

Rachel Plett's face darkened and the smile slipped slowly from her mask-like face.

"Samuel Shank."

"He retired?"

"Yes."

A lie.

"Where were you before that?"

It was an open question, one that she could not give a simple yes or no answer to.

The Pact

"My husband and I have travelled extensively on our missions."

The response was designed to annoy Locklear, to put him in his place. He remembered Carter's warning. *These people answer to no one but the Lord*. Well, Carter and the Pletts were wrong. It was time to stop wasting his time.

He waited.

"We ... our post here was supposed to be temporary until they found a permanent pastor. We wanted to be somewhere nearer to our children but ... well ... the bishop didn't feel there was anyone suitable to be pastor in Dayton at the time so ... for now, we're here."

"Why did your husband lie to me and say he was alone on the night someone tried to hang Andrew Fehr?"

Rachel Plett threw her hands up to her throat. "He ... he *was* alone."

"You were with him, Mrs Plett."

"Why ... why would you say that?"

"Because Mrs Wyss said you were there, in her house, when your husband supposedly drove to the Fehr farm to see what was happening."

Rachel removed her hands from her throat and returned them to their folded state on her lap.

"Henry lied to protect me. If people knew I'd been to the house of a shunned person – the women here, our congregation – it would just undo what we are trying to do here."

"Which is?"

"We're trying to change things. The people here have been so afraid for so very long. We want to put joy back into the community."

"Afraid of what?"

Rachel Plett looked like she was going to answer when they heard the front door opening. Then Pastor Plett was standing in the front room, Esther Fehr by his side.

61

"Rachel, go upstairs," Plett ordered.

Rachel Plett rose and walked quickly and almost without sound to the hallway. Locklear did not hear her climb the stairs.

Esther Fehr glared at him with her grey sun-flecked eyes.

Plett glanced her way and she disappeared out of the room without a word. He pulled up a chair and faced Locklear. There was a new expression on the pastor's face and, if Locklear had to name it, it would be anger.

For a full minute Henry Plett did not speak. His eyes, while focused on Locklear, seemed miles away.

"I miscalculated," he said then. "I really didn't believe that Mrs Wyss would speak with you."

"I gathered that – otherwise you'd have told a different story or else told her not to tell me you had been at her house."

"You don't understand that's going on here."

Locklear leaned forward. "Well, then – why don't you enlighten me?"

"You think it's that simple? You think you can come here, upset our culture, our private business and then walk out, leaving the good people of this town in pieces? Well, I won't allow it."

"Pastor Plett, neither you nor anyone else in this town are above the law. You know what happened to Andrew Fehr. You knew even before it happened. That's why you were there – on that night. You went to stop it."

"Yes."

"Who was it?"

"I cannot say because I do not know. I am here to protect these people. If anything happens to me or to Rachel, what will become of them?"

Locklear searched the pastor's face. "Who is it? Is it Samuel Shank?"

Plett stood up, his face panicked. "Stay away from Shank. He'll ..."

"He'll what? Pull the plug, so to speak, on Sara Fehr ... on buying the milk these farmers are so dependent for a living on?"

"How do you know about Sara?"

"It's my job and you are trying to stop me from doing it."

Plett sat down and crumpled into a ball on the chair.

"We are good people. You don't understand."

"Yes, you said that already, pastor. Give me more or I'll have the police come here and arrest you for obstructing justice."

"I knew what was about to happen to Andrew and I went there to stop it but I didn't see their faces. I couldn't risk being seen."

"*Their* faces? There were more than one?"

"There were about three – I think. I just heard their footsteps. They didn't speak – not one word so I can give you no names. The only sound I heard was Andrew pleading for his life."

Plett placed his hands over his face.

Locklear brooded. Why did these killers deliberately leave no ladder? That was another thing that bothered him. Whoever tried to hang the boy made no attempt to make it look like anything other than murder, as though the killing of Andrew Fehr was a warning. But for whom?

"You didn't think to phone the police and tell them?"

"And name who? An invisible enemy that is among us? A sickness borne of hate and blame? I simply knew where and when it would happen, nothing more."

"Why not warn Andrew? Take him somewhere safe?"

"I didn't know in time and when I did find out there was no way to reach him. He was already walking to Dayton to see Mrs Wyss."

"So you made an excuse to go to the Wyss farm?"

"I drove along the roadway first – Rachel and I – searching for him. When we didn't see him we drove up to the Fehr farm."

"And?"

"There was no one there. It was getting dark so we drove back to Wysses' and waited. He didn't show and that's when I saw the car lights going along the incline of Fehrs' farm. I immediately left the house and ... that's where I found him ..."

Plett broke down and cried openly into his large hands.

"Then who told you? Who provided you with this information?"

"It was Esther. Esther told me."

Esther Fehr was a textbook example of a hostile witness. In a stuffy, cramped back room in Dayton police station, she sat at the table facing the open window with her arms folded and her lips pulled tight into a thin, defiant line. The sun filled the room and reflected off the light in her stormy grey eyes. Tiny gold flecks in her mousy brown hair shone in the stifling room. Beads of sweat trickled down Locklear's face and body and on the female cop whom he had brought in from reception to witness the interrogation. Soaked with perspiration, the trooper stood against the open window, hoping to cool herself in the light breeze. Fehr, on the other hand, looked cool and calm. Her abrupt arrest did not seem to upset the young woman. She stared coldly at Locklear and nestled back into the chair, ready obviously for a long day of questions she would not answer. Locklear tried Mr Nice Guy but she sneered at him as though accustomed to such tactics. He tried coming down heavy on her, tried the age-old threats of charges, court, prison, but nothing worked. Esther Fehr was not afraid.

After an hour of trying to make her talk, Locklear sat back and returned the woman's stare for what seemed to be an eternity.

"I didn't have any brothers and sisters," he said at last. "It was just my mother and me, living from hand to mouth. It was hard. I spent a lot of time on my own, waiting for my mother to finish work. I couldn't tell you how many times back then I would have given anything for a brother or a sister. But you – you have four other people who I'd say care very much about you."

Locklear saw the slight thaw in the woman, a quiver of the lip so minute he might have imagined it.

The cop shifted her weight slightly, hoping that the nerve the sergeant touched in the ice-cold detainee might result in her escaping the heat of the room sooner than she'd thought.

"Someone tried to kill your little brother and now he's fighting for his life. That's gotta mean something to you."

Esther Fehr moved her lips slightly.

Locklear leaned forward.

"He's got Sara," she whispered.

Locklear moved closer.

The door opened and there stood the fleshy-faced cop minus the hot dog.

"Her lawyer's here," he said and, as he moved his girth sideways, a young, smartly dressed women entered. The style of her hair and the lack of make-up instantly identified the woman as Mennonite but her suit – sharp, grey, tailored – painted a different picture.

"Beth Stoll," she said as she threw her card on the desk in front of Locklear.

Esther Fehr stood and backed away. Locklear could see the terror in her eyes. It was the first time he had seen her show any sign of emotion – apart from rage.

"I did not tell anything!" she pleaded in a heavy Germanic accent.

The woman showed no sign of emotion and did not look at Fehr. Locklear noticed something else – her eyes. They were exactly the same as Esther's. This woman was a relative. A relative Esther was terrified of.

"Is she being charged with anything?" Stoll asked coldly.

"We're just asking Ms Fehr some questions."

"Then interview over," Stoll declared as she threw a document onto the table.

Esther backed further into the room, a look of panic on her face. Stoll moved forward and roughly grabbed her arm. Esther wrenched herself away.

"I don't think she wants to go with you," Locklear said as he stood and blocked the lawyer's path.

The assisting cop straightened and put her hand on her firearm, ready for whatever would happen next.

Stoll looked Locklear up and down, and a sneer washed over her face.

"Esther knows what's good for her – and for her family. You want to come with me, don't you, Esther?"

Esther nodded meekly and seemed to shrink before Locklear's eyes – the angry woman who had thus far treated him with contempt looked pleadingly at him as she was pulled from the room.

He followed the pair along the corridor, all the time looking at Esther who did not take her eyes off him.

She mouthed something as she was pulled out the station door.

Ask Abigail. Locklear was sure that was it.

Locklear watched from the station door as Stoll's driver got out and opened the back door to the blacked-out SUV.

Then a pickup truck, old and dusty, screamed into the lot, and halted in front of the SUV.

Luke Fehr was at the wheel.

Luke sat in his truck for what seemed to Locklear an eternity, his hat pulled forward, covering his eyes. He reached forward and took an item from the glove box. It was a small book, old, torn and tattered. He raised the book up and placed it tight against the windscreen and held it there for Stoll to see.

Luke opened the door and slowly got out of the truck, holding the book in his left hand. He pushed his hat upwards, revealing his eyes. Locklear squinted at the man – it looked like he had those same stunning eyes as his siblings and the woman in front of him. Locklear could not see what the book was but the expression on Stoll's face told him that Luke Fehr had just showed his hand and it was full of aces. Without removing his gaze from Stoll, Luke Fehr stretched his arm out and took two sideways steps towards the station as though his intention was to deliver the tome to the police.

Locklear heard a small yelp escaping from Stoll's throat.

Luke stared down the well-dressed lawyer who still held a tight grip on his sister's arm.

"No!" Stoll pleaded.

Luke did not speak but Stoll knew what it would take to stop him from handing the book over. She instantly loosened her grip on her captive who ran towards her brother and jumped into the truck.

Luke stood for a moment longer looking at Stoll but did not utter a word. He was sending her a message – a message she clearly understood. Slowly, he backed himself into his truck, the book still held tightly in his hand, and reversed out of the lot in a cloud of dust, almost crashing into Carter as he drove in.

Within seconds, the truck, and Esther, disappeared from view.

Locklear knew that it would be the last he'd see of Esther Fehr for some time. She was in danger and it would no longer be safe for her to be with the Pletts.

Carter parked and, armed with several documents from the library, looked briefly at Stoll but walked forward until he stood by Locklear, waiting to find out what was going on.

Stoll smoothed down her jacket and slid into the back seat of her car. She rolled down the window as her driver slowly moved forward.

"You haven't seen the last of me!" she called as they exited the lot.

Locklear sat down on a small wall at the front of the station house.

"Who was she?" he asked Carter.

"Bethany Stoll – she's Samuel Shank's granddaughter. What was she doing here?"

Locklear pulled at his thick mane in frustration. He had put Esther Fehr in danger by bringing her here. Carter was right – things had to be handled differently. Someone had told Shank that Locklear had taken Esther in for questioning and he sent his legal eagle granddaughter to silence the girl. Locklear had also brought the normally nocturnal Luke Fehr from his hiding place, placing the young man in danger also. It was also clear that someone was talking to Luke – someone told him Esther was here – Plett was an obvious choice. Locklear reasoned that it was probably Luke who helped Plett cut Andrew down from the rafters that night. What was also clear was that this was a feud between two families – the Shanks and the Fehrs – once part of the same kin but divided now by something Locklear could not get to grips with. Plett, for his part, was in the middle, trying to keep on the side of right but losing his battle against the might of the wealthy Shanks. Whatever Locklear did from here, it would have to be done quietly. He would have to have patient. He would have to listen to Carter.

As he pulled himself up from the wall, the fleshy-faced cop came out.

"The hospital phoned. Andrew Fehr is awake."

Chapter 8

The short drive to Rockingham Memorial Hospital seemed to take an eternity as Carter weaved through the late-afternoon traffic. En-route, Carter tried to update Locklear on his research into the Fehr family but gave up when it became clear that his boss's mind was elsewhere.

Locklear's mind was on the book Bethany Stoll obviously valued and, more urgently, the safety of Andrew Fehr. Now that he was awake, those responsible for his attempted murder had a lot to fear – that was if the boy's brain wasn't too damaged to point any fingers. Locklear lifted the radio and was put through to Harrisonburg's station. He waited three minutes to be put through to the station's chief and requested a twenty-four-hour guard be posted outside Fehr's room.

At the foot of Andrew Fehr's bed, Locklear was disappointed to find that the boy was asleep – deliberately tranquillised by Dr Bosch – reportedly due to the high state of agitation he displayed upon waking. Locklear walked up to the bed and ran his hand along the two tubes which fed sedatives into Andrew Fehr's veins.

"Which one is keeping him asleep?" he asked.

Bosch approached the bed and pointed to the clear liquid that dripped steadily into the boy's arm.

"Turn it off," Locklear demanded.

"But, he's –"

"Turn it off," Locklear repeated.

Bosch slowly turned down the medication and turned to Locklear.

"Often people who experienced a trauma wake remembering what they last experienced. He was terrified. I had to sedate him immediately. If he is to recover mentally, he needs to feel safe. He needs time to adjust."

"I understand that but I need to speak with him. After that, I plan to keep this boy very safe."

Locklear sat at the foot of Andrew Fehr's bed. Carter took the remaining chair while Bosch left to continue his rounds.

The pair sat together in silence, waiting for the boy to stir. Neither spoke as the clock ticked loudly above the door of the hospital room. Five hours passed slowly and by the time the heavy sedation began to wear off, Locklear had mentally mapped the case so far – who was involved, who might help him and who definitely would not – but most of all he thought about the book Luke Fehr had held up to Bethany Stoll and how the threat of it being handed over to the police had induced fear in the cold woman. The book, and its obvious value to the Shanks, was now the centrepiece in his puzzle.

Locklear's thoughts did not alter when he saw a slight flicker of movement from Andrew Fehr's little finger. Neither did they change when the boy's foot jumped twice before resting beneath the crisp linen sheet or when his left arm shot out in tremor and his teeth protruded as he began to gasp. It was when the boy opened his eyes that Locklear stood to meet the same amber-flecked Fehr eyes staring at him.

Fehr, now fully awake, began to thrash about, pulling at an invisible cord around his neck and gasping for breath. Carter jumped from his seat and stood over the boy, anxious to show him a familiar face.

"Andrew, it's Lee," he said but the boy did not appear to hear him.

Locklear pulled on the bell, hoping to summon Bosch. As much as he wanted to hear what Andrew had to say, he did not want the boy to suffer.

"You're safe," Locklear said.

A gurgle bubbled up from the Andrew's throat.

"*Es ist ...*" he whispered, his voice muffled and hoarse.

Lee Carter lowered his ear towards his mouth. "What Andrew?"

"*Es ist ... ein gutes ...*"

Andrew Fehr began to cough. Lee lifted his head and, without knowing if it was OK, put his own water bottle to Andrew's mouth.

Locklear could see the fear in the boy's eyes.

"*Es ist ... ein gutes Jahr ... un die ... Dinge ... richtig ... zu machen ...*"

Locklear watched as Carter mouthed the words over, as if trying to make sense of them.

"What did he say?"

"He said ... I think it was ..."

"What? God damn it, Carter. What did he say?"

"He said 'It's a good year to put things right'."

Locklear sank back down into his chair. Andrew had uttered the exact same words as his sister coming out of her absence.

When Bosch returned, he glared at the cops and rushed to the boy's bed, turning the drip back on. Andrew Fehr looked at Locklear as his eyes began to slowly close.

"Birthday," he muttered in English, as his eyes slowly closed.

"Well, did you get what you wanted?" Bosch asked sharply.

Locklear walked to the bed and held Andrew Fehr's hand. The boy's eyes jolted open again but this time he did not seem afraid.

"No. I don't think the boy's going to be much use to us," he lied, hoping Andrew Fehr understood and would keep up the charade. Locklear had no idea who to trust in the town and wasn't going to take any chances.

He remained with Andrew until a cop was placed outside the room and he felt it was safe to leave.

He returned to the station and completed his first task which was to phone Kowalski and have Andrew Fehr transferred to a hospital in Richmond until it was all over – until he had put all of the pieces of the sorry puzzle together. Several of those pieces were still missing but he knew where he might find the next one.

By the time he returned to Dayton, word of Locklear's visit to the Pletts' home and of the arrest and subsequent disappearance of Esther Fehr had spread among the homes and farms of the hinterland. As he drove slowly down the small country roads, he was deprived of the tipped hat from the men who had so far been polite, albeit wary, of him. Women working in fields or selling their vegetables to passing 'English', turned their back to him, afraid no doubt that he might stop to ask them questions and sentence them to the same fate as Esther Fehr. As he neared the Wyss farm he caught a glimpse of Helena Wyss pulling Abigail Fehr roughly from the roadside where she had been selling eggs.

In the car beside him, Carter sulked, no doubt angry with how Locklear was handling the investigation. The trust the small-town trooper had established with the community over years had been lost in one single day and it was Locklear's fault.

Locklear heaved himself out of the car and knocked lightly on Helena Wyss's door. Carter remained in the car and

Locklear did not ask him to accompany him. When she didn't answer he knocked again. He was about to leave when a note was slipped from inside the door to his feet. He looked towards the entrance to the farmhouse and noticed a small crowd of Mennonites gathered on the roadway, watching. He bent down and pretended to tie his shoelace and hoped that they could not see the note from their viewpoint. Locklear slipped the note into his pocket and returned silently to the car.

As Carter pulled away Locklear took the small white note from his pocket. He read it aloud.

"Mr Locklear, you have betrayed the trust of the people here. I cannot let you place Abigail in danger. She depends on me to keep her safe and I will not let her down. Please, please, for Abigail's sake, leave us alone."

Locklear sighed.

"What now?" Carter asked.

"I don't know," Locklear replied. He was stumped. There was no one left to talk to. He was facing a brick wall with no clue how to climb it or get around it.

"Where do you suppose Luke took Esther?" he asked.

Carter drew in a deep breath. "He has a shack out at Silver Lake but everyone knows that's where he does his poaching – he wouldn't go there."

"Have they any other family – anyone else they'd go to?"

Carter shook his head. "Just that old grand-uncle in the hills. Like I said, there's no way they'd go to him. Guy's as mad as a cut snake anyhow. Just speaks gibberish."

"How does he live?"

"Elder Shank runs a charity – they visit anyone in need of help, bring food, clothing, that kind of thing."

"And in return he expects?" Locklear asked.

Carter sighed. "Look, sarge, you're never going to get these people to go against Shank. I tried to tell you earlier – his people have been the pastors here for generations. You should see the references to the family in the archives. And he's rich. I mean *rich*. He provides scholarships, medical care, funds the elementary school, food for those in need – you name it, he does it."

"But yet he was demoted. He was pastor here until Plett arrived. How would something like that come about?"

Carter shrugged.

"Do you think he's clean, Carter? You don't say much. I gotta know which side you're on."

The look of hurt on Carter's face told Locklear everything he needed to know.

"No, I don't think he's clean," Carter said. "I think he's got his filthy paws into just about everything he can so that he can keep these people where he wants them. I heard he's even connected to a casino in town – he bought up a major shareholding in it. Now, gambling is something Mennonites definitely shouldn't be involved in. But one bad apple doesn't make the barrel useless."

"Meaning?"

"Meaning you've been going around here treating everyone like they're suspects. It frightens these people. You've got to know how to speak with them. They're gentle people but they're not stupid, sarge, and they deserve respect."

"OK, Carter. From now on I'll take your lead. Should have listened to you from the start."

Carter looked startled at this pronouncement.

They drove on, both pensive.

"Guess you know about me and Sara Fehr, huh?" Carter said then, breaking the silence.

Locklear nodded but did not look at the trooper.

"We were very young but I really liked her. She was smart and had her feet on the ground but she was terrified of Shank. She really believed that his ancestors had put a curse on her family and on the farm. We were together for a few years at high school and I thought because her family were shunned I might have a future with her, you know?"

"But her brother had other ideas?"

"Yes, I had it out with Luke one time. He said it was time to wake up and see nothing was ever going to come of Sara and me. He said they were cursed and being with her would only bring me bad luck. I thought it was just some crazy superstition. When I said I wouldn't stop seeing her, he beat me up bad, landed me in the hospital for three days. When I got back to school, Sara was gone. Luke had decided that they'd both leave school and Sara did whatever Luke said. I never really saw her after that – least not close up. When she had her accident, Luke wouldn't let me visit her."

"You could just go there – I mean, he's not there all the time."

Carter turned his head away and looked out of the window.

"I don't know if I want to, not any more. Too much time has passed. It'd be too hard to see her that way. I think it's best if I remember her as she was. I think she'd prefer that. I love my wife, sir, but Sara and me – it was different. I don't think I'll ever care for anyone that same way."

Locklear coughed, a coping mechanism he'd developed in childhood to manage the myriad emotions his mother forced upon him. He did it every time he was uncomfortable, every time he was expected to empathise when he had no words, no response, no idea what to say. He tapped his fingers on the clock on the dashboard: 16.30.

"Just drop me back to the station and you head on home to your son's birthday party."

"Thanks, sir. I didn't think you heard me earlier."

"I heard."

"Thank you, sir."

"I didn't know ... about your son."

Carter nodded. "Seth's real smart, you know, sir. People misunderstand because he can't walk. His kindergarten said he's top of his class. He loves puzzles and maps. He already knows all of his letters and he won't even be going to school for another year."

"Tomorrow – take your son to school – your wife doesn't seem strong enough to lift the ... you know ..." He coughed. "Then go straight to the library and focus on John Grant."

"Yes, sir. Will do."

When he reached the incident room, Locklear found Mendoza trawling through records on an old computer. She smiled when she saw him.

"I've got some interesting information for you."

Locklear poured himself a coffee and sat down.

"Shoot."

"The bad news first. I sat my backside down in the reception area of Shank Creamery for two hours, hoping to see the man himself or whoever signs the cheque for Sara Fehr's care but no one would talk to me."

Locklear sighed but he had expected that.

"So I headed to the cemetery. It turns out there are a lot of Fehrs in the local graveyard. Plett saw me there – he was going into the church when I parked the car but he just ignored me. Oh, by the way, I almost got myself another husband there. A young Mennonite man took a liking to me. Guess he won't be too happy when he finds out I am not the out-of-town visitor visiting her great-great-grandfather's grave."

"You don't think he noticed that you're Hispanic?"

Mendoza laughed. "Now – are you ready for this? There were a few Fehr graves from the late 1700s – you can hardly read the writing on the headstones – but the newer ones – well, when I say new I mean since the mid-1800s – a huge number of them died young – all male."

"From disease?" Locklear offered.

"No – there's too much of a gap between each death and there aren't enough other headstones in the graveyard with similar dates of death to signify an outbreak of disease. For example ..." she checked her notes, "I found Adam Fehr – brother of the brothers returning from war (1866), John Fehr (1701), Thomas Fehr (1727), Matthew Fehr (1752), Andrew Fehr (1780), Mark Fehr (1810), Isaac Fehr (1833), another Matthew Fehr (1870), Lucas Fehr (1901), and another Mark Fehr (1933), Isaiah Fehr (2007) – that's the last one I found. I checked the records and he was the Fehr children's father. He was the only one who didn't die so young, though he was only forty-eight years old. He died of cancer. Every one of the other Fehr men died in their twenty-first year."

Locklear stared at her.

"Yes, that's what I said: all of them died in their twenty-first year."

Locklear thought for a moment. "Andrew Fehr said *birthday* to me today."

"You sure? Carter said he spoke German?"

"He did but before he went back to sleep he looked at me and said *"birthday"* in English. Helena Wyss said it was his birthday that day and she was expecting him. She had a present for him."

"Maybe it was the first thing he remembered when he woke up?"

Locklear shook his head. "Look up the report on Andrew Fehr – see if it gives his date of birth."

Mendoza entered the case number and read the main sheet which recorded his vital information.

"July 14th, 1994. He was tw–"

"Twenty-one," Locklear said.

"Just like all of the others. But how could this happen over and over again? How come it didn't get out – become public knowledge?"

"Like Carter said, these people sort out their own problems."

"Till now."

"When did you say the first premature death occurred?"

"Em ... 1866."

Locklear thought for a moment. "A year after the end of the Civil War."

"You think that has anything to do with it?"

"It has everything to do with it, Mendoza. Everything."

"Type in one more thing. Search the police record for Sara Fehr's automobile accident."

Mendoza typed in Sara's name twice – once with a H and then without.

"Here it is," she said, swinging the screen around so Locklear could see.

He scanned the page until he found what he was looking for. Sara Fehr's date of birth. April 20th, 1987.

"Now – get me the date of the accident."

Mendoza followed the order. "You really need to learn how to use a computer, sarge."

She ran her a fingernail along the screen, squinting until she found what she was looking for.

"Here it is – date of accident – April 20th, 2008."

"Her twenty-first birthday," Locklear and Mendoza said in unison.

"But, she's the only female ... and it's recorded as an accident. Something about that doesn't add up."

"Check to see who the investigating officer was and talk to him."

"Or her!" Mendoza replied. "So, someone has been murdering the Fehrs for one hundred and fifty years – and all on their twenty-first birthdays."

"Not someone, generations of someones – and I bet I know who they are."

"But why?" Mendoza asked. "What feud could possibly last for so long?"

Locklear stared at the hard facts in front of him.

"This isn't a feud. I was wrong. The Fehrs have something the Shanks want only they don't really have it ... or ... they don't know where it is."

Chapter 9

Set high on an attractive lot on the south side of Richmond, the home of Bishop John Rahn was even plainer than the Pletts' house, except brighter and airier. The house, which overlooked the southern edge of the sprawling city, had stood in that spot when Richmond was no bigger that Harrisonburg was now. There was an air of peace and serenity to the small waiting area where Rahn's wife had placed Locklear half an hour earlier.

When he arrived, Rahn looked nothing like Locklear expected him to. The bishop was dressed in an ordinary grey tweed suit over a blue shirt and patterned tie. His short beard, slightly greying, was neatly trimmed on his thin bespectacled face. Rahn could be, Locklear reasoned, described as an attractive middle-aged man. He had a friendly face with sparking blue eyes and an open way about him.

He shook hands genially and took Locklear into his office where he settled down in front of a large oak desk.

"Can I get you a coffee or anything?"

"No, thank you."

"What can I do for you?"

Locklear thought about how he might broach the question of the demotion of Samuel Shank seven years previously. The forthright expression on Rahn's face told him that it would be best to just come out and say it.

Locklear explained the events in Dayton and watched as Rahn's face clouded over. He wondered what the man was thinking but continued with the story, finishing with a question about the placement of Plett in Shank's place.

Rahn ran his hands along the old wooden desk. He took off his glasses and rubbed them hard with a white-cotton, lace-trimmed handkerchief. He caught Locklear looking at it.

"It's my wife's," Rahn said with a smile. "She puts lace on everything. I took it accidentally yesterday. I've been trying to hide it ever since." He replaced the glasses, which did not look any cleaner, back on the edge of his nose. "In the past, Mennonite pastors were elected by the congregation. The system worked well for hundreds of years. They were unpaid and largely undertook their duties as a devotion to God's work."

"And now?"

"Well, depending on the size of the community, pastors are now hired, and paid, by the community. They are often seminary graduates. But this usually happens in the larger congregations who can afford to pay the salary of a pastor."

"And the smaller ones – like Dayton?"

"Dayton has a very small – and dwindling population. There was never money there to pay a pastor."

"So what changed? I assume Plett is paid for his work?"

"Yes, yes, he is – part-funded by other, larger congregations. Sometimes, the old arrangement just doesn't work in today's economic climate."

"Can you give me an example, Mr – em – do I call you Bishop?"

"John. On rare occasions, there are problems, a mismatch between the needs of the congregation and the pastor, a pastor trying to enforce old order ways on modern Mennonite groups ... an abuse of power ..." Rahn trailed off.

"Was an abuse of power the reason Samuel Shank was relieved of his duties?"

Rahn did not answer.

"Well, can I take it, John, that the latter reason would most fit the reason Plett replaced Samuel Shank?"

John Rahn nodded.

"Are you going to tell me what was going on?"

John Rahn's mouth smiled but his eyes mirrored his thoughts. "There were complaints. People who left the area to practise in other church groups complained to the new pastors. Eventually, it got back here and ... I had to take action."

"By installing Plett?"

"Yes."

"Can I also take it that what happened to Sara Fehr sparked your 'action'?"

"Yes," Rahn replied, meeker now.

Locklear knew the interview was coming to the end. He stood, as did Rahn.

He took the pastor's outstretched hand.

"Can I ask you one more thing, John?"

Rahn nodded but his face was more serious now, his smile gone.

"Does *'It's a good year to put things right'* mean anything to you?"

Rahn shook his head. "I'm sorry – no."

Locklear scanned the face of the man in front of him. Rahn was telling the truth.

Before he left Richmond to return to Dayton, Locklear had three things to do. First he had to sit down with Alex Kowalski and update his boss on the case so far.

After this, he went to check on Andrew Fehr who had been admitted to Richmond Memorial under an assumed name.

He found the kid sitting up in bed eating jelly, but with no memory of the night of his hanging. Either that or he was keeping up a charade that he didn't remember. Locklear was glad of that but frustrated to find that the charade extended to him also.

The third task he had to attend to was to check on the cactus plant in his apartment. It was the only living thing that depended on him and he had bought it because of its resilience – cacti needed little water and therefore little care. When he got there, it was fine but he watered it anyway – there was no telling when he'd be back.

Before he left he went to the closet and packed some more clothes. He reached into the back of the closet and retrieved a box he'd kept since his childhood. He blew the heavy dust from it to make sure he had the right one.

Five minutes later he was back on Route 64, thinking of what he'd do next.

Jo Mendoza didn't have far to go to interview the cop who investigated Sara Fehr's accident – he sat most days under the fan in the police station filling out traffic violations and court paperwork, a punishment for discharging his weapon without need, although he didn't see it that way at the time.

Trooper Ricci waited until Mendoza finished talking before telling her what he remembered from the day Sara Fehr was pulled from the Susquehanna River.

"We came upon the scene only a few minutes after she hit the water 'cause she drove right past us like the devil himself was chasing her. The road she was speeding on is a dead end and only leads to one place – Rockville Bridge – which is a railway bridge not open to traffic. We followed her. We thought she might be drunk. We got cut off when a truck jack-knifed so we had to go around. By the time we got there she was under water. You could say she was lucky that where she landed was shallow – only the driver side was actually in the water – rest of the car was stuck in silt. But she hit her head bad. My partner got in the passenger window and I called for services. He pulled her out but she was unconscious."

The Pact

"Is your partner still active?"

Ricci shook his head. "He was shot – five years ago. Died at the scene."

"I'm sorry. Did you see anyone chase her? Was there another car?"

"No. Guess she was depressed or something. The note we found – it was on the floor of the passenger side – was in German. We took a photocopy of it and got it translated but the note itself was lost before the coroner's court called the case."

"What did it say?"

Ricci stood up and went to the files at the back of the room. Mendoza waited while he banged the drawers of several filing cabinets open and shut. He returned and handed a photocopy to Mendoza. There were two lines on the page:

It's a good year to put things right. I'm going to put things right I'm sorry. The children need you more than me Sara

"Hell of a thing – a girl like that – her whole life ahead of her – trying to kill herself."

"The coroner ruled it attempted suicide?"

"No, that was the odd thing. Me and Billy – that was my partner – reckoned the group didn't want it to get out and exerted some influence. She was a Mennonite."

"A shunned Mennonite," Mendoza corrected him.

"Really? Well, the actual note was lost and no one seemed interested in the photocopy we had. They said it was an accident. I knew we were being told to shut up. It *was* suicide – I'm sure of that but we wondered if whoever drove the poor girl to it wanted to keep things quiet. We even had a witness said he saw her drive off the bridge. I moved the photocopy years back to an unsolved file. Had a feeling someday someone would come looking for it."

Mendoza studied the writing. There was something not right about it but she couldn't put her finger on it.

"Is that everything?" she asked.

"There was one other thing that was odd. When the ambulance took the girl away, Billy and myself drove to her farm to inform the family. First we thought there was no one there – there was no answer at the house so we walked over to the barn. We looked inside and there was a noose hanging from the rafter. Then we heard banging so Billy took out his gun – we thought we'd stumbled onto something. We walked behind the barn. There was a small outhouse and the door to it was blocked – someone had driven a car right up to the door and had locked someone inside. There were no keys in the car so Billy and I had to freewheel the car backwards and let the guy out. It was her brother – her twin actually – we found that out later. He mustn't have been well before we even gave him the news because he smelt of vomit real bad. The poor guy fainted when we told him. Strangest day I ever had and I've had a few."

"Did you ask him about the noose?"

"Billy did but he wouldn't speak – said not one word in the whole time we drove him to the hospital. We weren't sure if he spoke English or not so we left him alone and just figured the girl had changed her mind about the method she'd use to end it. It's men who hang themselves – not women – least not in my experience."

"There's no reference to Luke Fehr or the noose in your report."

"There was in the original report. Billy and me spent two hours working late writing it up and left it on the sarge's desk. Next morning, he came to us and said to take it out … so we did."

As dusk fell, an excited Lee Carter exited by the back entrance to Harrisonburg Library, pleased with what he'd found out about John Grant and the time he spent in Dayton at the end of the Civil War. The librarian, who he'd known at high school had been very helpful, spending a good deal of her day

The Pact

helping him find the records he needed, and then stayed on past closing. A day trawling though historic records reminded him of his old life, the one he knew before his son was born. For two years after Seth's premature birth, Carter continued in his research post in Richmond while his wife struggled at home with a child who needed twenty-four-hour care. When his wife's mental health began to suffer, he threw in the career he had worked hard for and returned to Harrisonburg to take up a post as state trooper under his father's then command. Even now he knew he'd made the right choice but that didn't stop him longing for a life in academia.

This day had been the happiest he'd experienced in the job and he felt satisfied as he threw the photocopies of useful records he'd found into the trunk. As he slammed the trunk shut, Carter heard a familiar voice behind him, a woman's, calling his name. He turned and instead saw the face of a man with a gun pointed at him. The gun fired and Carter instinctively shifted to the side. Searing heat spread through his left shoulder as he fell and slammed his head against the ground. As he gasped for breath he opened his eyes and looked upwards into the dark night sky. A click – the sound of a bullet moving into the chamber – ready to fire again. Unable to move, he clenched his eyes shut and waited for the shot which he knew would end his life, and thought of the loves of his life: his wife, his son, his father and Sara Fehr who even with the passing years was never far from his mind. He understood now what people facing death meant when they say time slowed down and a million thoughts came and went in an endless procession of photos and memories. He saw his life – a happy childhood despite the absence of his deceased mother, the love and devotion of his widowed cop father, a sense of belonging to his community, his love of sport and history – and theology, which he had avoided mentioning to Locklear. More important than anything, his faith that would hold him through whatever he now faced on the cold damp ground. Another sound and he began to pray. A scuffle, noise, grunting. He opened his eyes. A car screaming away, the rough pull of strong arms lifting him up. The smell of sand and the rough throw onto a hard metal base. He groaned in pain and as he drifted into unconsciousness the last sounds he heard were the screams of the librarian in the distance.

While Carter lay in the back of a truck in a pool of his own blood, Jo Mendoza sat four blocks away in the incident room alone, thinking out Ricci's story. She wondered if the other Fehr deaths were as a result of suicide and if perhaps there was a genetic predisposition to mental illness. If so, it would put paid to Locklear's suspicion of multiple murders of the Fehr family. She sat at the computer and, starting with the earliest dates, began typing in the names of the Fehr men whose headstones stated that they had died in their twenty-first year. Few of the deaths appeared in the state records, and those were recorded as farm accidents. Mendoza wondered if, like in her own faith, suicide was considered a sin and covered up by Mennonite families in the hope of their loved one being buried in consecrated ground. Carter, she reasoned, would know if there was any other way of finding out what happened to these men. She lifted her phone. Carter's phone was answered after only two rings – by a woman – a screaming woman at that.

"Hello?" Mendoza said. "Hello? Hello?"

"This is – Anabel Schumer – from the library. His phone was on the ground so I – he took him – *my God, he took him!*"

"Carter? Who took him?"

Mendoza thought the line had gone dead but realised the woman was sobbing silently into the phone.

"Luke Fehr."

Chapter 10

By the time Locklear reached Harrisonburg, an anonymous person had brought Lee Carter into the emergency room of the town's general hospital and had disappeared without giving a name. Locklear already knew that person was Luke Fehr and, unlike Mendoza, did not believe that it was Fehr who attacked Carter. Instead of going to see if his trooper was going to live or die, he drove to the station where the librarian was giving her statement.

Locklear pulled up a chair and listened as the shocked woman shook beneath a heavy blanket.

Frustrated by the cop's generic questions, he pushed his chair into the centre.

"I just want you to focus on this – you walked out the back door – then what? Just relax. Take it step by step."

The librarian's lip trembled. She preferred the other cop who was walking her through the whole day, who came in, who went out.

"I opened the back door to go to my car. It was dark. I was surprised that Lee's car was still in the parking lot. I let him park it there because it's free. No one else has access. I saw a light in his car because the door was open. I heard a woman's voice but I couldn't see anything. The outside light was broken. It wasn't broken last night. There were bits of glass on the ground but I didn't see it until I closed the door and stood on the glass. It cracked. I looked down at it and I heard a gunshot. I screamed. There were more voices and noise, a scuffle I think. A car took off. I looked down and someone was putting Lee into the back of a truck. I shouted and he looked up. It was ... it was Luke Fehr."

"You know Luke Fehr?"

"Yes."

"Are you sure it was him?"

"Yes, I was at high school with Luke. Lee also. I can't believe he'd hurt Lee. They used to be friends."

"So, there was another car, apart from Luke Fehr's truck?"

"Yes."

"Did you see the make, colour?"

"No, I didn't even know it was there until I heard it take off. It must have been parked round the side."

Locklear stood to leave.

"There's something else!" she said. "Before the gunshot I heard a voice. A woman's voice."

"What did she say?"

"It was muffled but I think she said ... *take all ... something ... Grant.*"

"John Grant?"

"She didn't say John or least I didn't hear her say John but that's who I was helping Lee research earlier – John Grant."

When Locklear arrived at the crime scene, Carter's trunk was empty and beside his vehicle lay a pool of the trooper's blood. Forensics had found the single casing on the ground, which did not match Carter's weapon.

In the hospital foyer he saw Nick Lombardi, hunched over in a hard plastic chair, crying into his hands. For a brief moment he considered approaching him to enquire if Rosa Lombardi was still alive but instead climbed the three flights of stairs to the floor where Lee Carter lay in a serious but stable condition.

Mendoza met him at the door and beckoned for him to remain outside. There were things she did not want to say in front of Carter's distraught wife.

"They're taking him to surgery in the next half hour or so. They're just waiting on the surgeon to arrive. Looks like the bullet fractured his clavicle and he's gashed his head badly but he'll be fine. I put out an APB on Luke Fehr."

"What? Without my order? Undo it. Fehr didn't attack Lee. It was Shank."

"Shank?"

"Not him personally but his people – the woman the librarian heard – I think it was Shank's granddaughter."

"Or Esther Fehr! Sarge – the librarian saw Luke bundle Carter into his truck."

"To take him here *obviously*! Come on!"

In the hospital's security room, Locklear and Mendoza watched as the security guard rewound the grainy video to the exact time Carter was dropped off at the hospital.

At 21.37, a tall man wearing a cowboy hat could be seen carrying Carter into the hospital foyer. The screen filled with hospital staff rushing towards him. A trolley came into view and the man waited for a moment, said a few short words to a doctor and turned away. A second camera kicked in and as he passed, the man glanced up it, revealing part of his face.

"That's Fehr," Locklear said. "Let's go see what he said to the doctor."

After a brief visit back to Carter's room, Locklear and Mendoza, satisfied that their colleague was not in danger, returned to the emergency department to look for the doctor Fehr had spoken to in the foyer.

When they found Adrian Haak he was asleep on a trolley, exhausted after a thirty-six-hour shift.

Locklear poked him until he opened his weary eyes.

"*What did he say?* You woke me for that?"

"Yes."

"He had an accent. He said, em … 'He's my friend … save him' or 'please help him' – something like that."

"Anything else?"

"No. Now can I go back to sleep?"

Locklear and Mendoza walked away without answering. Haak was already snoring before they had walked ten yards.

Nick Lombardi was nowhere to be seen.

"Feel like a beer?" Mendoza asked.

"I'll join you but …. no beer."

In the corner of O'Mahony's pub, Mendoza and Locklear drank quietly while Irish music played in the background.

"Ever wonder why Irish music can be found pretty much anywhere in the world?" Mendoza mused.

Locklear did not answer. At the moment, he wondered about nothing except who was killing, or trying to kill the Fehr family and anyone else who got too close to the truth.

"I think it's because it's happy," she said. "You know, it sounds happy."

Locklear laughed. "Doesn't take much to get you drunk!"

Mendoza put down her beer. "You worried about Carter?"

"Yes," he replied quietly. "Seems like I'm always one step behind Shank."

"You don't even know if it's him."

"I do. I know it's him. I just have to prove it."

Mendoza smiled, revealing the thin white scar beneath her lip.

"You gonna tell me now where you got those scars?" Locklear asked.

She lifted the bottle again and took a long, deep swig.

"Those," she said, "are courtesy of Manuel Santiago Garcia."

"A perp?"

"My husband. Ex-husband. And those are only the ones you can see. I got lots more."

"You didn't ring the cops?"

"He was a cop! Who was I gonna call? Ghostbusters?"

Mendoza laughed but Locklear could see the sadness in her dark-brown eyes. They reminded him of his mother's.

"How'd you get away?"

"I left one night. The first time he hit Santiago. I left."

"Your son?"

"Yes. It was one thing him hitting me but not my son. I would kill to protect him. My only regret is that I didn't leave earlier."

"You said you got them in the line of duty. What did you mean?

"You, sir, have a very good memory."

Mendoza pulled the label off her bottle and spread it onto the bar.

"When my brother told our parents he was gay, it nearly killed them, especially my dad. He was already upset that Diego wanted to be an artist and not a cop. Dad just didn't understand. They were devout Catholics and they felt so ashamed in the community. For a while Dad wouldn't allow Diego to visit. They only made up a few weeks before Dad died of cancer. He'd been battling his illness for months so when I said I was pregnant it was too much for them. There was no question of me being a single mom. Sad part is I already knew I didn't want to marry Manuel. He had already begun to hit me, even when I was pregnant with Santiago, but I had no choice. I did my duty. I did it for my parents and I stayed in that marriage through my dad's illness. I just couldn't tell them how unhappy I was or what was happening to me. I just couldn't tell them who I really was or what it was I wanted from life. I hadn't realised any of that until I had locked myself into a life that just wasn't for me."

"Religion!" Locklear replied, unsure what else to say.

"No ... you cannot blame religion. I love my God."

"Now I *know* you are drunk, Mendoza."

"No, I have my faith. People do things in God's name that he doesn't want."

"Are you sure it's not a She?" he said.

"Yes, maybe God is a woman!" Mendoza raised her bottle to the barman. "Another – *per favor*! Seriously, Locklear, it's true. Our parish priest talked my parents into making me marry Manuel – God didn't. Like Shank – we could think God's way is the Mennonite way but those people, they're so kind. Shank is one piece of poison among so much good."

"You sound like Carter!"

Mendoza didn't reply to that jibe.

"What about you? You ever been married?" she asked after a while.

Locklear visualised the many suitcases that had stood in his apartment hallway. Women who got tired of waiting for something he never pretended he would, or could, give.

"No."

"Well, tell me about you then."

"There's nothing to tell. I was an only child. My mother and me, we travelled around a lot. I joined the army, then joined the police. She died. That's about it really."

"Did you love her?"

"What the hell kind of a question is that, Mendoza?"

"A simple one."

Locklear sighed. His soda glass was empty.

"She was always running away from something. She ... it ... made my life hard."

"A man?"

Locklear shook his head.

"A woman never runs from a good life," Mendoza said. "She will always put her child first. If she was running, it was to protect you from something,"

A memory surfaced. The day after his mother bought him

a new school uniform. They had settled into a new town. She had found steady work, a steady boyfriend and a steady home in a trailer park on the outskirts of the small friendly town. Two days after his mother filled in the enrolment forms for his new school, he watched from the window as a man pulled into the parking lot in a mustard-coloured mustang. He had never seen the man before. His mother was sleeping on the sofa after a night shift in the local diner. He stood and watched the Indian run in and out of several trailers before barging into theirs. His mother screamed. She cried. They talked. He slept on the couch, she in her bed. Her boyfriend from the next trailer did not call. For two days the man pleaded, insisted, begged, cried – but his mother would not be budged. Locklear didn't understand what the man wanted her to do. Only once did the man speak to him, using words from his mother's language that he understood because she had said the same thing to him many times. *Paleface*. He never uttered another word to Locklear. On the third morning the man drove his mustang out of the trailer park, leaving a trail of dust behind him. Locklear never saw him again. When his mother stopped crying he asked her who the man was. She didn't answer. Instead she began to pack. The next day they left. He never got to wear his uniform, never got to go to that school and never enrolled in another school using his real name again.

Now, when he occasionally remembered the episode, he wondered if the man was one of her family. His family.

"You didn't answer my question," Mendoza said, waking him from his reminiscing.

"I know what my mother was running from, Mendoza, and it wasn't a man. It was herself."

Chapter 11

The following day, Locklear woke to the news that the town's library had been burned to the ground in the early hours of the morning.

"Dumb redneck fuckers!" he said to Mendoza who sat in the booth facing him and was unusually quiet. "You OK?"

"Yes. Look ... I'm worried that I may have told you too much last night ... I'm ... I'm a bit embarrassed. I don't usually tell anyone about my marriage. I hope you don't think me weak, or vulnerable. I'm neither."

"I know," Locklear responded.

"That's it? You know?"

Locklear turned from her and took his wallet out to pay for breakfast. He knew it was one of those situations when a woman wanted more and he never quite knew what he was expected to add to what he'd already said. He turned back to Mendoza, who was holding her head in her hands, and thought for a moment.

"I think it took more guts to stay in a marriage to keep your parents happy than it would have taken to leave."

"Thank you," she said quietly. "It was stupid though."

"Oh, it *was* stupid," Locklear replied, smiling.

Mendoza returned her boss's smile as he paid the check.

He shoved her hungover body towards the exit.

"OK, I need you to find where that librarian lives and ask her what Carter found out about John Grant. Then I want you to go see Plett and see if he has historic death records for the area. I want to know what those Fehr men died from. Most likely if Plett has them he won't show them to you. Probably doesn't have them. If so, go see John Rahn – he's the Mennonite bishop in Richmond. He's probably got copies of the records in his offices."

"OK, sarge. Is it OK if I go see my kid while I'm in Richmond?"

"Sure, stay overnight. I'll see you tomorrow morning."

"Where are you going?"

"I'm going to see Samuel Shank and, trust me, he won't leave *me* in his waiting area."

Shank Creamery was situated on the main highway, exactly equidistant from the towns of Dayton and Harrisonburg – a strategic location and one that was not lost on Locklear – the old man clearly kept one foot in the old world and one firmly planted in the new.

Locklear poured himself a coffee and lowered himself into the soft leather sofa in the reception area. A flyer on the glass table pictured Shank and another man in Old Order clothing driving a buggy along a Dayton slip road with several milking cows in the background. A caption said: "*From our humble farms to your table.*" Locklear grinned and placed the flyer in his pocket.

He had been hoping that he'd be kept waiting, at least for a while. He wanted to take in his surroundings. Every wall in the large glass-fronted foyer was adorned with expensive-looking modern art. Beside him, a large framed photo revealed the office's modest origins – it was an old black-and-white photo of a group of about twenty young Mennonite male farmers, staring into the camera with serious faces.

Locklear read the names of the men beneath the picture and locked in on one – Aaron Fehr, no doubt the man Carter said was a grand-uncle of the Fehrs, stood slightly apart from the group and the expression on his face said he did not want to be there. Carter had said the old guy was crazy and warned Locklear not to go anywhere near him.

A sculpture of a Grecian-styled semi-nude sat in the middle of a small water fountain in the centre of the reception area. Two elevators to his right brought frantic-looking employees to their floors and the air was one of general haste and anxiety – not the atmosphere you'd expect a Mennonite employer to support. One look around the area told Locklear that Shank did not lead a simple Mennonite life and that his black clothing and horse-drawn buggy were mere costume pieces dusted off on the occasion he visited the town of his roots. Twice he noticed the nervous-looking receptionist glance his way as she spoke quietly, yet urgently, into her phone.

Upstairs, a glass-panelled corridor revealed workers hurrying to and fro from their offices. After ten minutes, aware that he was being watched, Locklear glanced up and saw Bethany Stoll staring down at him. Her long, wavy hair was loose and hung about her shoulders. He smiled at her as she moved back from the glass and disappeared.

After twenty minutes passed, Locklear waved to other people sitting on adjoining sofas, business people waiting to see Shank.

"Must be a lot of money in milk," he said loudly.

Only one man smiled at him while two others drew their briefcases towards their chests and avoided eye contact with him.

Locklear began to whistle. The receptionist lifted the phone again and whispered into the receiver.

"I'm waiting to see the big man myself. Find out why he won't buy milk from shunned Mennonites while he lives in luxury."

Now his only supporter looked away from him but Locklear could see the faint smile on his lips. The man picked up the newspaper and snapped its large pages open.

"You know, that's another funny thing." Locklear raised his voice. "I'm a bit ignorant about the faith and I thought Old Order Mennonites don't read what's going on in the outside world. I was wrong – they do. Not everyone has respect for the written word though. Did you know that the library burned down last night? Doesn't matter though, they got copies of everything that was in there in practically every library in this country." Locklear was practically shouting now.

The neatly dressed receptionist left her seat and approached him.

"Mr Shank will see you now."

"I thought he might," Locklear replied.

When the door to the elevator opened on the fifth floor, Locklear found Bethany Stoll waiting for him.

"Mr Shank's office is this way."

"You mean your grandfather's office?" Locklear curtly replied.

Stoll ignored him. Locklear had to bite his lip to stop himself from saying he knew she was the woman in the parking lot of the library the night before, that he knew she or someone with her had tried to kill Carter and that she had arranged for the library and every piece of information on John Grant inside it to be burned to the ground. Locklear noticed the shortness of the young woman's skirt, which revealed two deeply tanned legs, and the way she deliberately accentuated the swing of her hips as she walked ahead of him. He focused his eyes on the door at the end of the corridor, knowing his nemesis sat just inside its heavy panelled door.

Stoll knocked lightly and entered.

"*Das ist Herr Locklear – ein Polizist*," Stoll said.

Locklear stood at the door and stared at the tiny man

behind the huge desk. Samuel Shank looked smaller than he had the first time Locklear laid eyes on him perched on top of his buggy. The bespectacled man with the large grey beard wore the same black coat and, despite being indoors, wore a large black hat on his tiny head. Locklear wondered if the hat and coat had ever fitted him and smiled at the charade.

Shank stood and offered his hand. Locklear ignored it and sat uninvited. Stoll remained at the open door until Shank began to shout at her in German. Locklear knew the old man's ire related to the length of his granddaughter's skirt as the woman pulled at the garment before closing the door abruptly behind her.

"What can I do for you, Herr Locklear?" Shank said genially.

"Sergeant," Locklear corrected him.

Shank shrugged his shoulders and opened his mouth to speak.

"I know, I know," Locklear interrupted him. "You answer to no one but the Lord. I wonder what the Lord would think of your nude statue in the entrance?"

Shank sat back on his leather chair and rocked back and forward.

"In the business world, one has to present oneself in a certain manner."

"And in your Mennonite world?"

Shank said nothing and continued to rock back and forth.

"You have questions for me?" he asked.

"I'm still waiting on you to answer the last one."

"It is true that my personal life and professional one are at odds with each other."

Shank stood and went to the window behind his desk. He tilted the blinds on his window and stared out, his back to the room.

"I learnt as a young man that the only way I could help my community would be if I was rich. So I set about building this business up to what it is today. I stopped my people being reliant on outsiders to buy their milk and gave them a fair price for it. Soon, English farmers wanted to do business with me and the business grew. As a result of my success I am able to pay for schools, for education, housing –"

"Healthcare?" Locklear interjected.

"Yes, that too." The old man released the blinds and returned to his desk to face Locklear.

"Including the medical costs for Sara Fehr?"

"An unfortunate accident," Shank replied.

"Not attempted suicide?"

Shank's grey wiry eyebrows rose up. His lips parted slightly, revealing a semi-toothless mouth.

"Or would attempted murder be more correct?" Locklear asked.

Shank ignored the comment but, this time, did not bother to feign surprise.

"She was a beautiful girl but, you probably don't know, there's a long history of ... psychological distress in the family."

Locklear did not speak in the hope it would make Shank nervous. It didn't.

"Her family can't afford it. They no longer even farm. They're distant relations of mine so ..."

"What is Luke Fehr digging for?" Locklear asked abruptly.

Shank had taken control of the interview and Locklear needed to put the ball back in his court. He knew this might be the only time he got to speak with the man and he could already picture his smart granddaughter typing up an application for a restraining order.

This time Shank's surprise seemed real. The man was a good actor.

"Digging?"

"Yes, you know. Digging – shovel-into-hole – that type of digging," Locklear replied.

"I've no idea."

"I think you do, Mr Shank."

Shank remained silent. The door opened and a man in a dark-blue suit walked in.

"Ah, Jacob! Come in. This is Mr – Sergeant Locklear. Mr Locklear, this is my son. He largely runs the business now."

Locklear recognised the man as the second occupant of Shank's buggy in the flyer he took from reception.

"And your granddaughter?" Locklear asked, anxious for them to know that he knew the identity of the woman.

"My sister's daughter," Jacob replied.

"I wasn't speaking to you," Locklear retorted.

"No, but you will be in future. Any further contact with this company will be through me – or through Ms Stoll."

Shank Senior sat down.

"Ms Stoll ... yes, I think my trooper mentioned he saw her last night at the back of the library," Locklear lied. "Not somewhere a registered lawyer wants to be identified, especially as someone shot him. I hear they don't treat lawyers too good in prison."

Samuel Shank stood quickly. Locklear could see the look of alarm in the old man's face.

"She didn't shoot –"

Jacob Shank raised his hand, silencing his father.

He smirked at Locklear who stood up.

"If you think you can prove that, Mr Locklear, we'll very happily see you in court. Shortly after you try to drag our name through the mud, we'll see your department in court for defamation. Am I making myself clear?"

Locklear walked to the door and turned.

"Crystal. But let me make *myself* clear. I know that your family have been killing the Fehrs for generations. I know you were behind the attack on Andrew Fehr and also, somehow, responsible for what happened to Sara Fehr and I will keep digging until I have enough evidence to prove it."

Locklear walked out onto the corridor and banged the elevator button.

When he reached reception, Bethany Stoll was idly standing at the desk. She walked up to him and whispered, "I really hope your trooper makes it. He's kind of cute."

As she walked away, Locklear could see that the woman had hitched her skirt back up.

He made his way into the heat of the parking lot and remained there for several minutes, thinking.

There was only one more place he could go.

On the other side of Fehr's farm, Locklear parked his car and climbed the north side of the steep incline to the old cabin he had seen on the day he climbed to the top of Fehr hill. Nothing told him this was where he'd find Aaron Fehr except instinct. He had called to the station en-route and found the old man was not listed on any database. No tax number, no utility company records. The man did not exist. Locklear checked Mendoza's notes and figured the man was a sibling or cousin of the Fehr's grandfather.

When the cabin came into view, Locklear hunkered down and moved slowly towards the back of the property, anxious to take Aaron Fehr by surprise. When he reached the building, he stood upright and glanced through one of the two back windows. The cabin, which appeared to consist of just one room, was sparse and basic. Fehr could be seen sitting in an old armchair, facing the open door of the cabin. To the right, a small table held a cup and plate. A swarm of flies buzzed around the leftover food and about the head of the cabin's only occupant. Locklear couldn't understand why Fehr did not move to shoo them. Slowly, he moved around the side, ducking briefly to avoid detection in the one dusty window that faced south. He stepped on a dry branch and held his breath as it cracked loudly beneath his feet. He looked at the ground and found Abigail Fehr's red rag doll lying in the dirt.

Convinced the twig had given him away, he remained there waiting for movement within the shack. He heard none. He moved forward and along the front of the building which contained only two small windows on each side of an open wooden door. Locklear hunkered down again and raised just the top of his head as far as his eyes to get a closer look at the man. Realising what he was looking at in the dim room, Locklear slowly stood to his full height. Aaron Fehr was dead. A short noose was tied around the old man's neck. Locklear stepped inside and placed a hankie over his nose and mouth. Fehr had been dead for several days and had obviously been beaten before someone strangled him with a short rope in the seat he was sitting in. Locklear stepped back outside into the air and picked up Abigail Fehr's rag roll. He phoned the station and then sat on a rock and looked down at the Wyss farm in the distance. Abigail Fehr had been here and he was both sickened by and enthused that the young girl might have seen or heard something that would be useful to him.

Two hours later the body was carried down the steep hill and removed to the hospital's morgue. Locklear was still sitting on the large rock as he gave his statement on the hill to the fleshy-faced cop whose name turned out to be Maguire. Crowds of Mennonites could be seen at the base of the hill watching and whispering, anxious about the drama unfolding in the normally serene village they called home.

Slowly, Locklear descended the hill and made his way down the dirt track to the Wyss farm. He knocked on the door and stood silently while Helena Wyss considered whether or not to let him in. The much-missed doll in his hand may have swung her decision.

"I heard about Mr Fehr," Helena said as she ushered Locklear into the kitchen where Abigail was busy podding peas. "It's so awful."

Abigail looked up and saw the doll in Locklear's hand. He held out the doll to her. Her lip quivered and Locklear thought she was going to cry. She looked to her foster mother for reassurance before reaching forward and snatching the doll forcefully from his hand.

"She's missing Esther," Helena offered as she gestured that he should sit at the table.

"She hasn't been seen since?" Locklear asked, sitting down.

Helena shook her head.

"Has Abigail been ... behaving strangely since the doll went missing?" he asked, anxious to know to what extent the girl witnessed the events in the cabin.

"You're wondering if she saw ... Mr Fehr?"

"Yes."

Helena placed her hands to her face. "I've told her a hundred times not to go up there."

"Has she said anything?"

"No."

"Can you ask her?" Locklear asked, unsure how to communicate with the strange girl.

Helena moved to Abigail's seat and turned the girl around to face her. She took the doll from her foster daughter's hands and held it in front of the girl's eyes.

"Abigail – where did you lose Red?"

Abigail turned away from her mother and lifted another pod.

Helena turned her around again.

"Abigail. Answer me."

Abigail Fehr dropped the pod and smacked herself on the face. Helena reached forward and held the girl's hands down.

"She does this sometimes during an absence," Helena said almost apologetically to Locklear. "Abigail? Did you go see Uncle Aaron?"

Abigail Fehr eyes rolled upwards and she began to laugh. *"Fuck you! Tell us where it fucking is!"*

Helena blushed. "She doesn't mean it. Can't think where she heard such words."

Abigail rolled her eyes back to their normal position and stared at Locklear. "It's a good year to put things right."

Locklear stood and went around to the other side of the table. He hunched down and looked into the girl's stunning eyes.

"Abigail – I need you to tell me where you heard those words. It's important – for Andrew."

Helena pursed her lips. Locklear could sense her disapproval.

"Please do not lie to her," she whispered.

Locklear didn't take the time to explain that he was telling the truth. Those words linked Abigail to her brother and if he could find out where she heard them, he would know why Andrew Fehr woke saying those same words.

Abigail looked at Locklear as though she had only just woken to find her foster mother and a strange man looking at her.

"*What?*" she snapped.

"Abigail – be gentle," Helena warned.

Locklear repeated the question. "Where did you hear those words, Abigail?"

"The men in Uncle Aaron's house said them."

Locklear moved closer to the girl. "When was that?"

Abigail rolled her eyes back and forward. Locklear, anxious that the girl was going into another absence, touched her arm. She jumped.

"When did you hear those words?" he repeated.

"The day of Andrew's birthday."

"Where was your uncle then?"

"Sitting in the soft chair Pastor Plett gave him with blood on his face."

Helena gasped. She walked to the kitchen wall and stood facing it. Locklear glanced at her as she lifted her apron to wipe tears from her face.

"Abigail – did you tell your uncle that Andrew was coming to this house that night?"

Abigail bit down on her lip. She raised her hand to hit herself but stopped. "Yes."

Locklear could see tears welling in her eyes.

"You're not in trouble, Abigail. If you tell me the rest it will help Andrew and Luke and Esther."

"Sara?" she asked.

"Yes – and Sara too."

Helena turned back from the wall and glared at him.

"It won't help her wake up but it will make her happier," he added. "Did Aaron tell those men that Andrew was coming here?"

"Yes."

Locklear patted her head although he suspected she was much too old for such comfort. He never knew how to interact with children, never having had any or even being one himself.

"What happened then?"

"Then they put a rope around Uncle's neck and pulled it tight and then they stopped and he coughed."

Abigail made a gurgling noise and poked her tongue out of her mouth, mirroring what she saw.

Helena let out a cry and ran from the room.

Abigail, unperturbed, stared at Locklear, waiting to give the next answer that would make everybody happy again.

"Where were you? Did they see you?"

Abigail shook her head. "I was looking through the side window."

Locklear knew the window Abigail meant. It was where he stepped on the dry twig and where he found Abigail's doll.

"What happened next?"

"One man put his hand on Uncle's neck and said 'He's gone'. But he wasn't gone – he was still sitting right there." She looked questioningly at Locklear. "Then I made a noise and a man came out to see. I was afraid. I dropped Red and hid behind a tree."

"Then what?"

"They left. I went inside and sat on Uncle's knee."

"What happened then?"

"Uncle played a whispering game."

"Can you tell me how it went?"

Abigail leaned forwarded and whispered into Locklear's ear – her voice changed into a hoarse rasp. *Tell Luke. Warn him – they're coming for Andrew. Tell him it's a good year to put things right.*

"Did you tell him? Did you tell Luke this?"

Abigail Fehr shook her head. "It was daytime and Luke only comes when it's dark."

"What did you do?"

"I walked to Pastor Plett's house and I told Esther. Uncle isn't playing with me anymore."

Locklear reached forward and pulled the girl to him, awkwardly patting her shoulders.

"No – but he's very proud of you." He pulled the flyer from Shank's office from his pocket.

"Was this the man you saw on the mountain?" he asked, pointing at Samuel Shank in the buggy.

Abigail shook her head. Instead she pointed at the younger man – at Jacob Shank. "It was that man."

Locklear stood and retrieved a shaken Helena from the hallway.

"Did you hear all that?" he asked.

"Yes. Now what?"

"Under normal circumstances I'd issue a warrant for Jacob Shank but ... right now, with Luke and Esther out there alone, it's too risky. It's better for now that Shank thinks he's in the clear."

Abigail Fehr followed Locklear to the hallway.

"Did I make everyone happy?" she asked as he exited the front door.

"Yes, Abigail. You made everyone happy, including me."

Chapter 12

Locklear had dozed off lying on his bed and woke to see the lights of a car driving into the motel lot. The noisy exhaust told him it was Mendoza who had obviously decided not to remain in Richmond overnight after all. He glanced at the digital clock on the television set and was surprised to see it was only a little after eleven. He swung his legs out of the bed and got up.

After he'd left the Wyss farm he'd returned to Harrisonburg to be served again by Marilyn Monroe and then had sat quietly by Carter's bedside. Twice the trooper opened his eyes and tried to mouth something but, dazed from painkillers, fell back asleep almost as soon as he'd opened his eyes. When the night shift arrived to guard Carter's room, Locklear checked that the cop knew his brief and then walked downstairs to the foyer.

On his way out he saw Lombardi again and sat with him for a moment. Neither man spoke. Thirty years ago Locklear would have thought such a scene impossible but here they were, two flawed men nearer to death than life, sitting together.

By the time Mendoza arrived with two cold Cokes in her hands, Locklear was standing in the open doorway.

"Thought you wanted to see your kid?"

"I did but he had a sleepover so it was either come back here or listen to my mom all evening talking about suitable Latino men I could marry."

Locklear laughed.

"I checked in on Andrew Fehr – he's still playing dumb," she said.

"Good for him," Locklear responded. "He's safer that way. Some men killed the old man, Aaron Fehr. And Abigail Fehr witnessed it – she was in hiding – she thinks Jacob Shank was one of them. I think it happened on the same day."

"How did they do it?"

"Strangled him, left him for dead – but he didn't die before he passed on a warning to Abigail for Luke Fehr. So much for Carter's theory that Luke didn't go near the old man. He was a lookout for them. I suspect it's been him, or him *and* Luke who's been watching us."

"So, the Fehrs are smarter than we've given them credit for?"

Locklear visualised the day Luke Fehr came roaring into the station lot, blocking off Bethany Stoll and rescuing his sister. The man was not afraid though Locklear felt that he should be. It suddenly came to him why Luke did not live on the farm – why no one really knew where he slept. It would make him a sitting duck.

"Luke Fehr's been fighting a lone crusade for a long time. From time to time he wins a battle but he can't win the war while the Shanks have power over a community that won't resist what he is doing to them. Shank is manipulating the gentleness of these people."

Mendoza sat herself down beside Locklear at the end of his bed. He stood quickly and sat on a chair, facing her.

"Don't worry – I wasn't trying to seduce you. You're not my type!" she laughed.

Locklear grinned shyly. "OK, what have you found out?"

"You're going to be disappointed."

The Pact

"I can't be any more disappointed at how this investigation's going than I am now, so just spill it."

"First Anabel Schumer – she wouldn't talk to me. She kept me at the door of her apartment until I talked my way in – woman's a nervous wreck. Just kept crying about what she's going to do now the library's burned down. But I reckon there's more to her nervousness than that. Before I left I spotted a business card on Schumer's coffee table. It was Beth Stoll's. Reckon she paid a visit to Anabel and frightened her off. I asked around at the station about Schumer – and guess what? Her father and two brothers work for Shank Creamery. They were originally German emigrants. They're not Mennonites but looks like her family have plenty of financial reasons to keep quiet."

Locklear stood and walked around the room.

"What about Plett?"

"Like you thought – Plett had no records – he said when he arrived to take over from Shank the archives had disappeared."

"That was convenient for Shank."

"Quite – so I drove to Richmond and Bishop Rahn was very helpful. I spent hours there and sorry to tell you but ... all of the deaths of young Fehr men ... they were all suicide. And all by hanging, on the farm, just like Andrew."

"Except someone else put the noose around Andrew's neck ... and he lived."

Locklear leaned forward and rubbed his hands back and forward through his thick mane. "There were no forensics back then so who's to say what happened?"

"True. But there's something else. Every one of them had a note pinned to their shirts, which said –"

"*It's a good year to put things right.*"

"Yes."

"Was it in their handwriting?"

Mendoza shrugged. "So, sarge, what now?

"Fancy a late-night stroll?"

"I hope you're not suggesting what I think you're suggesting."

Mendoza shivered in the cool night air at the edge of the Fehr farm. With only the moonlight to guide them, she followed Locklear on foot towards the cabin where old man Fehr was found. As she looked behind she could see only total darkness. There were no lights in any of the farmhouses below – the nearest lights were those of Harrisonburg in the distance. The only sounds she could hear were a barn owl hooting in the distance and an occasional cow bellowing from nearby farms. Twice she almost fell into newly dug holes along the northern face of the incline. She pointed them out to Locklear – whoever dug them had not bothered to fill them in.

Locklear noted the change in habit of their hole-digger. Someone was running out of time to find whatever it was they were looking for.

When they reached the spot, Locklear sat panting on the rock outside Aaron Fehr's cabin and caught his breath.

"So what exactly are we doing here?" she asked.

"Waiting."

"For?"

"Something. Anything. I don't know."

Mendoza looked into the darkness. "This place gives me the creeps," she said, blessing herself.

Locklear turned and stared at the silent cabin in the darkness.

"You believe in ghosts, sarge?" Mendoza whispered.

"I don't know," he replied. Not for the first time he wondered what his people believed about the spirit world. His mother had taught him nothing and he'd had no religious or spiritual education. He did not tell Mendoza of his visions of his mother which would appear when he was in danger. No one would believe him. He hardly believed it himself. The only real hauntings he'd experienced were conjured up by his own mind – his conscience exhuming the accusing faces of the dead whose killers he had never brought to justice.

"I do," Mendoza said.

"I thought you people weren't supposed to believe in ghosts?"

"You people?"

"Catholics."

"Well, we believe in angels and devils and exorcisms – and the holy souls in purgatory – so why not ghosts?"

Mendoza stood and looked into the blackness. Only once in her life did she experience such complete darkness. She was about ten when her family returned to the small rural village in Mexico where her mother had been born. Mendoza had never seen her mother look so at ease but she, a city girl, had known only street lights and busy streets and had hated every moment of the month-long vacation. Now, as an adult, she wondered how her mother had coped with the city she found herself in and how odd the electric street lights and activity of Richmond must have seemed to the seventeen-year-old hotel maid. Mendoza found the darkness suffocating where her mother found comfort and peace in her familiar surroundings. Her thoughts moved to one's sense of belonging. Mendoza spoke Spanish, looked Spanish, ate mostly Spanish food but in her heart she was an American who loved her country and dreamt of serving it someday as her father had done before her. She understood why the Fehrs did not leave this place after the family had been shunned. It was all they knew and this tiny village was so different from the outside world that there was little chance of them surviving outside of it.

In the distance, Mendoza noticed a small light dancing across the field at the back of Wyss farm.

"What's that?" she asked.

Locklear raised himself slowly off the stone and watched

the tiny light move forward into a small wooded area.

"It looks like a torch. Come on."

Together, Locklear and Mendoza crept quietly down the southern edge of the hill until they could get a better look at the torch-holder. When they reached a good vantage point, Mendoza took Locklear's lead and lay flat on the ground, looking at the night walker.

Locklear waited until the figure got closer but he already had a good idea of its identity. Helen Wyss's slight frame and curly hair were easily identifiable even in the moonlight. In her arms she carried a large bag. Locklear knew it was heavy as she stopped from time to time to readjust the dead weight in her thin arms.

"What's she doing?" Mendoza asked.

"She's visiting."

"In the dark in the middle of a field? Who?"

"Come on – I'm going to drop you back to the motel," he replied.

"Aren't we going to confront her? Or even follow her? What's she's hiding?"

Locklear shook his head. He knew who Helena Wyss was hiding and smiled at the fool she had made of him. "No, we'll only place her in danger. There's no telling who Shank has watching our movements. As far as the incident room goes – what we saw tonight doesn't go on the board, right?"

Mendoza nodded. "Saw what, sarge?"

"Kowalski was right. You're a good cop, Mendoza."

"So you've got over my not being a man?"

Locklear did not answer.

When they reached the car, Locklear eased the car slowly down to the main road without headlights.

"So, what now?" she asked when they were safely on the main road back to Harrisonburg.

"Bishop Rahn said several families left the area due to Shank," Locklear said. "First thing in the morning I want you to find out where they went and talk to some of them – see what their gripe was. I'm going to check in on Sara Fehr before Maria Whieler finishes her shift in the morning. She said her mother didn't like living here. I want to know why."

Locklear did not access Dayton Kindred Hospital by normal means. The front door to the facility was closed and a security guard sat at a small desk inside the front door, staring out into the darkness. He parked on the main road and made his way on foot to the back of the hospital. He reached the door that led into Sara Fehr's room and stood for a couple of minutes looking in at Maria Whieler, asleep on the hard chair, leaning on the side of Sara's bed. He slowly opened the fly screen and stepped inside.

She stirred. "Luke?" she whispered, but returned to her dreams as Locklear moved farther into the room.

Sara Fehr's still body lay in the same position as he had last seen it and a heart monitor beeped rhythmically at the side of her bed. Three clipboards hung from the end of the bed, recording the sleeping woman's vitals. There was something so serene about her that he found himself not speaking to Maria Whieler as he intended but standing at the foot of the bed, staring at Sara Fehr. Even in her vegetative state he could see that she was a beautiful woman but her face also looked kind. He reasoned that Sara had been a gentle and giving person, caring for her siblings after their mother's death. How vulnerable she was in this state and how utterly dependent on others to care for her. Dr Miller was right – this was no way to live.

He moved slowly to Maria and gently touched her arm. Startled, she jumped to her feet.

"What? I wasn't sleeping ..."

Locklear raised his hands up surrender-style to quieten the woman.

"I just want to ask you a few questions."

"I wasn't sleeping. I'm not allowed to."

Locklear looked behind him and retrieved a chair from the other side of the room. He brought it to where Maria stood and sat down.

"I'm tired, that's all – with day school and all," she said.

"I'd like to hear about Sara – about what kind of girl she was before the accident."

"Why?"

"I'm just interested, that's all. I think if I understand more about the Fehr kids, it might help Andrew, all of them, including Luke." He hoped the specific mention of the aloof man's name would put the anxious woman at ease.

Maria returned to her seat. "She was lovely … she was a good friend."

Locklear waited for more.

"She was always happy, always smiling. People said if she didn't have the same sparkly eyes as Luke no one would ever take them for twins. Luke was always quieter and more serious. Sara was good fun."

Locklear looked with pity at Maria. The lonely woman's face lit up talking about her only friend. He sensed she lived for the possibility that Luke Fehr would become more to her than a night-time visitor she had no actual contact with.

"You know she left a note. Do you think she intended to kill herself that day?"

Maria's mouth drooped as though she was about to cry. "I never heard about any note. I don't believe that. Mama and me left town several years before that but Sara and me always kept in touch. I wrote her almost every week. She was just the same in her letters as she was face to face and it cheered me up because I was really lonely in the town we moved to. It was so different. I didn't fit in."

"So she wasn't depressed?"

"Not until the last letter and I wouldn't even say she was depressed then. She was just different, is all. I got it about a week before her birthday and I sent back a card although I don't know if she ever got to read it. She said she wasn't looking forward to their birthday. She said that she was worried about Luke and that she couldn't think how she'd manage without him. I assumed he was in trouble again and that maybe this time Pastor Shank involved the police. Luke only poached because they had no money and the family needed to eat. He brought home everything they needed and Sara looked after the younger kids."

"So ... she said she didn't know how *she'd* do without him, not how *he'd* do without her?"

"Yes, she did. I've still got all the letters. Sometimes I sit and read them to her here and I know she hears me. Looks like she's smiling a little bit. If you want them, if it'd help her or Luke?"

Locklear repeated the line in his head. *She couldn't think how she'd manage without him.* It didn't sound like something a suicidal person would write.

"Sir?"

"Yes?"

"There's no way Sara would leave those kids. No matter what was going on, she'd never have left them."

Locklear looked at the vulnerable woman. Maria Whieler was a lost soul who was spending the best years of her life sitting in the dark bedside her dying friend.

"Why did you and your mother leave town? You obviously feel like you belong here."

Maria stood and fixed the sheet over her friend. She checked the monitors and wrote two or three words on one of the clipboards. Locklear knew she was stalling for time.

"You can tell me – in confidence."

Maria heard her mother's words of warning echo in the silent room. She had spent her youth caught between her parents' worlds – her simple farmer father's innocent and unquestioning commitment to the faith and his complete rejection of her mother's warning about Pastor Shank – and her mother who was intelligent, suspicious and increasingly paranoid about Shank for whom she worked in accounts. When it was clear that her father would not survive his illness, her mentally ill mother took her out to the barn one night and showed her something. It was a thick notebook filled with dates, prices and notes she had written – evidence that Samuel Shank was paying more for milk to English farmers than to the trusting Mennonite community. He was also paying less for prime pasture – the farms of Mennonites whose lives he made so difficult that they left and joined other congregations or sometimes none at all. Her mother also kept notes on people who were quietly standing up to Shank, people who would help Maria if anything happened to her: Mr & Mrs Wyss, the Fehrs – there were around four or five family names in all. The day after her father was buried, Samuel Shank and his son came to their home and asked to speak to her mother alone. He sent Maria out to the barn from where she could hear her mother arguing. She could still remember how torn she was during those moments. A part of her, the part that was her father, told her to do as Pastor Shank directed while the small suspicion that had slowly seeped into her blood told her to come to the aid of her vulnerable mother. Instead, she walked fifty steps towards the house and stood rooted at the halfway mark between the barn and the back of their farmhouse where she waited in the pouring rain. It was not lost on her that this was to become her position in life, that she would be neither Mennonite nor share her mother's dislike of the faith, that she would neither belong nor be the outsider her mother had been. She would spend her life on the fringes of two worlds, always looking in through other people's windows and other people's lives.

When Shank finally left the house, her mother appeared at the door, with a sheaf of papers gripped tightly in her hand – paperwork Shank had left on the kitchen table, Maria found out later.

The Pact

She called out his name and Shank turned around. Maria could still remember the look on his face.

"I've kept records – records of every dishonest deed you've done to your own people!" her mother called out. "It is not here. Unlike my husband, I am not stupid. It is with someone who knows what to do with it if anything happens to me or to Maria. If you ever come near me or my daughter again, the book will be given to the police."

When she slammed the door, her mother's composure vanished.

"Pack up your things," she said. "We no longer own this farm."

Maria was twelve at the time and, after all the years that had passed, it was those words that still hurt, still brought tears to her eyes. In an instant she was ripped from the place and the people she loved. Weeping, she helped her mother pack the few belongings she had and they drove from the farm in the darkness into a life she had neither knowledge nor understanding of. Cut loose, they drifted from town to town until her mother found work in the centre of Charlottesville. Maria was enrolled in a state school on a busy street where no one understood her. She barely stayed in that school a year and moved twice more to other schools that did not differ from the first. She was odd, she dressed funny, spoke funny, looked funny. By age fourteen she refused to return to any school and stayed at home, nursing her mother through her spells and working part-time in five and dimes to put food on the table during the times her mother's illness rendered her unable to work.

"Mr Locklear. I spent years outside of where I wanted to be, moving around with my mama. I didn't get much of an education. I'm not smart, I know that. But this is the only place I feel like I belong. It's the only place I can belong."

Locklear stood and took a few steps towards her.

"I understand, Maria. You and I are a lot alike. But listen,

Maria, we can protect you – so if there's anything you can tell me that could help Sara, or her brother, now is the time."

Maria sat down and fixed her eyes on her sleeping friend.

"My mother got a job at Shank Creamery straight out of high school. She met my father there and they fell in love. Her family disowned her. Not long after they married my father realised that she was unwell but it didn't matter to him. He loved her. She hated Dayton. She hated the faith and she really hated Pastor Shank."

"Why did she hate Shank?" Locklear asked.

Maria sighed. "Like I said, she imagined a lot of things ... there's no way to know if she was right about the things she said about him."

"I understand."

"She thought he was doing all sorts of illegal financial things here. My mother worked in the accounts section of the creamery. She began to keep notes. I don't understand much of what she wrote. She was real smart with figures. I'm more like my dad."

"Do you have the notes?"

Maria Whieler looked to the ground. "I forgot all about them. When she died I was going through her things and I found them. She said I was to use them if I was in trouble and she named families who would help me if anything happened to her. When I got back all but two of the families were gone."

Locklear stood waiting for an answer to his question.

Maria slowly raised her eyes to meet his stare. "I didn't want to keep it. Pastor Shank has been so good to me, paying for my studies, giving me a place to sleep, this job. It felt wrong to keep it."

"Did he ever ask you about the book?"

"No, but ..." Maria could hear her mother's voice again, warning her to be careful, warning her to be more like her, a voice her loneliness tried hard to ignore. "When I returned to the town, I found a place of my own in Harrisonburg, right near the bus station. I was only living there a few days when the landlord threw me out, said he didn't want the sort of trouble I'd bring to the house. Someone must have told lies about me. Same day Pastor Shank arrived and said he heard I was in trouble. I don't know how he knew but he brought me straight to a new apartment and then got me this job. The day after I moved in, I came home and my room had been disturbed. I was so upset. The only thing I have that is of any value is my mother's wedding ring and it was there. Nothing was missing.

"And the book?"

"It was never there."

"What'd you do with it?"

"I gave it to someone."

"*Who?*" Locklear asked, becoming frustrated.

Maria stood again and looked Locklear up and down – trying to decide if she could trust him, if her mother would have trusted him.

"Luke has it. I gave it to Luke."

Chapter 13

The sun was coming up over the horizon as Locklear set out for Luke Fehr's hideout to see if he could get the book he now knew was the book Fehr held out to Bethany Stoll at the station. Luke was obviously using the book to protect himself and his family and, in the meantime, he was searching the farm for something the Shanks wanted. He knew Luke was running out of time and the book was merely holding back the tide on the wrath of Samuel Shank.

As he drove by East Washington Street, a familiar figure hobbled by. The hunched form of Anabel Schumer, carrying a huge suitcase, rounded the corner and disappeared into the station. Locklear parked illegally and chased into the station, searching for her among the crowds of early-morning commuters. He found her at the ticket desk, paying for her ticket out of Harrisonburg.

"Going somewhere?" Locklear asked from behind.

Anabel Schumer let out a short, sharp scream. Locklear picked up the suitcase, took Anabel by the arm and led her out of the queue towards a half-empty coffee shop at the far end of the station.

"Please, I can't be seen talking to you," she pleaded.

Locklear half threw the young woman into the booth and

ordered two coffees. "Says who? Do you know that Lee Carter is lucky to be alive? That whoever attacked him outside your library tried to kill him?"

Anabel began to cry, attracting furtive glances from two middle-aged male tourists in the booth on the other side of the aisle.

"I know, I'm sorry, but I can't ..." she said, sliding out of the booth.

Locklear stood and blocked her path.

One of the men left his booth and stood in front of Locklear.

"Is this man bothering you?"

Locklear flashed his badge. "Richmond PD – this woman's wanted for prostitution."

The tourist backed off and Anabel gasped as a deep crimson flushed up her face from her throat. Locklear reached out and once again pulled forcibly on the young woman's arm. Embarrassed by the attention they were starting to attract, she complied with Locklear and moved swiftly on his heels to the back exit. He led her to a large parking space where several buses were leaving for their daily journey to the larger towns or to other nearby states.

"This is too open. Someone will see me," she said, walking on to a disused waiting room at the far end of the lot.

Locklear sat down facing the woman, inside the derelict building. He did not speak and waited for Anabel to talk.

"I used to hide out here as a kid," she said. "Sometimes Lee would be with us. He hung around with my brother. I liked him a lot. If it wasn't for the fact that he was besotted with Sara Fehr, I would have asked him out."

She smiled but Locklear could see the tears welling in her eyes.

"I'm so sorry he got hurt!" she cried. "It's all so messed up. My dad thinks the only thing to do for everyone's sake is for me to leave."

"Did Bethany Stoll threaten you?"

"She came to my apartment the night Lee got hurt, said she was representing him in court. But I knew who she was. She wanted to know what information Lee got from the archives that day so I told her it was about John Grant and local Mennonites in the Civil War. She became really agitated and I was terrified. Then she asked if I could identify anyone in the parking lot that night. I told her no, that I couldn't see in the dark and that's what I told the police."

"What happened then?"

"She left her card and said I was to phone her if I remembered anything and I wasn't to speak to the police again."

"And that was the end of it?"

"I thought so but later that night the library burned down. I knew it was them. She must not have realised until later that even local records would be kept in other libraries. Well, she can't have every library burned so the only thing she and her family could do was make sure I don't talk to anyone else. My dad and both of my brothers work for the Shanks. Shank's son, Isaac, brought Dad into the office and said if I open my mouth there wouldn't be room for the Schumers in Shank Creamery any more. My mom's real sick and my dad's insurance plan doesn't cover her care. Samuel Shank's been paying her medical bills for the last year."

Locklear pondered this information. "So, they must have intended that Carter wouldn't survive to tell me what he knew?" That was sloppy, he thought. Of course, but for Luke Fehr they would have finished the job.

"Guess so. Can't believe they'd hurt Lee. His father is a good friend of Shank's. They go back a long way."

Locklear sighed. "So, you're leaving?"

"Nothing else I can do." She began to cry again.

"Where will you go?"

"I have family in Minnesota. Thing is, I'm an only

daughter and my mom needs me. I can't bear to think of her struggling here without my help. But she's too sick to come with me so there's no other choice. Dad said he'd prefer that I am away from here and alive than for me to stay and die."

"He thinks Shank would have you killed?"

She looked at her watch and stood. Deep dark lines ran under her eyes and her young face had aged in the few days since he'd interviewed her.

"You need to open your eyes, Mr Locklear. Samuel Shank doesn't only kill Mennonites. His family have been killing people here for generations or forcing them to end their own lives and there's nothing you or anyone else can do about it."

Forcing them to end their own lives.

"Why are they doing this?" he asked. "Surely it can't be about the Civil War?"

"The Shanks have a lot to hide but what really motivates them is money."

"What do you mean by a lot to hide?"

"About ten years ago a man named William Jefferson came into town from New York. He was black university professor and was writing a book on John Grant. He spent all day in the library researching and also tried speaking to the locals in Dayton to see if any stories had been passed down about Grant. I helped him as much as I could. I'm a historian myself and Stoll knows I know a lot more about them than I've said but I'm not stupid enough to repeat it. I know things – things about when that same professor went missing."

"Then you need to tell me."

She laughed. "The only reason I'm alive is because all these years passed and I kept silent. I'm in more danger now than I was back then. Professor Jefferson left a lot of paperwork behind the library desk that he said he'd come back for. Before he got a chance to return, the police came in asking about him, what he was looking for, etc. They took his research notes and then I never saw him again. I read in the paper that his wife reported him missing. He never checked out of his hotel and his hire car was still in the hotel's car park. The police here turned a blind eye to it and to lots of other things. No one will ... or can, come up against Shank."

"The police were involved? Does that include Carter?"

She stopped at the doorway.

"Not Lee but look back a bit further – not that it will make any difference," she said as she left.

Locklear stood at the door and watched her go. A light rain began to fall as she crossed the lot to take a bus to her new, enforced life.

Locklear did not go back inside the bus station but walked the long way around the building. He got to his car just in time to stop Maguire from having it towed.

"Sorry, sarge – didn't know this was your car. Went looking inside for the owner. Fair warning and all that. I saw the Schumer girl inside. Looked like she'd been crying. She wouldn't talk to me. Seemed real upset. Did you talk to her? Did she tell you where she was going?"

"No, I didn't see her," Locklear replied. Now that he knew the police were somehow involved in covering up Shank's crimes, he didn't know who he could trust.

One thing Anabel Schumer said stood out for him: that Shank's family had been killing others *or forcing them to take their own lives* for generations. It would explain all the suicides of the Fehr men. But what, he wondered; would it take to force a person to take their own life? What did Shank hold over them? There was no way he would ever know the answer to that unless he got hold of the book he knew Luke Fehr had in his possession. He needed to go back to Dayton. He needed to see Helena Wyss.

Bishop Rahn warmly welcomed Jo Mendoza when she arrived unannounced at his house shortly after nine that morning. After a brief update, he led the cop to a small room in the basement of his home and directed her to two filing cabinets which tracked the whereabouts of the various congregation members.

Mendoza got to work. Two families had sold their farms to Shank and had moved to Richmond itself. Three more, whose farms were repossessed and bought from the bank by Shank, had moved to Harrisonburg. Two further families had moved to Arlington and one to Chesapeake and had found employment in factories or on farms in and around these towns. Three further families had left the community and their whereabouts were unknown.

Mendoza took down any addresses and, as she made her way to the stairwell, she noticed a young girl move quickly from a bathroom into a bedroom down the other end of the long hallway. Mendoza followed and knocked on the door but there was no answer and no sound could be heard in the room.

She made her way upstairs to the ground floor and Rahn's office.

She knocked gently and entered when he answered.

"Thanks, John – I have everything I need."

John Rahn stood and walked around his desk. He shook her hand.

"Happy to help."

"Do you ... do you have children?"

"Yes, two daughters – they're both away at college. Both studying to be teachers in our community."

"Oh – I thought I saw a girl go into one of the bedrooms. I thought she looked familiar."

Rahn stared at Mendoza. "Andrew Fehr is being discharged in a couple of days," he said.

Mendoza, feeling she was being fobbed off, nodded slowly. "That's good."

"The police have asked if he can stay here until he's well enough to return home."

"Yes, I know. My sergeant told me."

"Andrew won't be the first or last person my wife and I have offered sanctuary to, if you understand me."

Mendoza understood. She knew who was hiding behind the door in a basement bedroom.

Chapter 14

The short trip from Harrisonburg to Dayton was one Locklear was becoming very familiar with. As he neared the Wyss farm he saw Helena walking the roadway with some shopping. He slowed down and drove alongside her but the woman did not raise her eyes to greet him.

"Would you like a lift?" he asked.

Helena Wyss looked angrily at him. "You cannot talk to me here."

Locklear sighed and drove the rest of the way to the farm where he waited for her to walk the three miles to her home. As he wandered around the yard he decided now would be as good a time as any to see where Wyss was headed last night in the dark. He checked the main road to ensure no one could see him and made his way to the tree line. Slowly he moved through the dense scrub, looking for the small cabin or shelter Luke Fehr was living in. He searched the ground and ignored the worn pathway.

It would be the route Fehr would expect unwelcome visitors to use. Locklear preferred that the feral man was not at home when he arrived. The book was not something Luke would give up easily and Locklear did not want to come up against a man who was clearly living on the edge. As he moved deeper into the woods, the light faded and splintered through the tall trees in misty, amber beams. Locklear stopped and caught his breath against an ancient red oak, taking in the eerie silence of the majestic vista in front of him. There was a peace in this place that spoke to his heart. For a moment he almost envied Luke Fehr the silence that this place offered him.

Locklear pushed forward until he came to a small stream, trickling its way down to the farmlands below him. In the distance he could hear the song of the redbird and of the cuckoo. A hummingbird beat its wings nearby and a pair of mourning doves, startled by his sudden presence, outstretched their wings and flew in unison up to safer ground. Further and further into the lush, dark foliage he pushed until he stopped again to check his bearings. The sun, now almost at its highest, was barely visible thought the forest. He listened but could no longer hear the hum of traffic from the main road. A branch cracked somewhere to his left. He turned but saw only the grey hide of a fox squirrel scuttling up a moss-laden tree.

The feeling that he was being watched crept slowly up his body. Someone was following him, sideways, backways, forwards, whatever route he chose he felt eyes on him. He had been walking for almost twenty minutes but had seen no clearing where a small cabin might fit. Thirst began to overwhelm him. He stopped and listened for the stream but could no longer hear its slow steady descent down the hillside. Disorientated, he decided to climb a tree in the hope of catching a glimpse of the road and Wyss's farm. He placed his hands around its massive bulk and inched his way upward. His hands touched a smooth line in the trunk. He stopped. IF1861. It was the initials of Helena Wyss's ancestor carved in by his grieving widow over a century and a half ago.

A face flashed in front of his. It was his mother's – young and beautiful, her deep brown eyes looking sorrowful.

Around her neck was a string of pearls, something she had never owned in her life. Her eyes moved over his shoulder and he followed her gaze into a sea of green. He climbed further and further but still could see nothing except an ever-expanding wood.

"Where?" he heard himself asking the ghost who had now disappeared from view. A barn owl screamed – an omen, his mother would say, of evil. He slipped, plunging several feet down the damp bark, halted only by his shirt as it snagged on a sharp branch. He caught his breath and looked around until he saw it – the road, now tiny with dinky-sized cars meandering along the welcome grey sight. Locklear pulled his shirt from the branch and lowered himself towards the ground. The owl sounded again. He stopped. Fear overwhelmed him – ridiculous, superstitious fear. He looked down and reckoned he was no more than fifteen feet off the ground. Instinct made him look upward yet he hoped he would not catch a sight of the bird whose harsh scream had often terrified his mother. A spread of wings fluttered in the periphery – long golden-grey wings fluttered towards him. Locklear loosened his grip on the tree as his body entered free-fall towards the damp earth. Her eyes locked onto his again as he descended the short distance, only this time his mother was singing. He felt his body on the soft ground.

Something snapped. Metal. Sharp. Closed. A rock became his pillow. Hot liquid squirted from his head down his forehead.

He raised himself up and tried to free his foot from the trap. He tugged twice but it was useless. His eyes became heavy and his vision clouded over. He lay back and he closed them. He wanted to sleep but a foot gently kicked into his side.

"*Wachiwi?*" he called. Her first name.

He screamed as the rough hands pulled at his foot. He heard the metal snap again, teeth tearing, fluid flowing. He opened his eyes and tried again to raise himself up. A man circled him, surrounded him, watched him. More tearing, of cloth. Something was tied around his head, then around his foot. The oozing stopped. The hot fluid slowly cooled and hardened, cracking along his face and forehead. He closed his eyes. Another kick – harder now – a branch thrown at his side, feet treading on the ground, fading, then silence. He was alone. Twice more he drifted off and, when he came to, at his feet stood the broken trap, his sock still enmeshed in its rusted teeth. He moved his hands down and lifted himself from the blood-soaked rock that had welcomed him as his body met the ground. He flinched as he stood. The tightly wound bandage made it difficult for him to see how badly his foot was cut. He reached down and lifted the long thick branch left by his rescuer as a walking stick and slowly made his way in the direction he hoped would lead him to Helena Wyss's kitchen.

When he caught sight of the farmhouse, Locklear's strength seemed to leave him. He fell in the open plain at the back of the house and lay there until lifted by two men, Peter Wyss and a Mennonite man with kind, worried eyes, into Helena's kitchen.

She did not speak to him for the first twenty minutes of his arrival as she boiled water to disinfect his wounds. He caught her eye as she tightly tied a white bandage to his foot and her husband phoned Mendoza to come get him.

"It's only a flesh wound," she said, breaking the deafening silence between them.

"Thank you," he said.

Peter Wyss had left to attend to his evening farming duties. Locklear had noticed that the man had not spoken to him and that his glances had not been friendly.

Helena slammed the basin into the sink and folded her apron into a drawer.

"What were you doing up there?" she asked.

"Looking for Luke Fehr's hideout."

She swung around as tears filled her tired eyes.

"Are you completely without redeeming qualities, Mr Locklear? Do you not feel? Not love anyone, anything?"

Locklear thought about his lonely cactus sitting on the windowsill of his quiet, empty apartment. It was a ridiculous thought and one that annoyed even him. He lifted his coffee and finished the cup in one gulp.

"He has something I need."

"He has a right to safety!" she snapped.

"He saved me, you know, least I think it was him. Took my foot out of the trap and bandaged my head."

Helena smiled though watery eyes. She had put up a good act of pretending to dislike Luke Fehr intensely.

"For all his faults, Luke is a good man," she replied.

Locklear nodded. Luke Fehr could have killed him on that hill and buried him in a shallow grave but he didn't.

"Do you know what will happen to him if someone saw you? Do you know what will happen to Luke if they find him?"

"Do you trust the Mennonite man that helped lift me in here?"

Helena looked out the window. "He is a distant cousin. He will not tell."

"Why didn't you tell me you were hiding Luke?"

"Tell you? I do not know you. I have no reason to trust you."

"You can trust me."

"*I cannot!*" she screamed. "You placed Esther in danger. Luke worked hard to make sure they were all safe. As long as she was with the Pletts, Samuel Shank could not harm her – and now she is in hiding, away from her people, away from here. Luke chose that crook Lombardi for Andrew because he knew Shank's hoodlums wouldn't dare go after Andrew there. And as long as Abigail was with me ... I'd die for her."

"Is that why Andrew was pretending to be slow? In the hope that Shank would leave him alone?"

Helena nodded. "It was Luke's idea. It didn't work though. They came after him anyway."

"What's going on here, Helena? What is this all about?"

She stood again and looked out into field as her husband herded the few cattle they now kept. Abigail was beside him, playing with a dog.

"It started out as a penance handed down from the Pastor Shank of the time. He said the Fehrs brought shame on the community. I don't know much more about it than that. Samuel Shank has carried on that punishment but it has turned into something much more evil, more greedy and destructive. He won't be happy until every last one of those children are dead."

"Mrs Wyss – I'm trying to put an end to all of this so the Fehrs – and you – can live in peace."

Helena Wyss laughed. There was hysteria to her voice that Locklear had not heard before.

"You cannot change anything here! All any of us can do is to get through each day and to keep the Fehr children living."

"Do you call this living? Luke hiding in a cabin, waiting for you to bring him food and clean clothes in the dead of night?"

"You were watching me?" she asked as an expression of terror spread over her face.

"I saw you last night in the dark. From the Fehr farm."

She turned from the window and placed her hands over her mouth. Hot tears ran down her thin face.

"You are safe," he said. "We will protect you."

"I am not worried about me!" she spat. "It's Abigail. I am the only mother she has. If anything happens to me, what will become of her? What will become of Andrew?"

A car pulled into the driveway. Locklear stood and saw the patrol lights of Mendoza's car. He forced his bandaged foot into his mangled shoe and limped over to the doorway.

Helena opened the door and stood to one side.

"Never come here again, Mr Locklear. You are not welcome."

"I'm sorry," he said as the door slammed loudly behind him.

Mendoza looked at Locklear's foot as he groaned his way into the car.

"Hospital?" she asked.

"No hospital. I'm fine. Caught it in a metal trap."

"I'm taking you to hospital. You need a shot for that foot."

Locklear did not reply and rested his dazed head on the headrest. He closed his eyes.

"Hey – don't sleep – you might be concussed," she ordered.

"You going to tell me what happened today?" he asked. "You look like shit."

"How about you tell me?" she said angrily. "You were looking for Luke Fehr, weren't you?"

"Yes, I was."

"You shouldn't have gone up there alone, sarge. Luke Fehr could have killed you."

"Luke didn't do this to me. I heard my mo–"

"Heard who?"

"Nothing. Actual fact, he freed my foot from a trap and looks like he tore the shirt off his back to stop the bleeding."

"Regardless, you should have waited for back-up."

Locklear stared out the window as he rubbed his throbbing head. It was the first time in days he felt like having a drink.

"What happened today with Rahn?" he asked.

Mendoza swerved onto the main road and sighed.

"First off, I think he's hiding Esther Fehr there. I think I saw her."

Locklear nodded. "We don't need her anyway. She's safer there."

"He talked about taking care of Andrew when he's discharged from hospital. I'm thinking that will put Esther at risk."

"Yes, well, apart from Rahn and his wife, only three other people will know Andrew's whereabouts. You, me and Carter."

"I started with the two families who moved to Richmond. Neither of them would talk to me even though Bishop Rahn phoned ahead to tell them it was OK. I then went to three families in Harrisonburg. In one house there was definitely no one home. But the other two – I saw signs that the houses weren't empty so word is out not to speak to us."

Locklear thumped the dashboard, frightening the trooper. *"Don't these people know we're trying to save their lives?"*

"There's a family in Arlington and the father sounded real scared when I phoned. He asked after Andrew Fehr and said he and his family were praying for him and for all the Fehr children but he wouldn't say a word against Shank. All he said was he and his family slept better at night being away from Dayton. There was no answer to the Chesapeake family's phone. I left a message but I doubt anyone will be calling me back soon. The last three families – they've all left the faith and their whereabouts are unknown. I think they're the families we need to talk to most."

"Where can three Mennonite families hide without being noticed?" Locklear growled.

"Well, if they've left the church chances are they're just fitting into mainstream life."

"With those German accents?"

Mendoza inhaled deeply. "OK – I'll dig deeper."

Chapter 15

After a brief visit to the emergency room where Locklear had to endure the embarrassment of a tetanus shot while an amused Mendoza looked on, he had slept for the entire journey back to the motel. The pain medication the doctor had given him had kicked in.

He leaned heavily on crutches too short for his height, which the hospital had given him, as they made their way into his room.

Mendoza pulled back the covers on the bed and sat him down on it. She carefully took off his shoes and his one remaining sock, then reached forward to remove his pants.

"What are you doing?" Locklear slurred.

"Don't worry – you're old enough to be my father. I'm just helping you into bed."

Locklear mustered up as much strength as he could to shove the young woman's hands away and lowered himself back onto the bed.

He closed his eyes. "Mendoza?"

"Yeah, sarge?"

"Do you think I'm without redeeming qualities?"

Mendoza frowned at him.

"Helena Wyss said that to me today."

"And that hurt you?" she asked, confused by her boss's sudden vulnerability.

Locklear didn't answer. Then he said, "I heard my mother today, singing to me."

Mendoza pulled the covers up over him and sat down on the bed.

"Did she sing to you often?"

There was a faint smile on his lips.

"Never," he said with a laugh.

Mendoza smiled. "Then she was definitely singing to you now – making up for lost time."

She sat a while longer until she began to hear a faint snore. She leaned forward and kissed him on the cheek. Then she stood and quietly left the room, hoping that in the morning Locklear would have no memory of the vulnerability that he had shown to her or the affection she had demonstrated.

At breakfast the following morning, she found Locklear already sitting in the diner, crutches at his side. She sat down in front of him and ordered her usual breakfast.

"You still eating that crap?" he barked.

Mendoza smiled. He didn't remember.

"I suppose you're going to tell me how to drive all the way to the station too?" she said. "I wouldn't if I were you. Can't see you walking the distance if I throw you out of my car."

In the event, Locklear remained silent for the short drive but kept his good foot on an imaginary brake on the passenger side of the car. As they passed Lombardi's car yard he noticed that every curtain was drawn in the house. Rosa Nardoni was dead. As they rounded the corner he saw Lombardi sitting outside the house, staring into space. Locklear felt pity rise up inside him. He swallowed. He did not want to pity Lombardi, not with everything he had done.

When Mendoza helped Locklear shuffle on the short metal crutches into the incident room at Dayton station, they were startled to find Lee Carter sitting at the table, his arm in a sling. Mendoza approached him and put her arms around him. Locklear watched the scene, amazed at how affectionate she was with a person she'd known only days. He could never be like that. He could never let his guard down.

"Shouldn't you be in hospital?" Locklear asked gruffly.

"I signed myself out. Couldn't stick it any longer." Virginia dropped me off. Thought I'd see how things were going. I found these –" He lifted a pile of letters off the desk. "Maria Whieler dropped them by so I thought I'd make myself useful."

"You sure you're up to reading them?" Locklear said. "They're from Sara, you know?"

Carter nodded. He had read about fifteen of the oldest letters in the pile and was glad there was no one in the room to witness the effect Sara's description of her feelings for him had had on him.

"It's no problem, sarge."

Locklear pulled out a chair and lowered himself into it. He groaned as he tried to move his foot under the desk.

"Should I ask?" Carter laughed.

"Luke Fehr gave him a going-over," Mendoza replied. "It's like working with the walking wounded. I'm the only healthy cop on the team now."

Carter raised his eyebrows and stared hard at Locklear.

"He didn't," his boss finally responded. "I stepped into a trap and he freed me."

"You saw him?"

"Not exactly – banged my head off a rock."

"Well, I don't trust him," Mendoza offered.

"I do," Carter replied. "He saved my life that night. I hope I get a chance to thank him."

"Find anything in those letters yet?" Locklear asked.

Carter shook his head. "Mostly just teenage girl stuff."

"Well, you let me know if you find anything useful."

Carter placed another letter into its yellowed envelope and pushed back his chair.

"Is now a good time to tell you about John Grant? Better update you before someone else tries to shoot me."

Locklear and Mendoza sat quietly as Carter told the story of John Grant, a fifty-year-old black Union solider from New York caught behind enemy lines at the end of the Civil War. Incarcerated in a Confederate prison at Camp Sumter in Andersonville, Georgia, he befriended the gullible Fehr brothers who were imprisoned for fighting with the Union.

"I found most of this stuff in a history book on the Civil War written by a Northern writer called Hennessy who'd interviewed Grant in prison in New York," Carter said. "The South refused to acknowledge black Union soldiers as free men and believed those who had originally been slaves should be returned to their owners."

"But Grant would surely have been a free man even before the war began?" Locklear asked. "He wouldn't have had an 'owner'."

"Correct – but he had other reasons to escape – I'll come to that. So he broke out of prison and, on foot and without any money, had to live off the land and travel by night."

"He couldn't have got far," said Mendoza.

"He didn't. He told the writer that he hid in the house of a blind widow and did work for her in exchange for food and shelter. The woman was well off and lived alone. Doubt she realised he was black."

"As a black Union soldier in the south, how did he hope to ever make it home?" Locklear wondered.

"Well, he must have known his chances were slim, but he took the risk anyway. And, as I said, he had his reasons."

"What reasons?" Locklear snapped.

"I'm coming to that. Eventually his cover was blown in the widow's place. Some relatives came to check on her and he had to run. Then he walked for days in the wrong direction without realising it and survived by teaming up with others in the same situation. Something odd about this – how could he walk south, east or west thinking he was going north? Couldn't he see where the sun was rising and setting? And not just him – the 'others in the same situation' all made such a basic error? He also claimed they gave him a horse – wonder if he stole it from the widow? Then, somehow – and this really makes me doubt certain features of his story – when the Fehrs were released, he met up with them on the road and latched onto them as they faced the nine-day march for home. Could that really have been a chance meeting? I'd say he knew the Fehrs were soon to be released and lay in wait for them. I suspect he had decided to use them for what they could give him. Sanctuary."

"Makes sense," Locklear said.

Carter looked gratified at this. "Then on the road they met with up with another Union solder returning from war – Eli Shank. But Shank wanted nothing to do with Grant. He was a lot smarter than the Fehrs and sensed what kind of a man Grant was. Eli of course knew that he was not going to receive the welcome home his northern-based fellow-soldiers would enjoy but, battle-hardened and homesick, he headed south in the hope that he would appeal to his religious father's Christianity."

"Was he right?" Locklear asked.

"Turns out he wasn't."

"Seems harsh," Mendoza mused.

"Now here's the thing … Grant, on the other hand, had a problem about going home because he was wanted for shooting his captain on the same day he was captured by the Confederates in battle."

"Ah! The 'reasons' at last," Locklear said.

"Yes. Some say he deliberately got himself caught by the Confederates to avoid the firing squad. And that wasn't all. Hennessy's book included a copy of an old newspaper clipping from New York which said Grant had already been to prison for horse theft and multiple charges of relieving people of their savings to invest in fictitious business ventures. So he needed a place to hide. He knew it had to be somewhere remote, somewhere he could stay unnoticed in the South until he came up with a plan."

"So that's where the remote Fehr farm came into it," Mendoza said.

"Exactly."

"So how does Eli Shank fit into all this?" Locklear asked.

"The book said he only travelled with them for about three nights before a row broke out between him and Grant – they had to walk at night to avoid detection of course. Remember all four were dressed in Union uniform with the badly wounded Joshua on the horse. Grant said in the book that Shank accused him of stealing from him. Said Shank beat him to a pulp."

"Money?"

"No, something Shank had brought with him from home in a metal box. Something that was not of great value but was of huge importance to his people. That's what Shank told Grant when he pleaded for its return. Grant, headed for Dayton and desperate for leverage, denied taking it. The Fehrs sided with Grant. Of course Daniel needed Grant's horse to carry his injured brother. But they did believe Grant. He must have been very convincing. So Eli accused them of bringing shame on him."

"A box! What was in it?" Locklear asked. The box was important. He could feel it.

"Don't know, sarge. He didn't say."

"Do you believe Grant?"

Carter shook his head. "Nope."

"What happened next?"

"Grant said the Fehrs hid him in an old cabin on the farm. When Shank arrived back in Dayton his father, who was the local pastor, disowned him and said he was shunned until he returned the item treasured by the Shank family."

The Pact

"So after enduring war and seeing God knows what, Shank is out on his own and desperate to retrieve what Grant stole from him?" Locklear said.

"That's right, sarge."

"So when he hears that the Fehrs are hiding Grant on their farm, he goes there and threatens to kill Grant. Only Grant won't give up the prize and tells Shank he buried it on the farm."

"Which explains the digging," Locklear said.

Carter nodded.

Locklear pondered this. For exactly one hundred and fifty years the Fehrs were trying to return whatever it was that Grant had taken from Eli Shank.

"Grant said that Shank went crazy and for days he held a rifle on them while Grant and Daniel and Adam Fehr dug up the farm. First chance he got Grant escaped, leaving the Fehr brothers at the mercy of Shank. Grant did make it home but he was captured and imprisoned five months later."

Carter paused.

"He always knew that at some stage he'd probably face consequences for killing his captain … but he was surprised to be also charged with the hanging of Adam Fehr."

Locklear sat upright. "*Hanging?*"

"Yes."

"So that's how it all started," Mendoza said. "The first hanging of many more to come."

"Yes."

"Joshua would have died from his war wound by then so that just leaves Daniel Fehr alone on the farm after that," Mendoza added.

"There's more," Carter said. "I checked the local newspapers and an article from Harrisonburg reported the death of the eldest Fehr brother and said that mysterious holes had appeared on the farm and that when the sheriff recovered his body there were about fifty shallow holes dug all around the barn. It was fascinating to read."

"Will you fascinate me by finishing the story, Carter?" Locklear asked as he rubbed his throbbing foot.

"Grant admitted to shooting his captain but throughout the trial he continued to plead his innocence of the murder of Adam Fehr."

"So then it was Shank?" Mendoza said.

"Must have been. He must have hoped Daniel Fehr knew where the item was buried and if he threatened to hang Adam Fehr, he'd confess."

"But Daniel didn't know."

Carter shook his head. "Grant was shot by firing squad a month later."

Locklear leaned forward and rubbed his hands over his craggy, unshaven face. Something still didn't add up. Schumer had said that greed was behind the Shanks' misdeeds but this didn't sound like greed to him. It sounded like revenge killing.

Locklear visualised the case in his mind. Gone from its centre were Andrew and Luke Fehr – the brothers were merely pawns in a row that had begun one hundred and fifty years ago. Instead the centre was occupied by Eli Shank, Grant and the two boy soldiers. It all started with them and until he found out what was in the metal box Shank tried so hard to find, he would never stop the Shanks from killing the Fehrs or from Luke Fehr digging for something that was probably never actually there.

Slowly, the conversation died and the group settled down to work.

Carter returned to the desk under the far window and settled down to read the rest of Sara Fehr's letters to Maria Whieler. Mendoza, charged with finding the three missing Mennonite families, logged onto the station's system and started with the first name: Eric Stoll.

Locklear was the only one who did not appear to be working. He stood and slowly negotiated his way over to the window on the crutches. He stood there, gazing out unseeingly.

He had set his team tasks which he hoped would uncover smaller pieces of the Dayton puzzle but felt it remained to him to figure out what was happening in the town on a broader scale. In his mind he visualised Helena Wyss, Pastor Plett, Esther Fehr, Abigail, Maria Whieler, Anabel Schumer – they had all helped him in their own ways but there were too many missing pieces for him to make sense of any of it. He needed the book Luke Fehr had and he needed it badly.

The low tone of voices began to drift down the hallway to the incident room, slow at first, then urgent, several voices at once and then only one. The volume of that one voice increased more and more until Mendoza left her seat to see what the commotion was. Carter and Locklear followed.

In front of the desk, a cop was trying to calm a middle-aged man down while struggling to stop him from charging down the corridor. Two younger men were also trying to hold the man back. One of them shoved the cop away.

"*You did this! My daughter, my daughter!*"

The man buckled over and cried openly. His two young companions, with tear-filled eyes, tried to hold him upright.

"That's Albert Schumer. He's Anabel Schumer's father and they're her brothers," Carter whispered.

Another cop, the woman who was usually sitting just inside the front door, tried to get Schumer to sit down but the man would not be calmed.

Locklear moved forward and stood in front of the group.

"What's going on?"

"His daughter's missing. She never turned up at her relatives," the woman cop said.

"I told her to take the bus – I told her it'd be safer!" He pointed a shaking finger. "*You* did this! *You* did this!"

Locklear followed Schumer's eyes to the group behind him. Standing there were Maguire, a new cop he didn't know, Mendoza and Carter. Locklear turned again to Schumer to check who the man was accusing. He was not looking at Maguire or the new guy and he was not looking at Mendoza. Neither was he looking at Locklear. Schumer was looking at Lee Carter.

Chapter 16

Lee Carter sweated in the incident room across from Locklear.

"Do you really think I had anything to do with Anabel's disappearance?"

Locklear did not reply. He was studying the fresh-faced trooper's facial expressions. Tiny lip quivers, nose twitches, minute mouth movements all told him if a person was lying or not. There were other tells, too many to mention, and he knew them all. The training had served him well in the course of his career.

"Did you see Anabel since you were attacked?" Locklear asked.

Carter blushed, preparing to lie. He shrugged, purchasing time. "She came to see me in the hospital." He knew there would be no point in lying about this. Every visitor had to sign in and the hospital was full of security cameras.

"Did she tell you she was leaving town?"

Carter's shoulders visibly rose. His mouth turned downward. He blinked three times while formulating his response.

"Yes."

"Did she tell you where she was going?"

Carter stared hard at his boss. "She said she was leaving town."

"That's not what I asked you, Lee."

Carter looked out of the window. "Do I need a lawyer?"

"Do you want one?" Locklear asked.

Carter said nothing.

"She could have told loads of people where she was going," he finally replied.

"But she didn't," Locklear replied. "She told me. I've already made my statement to that effect. Her family knew but according to her father no one else knew. He said Anabel has been hiding out in her parents' home for the past few days and that she saw no one in that time and made no phone calls."

Locklear had interviewed Maguire who had also been at the bus station that morning and the man definitely did not know where the girl had been going.

"Carter, you better tell me what you know and you better do it now. Otherwise you'll leave me with no option but to think you had something to do with her disappearance."

Carter's eyes opened wide. His mouth dropped simultaneously. Locklear was getting somewhere.

"She was upset. She told me Beth Stoll came to see her and threatened her, made me promise not to say a word to anyone."

"Did she mean me?" Locklear asked.

"Yes, she mentioned you specifically, but I got the impression she really meant everyone. She came across real paranoid. Looked like she'd lost weight in the few days since I'd seen her. She looked awful."

"What else did she say?"

Carter took a deep breath. "She said that her dad was forcing her leave town and had arranged for her to stay with relatives in Minnesota."

"And she told you when she was going?"

Carter nodded. A look of fear spread over his face. Something had just dawned on the innocuous trooper.

"It wasn't me, sarge, you must know that."

Locklear offered the man no reassurance. He leaned back in his chair and folded his arms.

"Who did you tell that Anabel was leaving?"

Carter swallowed. His lips parted slightly but no sound came out.

Locklear leaned back to the table top and banged his fist off the table. Carter flinched.

"*Who did you tell?*" Locklear repeated.

"My dad," Carter finally whispered.

"No one else?"

Carter shook his head.

Locklear stood and walked back to the incident room on his crutches, leaving Carter sweating in the tiny interview room. Something was scratching at his brain, something he had read in one of Mendoza's lengthy reports. He riffled through his desk. He scanned one or two documents until he found what he was looking for. It was Mendoza's report on Sara Fehr's accident and her interview with the cop who came on the scene. Locklear flicked the pages until he came to the third paragraph on second last page. He read the line again.

"Sarge said to take it out ... so we did."

Why had he not realised what that had meant at the time? He left the room and hobbled back without his crutches to reception where Ricci was sitting at his desk, eating. Locklear placed the report onto the desk in front of him and leant into Ricci's face. The cop put his burger down and looked at the line Locklear was pointing at and waited.

"You said this to Mendoza?"

Ricci nodded. "Yeah."

"Who was your sergeant at the time?"

Ricci looked over his shoulder and then scanned the desks round him. There was no one around except Locklear and Williams who was busy hiding his increasing deafness from his superiors to avoid forced retirement.

"Sergeant Carter."

"Lee's father?"

"Yeah."

Locklear stood upright and lifted his throbbing foot from the floor. That's what Anabel Schumer meant – look back a bit further than Carter. She meant back a generation – she meant Carter Senior. He wondered for how many years Lee's father had been feeding Shank with information on people Shank had a grudge against.

"Ricci – keep Carter here and do not let him make any calls."

"Is he under arrest?"

"No, but just stall him."

"Mendoza!" Locklear called.

"Sarge?"

He threw her the keys to Carter's patrol car.

"You're driving."

Jeb Carter's house didn't look like a house occupied by a long-time widower. The front garden was trimmed with rows of multicoloured flowers and the lawn was thick and neatly cut. A small leafed hedge grew a foot over the white picket fence and was so neat it looked like Jeb Carter had trimmed it with a scissors. This was not the kind of house Locklear was expecting a retired single cop to live in. He was also not expecting Carter Senior to open the door and walk back down the hallway, leaving it wide open.

"He thinks we're Lee. He saw the bonnet numbers," Mendoza said.

When they reached the front door, Mendoza pulled her firearm and stood to one side. Locklear grinned. "You really think there's any need for that?"

Mendoza put her pistol away and shrugged.

"You first then!" she said, stepping back to one side to allow her boss room to manoeuvre his ill-fitting crutches down the hall.

When they reached the end of the passage, Locklear stood at a door which led into a dark kitchen where Jeb Carter sat beside an empty fireplace.

"Who are you?" the man asked, alarmed by the stranger in front of him.

Locklear moved slowly and painfully forward and introduced himself and Mendoza who waved weakly from the kitchen doorway.

Locklear glanced quickly around. The blinds on the two large windows in the room were closed and the kitchen was in almost complete darkness.

"Mind if I pull these?" Mendoza asked.

Locklear was on the same page. A darkened room meant that they would not be able to see if Carter Senior had a gun pointed at them.

Jeb Carter did not answer which Mendoza took as a yes. She pulled the cords and the room lit up like a Christmas tree.

Locklear took a seat facing Carter and noted that he was not unlike his son. Locklear had often wondered if there were people in his country who looked like him – relatives that shared the same DNA, had the same hair, eyes, traits, as him. He would never know this because the short search he undertook after the death of his mother led to a dead end and it did not occur to him to keep looking. He didn't care that much.

Jeb and Lee Carter had the same foppish thick hair and piercing blue eyes. They also had the same complexion, being lightly tanned and big toothed in that all-American way. But there was one exception. Jeb Carter had two black eyes and a swollen jaw.

"You're the Indian Lee's working with."

Locklear did not answer. He could see Mendoza staring at him on the periphery as though she was seeing him for the first time.

"Palest Indian I ever saw," Carter quipped.

Locklear did not bite. "Who beat you up?"

Carter swallowed but not in fear. Drool flowed uncontrollably from his mouth. His jaw was broken. Locklear noticed the top of a long, angry, narrow scar on his chest. Carter had obviously had recent enough heart surgery.

"You better get that jaw seen to."

"I knew you'd figure things out sooner rather than later. I told Lee not to come here for a few days. I said I had a virus – that Seth and the girl might catch it."

Locklear noticed Carter did not use his daughter-in-law's name and wondered if the old man had not approved of the interracial marriage.

"You didn't approve of Lee's choice of wife?" he asked.

"Damn right I didn't."

"Would you have preferred if he'd married Sara Fehr?"

Carter's face darkened, answering Locklear's question.

"So, then," Locklear said, "what you wanted was a nice white, Baptist, wholesome, Virginian girl?"

Mendoza grinned.

"So, you're a racist and a bigot but yet you were friends with a crook like Samuel Shank?"

Carter turned his face away from the company and spat into the empty fireplace.

"Don't worry," Locklear went on. "You're in good company – my trooper here thinks I'm a misogynist and I've been told I'm an atheist who hates everyone including a god he doesn't even believe in." He glanced at Mendoza.

"I'm not like you – I love my son and my grandson and I love my God," Carter answered. "I devoted my life to Lee and to my job. They were all I had in my life when his mother died."

"Who beat you up?" Locklear repeated.

Carter moved his tongue around his mouth and tried to swallow more spit.

Locklear waited. Nothing.

"Did Lee tell you that it was the Shanks that tried to kill him?"

Carter looked away again.

Mendoza saw the sparkle of tears begin to well in his eyes. She moved forward and took the seat beside Locklear.

"What if they had killed him?" she said. "Would you stay silent then? When they'd taken what matters most in your life from you?"

Carter's chin quivered slightly.

Locklear went in for the kill.

"By the state of your face, I'd say your friendship with the Shanks has recently come to an end. What did they want? To know what you knew about Anabel Schumer? Do you know she's missing? I'd most likely say she's dead, buried in some shallow grave off a highway."

Carter's composure wilted. Hot heavy tears welled in the man's eyes.

"They said they just wanted to talk to her."

"And you believed them?"

"Beth said she might have a job for her."

"I don't believe you," Mendoza said.

Carter shot her a sharp glance. His tears dried instantly.

Locklear leant forward. "We have Lee locked up in an interview room at the station. Anabel's father pegged him for the last person she talked to and the only person who knew exactly where in Minnesota she was going. If you don't talk, Lee will be implicated in her disappearance."

Carter lowered his gaze. Locklear could see the old police sergeant ruminate over his options. Save his son or himself. He was hoping Carter would choose the former.

"I want to talk to him."

Locklear took the phone out of his pocket and dialled the station. He directed Ricci to put Lee on the phone. The call took about thirty seconds. Jeb Carter was ready to talk.

Chapter 17

Jo Mendoza placed two painkillers into water and handed them to the retired cop. He swallowed them quickly and wiped the drool that continued to drip from his mouth.

"Samuel Shank and I aren't friends. Haven't been for a long time."

"But you were? Once upon a time?"

"My father was the vicar here and Samuel and he met regularly for inter-faith work in the community. My grandfather had also been the minister so my family and the Shanks go back a long way."

"But you had a falling out?"

Carter shook his head and grimaced at the pain the movement caused him.

"Is this off the record? I don't want Lee knowing anything about this."

"Sure," Mendoza replied before Locklear had a chance to refuse.

"We didn't exactly have a falling out. We got along fine for most of my career. About fifteen years back I was working on a murder case. The perp was a drifter named Doyle and he'd been spotted previously trying to lure young girls into his car along the highway just outside town. Lots of young kids would wait there after the school dance for their parents to collect them. No one would think anything of a car pulling in to pick up kids. It was real clever. We came out and ran him but Doyle was persistent and came back only a couple of hours later. He abducted a nineteen-year-old girl and raped her only a few hundred yards from her home then dumped her on the side of the road. We picked him up out further on the highway with a flat tyre and no spare. Tested his DNA on what we got from the girl and it was a match. Shank's granddaughter wasn't long out of law school then and was cutting her teeth defending no-hopers before she took up her post with the family. She defended Doyle – the case was a no-brainer for her. If she lost no one would think it was her fault – there was enough evidence to convict him. If she won, she'd have proved her abilities from a young age. Well, she won and he walked because the girl had what Stoll described as a 'reputation'. A few weeks later Doyle struck again, only this time he took a fourteen-year-old girl – he took the girl into the woods where he repeatedly raped her and then strangled her. She was only fourteen, a baby. She was the daughter of a friend of mine, Burt Gunderson. Burt lost his mind after she was found. He'd been fishing that day and was late picking her up. Blamed himself. A few days later he was found floating on Silver Lake. He'd drowned himself. He just couldn't live with it. By the time we found the girl's body, too much time had passed. The DNA was useless."

"So you planted Doyle's DNA from the first case on the body?" Locklear asked.

"Yes, and I don't regret that decision. It was the right thing to do."

Locklear inhaled deeply. "Only Bethany Stoll was on to you?"

Carter nodded. "She knew how long the body was in the woods because you can be sure he told her everything. Doyle was a monster and she saw nothing wrong with defending him against her own community."

"So she blackmailed you?"

"Not her – Shank did. Said he'd tell her to make Doyle plead guilty in exchange for favours."

"Did he say what those favours would be?"

"No."

"Yet you agreed?"

"My career was at risk and the careers of the two cops who went along with it. They had families to think of and I ... I couldn't handle the shame. I couldn't face Lee. I raised him to be upright, honest. I didn't want him to know what I'd done. But there's more. A few months after the case was over, Doyle appealed his sentence and was defended by a different lawyer. He didn't want Stoll near him – told anyone who'd listen that she sent him down the river. Burt's wife was convinced Doyle would get off this time. Mary Gunderson went to court on the last day of the case. No one knew that she had brought a gun in with her. No one would ever have suspected someone like her to even own a gun. When the verdict was read out, Doyle's sentence was reduced to manslaughter. Manslaughter! He crushed that girl's windpipe with his bare hands! Mary stood up and shot him dead there and then in front of the entire court. Guess she felt she had nothing left to lose."

"Where's Mary Gunderson now?" Mendoza asked.

"She's in Wallens Ridge maximum security prison. It's a tough place. Caters for serious offenders, mostly murderers. Last I heard Mary's become as tough as the other inmates. Gives as good as she gets."

Locklear sat a while and ruminated over the story. He needed to know how his gullible trooper fit into the case.

"Did Shank insist that Lee was on this case?" he asked, remembering how Kowalski had insisted that Carter stayed on. It was clear now that someone high up had put pressure on his boss.

"Yes."

"And you made sure your son was stationed here so he

could continue to feed you information that would be of use to the Shanks?"

"You're wrong. I never wanted this for Lee – a life in the force – he certainly wasn't cut out for it. Lee's not tough, he's no cop. I'm sure you've figured that out already. I was proud when he left this crummy town for university on a sports scholarship. He took three degrees. Majored in theology."

"Theology?" Locklear was startled. Lee had kept that quiet.

"Yes – he also took history and anthropology and he was a great baseball player – an all-rounder. He loved theology but he knew I didn't want him to be a minister like my father and grandfather. I didn't want him working alongside Shank in this community or with whoever came after him. Only reason he came back here was because of his kid and his wife – she's weak-minded. Took to her bed when the kid was born. Couldn't cope with the fact that he would never walk. There was nothing much else to do around here. Lee had to give up everything he worked hard for and take a job in the very place I never wanted him to end up."

"So, why did Shank have someone beat you up?"

Jeb Carter rubbed his throbbing jaw as though the blow had just happened.

"After they tried to kill my son ..." His chin began to tremble.

Mendoza leaned forward and patted his knee.

"I said that was it," Carter said. "Let them expose me. I didn't care anymore. Both of the cops I was covering for are dead now anyway. One to cancer – the other was shot in the line of duty. It's just me now and as long as Lee is safe they can do what they like to me. But they came over a couple days ago and asked about Lee, said they might pay him a visit."

"They?"

"Beth Stoll and her uncle."

"Jacob Shank?"

"Yes. They had a couple of goons with them – I expect

they're the ones who shot Lee. The Shanks aren't stupid enough to get their hands dirty."

Jeb Carter stopped speaking and looked into the empty fireplace.

Locklear could guess what he was thinking. The Shanks' visit was a chance for him to do something different but he didn't take it. He kept on letting the Shanks use him and it had got Anabel Schumer killed.

"They asked about Anabel, said she was gone into hiding and asked if I knew where she was. They already knew that she had left Harrisonburg but they didn't know where. God help me but I told them – not because they hurt me but because of Lee. I couldn't risk them killing him because I made a mistake all those years ago."

"And the suicide note from Sara Fehr? What did Shank have to lose by that getting out?"

"Samuel said it would devastate the family, that it was easier if no one knew that she'd planned to kill herself. I didn't see any harm in that so I buried the note. I also didn't want Lee to know. He loved that girl very much."

"She didn't try to kill herself by her own volition, Carter. Someone forced her to do it and you helped cover it up."

"Shank?"

"Yes."

Jeb Carter returned his gaze to the empty fireplace.

Locklear and Mendoza stood and made their way to the front door. They had what they needed, another piece of the puzzle but where it fit Locklear didn't yet know.

When they got back to the station, Locklear opened the door to the room where Lee Carter was still being held.

"You can go – and your father needs to be taken to a hospital."

A look of shock registered on Carter's face. "You hurt my dad?"

Locklear stepped forward. "It wasn't me, you dumb bastard!"

Mendoza moved between the pair.

"By the way, you're off the case," Locklear said. "And you're suspended until I figure out what to do with you."

"Why?"

"Because I said so."

"Sarge, I've worked hard on this case. I even got shot and now ... now I'm out! The least I deserve is to know why."

"Ask your father."

Chapter 18

Eric Stoll was the first of the three "missing" people Mendoza needed to track down and it wasn't hard to find out that the man was working in a sawmill over a hundred miles away in the town of Bedford.

Locklear insisted on coming and, as the pair headed southwest on the 81, they settled into an uncomfortable silence.

"You don't think you were a bit hard on Carter?" Mendoza asked eventually.

"Senior or junior?"

Mendoza frowned at him.

"He was feeding info on the case to his father!" Locklear said.

"Not maliciously. He didn't know that his father was passing it on."

"Doesn't matter, Mendoza. It was classified information. Period. He's out."

Mendoza wrapped her fingers around the wheel tightly and focused on the grey expanse of highway ahead of her. She tried to think of something else to talk about.

"So ... you're Native American, huh?"

Locklear blew out. He had hoped the trooper wouldn't bring it up. He wasn't even sure how Carter had figured it out. Not many people noticed and it wasn't something that he ever discussed. He was ashamed that he knew nothing about those proud roots. He knew nothing about his tribe or where they were from so he avoided any conversations that might lead to questions about his nomadic mother and the unstable, rootless life she had subjected him to.

He had noticed Mendoza was out of uniform. "Why are you wearing that long skirt?" he asked.

Mendoza knew the conversation was over before it had even begun. "I figured Eric Stoll might not be comfortable with the uniform. I thought a skirt and jacket might be less intimidating." She looked her casually dressed boss up and down. Locklear never wore a uniform – another thing she intended to ask him about but which she knew she probably wouldn't get an answer to.

"Tell me about Eric Stoll," he said.

Mendoza told Locklear as much as she knew about the man who, according to Bishop Rahn, had moved his family practically overnight from their farm outside Dayton and had disappeared. The town of Bedford where Mendoza had located him through tax records had no Mennonite church or congregation. According to Rahn, Eric Stoll was a quiet, unassuming man who lived an Old Order life. He was married to Rebecca and had two daughters, Marta and Bethany, both now in their early twenties.

"Bethany Stoll is his daughter's name?"

"Yep, he's actually a brother of our friend the lawyer. I checked back and Beth was also their mother's name. Before she married, Beth Senior was Beth Shank – Samuel Shank's daughter."

"And you say Eric Stoll is living an Old Order life?"

"Yep."

"What could make two siblings take two very different paths like that?"

"Guess we'll find out when we talk to him. I think we

should record the conversation. No one knows Beth Stoll better than him. He might give us something we can use in court."

Mendoza leaned across and pointed to the record button on Locklear's phone.

"It's that one – in case you didn't know."

Locklear frowned at young trooper. "We're not taping anyone, Mendoza. We have no authority to record so we won't be doing it. Stay within the law – always."

Mendoza shrugged and skirted roughly off the highway onto a secondary road that would lead them to the tiny village. Locklear groaned as his foot slid painfully towards the door. He placed his hands flat to the ceiling and pressed up hard to steady himself.

"God damn it, Mendoza! Take it easy."

As they drove into town, Mendoza and Locklear passed a small convenience store which appeared to be closed. The sawmill also showed no signs of life. At the end of town the sign on a small diner creaked in the breeze. A dog outside the diner stood and barked twice at them then returned to its supine position to pant in the heat.

"I'm expecting tumbleweed to pass by any moment," Mendoza said.

"I like these places," Locklear replied. "They're peaceful."

Mendoza got out of the car and squinted into the midday sun.

"Maybe you can buy a place here when you retire."

Locklear placed his crutches out of the car and gingerly raised himself onto his feet.

"I don't plan on retiring until Kowalski forces me to. Come on, let's check out that diner."

Locklear chose the seats nearest to the door and their waitress Bonnie brought them coffee. They ordered lunch and when she brought it she wished him and his daughter a pleasant day.

Locklear grimaced. "Guess you were right. I do look old enough to be your father."

Mendoza blushed. So he did remember the conversation they'd had the night she put him in his sedated state into bed. He most likely also remembered that she had kissed him on the cheek.

Locklear grinned and settled back into the seat to eat.

When Bonnie returned with their bill, Locklear felt he had been pleasant enough to get answers to some questions.

"Why is the sawmill closed?"

Bonnie looked across the dusty road to the mill which sat across the street.

"It's just closed for lunch, honey. It'll reopen at two."

Locklear glanced at his watch. It was only 1.15.

"Where would I find the workers from the mill at this time?"

Bonnie glanced down the counter at two men sitting side by side.

"Those men there are the owners."

"I'm looking for one of the workers – Eric Stoll."

"Oh, that nice man? He's so quiet. He always goes home for lunch."

"Which is where?" Locklear flashed Bonnie his craggy-faced smile and placed a twenty-dollar bill on the table.

Bonnie placed the money in her apron pocket. "It's a small single-storey about two miles out of town. Red tin roof – green door."

Locklear pushed forward, placed his crutches on the ground and stood.

"You have a lovely day, honey," she said as he inched past her with Mendoza on his heels.

"Honey?" Mendoza teased as she helped her boss into the car.

It was not hard to find Eric Stoll's green-doored house in the sparsely populated outskirts of the village. Stoll had

The Pact

picked a good place to rent. Right next door was a police station – a one-manned outpost with a large hound stationed outside on a long chain.

"Smart," Mendoza mused as they parked the car far enough away from the dog for safety.

A plain black bicycle lay flat on the ground at the front door and a long line of crisp linen sheets blew in the light breeze at the side of the house. Mendoza knocked and waited until a woman answered.

Rebecca Stoll epitomised the kind of woman Locklear had expected to find living in the town of Dayton. She wore a long, plain grey dress and a white lace bonnet covered her fair hair. The woman wore no make-up or jewellery save a narrow silver wedding ring on her left hand.

Locklear was immediately taken by her smile and the radiance that oozed off her. He expected her to speak, to enquire what their business was but the beautiful woman simply stood and waited for them to do the talking.

Mendoza quickly and very briefly flashed her badge and, aware that their presence might cause the woman difficulties, asked to speak with her husband. Locklear stood back and let Mendoza take the lead and watched the light in the woman's face slowly dim. She stepped outside and closed the door tightly behind her.

"Come this way," she said as she directed Locklear and Mendoza around the back of the house.

Locklear walked beside the two women and watched Mendoza push her jacket back and place her hand on her gun which was placed in a shoulder strap. His trooper was always ready for conflict even when he himself could see no cause for alarm. He glared at Mendoza until the trooper moved her hand into her pocket.

Around the back of the house Locklear waited in the background and watched Eric Stoll, dressed in a plain black trousers and a white, collarless shirt, mending a broken bicycle. They listened as Rebecca Stoll nervously told her husband of the English strangers who had come to ask him questions about a life he had chosen to forget. They could not understand the language but it was clear to Locklear that Eric Stoll was refusing to speak with them. Locklear moved forward, inching his way painfully on the uneven terrain.

Eric Stoll stood up to his full height and placed his black hat firmly on his head. He did not move.

"Andrew Fehr is lucky to be alive and we believe your grandfather is involved," Locklear said.

The couple looked at each other and then returned their gaze to Locklear. Eric spoke but not to Locklear. He stared at his wife and the couple seemed to be arguing. Locklear watched to determine which of the couple was on his side. Rebecca Stoll, he decided, was trying to encourage her husband to tell the visiting police what he knew. Locklear wished it was the other way around. Eric Stoll wasn't budging.

"Please, husband," Rebecca Stoll said in English. "Please tell him and maybe someday we can go home."

Eric Stoll threw down his spanner and moved towards Locklear from whom his gaze never wavered. As he neared, Locklear realised how big the man was. He stood a good four inches taller than Locklear and was a good deal younger and stronger. However, Locklear had no intention of fighting him so the man's size was of no consequence to him.

"Come," the giant said when he reached Locklear.

They entered the house through a back door. Two teenage girls were busy preparing lunch in the kitchen. Stoll glanced at them and they disappeared down the corridor without a word.

Stoll directed the visitors to sit. Rebecca Stoll took glasses from a cupboard and poured cold lemonade for the visitors. Locklear watched as her small hands shook around the large pitcher. Her husband reached forward and wrapped his huge

The Pact

hands around hers to steady her grasp. Something about the scene roused feelings in Mendoza – feelings of loss – the awareness that in front of her was something she wanted but had never found. Love.

When all the glasses were filled, Rebecca Stoll took the seat beside her husband but kept her eyes firmly fixed on the table top. Eric Stoll placed his hat down in front of him and stared at Locklear. He did not look at Mendoza who sat beside her boss, directly across from Rebecca. Locklear took in the kindly visage of the Mennonite, his sandy-coloured hair and his eyes, the same eyes as the Fehrs and as Bethany Stoll.

"You have the same eyes as your sister," Locklear said.

"My sister is lost," Stoll replied in a quiet, Low German accent.

"I saw her recently in Harrisonburg," Locklear offered.

Mendoza touched her boss's arm, knowing that that was not what the softly spoken man meant.

"She is lost to God," Stoll explained.

Locklear nodded. He looked around the simple room and wondered where he'd begin.

"Can I ask why you left Dayton?"

Rebecca Stoll moved her hands to her husband's and held them. He searched her face and she smiled at him. Mendoza felt her heart lurch.

"We could not live in peace there anymore."

"Why?"

Stoll stalled and took a deep intake of breath. "How did you find us?" he asked.

"Tax returns," Mendoza replied.

"Ah, the English world," Stoll replied, his voice almost a whisper.

"You could have changed your name," Mendoza replied.

"We are honest people."

"I understand ... but if we could find you, then so can others," Mendoza said.

"But if your family wanted to harm you, they would have done so by now," Locklear added, hoping to reassure the gentle couple. He glanced at Mendoza, hoping she understood his point. He needed the Stolls and reminding them of how much danger they could be in wasn't conducive to getting them to talk.

"My sister and I – our parents died when we were young," Stoll said. "I was almost fourteen but Beth was only nine. Uncle Jacob took us to live with him and his wife but we were not happy. He lived a different life to the one our parents lived."

Locklear waited for Stoll to continue. He could see the retelling of his story was painful for the gentle man.

"When I was eighteen I returned to the farm and began to manage it on my own. Beth was too young so she remained with our uncle and aunt. They had no children. Their son died in infancy. Now …" Stoll fixed his eyes on his large, work hardened hands, "now I wish I had taken her with me."

"Why?"

"Because Uncle Jacob poisoned her heart and her mind, sent her to college to learn things a woman did not need to know, things she did not need to be exposed to."

Mendoza stiffened and Locklear touched her leg with his, hoping she would understand that now was not the time to express her feminist opinions.

Stoll focused his eyes on Mendoza. "In our faith men and women are equal. But we avoid all things that darken the heart and the mind – men and women alike." He paused. "When I refused to be part of his life, uncle and grandfather refused to buy milk from my farm. I just wanted a simple life. I wanted to farm, go to church, love my family and honour God. This is the life I wanted but they would not let me have it, they would not leave me in peace. I was already married and had a family to care for. I sold the cattle and made furniture but my workshop was burnt to the ground. I walked to Harrisonburg to work on other farms and my windows were broken with my wife and daughters inside. We had no choice. We had to leave. My wife had to leave her sister and I had already lost mine."

"But you moved to a place that does not have a Mennonite church or pastor?"

Rebecca Stoll's eyes filled with tears. "We could not risk being found."

"Do you know why your grandfather has a grudge against the Fehrs?"

"Because they shamed his family," Stoll replied.

"It happened a long time ago and it wasn't them – it was their ancestors," Locklear replied.

Stoll remained quiet for a moment. "Many generations past, my ancestor Eli Shank cursed the Fehrs. They had shamed him. They wronged him but he had no forgiveness in his heart. He cursed them and said their land would never bear fruit and would dry out."

"Do you believe that is possible?" Mendoza asked.

"It was true. Their soil turned to sand and the grass does not grow. It is worthless."

"Do you know what it is that your grandfather thinks they have buried on their farm?"

Eric Stoll pushed his fair eyebrows downwards. Deep long lines appeared above his nose and narrowed his eyelids around his extraordinary pupils.

"I do not know."

Locklear believed him.

"Luke Fehr is not a godly man," Stoll replied.

Rebecca turned to face him. "Husband, he is a burdened man."

Stoll lowered his eyes and nodded. "Forgive me."

Mendoza tapped on the table, anxious to ask any questions that might move the case forward.

"How close were you to Sara Fehr?"

"The family were shunned so we were not permitted to be in the Fehrs' company," Stoll replied.

Mendoza expelled her breath through her nostrils. "And the same with the Wyss family?"

Rebecca nodded. There was a look of guilt on her face. "Helena Wyss is a kind and godly woman. We feel her loss."

"And now you are in the same boat," Mendoza said. "But you didn't feel the same about the Fehrs?"

Stoll shifted uneasily on his seat. "I have told you – Luke Fehr is not a man of God."

"Did you know that Eli Shank fought in the Civil War?"

Rebecca Stoll turned swiftly and stared questioningly at her husband.

"Forgive me," he said. "I made a promise to my uncle never to repeat this."

Rebecca Stoll squeezed her husband's hands.

"Eli was not a good man even before he witnessed cruelty in battle. It was my mother who told me this but, to Uncle Jacob and my grandfather, Eli was wronged by the Fehrs. When he returned from war, his heart had darkened even more. He had lost something given to him by his mother and was not permitted to return to the family until it was returned."

"Do you know exactly what it was?"

"I only know that it was something my ancestors brought with them to this country when they fled persecution from their homeland. An heirloom. I was never told what it was. I was ... out of favour with my grandfather when it was time for me to know."

"Out of favour?" Locklear asked.

"Not trusted," Stoll replied.

"What happened when Eli returned to Dayton?"

"He was shunned by his father and was not permitted contact with his family until the heirloom was returned."

"But he didn't know where it was?" Locklear interjected.

"He said it was stolen from him and that the Fehrs assisted the thief."

"I don't think that's quite what happened," Mendoza offered.

Stoll did not argue. "I am simply telling you what I was told. Eli's father was an old man and he was very sick. He had many daughters and his two sons were born last when he was already an old man. Eli did not return the item and lived alone in the woods. My mother said he had poor thoughts. Eli found out that his father was planning to put his younger brother forward as pastor."

"What did Eli do?"

Stoll looked at his wife and then lowered his eyes to the ground. Locklear noticed how guilty the man now looked, as though the sins of his ancestors were also his.

"The old man died suddenly and ... Eli's younger brother was found hanging from a tree in the woods."

"You think ...?" Locklear began.

Stoll's eyes met the sergeant's. "I cannot bear false witness against a man when I do not know the truth but Eli told the community that the Fehrs had killed his brother."

"Do you believe that?" Mendoza asked.

Stoll returned his eyes to the table top. "No."

"And his mother welcomed him back?"

"Yes. He became pastor immediately even though ..."

"Yes?"

"In my heart I believe Eli Shank had blood on his hands and not just the blood of those he met in battle."

"Yet you hold a grudge against the Fehrs?" Locklear said. "Don't deny it. I can see it in your eyes."

"I don't know what happened back then, Sergeant Locklear, but if the Fehrs had helped my ancestor, if they'd stopped him from being robbed, history would have been different for generations of Shanks and Fehrs. We would have had peace."

As they drove the car out of the Stoll driveway, Locklear waited on Mendoza's appraisal. With Eric Stoll out of the picture, his childless uncle was reliant on Beth to continue on with the evil empire and it looked like the woman was shaping up to do the job well.

"Well?" he asked.

"Eric Stoll is a good man. He's telling the truth about not knowing exactly what the feud is about. His heart is broken about his sister. He misses home, they both do – and, like me, he doesn't trust Luke Fehr."

"You're right about everything, Mendoza, except one thing – Luke Fehr is not a bad person. He's simply trying to survive in a place that you either submit to or leave and he's applying his own brand of justice that these gentle people just don't understand."

"OK, sarge, but when I'm proved right you owe me a beer," she said as she rocked the car back down the narrow road towards the highway.

"It's a deal. Now, take it goddamn easy on the road."

As they merged with the highway, Locklear's tension eased and he removed his hands from the roof of the speeding car.

"Where to now?" he asked.

"Christiansburg. It's about an hour further south."

"OK, shoot." Locklear pushed the seat back into a semi-supine position and closed his eyes to block out the sun.

"You sure you're comfortable?"

Locklear grunted in response.

"OK – next are the Yoders. They're a retired sister and brother, neither married. No kids. No jobs."

"How did you find them?"

"Well, I figured that at one point they were farming here so I checked property registration records. The Yoders sold a very valuable farm halfway between Dayton and Harrisonburg to Jacob Shank around the same time that he and his sister left the area. Now get this – they sold the fifty-acre farm for $120,000. I checked local prices and it was worth twice that much."

"Good work. Got a contact number?"

"I only have a building and street name. No number. I tried to Google it – oh, for you older people that means *search for it online*."

"Very funny."

Mendoza drove steadily down the highway, her mind focused on the affection and intimacy she had witnessed passing between the Stolls. When her divorce came through, she thought that her son and her job would be enough to fill her life but there was an emptiness that neither her child nor her career could fill.

"You ever get lonely, Locklear?" she asked but her question was answered only by quiet snores rising from the seat beside her.

Chapter 19

"It's a nursing home," Mendoza said as she stood on the pavement outside Mercy Building.

Locklear stood back and ran his eyes as far as the long, grey building would allow.

"It's a dump."

When the pair entered the reception area, they were met with the smell of urine and boiled cabbage.

"Jesus!" Locklear exclaimed.

When a tall, stern woman approached them, Locklear took out his badge and asked to speak with the Yoders.

The woman, who introduced herself as Joseph, seemed surprised to hear the name.

"They're not here."

"Well, where *are* they, *Joseph*?" Locklear asked, accentuating the name which he thought was ridiculous.

"Well, that was years ago. They never arrived."

Locklear blew out and took a seat beside an old man who was laughing into thin air. He took off his shoe and stretched his painful foot. He had abandoned the crutches, probably too soon.

"You'd better come into my office." She led them to the door and, ushering them in, said, "I'll join you in a moment."

The Pact

"Do you think this a Mennonite nursing home?" Locklear asked Mendoza as they waited in the office for the woman to join them. Mendoza snorted and pointed to a large statue of St. Joseph in front of the stained-glass window above them.

"You're an idiot, Locklear. This is a convent-run home. Joseph is a nun."

Sister Joseph returned with another, older woman who wore a long brown habit and veil. Joseph sat at the desk while the more formally dressed nun stood behind her with a pile of small brown envelopes in her hand.

"This is Sister Thomas. She manages the patient records here."

Sister Thomas then told the story of the siblings who had come to see the facility years previously. They had booked two rooms, side by side, and paid a deposit for their care which would be then paid monthly from a bank account in the brother's name.

"Why come here? Surely there are retirement villages for members of their faith?" Locklear asked.

"I got the impression they wanted to go somewhere no one would think to look for them," Sister Thomas replied. She moved forward and placed the letters in Locklear's hands. "We wrote to their bank and told them to stop the payments. We had no other address for them and had no contact details for any next of kin."

Locklear opened the first letter, a bank statement from Harrisonburg stating that the Yoders had €125, 561.00 in their bank account.

"They said they'd sold their farm and were looking for somewhere to retire," Sister Thomas said.

"That amount wouldn't have lasted them very long," Mendoza said. "They were only in their sixties."

"I knew something wasn't right about it. I felt they were running from something."

"It was clear that money wouldn't last them long," Sister

Joseph added, "but they would have received care here even when the money ran out."

"So, they never arrived." Locklear ripped another envelope open, dated two years later. He clenched his jaw and shoved the bank statement into Mendoza's hands.

"It's empty!" she exclaimed.

"We sent so many of these back but they kept coming until a few years ago," Sister Thomas said. "Eventually Mother Superior wrote to the bank and they replied saying that they had informed the Yoders' lawyer and would pass on their mail to them. We only kept these because … well … as I said, something didn't seem quite right."

"Did you ever hear from the lawyer?"

"Yes, she came here with a man."

Locklear looked at Mendoza.

"Do you remember her name, Sister?" she asked.

Sister Joseph looked at Sister Thomas who shook her head.

"It was a long time ago."

"Was it Stoll – Beth Stoll?"

"Yes, that was it! Stoll. That's right," she replied. "Ms Stoll said the Yoders were very ill and had decided to take up residential care nearer to their home. She told us that they were no longer able to advocate for themselves and all future correspondence should be directed to the legal firm."

Locklear stood and thanked the women for their time.

As they passed the reception area two old ladies were fighting over a newspaper.

"I'd rather hang myself than end up in one of these places," Locklear said as he and Mendoza exited the depressing building.

"If you wait long enough I'd say the Shanks will do that for you! Listen, we are getting nearer to the truth, Locklear. We'd better be careful. Very careful."

As dusk fell, Locklear and Mendoza stopped for a coffee in a roadside diner about halfway through their journey back to Harrisonburg.

"So, you think the Shanks killed the Yoders?" Locklear asked.

Mendoza put down her coffee and looked out at the darkening sky. The midnight-blue canopy was streaked with long purple veins as the sun disappeared for another day. It was a beautiful sight.

"It's hard to understand why there has to be so much cruelty in the world," she said. "Shank forced the Yoders to sell the only thing they owned and probably loved, paid them a pittance for it and … I just don't understand why he'd need to kill them."

Locklear beckoned the waitress to fill his cup.

When she left, he said, "I reckon when the Shanks bought the Yoders' farm, the fact that they had to leave meant no one would notice them disappearing. They had no other relatives so no one would be looking for them. It was a perfect crime."

"I want to know what happened to their money. I want to find their will, see who the benefactors were."

"You mean you want to confirm that it was the Shanks who'd inherit the money on the Yoders' death?"

Mendoza nodded.

"OK," he said. "Tell me about the last of the missing families."

Mendoza told the story of pensioners David and Anna Ropp who eight years previously left their farm before dawn with only the most basic necessities and were never seen nor heard of again. Mendoza still wasn't sure that the couple she'd located in New York were the right people and had only happened on them from a newspaper article reporting on an accident at a subway station where a man named David Ropp had slipped off the platform and had been seriously injured. She had arranged for Irene to book flights to New York to interview the couple but had not phoned ahead, hoping instead that surprising the couple might result in looser tongues than could be expected from those given prior notice.

"I'm coming with you," Locklear said as the pair parted company outside their motel rooms. He could use the time to meet with the widow of the university professor who disappeared halfway into his research into John Grant's time in Dayton.

And there was one other thing he needed to do in the city he used to call home. Something he wasn't looking forward to.

Chapter 20

The exit from JFK airport onto the main highway was an assault on the senses that Locklear had almost forgotten about. It seemed like every vehicle on the packed highway was beeping its horn simultaneously.

"This place is nuts," Mendoza said, as she waved yesterday's newspaper in front of her face in the cab which appeared to have no air conditioning. Its driver, a Haitian man with a quick smile and loud laugh, sniggered when they asked him to open, then close, then reopen the electric windows – the controls for which had been ripped off the back-seat doors.

When they checked in, Locklear's ire rose as Irene had forgotten to change the booking to two rooms in the fully booked hotel. Mendoza, unperturbed, slung her bag on the bed under the window and lay down, panting in the heat until the AC kicked in.

"Will you not do that?" Locklear barked.

"Do what?"

"Breathe like that."

Mendoza laughed and went to the bathroom for a shower. She pulled fresh underwear from her bag and waved it at Locklear who sat bolt upright on his bed, barking at Irene who Mendoza guessed was enjoying his annoyance.

When she returned to the bedroom her boss was quieter and his mood seemed to have improved. Mendoza sat at the edge of his bed, drying her hair with a towel and showed no reaction when he stood abruptly and moved to the window to look out on the busy street below.

"I'm going to see Jefferson's widow," he said quietly. "And then I've some other business to see to."

Mendoza stood and went into the bathroom to change. When she returned five minutes later, Locklear was gone.

The 5th Avenue apartment of Mrs Norma Jefferson was the sort of place Locklear felt most ill at ease in. He realised that he could add a dislike of rich people to his list of personality traits. Mendoza was one thing he didn't dislike. What he hated was the effect she had on him. The tough Latino made him feel protective, affectionate, vulnerable, old, but most of all she made him feel lonely. The pretty trooper reminded him of what he had lost out on in life, what he could have had but rejected time and time again so that he could be free.

As he stood in the apartment's expansive entrance hall, he took in the oak-lined walls and gilded ceiling. The maid, who had left him standing in the impressive surroundings, returned and took him to a drawing room where he was again left to wait. He wandered around, lifting ornaments which probably cost a year of his pay. Two photos sat on top of an antique sideboard. One was of the couple on their wedding day. The African-American husband and wife made a handsome young couple. The second photo was taken at Christmas time with their three young sons. They looked happy, Locklear mused as he replaced the photo and took a seat on a crisp, white sofa. Another fifteen minutes passed and he had made a decision to leave when the door opened and Norma Jefferson entered. Locklear stood and tried not to show his disapproval of her show of wealth. Large gold rings fitted with gems of various

The Pact

colours adorned most of her fingers and a heavy gold chain hung from her wrinkled neck. He had not expected the glamourous black woman in the photos to look so old.

She immediately noticed that the photo had been moved.

"Yes, I've changed, haven't I?" she said, reading his mind.

Locklear searched for words. None came so he looked into the fireplace and waited for her to speak again.

"My husband's disappearance changed everything – including me," she added quietly.

Locklear returned to his seat and explained the purpose of his visit.

"Bill was everything to me."

"Can you tell me what happened?"

The maid knocked and brought in a tray with coffee. Norma Jefferson poured without asking and offered the coffee in a tiny, bone-china cup. Locklear tried to push his large fingers into the handle but gave up and lifted the cup by wrapping his large fingers around it.

Norma smiled. "You remind me of Bill."

Locklear glanced back at the photo of the black man with a toothy smile and kind eyes. He saw no resemblance.

"Bill wasn't born into wealth. We met at college and I fell madly in love with him. My parents weren't happy of course, they thought Bill was interested in my inheritance but I never even told him about it until we were dating for about a year."

"You never brought him home?"

"I didn't want him to be put off by the money. I was afraid I'd lose him."

Locklear grinned. He had never quite heard of things working that way before.

"We were both studying American history. I chose it because I didn't know what else to do with myself but Bill chose it because he was passionate about history, especially Black history."

"Why was he specifically interested in Grant?"

"Bill was on sabbatical from his position as Professor of Modern History at NYU and he was writing a book about black men who fought for the Union during the Civil War. He was an expert on the subject. He was particularity interested in the story of the Confederate gold that supposedly went missing in the aftermath of the war. He came upon a book by a writer named Hennessy about the experiences of soldiers during the Civil War. There was a letter in the book written by Grant. Among the many charges he faced, Grant had been accused of stealing Confederate gold. Bill became intrigued by the man's life. He wanted to know more about him and to include a chapter on Grant in his book."

"So that's why he went to Dayton?"

Norma nodded. She walked to a bookcase and lifted an old, tattered book from the third shelf.

"This is the book. The letter written by Grant is marked. Please, take it. I hope it will be of some use to you. You can return it when the investigation is over."

Locklear took the book and placed it on the sofa beside him.

"Thank you. You were saying ..."

"Yes. Bill was staying in a hotel in Harrisonburg. I never dreamed it would be the last time I'd ever see him."

"Did he talk to you while he was there?"

"He called me every evening when he'd got back to his hotel."

"The evening he went missing, did he say anything, did anything unusual happen?"

"I told the police all of this," Norma said.

Locklear could hear the emotion in her voice.

"I understand that it's hard but it might help shed some light on this case I'm working on."

"Most days were the same. He'd spend the day in Harrisonburg library – he said they had an excellent reference section on the Civil War in the area."

Locklear nodded. He didn't bother telling her that the library was burned to the ground, its excellent references along with it and its librarian missing, most likely dead.

"Some days he'd meet people who had local knowledge of the war. He said it was the sort of place that had a long memory – a stable population whose history went back generations in the area."

"That's true."

"Well, the night Bill went missing was unusual. Bill never drove at night because he had dreadful night blindness. He was due to meet a man who knew a lot about Grant. He said his ancestor had known Grant personally. He'd come into the library one day and they struck up a conversation. He offered to pick Bill up that evening and drive him to the spot where Grant had lived. Bill had hoped that he could see it by day to take photos for the book but the man said he was going out of town and wouldn't be back before Bill left town."

"So your husband agreed to meet him?"

"Yes."

"Did he say anything about the man, his name, age, anything?" Locklear was beginning to sweat. He was afraid that she would name Luke Fehr. Deep down he knew Luke Fehr was an innocent man and he was never wrong. Mendoza was getting under his skin.

"I don't remember Bill ever telling me his name but he said the man was of the Mennonite faith."

"Old? Young?"

Norma moved her dark-brown eyes upward as she tried to recall the last time she had heard her treasured husband's voice.

"It's been more than ten years, Mr Locklear, but I can still remember him saying that he loved me and to kiss the boys. The boys! They were all at college then!"

Locklear waited.

"Yes, he was an older man and I remember that he owned

a milk company or something to do with milk, Bill said."

"Did the police interview the man after your husband disappeared?"

"As far as I know they did but he said he'd never heard of Bill – never met him. It seems he was a local priest or a holy man of some sort so I doubt he'd lie about it. Bill left his hotel that evening and was never seen again. I know he's dead. I can feel it. I just want to know what happened and to give him a decent funeral. He deserves that."

Locklear put the precious china cup carefully down on the saucer.

Norma watched the large man's hand's shake around the antique cup.

"They were my grandmother's. They're invaluable, I'm told," she said.

Locklear stood and offered the woman his hand. He took one last look around the extravagant room. She followed his eyes.

"I'd give all this up in an instant to have Bill back. It's a lonely life without him and priceless china doesn't talk to you in the evening."

Locklear walked down the hallway until he reached the front door to the apartment. The maid opened it and stood to one side.

"There's a descendant of Grant that my husband was trying to get hold of, a young woman – Letitia Grant I think her name was. He wrote to her a few times but she was always moving. I think she had some social problems – well, drugs. You might like to try track her down. Perhaps she can help you."

Locklear thanked the woman and waited while the portly doorman hailed him a cab.

"East Harlem – Corner of Lexington and 119th," he said, and the driver swung around and headed for the darker side of town.

Chapter 21

As Locklear's cab passed the edge of the park, he could feel his heart start to quicken. He was not afraid of the Lombardis but he knew they were capable of anything. Why he was even making this trip he didn't know. Perhaps it was for Rosa. The woman's quiet resilience spoke to him and when they were both younger he sometimes wondered whether, if their meetings had not been across courtroom halls, if they had both been born into different lives in different places, he might have loved her.

Bile bubbled up his throat as the cab came to an abrupt stop outside the yard. He got out and scanned the rundown shop which had served as a front for Lombardi Senior's car-theft business for decades. Now, the shop looked abandoned. The trademark Italian flag painted on the outside wall was cracked and faded and the metal shutters were covered in soot and litter from the busy city street. He looked down the laneway that ran along the east side of the shop. There were no cars parked there.

Locklear knocked on the door of the small house that Nick Lombardi and his brothers had been born in. Without warning the door opened and a short, skinny youth reached out and punched Locklear in the jaw. Locklear lunged into the hallway and grabbed the teenager, tying him in a headlock and punching him twice in the stomach until, winded, he cried out in pain and fell to the floor, gasping.

"*Hey, Running Bear – go smoke a fucking peace pipe!*" the kid hissed.

Locklear punched him one more time for good measure.

A door at the end of the long, curved hallway opened. Locklear pulled his gun and flattened his back to the wall and waited. Thirty seconds passed and he heard nothing. A minute. Two. Locklear took a deep breath and wondered would this, an act of kindness, be the reason he would lose his life.

The boy tried to stand and Locklear kicked him in the ribs. "Stay down."

"Who's there?" a weak voice finally said.

"Go back inside, Grandpa!" the boy cried.

"Nicky?" the old man said. "Are you OK?"

Locklear pointed the gun at the boy's head. Nicky did not answer.

He listened as the old man made his way down the long narrow hallway. Short shuffling steps and hands rubbing their way along roughly painted walls. When Lombardi arrived, Locklear could see that the old man was no threat as two cloudy hazel eyes greeted him.

Vincent Lombardi was blind.

"*Who else is here?*" Locklear barked.

"No one," Lombardi replied quietly. "That you, Locklear?"

"Yes."

"Well, then, you better come in."

Locklear did not take his eyes off the sullen youth as Vincent Lombardi poured them both a Jameson. The boy placed it in front of Locklear and gave him a look that only someone young and stupid would do. A look of defiance in the face of unbeatable odds. Locklear was big and had a gun. The boy had tiny fists and a ten-stone body.

Locklear ignored the drink and fixed his eyes on the old man. It was more than thirty years since he'd laid eyes on him and was surprised that he was even alive. Locklear looked around the room that was once filled with the Lombardi family. He had arrested Nick in this very room countless times and had dragged him down from the tall boundary wall as the young criminal tried to escape. It was the same four walls but everything else had changed. The lace curtains on the window were grey and dirty and the room was filled with empty bottles of whiskey. The smell of stale smoke hung in the air.

"Where are all the family?"

"All gone," Lombardi replied quietly.

"Gone where?"

"I heard you were dead – shot somewhere in Virginia," Lombardi said.

Locklear shook his head. "No, I survived that."

"Pity," Lombardi replied.

The old man grinned and lifted the amber fluid to his lips. He put the glass down and pulled a pack of cigarettes from his pocket. The boy reached forward and tried to take one from the pack. Using what little sight he had, Lombardi raised his hand and slapped the boy before his light fingers reached the packet.

"So?" he said as he dragged heavily on the cigarette. "What do you want?"

"Where is the rest of the family?" Locklear asked again. He had to be sure none of Lombardi Senior's three other sons would arrive and finish what their weak nephew tried to start.

Lombardi blew the smoke in long, even puffs. It reached Locklear's face. He coughed.

Thick sticky phlegm shot out of Lombardi's mouth and landed on his creased shirt. He felt around until he found the spot, took a dirty hankie from his pocket and dried the drool with it.

"Lung cancer. Doc says I got months, tops."

He took a deep breath, spat again and placed the hankie back into his trouser pocket.

"It's just me and the kid now. I don't know what's going to happen to him when I'm gone."

"Whose kid is he?"

Lombardi leaned forward and placed his hands over the boy's ears. The boy tried to pull away.

"Ah, Pops, I'm nineteen! Twenty in the fall."

"No one knows how old you are, kid, so quit it!" The old man looked at Locklear. "About fifteen or sixteen years back this tramp knocks at the door. Looked like a whore. Pushed the kid up to the front door and took off. Note on him said he's Nick's kid. Never saw her again."

Locklear studied the kid. He was the image of Nick Lombardi.

"We didn't even know what his name was. Nona said he was about three years old. Didn't look for a birth cert because the whore couldn't have registered him as a Lombardi if she registered him at all. Kid was too young to tell us his name so we just called him Nicky. Celebrate his birthday same day as Nick's." Lombardi took his hands off the youth's ears and tossed his hair.

"Pops!"

"I don't know where my Nick and Rosa is. Nona's gone now – she died not knowing what happened to our eldest boy. Fredo is away. Doing twenty-five in Rikers."

"How about Alfie and Leo?" Locklear asked. Lombardi's two youngest sons were more troubled and more dangerous, more ruthless, than Nick or Fredo ever were.

Lombardi took another puff on the cigarette. "They're where you can't do them no more harm."

Locklear looked away and focused his eyes on a fly caught behind the dull net curtains.

"What happened?"

"They were hiding out in Sicily, waiting for things to cool

down here. There was trouble here between them and the Lucchesi family. Lots of accusations, most of it untrue. I sent them away until things blew over."

"And someone got to them?"

"Not just them – their wives – Alfie's kid, my granddaughter – she was just eleven. All dead. Leo's wife was pregnant. She was going to have a boy."

"I never heard about it," Locklear said.

"They was all in a limo. Tyre blew out. They went over a cliff. Looked like an accident. A guard I sent with them survived. He said he saw someone on the highway shoot the tyre. Police there said there was no sign of a bullet in the tyre. Case closed. No one cares who killed almost an entire family. People is just happy they're gone."

"What happened to the guard?"

Lombardi looked in the direction of his grandson. "Go upstairs, Nicky."

"Ah, Pops!"

"*I said go upstairs!*" Lombardi shouted.

The door banged shut. Lombardi waited until the boy's feet banged heavily up fourteen stairs and a door slammed. He flicked his ash onto the floor and took a deep swig of whiskey.

"I want the boy to go straight. It don't help hearing me talk about what is the past. What happened to the guard, you ask? I heard he met with an unfortunate end."

"Because you didn't trust the fact that he survived?"

"*Di preciso.*"

"I'm sorry."

"No, you're not," Lombardi said quietly. "I was fifteen when I came to this country with only the clothes on my back. Mama sent me to her brother but when I got off the ship he was already dead. Shot in a street fight between his gang and some Irish hoodlums. His boss took me in. I slept in a car in his garage at night. He taught me everything I knew and mechanics along with it. If it wasn't for him I'd have died of starvation. I tried to go straight. But everywhere I went doors closed in my face. I was too dark, didn't speak right, too Catholic, too foreign. I understood early that I wouldn't ever fit in – that what I wanted I had to take by whatever means I could. I brought up the boys to think that too. Take, take and do as little as you can to get what you want."

Lombardi felt for the top of his glass to pour himself another whiskey from the open bottle beside him.

Locklear stood to help him.

"Sit down, god damn it. I can get it myself."

"So you regret bringing your kids up like that?"

"I regret nothing!" he spat. "You gotta do what you can to get by in this life. I wanted more than ten hours a day under the hoods of rich people's cars, only getting by on measly wages. I wanted to buy my Christina nice things. I wanted a house, education for the boys – but it don't work like that for people like me … or like you." He raised his glass. "It don't work like that."

"I know where Nick is," Locklear said.

Lombardi put his glass down on the dirty coffee table. He coughed. Phlegm rose up into his throat. He pulled the hankie from his pocket and spat into it. His eyes welled with tears. He tried to speak but could not formulate the words he wanted to say.

Locklear eased his pain.

"He's living in a small town in Virginia. Rosa is dead."

"But … why … when … we thought they was dead."

"He wanted a better life," Locklear replied.

"Did he get it?" Lombardi asked.

Locklear pondered this. No, he didn't think Nick Lombardi got the peace he was looking for. It was too late. Too much had happened. All Nick Lombardi got was a few years in the desert to cogitate his crimes. Even so, it was an opportunity neither of his younger brothers had had a chance to experience. "Maybe," he answered.

"Does ... does he want to see me?" Lombardi asked.

"He doesn't know I'm here but ... he's alone now. I'd say he'd like it very much."

Locklear stood and slipped a piece of paper into Vincent's hand. "Nick's address." As he passed the stairwell he saw the boy sitting at the bottom of the stairs.

"So long, kid, and next time don't pick fights you can't win."

"Fuck you, mister!"

Locklear laughed and opened the door onto the busy street. The smells of New York City greeted him. The aroma of pizza shops and hot-dog stands, the whiff of clogged-up sewers, the scream of cars and the hot, suffocating summer air.

Locklear headed west until he reached Park Avenue and walked along the side of the park until his foot ached. He weaved in an out of the crowded sidewalks, heaving with home-time commuters, all battling their way back to tiny apartments all over the crowded city. He did not miss this place or its chaos, its noise, its constant tension. He stopped for dinner in a familiar diner.

As dusk fell and the crowds dispersed, he hailed a cab to the hotel. Tomorrow he would track down Letitia Grant and hope that the woman could fit another piece into his never-ending puzzle.

When he returned to the hotel, Mendoza was lying in a white cotton nightdress on her bed in the darkened room. He tiptoed in and lay down fully dressed in the next bed. Within seconds he realised that his trooper was not asleep.

Mendoza got up and pulled on a dressing gown.

She flicked the switch on the electric kettle and made herself a coffee.

"Want one?"

Locklear shook his head.

She sat at the end of his bed and told him about her search

for the Ropps – the last family on her "missing" list. This time he did not move away.

The address she had was a dead end, as were two further addresses given to her by the occupants of places the Ropps had previously lived in. A mailman sent her to a church across from the last apartment she visited to a Father Fernandez who he thought knew the Ropps. The priest was helpful but unfortunately Anna Ropp, when she found her in Creedmoor psychiatric centre, was not. The Ropps had not been siblings as Mendoza had previously thought but were actually father and daughter. Anna's widowed father was only seventeen when she was born and the two shared a closeness that was broken only when her father died of his injuries three weeks after he fell onto the subway line.

"How come they ended up in New York?"

"The priest seemed to think David had a cousin there, but I couldn't find any record of that. I went to the nearest police station to where the accident happened and spoke to a cop named Petros. He interviewed Anna straight after the accident. Witnesses said she started to scream and was pointing to a woman on the other side of the track. Another witness said he saw two men push David Ropp onto the tracks."

"Did they give a description?"

"Yeah, but it was too general – two fat men with black coats – New York in winter, most of the men at the station would probably fit that description."

"What about the woman Anna was pointing at?"

Mendoza shrugged. "Long fairish hair, slim. Young. That was about as much as they could say from what they saw across a crowded station. But you and I know who it was."

"We do – but we can't prove it."

"True. I phoned the transit company – they don't keep tapes that far back so there's no way to view video footage now. Anyway, David died three weeks later. Father Fernandez said Anna was lost without him. He put her up in a new apartment because she was afraid to go back to hers. He came to bring her food once and she had slit her wrists. He took her to hospital and shortly after she recovered she took an overdose and was hospitalised again. Fernandez said Anna became paranoid – thought someone was after her. Said the money in her bank account was gone. She had a nervous breakdown and tried to kill herself twice after that. Last time she went back into Creedmoor she never came out."

"Was the money gone?" Locklear asked.

"Every penny of it," Mendoza replied.

"Fernandez believed that her funds were missing. He thought everything else was fantasy. Turns out she's had a history of mental illness even before they left for New York. He went to the police and filed a complaint. Petros looked into it and about three days after David died the money was wired to an overseas account. From there it was routed through Switzerland, Cayman Islands and then to –"

"Samuel Shank's account?"

"Correct. I went to the probate court to confirm this. David Ropp left Shank everything in his will. The account was in his name alone. It was watertight. Legit. The attorney wired the money to Shank after Ropp died. I phoned the station and spoke to Ricci. I asked him to check the Yoders' will at the probate office. Same thing – Samuel Shank inherited every penny they had."

"Were there any complaints to the police?"

"No – but get this – a few days after the Yoders' disappeared, Samuel Shank made a complaint to the cops about Luke Fehr."

"Saying what?"

"Saying Luke threatened to burn down Shank's offices. Guess he was trying to defend the Yoders. The night security guard caught him throwing a package into the mailbox."

"A bomb?"

Mendoza grinned. "No – inside the package were thirty

one-dollar coins and a passage from the bible."

"What?"

"Matthew 27."

"Which is?"

"My mom wouldn't be too pleased if I told her that I had to look it up. It's where Judas hangs himself after being paid thirty pieces of silver by the High Priests and elders for betraying Jesus. The police investigated. Luke's prints were all over the envelope. He only received a caution because there was no evidence that he had threatened arson and putting religious verse into people's mailboxes isn't against the law."

"So there's some semblance of law operating here after all," Locklear said dryly.

"So it seems. But there's more. And Ricci asked me to keep this quiet. He doesn't want it getting out that he told us any of this. Luke wasn't only annoyed about what had happened to the Yoders. Seems like Luke was retaliating for something the Shanks did weeks before he delivered the coins to Shank's offices. The cops arrested Luke for firing at Jacob Shank when he came onto the Fehr farm with a couple of goons, all three were carrying shovels. Seems like they were about to give up on him finding whatever it is that they are looking for and wanted to take matters into their own hands."

"What happened?"

"Luke fired at them and they left. Shank made a complaint and the cops arrested Luke but they couldn't hold him on anything because Jacob was trespassing. Luke went to court and tried to get a restraining order to prevent any of the Shank family or their employees coming onto his land. Ricci was in the court the third time Luke showed up there. He said he remembered it because no one hardly saw Luke Fehr anymore. Ricci reckons it took a lot for a man like Luke to go there. He must have been desperate."

"Did he succeed?"

"No. Three times he filed for the order and each time his

application was supposedly lost by the court clerk whose father, according to Ricci, is an employee of Shank. Fehr couldn't win. Fehr then sent Shank another message. A handwritten note saying that if Shank or anyone involved with him came onto his land he would shoot and that next time he would fire more than warning shots."

"I wouldn't say Shank took too well to the threat."

"He didn't. He went back to the police but he was told to stay away from Fehr and to make sure Jacob did the same. There was already a record of them trespassing and, while the police wouldn't exactly help Luke, they were sick of it and told him that he had no business coming onto the man's land."

Locklear smiled. "Now do you think he's guilty, Mendoza?"

"Yes, sarge, sorry but I do. Luke Fehr is no shrinking violet. He's tough. You think he's some sort of maverick out there fighting his cause but I think he's dangerous. I think he's a man who's capable of anything."

Locklear absorbed the information. Regardless of what his trooper thought, and indeed members of the man's own community, he couldn't help but admire Luke Fehr.

"OK – back to the Ropps. Do I need to ask who the lawyer representing the Ropps' estate was?"

"No."

"Beth Stoll made it watertight. Anna couldn't contest it because –"

"Because she doesn't have the capacity to understand," Locklear interjected.

"Exactly."

"Isn't there a clause where the lawyer can't be related to a benefactor of a will?"

"I don't know, sarge, but these people ... they just keep getting away with murder."

Locklear tapped the bedside locker. Mendoza was right.

Everywhere they turned, every lead they got, told them something but none of it added up to a whole lot. None of what they knew would result in an arrest.

"Seeing Anna there – in that state, all alone and knowing how her father tried to protect her, it made me miss my son."

"Take the red-eye home – go see your kid and meet me back in Dayton."

Mendoza stood and pulled the dressing gown around her thin body.

She reached out her hand and touched Locklear's arm.

"Thanks, sarge. You're a good man, no matter what you tell yourself."

When Mendoza had packed and walked out the door, Locklear's tension eased. Her perfume lingered in the air. He was glad she was gone. He undressed and lay down on his bed. Tomorrow he would track down Letitia Grant and hope that somehow the woman would move this sorry case forward before anyone else got killed.

Chapter 22

Locklear had hoped to avoid a visit to his old station in East Harlem but Maguire, who could tell Locklear how many times the long-term heroin user had been arrested, could not offer him the type of information he needed on Grant's descendant. He needed local knowledge and there was only one place that he could get it. He had never been popular there – or in any station he had been based in. His aloof nature and squeaky-clean reputation made cops nervous of and ironically distrustful of him and, while this did not cause him to lose sleep, it did impact on his ability to request favours when the need arose.

He ordered the cab driver to pass the 28th Precinct on the corner of W123rd and Frederick Douglas Boulevard so that he could check things out before deciding if he would actually enter the place where he had begun his career in narcotics and from where he had waged and partly won his battle against alcoholism.

Locklear got the cab to stop just beyond the station and surveyed the entrance from there. Six police cars stood idly outside the two-storey, grey concrete building. Save two, he did not recognise any of the cops standing against their cars, waiting for a callout.

Four of the cops were young – rookies who were probably

not even born when Locklear first entered the dreary building as a young, man, fresh and armed with a naivety that saw him through the first few years in narcotics. Within two years, drink and not his moral standing helped him through each day of trying to push back the tide of illegal drugs in a city whose economy – from lawyers, doctors, high-end criminals and pimps – depended on the neediness of addicts to line their pockets. It was a battle that Locklear eventually realised would not be won on the streets but in schools, in homes, in churches, in any place where people could learn before they took that first injection, that first high, that last.

He got out of the cab, groaning as his foot hit the pavement – despite its improvement it was still sore. He walked back to the entrance.

The cops looked up. A broad smile washed over the face of a heavy-set, moustached man.

"Well, lookey who we got here!"

The cop walked forward and stopped a few feet from where Locklear stood. He leaned backwards, pushing out his large chest like a rooster competing for the attention of hens.

"It's our old friend Locklear. Heard you were dead."

"That's what I always admired about you, Smith – your sharpness."

Smith's smiled waned. His chest deflated and he seemed to shrink before Locklear's eyes.

"Fuck you, Locklear."

Locklear passed Smith and walked over to Robbins who had not moved from his position. If he could have said he got along with anyone in the station it would be Mike Robbins who, apart from the slight greying of his black hair, had not changed much.

"Robbins," Locklear said.

"Sarge."

Robbins knew Locklear well enough to know this wasn't a social call.

"What do you need?"

Inside the station, Locklear eased himself down beside the computer parked sideways on Robbins' desk which was covered with unfiled paperwork and leftover meals. Two cold coffee cups hung precariously on the edge of the disorderly desk.

The room, in which Locklear had spent a significant portion of his youth, was cramped with desks and filing cabinets and the three phones on the desk rang continuously. A photo stuck on the far righthand corner of the computer showed Robbins holding a small boy.

"Nothing much has changed here," Robbins said as he typed Grant's name into the system.

"That your grandson?" Locklear asked.

Robbins smiled. "No. I'm not quite old enough for that yet! It's my kid sister's kid. He's fifteen now. We're buddies. Must get a new photo."

"Linda's a mother?"

Robbins shot Locklear a look. He was surprised that the distant man had remembered his younger sister's name. Locklear, for his part, hoped Robbins wouldn't ask him how exactly he had remembered the cop's wild-hearted sister.

"She still a cop?" Locklear asked, remembering the flame-haired beauty who had shared his love for whiskey and the nights she spent in Locklear's apartment that her brother never knew about.

"A lawyer," Robbins replied.

"I'm sorry for your loss," Locklear joked.

"Right!" Robbins chuckled.

The computer beeped and a photo of Grant appeared in the righthand corner. Locklear leaned into the screen to get a better look at the gaunt black woman who had spent her life on the streets fighting heroin addiction and herself. Letitia Grant had huge doleful black eyes and nappy hair. She was dressed in a thin cotton blouse and equally thin cardigan. The mug shot, taken several years previously, told Locklear that the woman might not even be alive now.

"What do you know about her?" Locklear asked.

"Depends on who's asking," Robbins replied.

"Come on, Robbins. I'm working on a case in Virginia – the girl is somehow connected. Don't ask. It's a long shot but she's all I've got right now – so, will you help me?"

Robbins sighed as he pressed the print button on his keyboard. He got up and collected his paperwork from the printer behind the reception desk and handed it to Locklear.

"It's got her last known address and her rap sheet. Be careful, that bitch bit me one time – had to get shots."

Locklear glanced quickly over the three-page document which listed the thirty-two-year-old woman's many misdemeanours: breaking and entering, deception, prostitution, dealing, car theft, DWIs and aggravated assault.

"I'll tell Linda you said hi."

Locklear waved and left the station. As he passed the car park, Smith gave him the finger. Locklear returned it and hailed a cab at the corner.

"306 West 102nd Street."

When he arrived at Saint Luke's Halfway House, Locklear climbed the four stone steps and opened the door into the facility which had been in its former life an old New York brownstone. The large city houses had been mostly turned into businesses of some kind and could now rarely be afforded by people as a family home. He walked six feet into the facility but found the inner door locked. He rang a buzzer and waited while an overweight Asian woman made her way down the long corridor. When she opened the door Locklear smiled at the badge the woman wore on her purple flowered shirt. *Don't yell at me. I'm just the probation officer.*

"Good badge."

"The girls here got it made for me," she said.

"I'm –"

"A cop," she said.

"You've been doing this a long time!"

"Too long," she said as she opened the door wide, allowing him entry. "I'm Ling."

She thrust her hand forward.

"Locklear," he responded, taking her hand.

"First name or last?" she asked.

"Last. Yours?"

"Both. Ling Ling, can you believe that? My parents must have had a sense of humour."

"Must have had? You don't know?"

"Long story," she replied, ushering him into her tiny office. "Come on in." She sat behind her desk.

Locklear settled down on the only other seat. He looked at the walls which were covered in framed photos of young women of all colours graduating from college.

"These all detainees here?" he asked. He stood to take a closer look at the photos. Ling was in most of them, smiling proudly.

"Residents," she corrected him.

"Looks like they're doing OK."

"Yes. Some make it – some don't."

"I'm here about Letitia Grant," Locklear said as he returned to his seat.

He waited as he watched the smile fade from Ling's face.

"What has she done?"

He could see the genuine look of upset on the probation officer's face and wondered how a repeat offender like Grant could get the woman in front of him to care so much.

"Nothing – least not that I know of. I'm working on a cold case. A relative of Grant's was involved. I thought she might know something. That's all."

Ling relaxed and eased herself back into the faux-leather chair.

"How long has she been here?" Locklear asked.

"She's been here four times in all. First three times she was taken back to prison. Kept breaking the terms of her parole. She's been here now eleven months and she's making good strides at getting herself straight."

"She still using?"

"No – she went through detox in prison. We don't take users here."

Ling pointed to a sign on the wall above her head.

No drugs. No alcohol.

"What else can you tell me about her?"

"Well, she's had it real tough. Spent the first two years of her life in foster care. Both parents were users. Father was in an out of jail. Mother worked as a stripper and sometime prostitute. After that she lived with her father's mother but the old woman went into State care when Letitia was seven. She kept in contact with her though, saw her a few times a year. She died when Letitia was fifteen. Letitia still talks about her grandma. Every time her parents cleaned up their act and got her back she'd be happy to be back where she felt she belonged, but it wouldn't be long before one or other of them would fall off the wagon and then she'd be back in State care. One time she was found alone in an apartment. Neighbours heard her crying. Reckon she hadn't eaten for three or four days. She was eight years old, can you imagine that? It's no wonder she took the road she did. She felt it had been all set out for her. My job is to show her that there is another path for her, if she wants it."

"Is it OK if I talk to her?"

"If she's happy to talk to you then it's fine with me. Letitia's at work but she should be back soon. She packs bags down at the Westside market and she goes to college at the local college two afternoons per week. She's studying to be an artist. You should see how she paints. She's a talented woman."

Locklear leaned back in his chair and studied the woman

in front of him. He found it hard to understand why someone would choose to do such a difficult job when the odds of success were so low.

"How did you end up here?" He immediately regretted the question. It had come out wrong and sounded offensive. The look on Ling's face told him he was right.

"Sometimes a job chooses us, don't you think?"

"I do."

"Coffee?"

"Thanks."

Ling left the room and returned with two stained mugs of steaming coffee. How different this was, he mused, to the reception he had received from Norma Jefferson on 5th Avenue. There were no china cups here, no maid and no gilt furnishings. These were the sort of surroundings he preferred. It was what he was used to.

"I was a resident in this very home when I was not much more than eighteen years old," she began.

Locklear put the coffee down on Ling's desk and shook his burning hand.

"I was brought to this country thirty-two years ago when I was eighteen months old. I'd been in an orphanage in China, the result of the one-child policy. Because I was a girl and my parents were farmers, I was no use to them and so they left me on the doorstep and walked away."

"I'm sorry," Locklear offered.

"Don't be," she replied. "It is what it is. They were in that situation and I am now in mine. A Chinese American couple adopted me and took me to California. I didn't know I was adopted until I was almost fourteen years old. It came as no surprise to me. I always sensed it, somehow."

"Did they have other children?" Locklear asked for reasons unknown to himself.

"No, it was just me. Unfortunately. I was twelve when my father started having sex with me. Fourteen when my parents took me out of the State for a secret abortion when I was carrying his child, fifteen when I ran away and took my first injection of heroin and sixteen when I arrived in New York to work as a prostitute to feed my habit."

Locklear shifted on his chair. "Didn't you tell anyone, your school?"

Ling smiled. "I'm not telling you this, Mr Locklear, to make you uncomfortable. It is simply to help you understand what it is like to come back from something like that. I want you to treat Letitia gently. You'll get further that way."

Locklear tried to think of something to say.

"How did you get out of … your situation?"

"I had a daughter and my life changed. She was taken into care. I came here. Every night I kissed her photo and told her I was coming for her. I got a job, went to college and saw her as often as I could. When she two and a half I got an apartment and got her back. I graduated law school with honours and went on to further my education. I started volunteering here while my daughter was at school and when a job came up I forgot all about being a lawyer. This is where I was destined to be. That was nine years ago now and I've been here ever since."

The front door opened and the bell buzzed in Ling's office. She rose and Locklear followed her. At the door, waiting for entry, was Letitia Grant looking healthier than she did in her mug shot. She looked fleetingly at Ling and then fixed her eyes on Locklear. The moment seemed to Locklear to last a lifetime. In that one moment, something told him that this woman, hundreds of miles away from Dayton, Harrisonburg and the Mennonite community, could unlock the secrets of the Fehrs' isolation. He saw it in her eyes. And then she was gone. Grant had dropped her shopping and had run from the porch.

Locklear instinctively gave chase to the pleas of Ling not to follow her. He chased the lithe woman to the end of 102nd and right onto Broadway, ignoring the pain in his foot. He stopped to catch his breath and rest his foot. Then he forced himself to run on. By the time he caught up with her again, all he saw was a glimpse of her bright-green shirt as she turned left onto W100th no doubt heading for the park.

He stopped and bent forward, waiting to catch his breath, then made his way painfully on foot back to the house.

"Where does she go to school?" he asked Ling.

The woman pursed her lips. "I asked you not to chase her. When these girls see a cop, they just think they're about to be blamed for something they didn't do."

"Which school?" he repeated.

"Edward H Reynolds – Westside," Ling curtly replied.

Locklear sat down and pulled his shoe and sock off. The bandage had come undone and one of the cuts on his foot had started to bleed.

"Tell her," he panted, as his breathing slowed. "When she comes back – tell her she has nothing to fear. I just want to talk to her about John Grant – tell her that, OK?"

Locklear had barely got his breath back when his phone rang. It was Maguire.

"Sarge, you better come back to Dayton right away."

"What's wrong?"

"Helena Wyss is dead."

Chapter 23

The short flight back to Richmond seemed interminable as Locklear stared out the window. Maguire had given him little information on Helena Wyss but had contacted Kowalski who had a helicopter waiting at the airport to take him to the scene. He phoned Mendoza and ordered her back to Dayton. He noticed how quiet she was when he phoned. She'd had only a few hours with her kid.

When his plane landed, Mendoza was already waiting at the helipad in Richmond in the pouring rain, uniform on, hair pulled back tight. He reckoned her deceased cop father would have been proud of her.

Neither spoke during the flight. The helicopter landed in a clearing between the Wysses' house and the forested area to the north. The rain had not subsided and soaked them as they followed a sodden Maguire up the twenty-minute hike through the dense forest. Mendoza marched ahead, wiping away the mascara that had begun to weep down her tanned face. Locklear was limping a little as his foot had become more painful on the short plane trip.

Soon they reached the spot where five cops, including Maguire's new young partner Jones, stood in shock at the sight before them. Helena Wyss was hanging by the neck from a tall tree. Locklear looked at the ground and saw the snapped trap that had only days ago held his injured foot and with it, his DNA. Several dollar coins had been thrown around the base of the tree. Her cotton dress had been pulled down to her waist, baring her upper body. Rain had broken through the canopy and had washed away some of the red writing emblazoned across her naked breasts. Her open eyes bulged forward and appeared to be staring in the direction of her farm. Locklear reckoned her throat had been cut immediately after the killer had strung her up and that he or she had used Helena's blood to write a message.

Locklear stood back and tried to read the writing: *ud s s ca ot*

"Can't believe she hanged herself," one cop said behind him.

Locklear's head snapped around until he found the mouth from which the sentence had been uttered. It belonged to young Jones, Maguire's new partner.

"Do you see a ladder around here, Jones?"

"No, sir."

"So you think she shinned up there?"

"No, sir."

"And tell me, trooper, did she paint that writing on herself before or after she cut her own throat?"

The rookie flushed. He looked fleetingly at Maguire and, embarrassed, rested his eyes on the dense woodland to his right.

"Jesus!" Locklear sighed, wondering if the kid had a brain at all or ears to hear – surely Maguire and the others had been discussing the situation?

He turned back and took a closer look at Wyss. Her head had now fallen slightly forward and her open eyes seemed to be staring at him. He looked away. Helena Wyss had endured a terrible death. He didn't need an autopsy report to know that the woman had fought for her life. It had been a violent death. He looked at her bare feet and noticed that they rested exactly where her ancestor's initials had been carved into the ancient tree more than a century and a half before. IF1861. The significance of this was not lost on Locklear. Like Isaac Falk, Helena Wyss had died for what she believed in. He tried again to read the words which continued to drip downwards, soaking into the ground below which held a pool of Locklear's own blood.

"Does anyone know what this writing means?"

No response.

"Maguire – get Carter up here."

"But, sarge, he's at the hospital. The old sarge isn't doing too good. They had to operate on his face, he got an infection and his heart didn't cope so well. He's in intensive care."

"But he's alive?"

Maguire nodded.

"And he's in hospital being cared for?"

Maguire nodded again.

"*Then get me goddamn Carter and get him here now!*" Locklear bellowed.

Maguire threw his keys at the blushing rookie who happily set off to collect Carter.

"Where's her husband?" Locklear asked.

"He works in Harrisonburg. Trooper went immediately to inform him but found he was out of town – his company has sent word for him to return at once."

"Where's the girl?" Locklear asked, referring to Abigail.

Maguire looked down at the blood-soaked earth. "Trooper out on the highway saw Luke Fehr's truck speeding in the direction of Richmond at dawn. He said there were two people in the truck and, from what he saw, the passenger was a young girl. He gave chase but lost him."

Mendoza eyed Locklear from the periphery.

He looked away. He wasn't wrong. He was never wrong.

Luke Fehr did not kill Helena Wyss. Locklear had a sense of grass growing under his feet. He squirmed and moved from foot to foot. The rain was breaking through the trees. He was losing time. He moved back from the body and stared at the brow of the hill that ran down to the Wyss farm. He tried to imagine how her killers carried her body up to this spot or if his suspicions were right and she was killed right here. He felt that he throat had been cut after she was hanged and that the lack of blood could be explained by the heavy rain which had washed Helena's blood into the earth beneath her – a fitting death, he reckoned, for the woman who had fought hard to remain on the land she loved despite the ever-present threat from Shank. Twenty further minutes passed with Locklear staring into space. He did this at every murder scene, spent time in silence ruminating over the minutes or hours leading up to the point when the person took their last breath. He pictured himself there – in the middle of the scene, invisible to the victim and murderer and in that time visions would come to him, imagery of what had happened. Then all he had to do was prove it.

"Shouldn't we cover her up?" a voice asked.

Mendoza cut in before Locklear unleashed his ire on another cop.

"That would infect the crime scene," she said gently.

Locklear paced up and down like a caged animal.

"Where the fuck are forensics?" he barked to no one in particular.

At last Lee Carter made his way into the clearing with Jones. A silence fell among the group. Carter looked like a shrunken man. Dark rings appeared under his eyes and deep lines ran along the sides of his downturned mouth. Everyone felt sorry for the trooper whose father's life hung in the balance and whose job was under threat.

Locklear lifted his guilty eyes from the earth and looked at Carter. A brief moment of eye contact occurred between the pair, a reconciliation, an understanding.

Carter walked up to his boss

"Dad told me everything," he said quietly.

"Don't judge him," Locklear replied.

"I don't. But I want to come back. I want to help sort this out once and for all."

"Deal," Locklear said as he shook the trooper's hand.

Locklear led Carter closer to the body of Helena Wyss. He felt the younger man stiffen and slow as they approached the tree. Carter Senior was right. His son was no cop and Locklear hoped that when the case was solved the bright man would return to the work he had been born to. Carter focused on the dollar coins littered on the ground around the giant tree. Locklear directed his eyes upwards. He knew little about religion but he did know that Helena Wyss's death had some sort of sacred meaning or that someone had worked hard to make it look that way. He was anxious to know what the theologian thought about the fading writing on the woman's breasts. The coins were going nowhere.

Carter stood back and focused on the letters. Locklear saw his throat jump and knew the man wanted to vomit. He put his hand on his back.

"Take a deep breath. It'll pass."

Carter shot a look at Locklear.

"I didn't mean to ..." Locklear stopped talking. He always managed to say the wrong thing without intending offence.

The group were intent as Carter read the letters. He finished and even though he didn't need to, he knelt on the wet earth to count the coins on the ground. There were thirty. He stood and wiped the dirt from his jeans.

"It says, or it did say: *Judas Iscariot*. Judas is known for the kiss and betrayal of Jesus for thirty silver coins."

"Matthew 27," said Locklear.

Carter looked at him in surprise.

Locklear didn't enlighten him.

Mendoza sidled up and murmured into Locklear's ear. "Looks like you owe me a beer."

"Whoever killed Helena is saying she betrayed them," Carter summed up unnecessarily.

Raised voices sounded through the trees. Recognising one of the voices, Maguire ran through the trees to stop Peter Wyss from seeing his wife. They all stood silently in the rain, praying that Maguire, who knew Wyss well, would convince him that it was better to remember his wife as she was.

Maguire failed. Peter Wyss rushed to the tree and fell to his knees under his wife's body.

"*Nooooo! Helena, nooooo!*" he screamed.

Mendoza ran to him and tried to lift the man off the muddy ground which was sodden with rain and the blood of his beloved wife.

Wyss moved his eyes around the group.

"*Stop looking at her! Stop looking at my wife!*" he screamed.

Slowly, the cops, including Locklear, turned one by one and faced away from Helena's semi-naked body.

Peter Wyss ran to Locklear.

"Please cut her down! Please! Haven't you done enough to her?"

Wyss grabbed Locklear by the shirt and tried to swing him around to look at his wife. Mendoza put her arms around him and tried to detach him from her boss who did not move a muscle to defend himself but the man could not be moved.

"*You did this!*" he screamed. "Following her about at night when all she was trying to do was to keep a man alive, to be a good Christian. But you're going to let him get away with murder. You can't stop him. No one can stop him!"

Mendoza hushed him. "We'll get Luke Fehr, Mr Wyss. Don't worry about that."

Peter Wyss's mouth open opened wide and he began to cry. He looked around at the cops, the cars, the siren lights and his dead wife and between his tears began to laugh hysterically.

"Luke? You fools! *Shank* did this! He killed my beautiful Helena!"

Wyss circled the cops who still stood with their backs to the body. He moved closer into each of their faces.

He stopped at Carter.

"And I don't care what you tell Shank. He has taken all that mattered to me. There's nothing else he can do to me."

Wyss turned and looked again at his wife. His chin quivered. He moved to her and placed his arms around her bare feet.

"She's so cold," he said.

He stepped back for a moment and took off his shirt. Locklear moved to stop him but Mendoza held him back.

Peter Wyss climbed the tree until he reached his wife's upper body. Gently he placed his shirt over her breasts. He reached one hand over and cupped her face and then kissed her gently on the lips. He moved his mouth to her ear and whispered something. Mendoza turned away as heavy tears fell down her stained face.

Wyss climbed down and stared at Locklear and then disappeared into the trees, away from the direction of his house and away from the life he had known.

Chapter 24

The call to Bishop John Rahn revealed nothing that Locklear hadn't already known. He and his wife had woken that morning to an empty house. Andrew and Esther, who he now admitted to hiding, were gone. Four of the five Fehr children were on the run. Luke Fehr was not stupid – the man knew that his DNA would be all over Helena Wyss's body. Samuel Shank would have made sure of that.

In the incident room of Dayton police station, Locklear went over his notes, nursing a semi-warm coffee to rouse him after what had been a sleepless night.

Mendoza, equally worn and dazed, sat in Carter's seat under the window and studied Sara Fehr's letters to Maria Whieler. When she tired of the banality of the correspondence, she moved to the large table in the middle of the room to study Sara Fehr's suicide note. She still felt something about the note, about how it was written, was wrong but although she came back to it over and over, she could not figure out what was bothering her. She slumped down and eased her feet out of her shoes.

"I slept in these last night," she said.

Locklear looked up from his notes.

"I was so tired I just lay down on the bed and didn't wake

up until this morning."

Locklear took his reading glasses off and inhaled. "I didn't sleep at all, so ... lucky you."

Mendoza leaned back and stared at her feet. A memory of how Peter Wyss had touched his wife's feet surfaced and brought tears to her eyes.

"Has anyone seen Peter Wyss since yesterday?" she asked.

"Nope, Maguire saw him heading on foot towards the Fehr farm yesterday evening. He called him but he didn't answer."

"Poor guy!"

Locklear shoved his glasses roughly back on his face and studied the notes in front of him. Mendoza watched. "It's not your fault, you know."

Locklear tensed and kept reading.

"I mean it – you couldn't have prevented this."

Locklear swallowed hard. Helena Wyss's death *was* his fault. Someone knew he'd been watching her bring food and clothes to Luke Fehr but that person or persons had known that she'd been doing that all along. They had simply used Locklear and his revelations to Wyss to kill the woman, thereby throwing suspicion on Luke in the process. They had simply used Locklear's visit to the farm that night, and his new-found information that Helena Wyss was caring for and regularly saw Luke Fehr, to place suspicion on Fehr. The silver coins were an awkward and ill-thought-out "clue" which the killer hoped would place Luke under police suspicion – and, more importantly, under Locklear's suspicion. Someone very clever was using Locklear as a puppet and it was time to cut the strings and solve the case once and for all.

The door opened and Carter walked in. Locklear looked up.

"Lee," he said.

Carter shyly took a seat on the other side of the room. Locklear looked at Mendoza.

"What time is it?

She checked her phone. "Nine thirty."

Locklear stood and stretched. He walked to the window and leant against it, facing the room.

"Nothing we've found out so far has progressed this investigation. We're finding stuff out, sure – but none of it fits together enough to put Shank behind bars for the attempted murder of Andrew Fehr. Now, remember that was where our investigation started and a whole lot has happened since then. We need to figure out what's driving Shank to keep people quiet – what it is that he is hiding. If we don't we'll never figure the rest of it out. Carter – no offence but it doesn't look like these people trust you any more so you're more use to me here. I want you to get back to studying the letters between Sara Fehr and Maria and phone me if you find anything useful."

"Yes, sir."

"Mendoza – there are scores of small farms in Dayton yet the Shanks have only pressurised the Yoders, Ropps, Wysses and Eric Stoll to get out. I want to know why. I want to know what's different about those farms or about those people. I want you to knock on doors – they must have distant relatives here. Appeal to their sense of righteousness. Sell them the idea that we want to put an end to the fear they're living under but we can't do it without their help. And take Maguire with you. Now, don't get all irate with me. I know you can handle yourself but Shank is getting desperate and therefore more dangerous."

Mendoza nodded. "Where are you going?"

"I'm going back to New York. I've got a date with history."

The hour-long drive to Charlottesville Airport gave Locklear time to think about how he'd approach Letitia Grant at the school she attended in Westside. Landing in Newark, he hailed a cab to take him the last twenty-five miles of his journey towards what he hoped would be a significant lead in the investigation.

As he waited in the foyer, he read the flyer advertising the school which catered for people for whom mainstream education had not worked. Locklear placed the flyer back into the plastic shelving and walked out the front door of the Edward H Reynolds School. He crossed the street and waited for Letitia Grant to finish her afternoon classes, hoping that if she could see him, if he didn't surprise her, the woman might feel less threatened and might tell him what she knew about her ancestor and the time he spent in Dayton. Locklear leaned against the black metal fencing that ran along the park opposite the school and placed his hands in his pockets, feigning the look of a relaxed man who posed no threat to her or to anyone.

The bell rang and scores of students filed out of the three front doors of the large school. The crowds dwindled and he watched eagerly as stragglers drifted out by him. Letitia Grant was nowhere to be seen. He turned towards the metal railing, lifted his phone and dialled Ling's office number. It rang twice before he heard a voice behind him. He closed the phone and turned.

"What do you want?" Letitia Grant asked.

Locklear looked about, wondering where she had sprung from.

"I saw you from the window," she said. "Thought *I'd* surprise *you* this time."

Close up, Grant looked older than her thirty-two years. Her face looked fuller than in the photo Robbins had given him and she certainly looked healthier but her eyes were old. They were the eyes of someone who had seen more in one short lifetime than people twice her age.

"Ling said I should talk to you." She moved three heavy art books from one arm to another. Long needle tracks were still visible along her left arm, a canvas of her life. No matter how the woman put the past behind her, the scars were etched forever on her body.

"I want to talk to you about John Grant, your ancestor," he said. "You hungry?"

Letitia settled into the booth of McDonald's and ate her meal ravenously.

The Pact

"We could have gone somewhere better," Locklear said as he lifted his coffee.

She spoke with a mouth full of food. "This is the only place I can afford."

Locklear knew there was no point in telling her that he would have paid. The woman had lived on the streets for years. She understood the rules. There was no such thing as a free lunch. This way she owed him nothing and could leave anytime she wanted. She took a loud slurp of her Coke and shoved some fries into her mouth.

"I don't know anything," she said.

"I haven't asked you a question."

She shoved another handful of fries into her mouth.

"Look, mister, the only reason I'm talking to you is because Ling asked me to. She said I can help you with something but I can't. I'm just sitting here so I can tell her least I tried. Ling's been good to me."

"You don't know anything about your ancestor John Grant?"

"He was a horse thief. I took a pony once from a fancy house upstate. Guess it runs in the blood."

"He was also a war veteran. He fought for the freedom of black people in this country."

She swallowed her food and took another gulp of Coke. She thought of her 8pm curfew and of her convenience-store boss who was itching to phone Ling about even the most minor misdemeanour.

"I look free to you, mister?"

"You know what I mean."

Grant finished her fries and wiped her greasy hands on her jeans. She sat back and began tapping her foot against the metal leg of the table.

Locklear waited but the woman said nothing and stared at the mirrored wall on the opposite side of the brightly lit restaurant.

"Ling said you were close to your father's mother," he said then. "I checked her out and she was never married – Grant was her birth name so she was a direct descendant of John. Didn't she ever mention him?"

"Just to say that he was no good."

"What did she mean?"

Locklear watched as Letitia's face hardened.

"Wasn't ever anyone any good in my family except my grandma. Only one ever cared about me. All she said was that John was shot for treason or something like that. Any Grant came after him was no good neither. We all been to prison. All thieves."

"It doesn't have to be your story."

"It's already my story, mister."

"Well, it doesn't have to end that way." Locklear looked down at the art books on the seat beside her. "Ling says you're a talented painter."

A weak smile washed across her face. "She believes in me. Sometimes she believes in me so much it hurts. Feels like I might let her down. Feels like I need a lot of strength not to let her down. Don't want to. Want to finish my course, go to college, go straight – but it feels like all these bad Grants are always pulling me towards them, pulling me down. My grandma said we be cursed because of John Grant."

Locklear's attention focused. "Cursed?"

"Yep. She said she remember her grandma saying someone cursed him and now we all cursed as well."

"Did she say who?"

She shook her head and looked at the food counter.

"Are you still hungry?" Locklear asked.

"No," she said.

A lie, he thought.

"Did your grandma say anything about John Grant leaving behind an old box?"

She stared hard at him and then returned her gaze to the

mirrored wall. Her lips moved slightly. He could see he had the woman's attention.

"No."

Another lie. Locklear would have expected questions, what was in the box, what did it look like, but the woman did not look at him and did not move her eyes from her reflection.

"Come on, you know all that but you don't know that John Grant stole a box from a young soldier and took it back to New York before he was arrested? I think he knew it was valuable but he didn't know why. He probably never figured out why. I think he passed it on to his wife and that she passed it on to her children and so on, and that the story of its origins was lost. Now, someone has the box and thinks it's a family heirloom. Fact is – it is an heirloom but not what you'd think."

"What is it then?" she asked without even looking at him.

"It's a box that has resulted in generations of a family committing suicide and is responsible for the murders of several more. Getting that box back will stop this."

"Must be valuable to cause all that."

"It isn't. It isn't valuable at all. Not in a monetary sense anyway. It's only valuable to the people from whom it was taken."

"I got nothing, mister, and that's the truth. I don't even got a photo of my parents. Got no brothers, sisters. No aunts, uncles. Don't have another living relative in this world and got nothing of theirs neither."

Locklear knew the woman was lying but he didn't know why. The Grants would have realised decades ago that the box was worthless. There must be, he reasoned, another reason why they had kept it.

"If you can help," he said, "then now is the time to do it. If you don't – and you continue to hang onto stolen property ..."

He saw her eyes widen. The woman did not need any heat.

"Look, mister. If I had some antique metal box, I'd have sold it for a fix years ago."

Locklear looked down at the woman's tattered jeans and focused on the nervous tic in her legs. He knew there was no point in pushing it – not right now. He would take Ling's advice and treat Grant gently.

He stood and threw his paper coffee cup into the bin and turned to stand directly in front of her. She looked away, unwilling to meet his eyes. He threw his card onto the table and pointed to his number.

"I never said it was metal."

It was almost eleven by the time Locklear drove from the airport in Charlottesville to the Dayton Kindred Hospital, the four-hour wait for his flight from Newark having delayed his return to base. He hadn't intended going to the hospital but somehow found himself driving down the narrow back streets towards its back entrance. He tapped gently at the screen door of Sara Fehr's prison and went inside. Maria Whieler was, as usual, at her post. She stood and flung herself at him and cried in his arms.

Surprised at the woman's sudden affection, he had no idea what to do except raise his hands to her head and soothe the lonely woman as best he knew how.

"He's gone," she said.

Locklear moved back and looked at the sleeping woman in the bed.

"I know," he replied.

Marie Whieler returned to her seat and lifted a large sealed envelope from her bag which had been hidden under her chair. She stood and walked the few paces to Locklear who had placed himself at the end of Sara Fehr's bed.

She locked her fingers around the end of the bed frame and looked at Sara.

"I think she knows they've all gone. She's been running a fever since. It's like she's got nothing to live for and she's giving up. I've been talking to her, telling her to hang on –

that Luke will be back. Sir, he didn't kill Mrs Wyss and he's anxious for me to say that to you."

"You saw him?"

Whieler raised the envelope up, on both her palms like an offering.

"He said to give you this."

"What is it?"

"It's the notes my mama kept. Luke said it's everything you need."

Locklear thought about the moment he walked away from Letitia Grant. The book was not everything he needed. It would help, he was sure of that, but Maria's mother was dead so she would not be here to be a witness in court and, even if she were, Shank's lawyer's would tear the mentally ill woman to pieces. He needed that box and, if he had read the woman correctly, he expected that he would hear from Letitia Grant, sooner, he hoped, rather than later.

Tears formed in Maria's eyes. She moved closer to Locklear and wrapped her arms tight around his body.

"If she dies, I've got nothing. Got no one. I'll be alone."

Locklear placed his hands around his back and loosened her grip.

"She won't die," he lied.

Marie Whieler rubbed the tears from her face and wiped her nose into her light cardigan.

"Thank you," she said weakly as Locklear opened the screen door and disappeared.

Maria returned to her station. She lowered her tired body into the hard seat and listened to the beats of her friend's heart on the monitor. She knew those beats, that rhythm, by heart. She closed her eyes and listened to the deafening sounds of Sara's pulse as it slackened, as it dimmed, and slowed.

Chapter 25

Locklear arrived at the station before dawn, anxious to get to work, and found Carter already at his desk, once again studying Sara's letters to her friend.

Locklear had dreamt of Sara the night before, sitting up in her bed, staring at him with eyes identical to those of her siblings.

He growled a greeting.

Carter looked up and seemed to be about to say something.

"*What?*" said Locklear irritably.

"Later," Carter said and turned back to the letters.

Locklear sat at his usual seat and began poring over the book given to him by Maria Whieler only hours before.

Mendoza joined them an hour later and placed a hot coffee in front of each of the two men. Carter drank his coffee then stood up and walked to the table in the centre of the room. He picked up his former girlfriend's suicide note. Mendoza sidled up to him and looked at the note as he studied it.

"I've been trying to work out what's wrong with the note since I first laid eyes on it," she said.

"Something is," said Carter.

He went back to his desk, retrieved one of Sara's letters and brought it back to the centre of the room.

"It's not her handwriting," he said.

Locklear, deep in thought, looked up. "What?"

"That's not Sara's handwriting."

Mendoza looked intently at the two pages he held. "Lee, it looks the same to me."

"It's very similar – but I know it isn't hers. And that's not all."

"What else?"

Carter read the second line of the note aloud: "'*I'm going to put things right I'm sorry. The children need you more than me Sara*'."

He looked at Locklear.

"*And?*" Locklear snapped.

"It's not *from* her but *to* her," Carter said. "See? There's no full stop after *me*. There's a gap and the handwriting is shaky, as though the person writing the line was upset or in a hurry but 'Sara' is not a signature – the writer meant: '*The children need you more than me, Sara*'. The gap was unintentional and, properly punctuated, there should be a comma."

Mendoza took the note from his hands and read the line quickly. "That's why it bothered me. I knew something wasn't right." She looked up at Carter. "Then who wrote it?"

"Luke Fehr wrote it," Locklear said.

"Sarge," said Mendoza, "Ricci said when he and his partner got to the farm to tell the family about Sara's accident, Luke was locked in an outhouse – a car had been driven up to its door so he couldn't have killed himself if he wanted to."

Locklear stood and took a seat at the centre table.

"Exactly. It was Sara who locked him in there. I read your notes. Ricci said there was also a noose hanging in the barn and that Luke had been vomiting. I think he wrote that note and left it for Sara. I think he then couldn't face what he had to do and ran to the outhouse where he was sick. That's when she drove his car into the door, that's when she decided that she'd do the 'honourable thing' and take his place. They were twins."

"And they were both 21 years old that very day," Carter said quietly. "When Luke heard about Sara he couldn't kill himself. He had to take care of the children."

"The noose was Luke's!" said Mendoza. "Maguire said that! He said women don't normally hang themselves."

"Rarely anyway," Locklear added.

"But why, Sarge?" said Carter. "What could possibly make two young people want to take their lives?"

"That's what we have to find out, Carter. Whatever insane pact was, and is, going on between the Shanks and the Fehrs, it was strong enough for them to come after Andrew on his 21st birthday."

Locklear walked back to his desk and lifted the book. "I got this from Maria Whieler last night. Luke Fehr gave it to her for me."

Mendoza and Carter each took the thick tome in turn and leafed through it.

"At the front there's a note from Maria's mother to her only child. She says that in the event of her or Maria's father's death, there are four families she was to go to for protection."

"Let me guess," Mendoza said. "The Yoders, the Ropps ..."

Carter attempted to finish the sentence. "The Wysses and –"

Locklear beat him to it. "Eric Stoll."

A silence settled into the room while the group absorbed the revelation.

"The book provides evidence that they were organising to have Shank removed from ministry. They'd written to Bishop Rahn and asked for a meeting."

"But they never got there?" Carter asked.

"No, but they had told him enough for him to send the Pletts in to minister until he found a permanent replacement."

Mendoza sat down and drank her coffee which had gone cold.

"Then, someone must have been telling Shank about them … someone close to them."

Locklear and Mendoza both moved their eyes to Carter.

He shook his head violently. "No, my father knew nothing about this. He would have mentioned it. I'm sure of it!"

"Then who?" Mendoza asked.

Locklear sat back down to study the next section of the book. "We'll soon find out."

Mendoza fanned herself and pulled her desk up beside Carter under the only window that would open and took half of Maria's Wheeler's letters from her colleague. The trio settled down to study what were now their only leads in the investigation in the stifling hot room. They read until the shrill drill of phone calls began to cut into their consciousness. Carter walked to the door and closed it tight to try to dim the noise. He had barely got back to his seat when the noise rose to a deafening level and it seemed like every extension in the station was ringing off the hook.

The three stood in unison. Something was wrong. Carter was the first down the corridor. He stopped at reception and listened as three cops answered 911 calls. Another phone rang continuously so he answered it. It was Karen Mason, a receptionist at Shank Creamery. Carter cupped his hand over his other ear as he tried to listen to the hysterical woman. All over the room he could hear the same words, over and over: Shank Creamery, Peter Wyss, gunshots. He handed the phone to another cop and followed Locklear and Mendoza outside. Already cars were screeching off the lot, sirens screaming.

The first thing Locklear noticed about the reception area of Shank Creamery was that the semi-naked statue, once pride of place, had been shot through. The upper segment of the naked woman lay face down in the water fountain and the lower half of the fake marble sculpture lay in pieces on the floor. He followed behind heavily armed riot police as they tried to move trapped staff from the building. A familiar man passed him carrying a briefcase with two bullet holes in it. Locklear stopped. He was the same man who had been amused by Locklear's ramblings in the foyer when he had come to visit Shank for the first time, except this time he was not grinning. The bespectacled, balding man was pale as a ghost and was clinging onto to whatever was in his briefcase. Locklear stopped and the man's hands shook as he handed the sergeant a business card. Locklear glanced at it quickly. J. Stein- IRS. It was clear from his expression that Stein expected Locklear to call him. He placed the card in his trouser pocket.

"Now is the time to handle your weapon," Locklear said to Mendoza. He suppressed an urge to tell her to stay outside and away from danger. His trooper would accuse him of sexism and she was partly right, but it was mostly because he cared about her and didn't want her kid growing up without a mother. Peter Wyss was armed and, having emptied two rounds from a semi-automatic rifle into the walls of the foyer, was somewhere in the building, presumably looking to kill Samuel Shank.

Maguire, dressed in a bulletproof vest, came from the elevator and informed them that two further shots had rung out from an upstairs floor since Wyss had rushed the stairs of the building forty minutes earlier. Locklear removed his gun from its holster and began to climb the stairs to Samuel Shank's offices. When he reached the top of the stairs, he motioned for Carter, Mendoza and Maguire to stay low.

Two heavily armed police brought Locklear to a windowless room and updated him. It was over twenty minutes since they'd heard the last shot fired. All staff had been evacuated from the building and, as far as they could tell, only Jacob Shank and his father Samuel were unaccounted for and according to Shank's secretary most likely trapped in the suite at the bottom of the corridor. Wyss, as far as they could tell, was in the room with them and was insisting on speaking with Locklear alone.

Mendoza's face was telling him not to do it while Carter remained silent.

"It's a trap, sarge," Maguire said. "He says he wants to tell you something but Peter knows he's not getting out of here to go home. He's got nothing to lose. He's here to settle scores and you're one of them."

"Carter?" Locklear asked.

Lee moved his gaze from Maguire to Mendoza and then rested his eyes on his sergeant.

"I say talk to him."

Mendoza's mouth dropped open.

"Carter, I reckon this is the first time you and I have ever agreed on anything," Locklear replied.

Mendoza moved to the front of the small group.

"Don't do it, sarge, please!" she begged.

"You want to get home to your kid or not?" he asked.

Mendoza didn't answer.

Locklear followed the lead riot cop to the end of the bright corridor. "Burke" was sewn into his jacket. He wondered if Burke had said goodbye to a family this morning and if he'd wondered if he'd be coming home that night.

Burke pressed the button on his phone. It rang three times. Locklear could hear it ringing on the other side of the door. It answered. Locklear couldn't hear what was said but Wyss's voice sounded urgent, angry, afraid, dangerous.

Burke snapped the phone shut and held his gun up. He motioned for Locklear to move to the door. Burke stood back as the door slowly opened.

Peter Wyss stood on the other side with his automatic pointed directly at Locklear's chest.

"Get in," he said.

Locklear obeyed.

"Sit on the floor there," Wyss ordered.

Locklear did a quick reckoning of the room before his view would be marred by his position on the floor. Samuel Shank was seated at his large wooden desk. His hands were loosely tied and he was writing on a large pad. Blood oozed from a bullet wound in his left shoulder. He'd survive. On the floor at the far end of the desk was Jacob Shank in a supine position. The single shot to his head most probably killed him instantly.

Locklear sat on the floor facing Shank and willingly raised his hands while Wyss bound them tighter than he had bound the old man's. Locklear was far more of a threat. He looked under the desk at the old man's legs which were bound tightly with a rope.

Wyss followed his eyes. "I would have used the rope from my Helena's neck but I doubt they'd have given it to me."

Wyss looked up to the ceiling. Locklear knew what he was thinking. If there was anywhere that Wyss could have swung a rope, Jacob Shank would have got a much slower death.

He turned to the elder Shank who was looking at Locklear.

Locklear recognised his expressions: fear, hope, pleading. "I'm not here to help you," he said. "*Write!*" Wyss screamed at Shank.

Shank looked away and stared out the window.

"*I said write!*"

Shank lifted the pen and returned to his prose. Wyss stood over his shoulder and watched as the old man wrote several lines. Locklear could see his chin tremble.

"Now read it. Read it aloud so the sergeant can hear."

Shank shoved the paper away and looked at the body of his only son on the floor beside him.

Wyss pulled a chair up beside the insolent old man. He

reached into his pocket and pulled out a small handgun and held it to Shank's temple.

Samuel lifted the page and read the first line. "*I, Samuel Shank, am responsible for the deaths of Noah and Eva Yoder.*"

Locklear moved to his knees.

"Sit down!" said Wyss.

"It won't work – he'll say you forced him to confess to things he didn't do. It won't work, Peter," Locklear said.

"I know what I'm doing!" he spat.

"Am I your witness?" Locklear asked. Now was as good a time as any to find out what plans Peter Wyss had for him.

"Yes."

"I'll have to say you forced him to write it."

Wyss moved towards Locklear and raised the gun. He swung back to strike him on the face but stopped halfway.

"My wife liked you. She was upset that she said you had no redeeming features. She didn't mean it. She said you had a gentleness to you that no one could see. But she could see it. Helena will be glad that I got a chance to tell you that."

Locklear, tense and ready for the blow, relaxed.

"We'll see what you have to say when he finishes his speech," said Wyss.

Wyss moved back to Shank and returned his gun to its position at his temple.

Shank squinted at the writing and read. "*I forced them to sell me their farm. I forced Noah Yoder to make me his sole beneficiary to his assets. My granddaughter Bethany Stoll assisted in this matter.*"

Locklear's stomach churned. He already knew, or suspected, everything Shank was saying but the sheer evil of the man dressed in Old Order Mennonite clothing in front of him sickened him.

"Next read about the Ropps."

"*I organised for the killing of David Ropp and forced*

him to name me as sole beneficiary in his will." Shank stopped and swallowed. "My... my granddaughter ... Bethany Stoll assisted in this matter."

"Forced him?" Wyss snapped. "That's not the word I told you to use. David Ropp and the Yoders were kind, simple people. They would not have understood what they were signing. You didn't *force* them. You lied to them. You cheated them." He tapped the gun against Shank's temple. "Go on."

"*I direct my estate to return the entire sum to be used for the care of his daughter.*"

Locklear's focus sharpened. Wyss was going to kill Shank and he was going to do it soon.

"Next!" Wyss screamed.

Locklear sensed the man's anxiety rising. Wyss knew that the riot police were at this very moment planning to storm the room. He was running out of time and he knew it.

Shank began to read.

"*I arranged for Helena ...*"

"Not us – leave me and my wife until last. The Fehrs."

Shank looked at Locklear. His expression told the sergeant the man still thought he was going to get out of this room alive.

"*Read it*," a voice said only this time it was coming from Locklear.

Shank was going to die soon and Locklear needed to know what the Shanks had against five orphaned children.

"*I ... arranged for the killing of Aaron Fehr. I arranged for the assault on Andrew Fehr and I intended to kill him. I ...*"

Shank threw the paper across the room. It landed at Locklear's feet.

"I'm not reading this. Just kill me. Just get it over with."

Wyss started to laugh. He lifted the pages from the floor and slapped them down in front of the old man.

"Read!"

Shank swallowed. It was the first emotion the man had shown reading his litany of crimes, his despicable acts.

"*I forced Sara Fehr to attempt suicide.*" He looked at Locklear. "It's not true!" he cried. "He made me write it! It was the boy we were after ... but I don't know what happened ... she drove herself off the bridge!"

"So you admit everything else?" Locklear asked.

"Yes," he said meekly.

"Why? Why did you do all these things? What drove you to these ... to this evil?"

Peter Wyss lunged towards Locklear. He knelt beside him and moved his angry face inches away from the sergeant's.

"He won't tell you why because there is a little piece of him that is ashamed. A tiny piece of God that speaks to him. But I will tell you why, Mr Locklear. Gold is why. Gold. Money and power are Pastor Shank's God. Isn't that so, Pastor?" He got to his feet gain. "*Now, read about me. Read about Helena.*"

Shank's lips trembled.

"*Read! Read! Read!*" Wyss screamed.

Shank lifted the paper. His hands shook.

"*I forced the Wysses out of the life they loved. I refused to do business with them. I forced others to turn their backs on them. I ...*"

Locklear's phone rang.

Wyss swung around and raced to him.

"Don't answer that."

Locklear raised his bound hands upwards.

"I can't – but, Peter, I asked Maguire to phone me if the results of Helena's autopsy came in. The phone is in my pocket. Answer it, please."

"The results do not matter to me. They can't help my wife. Only I can now help my wife and this is why I am here."

"Don't you want the police to catch her killer?" Locklear asked.

"I am looking at him."

The phone fell silent.

"*Read!*"

"*I killed Helena Wyss.*"

Shank finally crumbled.

"*I didn't do it!*" he cried.

The phone rang again.

"*Don't you dare deny it!*" Wyss screamed. "You may not have cut her, you may not have strung my beautiful wife up but you are as guilty as the one you got to do your dirty work. *Say it!*"

Samuel Shank's red eyes implored Locklear.

"Don't do it, Peter," Locklear begged. He knew what was coming. He knew it.

"*Say it!*"

"*I arranged to have Helena Wyss killed.*"

"*Why?*" Wyss shouted.

Shank began to sob. He lowered his face onto his bound hands. Gone was the script. He didn't need it. These were fresh acts, fresh evil. He needed no reminding.

"To frame Luke Fehr. To put an end once and for all to the man and to the Fehrs."

Wyss turned and looked at Locklear.

"Have you got all that?"

Locklear nodded. "Peter, if you kill him I will never find out what is going on here. I won't be able to protect the Fehrs so they can come home. You don't need to do this. Stop, please. Put the gun down … for Abigail's sake."

Wyss's eyes filled with tears at the mention of the vulnerable girl who had known him as her father. "I am doing this for Abigail. I have to do it, Mr Locklear, because the law will not stop him. He will get away with my wife's murder the same way he got away with all of the others."

Wyss lifted the pages and placed them into Locklear's hands.

"There's more there. Everything you need. Get Beth Stoll. Put her behind bars. The confession was for me and for Helena. Somewhere, she can see me. Helena can hear me."

"No! Peter, no!"

Wyss turned and pointed his gun at Shank and fired one close-range shot into his chest. He turned and smiled at Locklear.

"My wife liked you. Do the right thing," he said as he raised the gun to his head.

He took one last look at Shank and his son, pulled the trigger and fell with a dull thud onto the ground. From his position Locklear could see the open, lifeless eyes of Peter Wyss staring at Jacob Shank from the floor on the opposite side of the desk.

Samuel Shank's still body lay over his desk. Locklear saw the old man twitch – the last murmurs of life and with it his hope of solving a one-hundred-and-fifty-year-old case.

He did not hear the outside door smashing or notice the crowds of riot police pour into the room. He was blind to the medical staff whisking Samuel Shank away, the worried faces of Mendoza and Carter. He was oblivious to the adrenaline rush and subsequent drop, the weakness, the paralysing shock that rose up his body in the minutes after he walked alone from the building, past the bald man who had wanted to talk to him, past his troopers, past the crowds, the noise and the blinding blue sky.

Locklear sat in Mendoza's car and in a daze, drove the car to Harrisonburg alone in search of quiet, calm and intoxicating peace of mind.

Chapter 26

The bar on S. Main Street was exactly the sort of place Locklear was looking for. Aside from two old men playing chess in the corner, Jack's Hideaway was empty, dark, quiet and cool. He took a seat at the bar and ordered a Jameson. Neat. No ice. Locklear clenched his hands which were still shaking. He threw a bill on the counter and returned them to his lap out of view. The barman placed the amber liquid in front of him and Locklear inhaled the bitter-sweet aroma. He did not lift the drink but fixed his eyes on his reflection in the grubby mirror behind the bar. At times like this he would ring Kowalski, his mentor, but he didn't think his boss would want to hear from him right now and the only conversations they would be having would be to discuss the rising body count since Locklear took on the case. Both men were recovering alcoholics but Kowalski had developed his disease from his one-time party lifestyle. Alex was a family man now and had replaced his habit with his love for his wife and children. Locklear was different. He was a stress drunk, a man who could not handle his emotions, good or bad. Locklear believed he had the worst kind of alcoholism – the world was full of emotion so he had worked hard to protect himself from such by avoiding connections, strings, from

The Pact

hurt. He could see the barman eye him carefully from the corner of the bar.

"Something wrong with your drink?" he asked.

Locklear pretended not to hear him and fixated on his image, sitting on a barstool with a drink on front of him. The smell of the liquid continued to waft up towards him. His forearm twitched nervously, his fingers imagined themselves wrapped around the cool glass. His mouth opened. His throat practised the beautiful swallow, the rush, the bite, the killing of feelings, the drowning of anger, regret. Another and then another. And then oblivion. Beautiful oblivion, nothingness, silence, void. Peace. He knew if he lifted the glass, it was over. His struggle for sobriety, his thirty-year quest for a straight life, a better life, a life free from the captivity of addiction. He had been here before, in this exact position, sitting on a barstool staring at the short gap that stood between control and powerlessness, between peace and hell. His throat was dry.

"Water," he said.

The bar tender put down his newspaper and poured Locklear a tall glass of ice-cold water. He lifted it and downed the entire glass in one gulp.

Twenty minutes passed and Locklear had still not lifted the drink as an internal war raged deep within him. His mind, for the most part, wanted to relent, to take that step into forgetfulness. But one part of his brain knew better, knew that if he lifted that drink it was over. It spoke silently to him, quietly, gently. But he was losing. His hand reached forward and shook as it touched the glass. He pulled back and watched his reflection as his face creased and crumbled. The coward in him rose up and shouted, his failing strength whispered back.

The door opened and someone was beside him. Mendoza. She struggled to lift herself onto the high stool beside him and sat in silence. He saw her glance at the untouched whiskey. She moved her fingers to his lap and squeezed his trembling hands.

"Kowalski said this would be the kind of bar I'd find you in."

Locklear ignored her.

"Are you OK?"

Locklear trained his eyes once more on the mirror and imagined himself lifting the glass to his throat. It was a method he'd developed during the rough times he'd faced since he'd quit. He imagined the feelings that would surface after that first swallow, that first embrace, the warmth, the poison. He inhaled deeply and pictured the chaos that would ensue because he knew it would not be one drink but several and it would not be one day but a daily battle to return to sobriety once he'd given it away.

"You want me to go?" Mendoza asked nervously.

Locklear stood abruptly and made his way to the door, leaving his worried trooper behind. On the street, he could see Carter sitting in the passenger seat of an unmarked car on the opposite side of the road. Back-up, Locklear reasoned. He rounded the corner and made his way on foot to his motel. He lay down on the bed, placing his shaking hands underneath his body. He willed himself to sleep but the vision of Peter Wyss's body crumpled on the floor of Samuel Shank's office thwarted his quest for quiet. The itch he had felt beneath his skin earlier slowly calmed. He had won – again – and only for now.

When he woke four hours later, Locklear was surprised to find that he had slept and that his dreams were not filled with the events of the day. He rose and drank a cold coffee from the pot in his room while he pondered his next move. On his way to the station, he passed Mendoza's car parked outside a diner. He slowed and saw her sitting in the booth with Maguire and a couple of cops he did not know. She had

The Pact

obviously recognised his need for space and was leaving him to come out from whatever spell she had found him in earlier.

When he reached the station, he found Carter sitting at the desk in the incident room.

He looked Locklear up and down and, seeing the man was sober, smiled.

"I'm glad you're OK, sarge."

"Where are we at?" Locklear responded, not wanting to admit to, or discuss, his moment of weakness with the clean-living trooper.

"I've been to the morgue. Peter Wyss and Jacob Shank were lying side by side. Life's strange, isn't it, sir?"

Death – Locklear thought – the Great Leveller.

"Samuel Shank is in surgery. Mendoza went to the hospital. It doesn't look like he'll make it. We've an APB out on Bethany Stoll. So far no sighting of her. Looks like she slipped away."

"We'll find her."

"Any sign of the Fehrs?" He was aware now the Luke Fehr would soon be the only person that could answer his questions.

Carter shrugged. "Whole state is looking for them."

"How can a man with three siblings and no money disappear?"

Carter had no answers.

Carter stood and placed the results of Helena Wyss's autopsy in front of Locklear. He pointed at one line on the second paragraph. Tissue had been found under three of Helena's finger nails. Foreign tissue. Female tissue.

"Please let it be Beth Stoll's," Locklear said aloud.

He looked up at Carter.

"How's your father?"

"He's hanging in there, thanks, sarge."

Locklear knew the innocent trooper had seen more in the

last few days than most rural cops saw in a lifetime. Gone was the boyish smile and the ever-present ball was missing.

"Are you OK, Lee?"

"Sara has pneumonia. It doesn't look good."

"I'm sorry," Locklear replied although he didn't mean it. He hoped she would die soon. He hoped Sara Fehr would pass on and find peace and that those who had loved her could move on with their lives.

Locklear stood and slowly paced the room while his trooper looked on.

He glanced at the clock over the door. It was only four o'clock.

"You can go home, Carter. Phone Mendoza and tell her to head back to the motel if she wants. Before you go, I have something here for you."

He reached under his desk and handed the trooper a box that he had meant to give Carter days before. A puzzle he had favoured as a child for Carter's son. A map of America. Lee opened the battered box and shook its contents.

"Why are there red dots on some of the pieces?"

"I put a dot on every state I lived in as a kid."

Carter whistled. "Boy! There's an awful lot of dots, sarge!"

"I lived in an awful lot of places."

"Thanks, sarge."

"Carter?"

"Sarge?"

"Go see Sara. Go before it's too late."

Carter nodded and left the room.

Locklear watched from the window as the trooper's car drove slowly off the station's lot and headed south in the direction of the Kindred Hospital.

Locklear returned to his seat and put his reading glasses on. He began to pore over Shank's confession which contained information on the burial places of the Yoders and

The Pact

Bill Jefferson and four names of other people he did not know – crimes obviously committed by Shank during the decades he persecuted his community. He picked up the phone and began the process of arranging the exhumation of their bodies. He thought of Norma Jefferson sitting alone in her Fifth Avenue apartment and the closure she would get from bringing her beloved husband's body home.

There was no mention of Anabel Schumer. Locklear sighed alone in the empty incident room. He'd been hoping to give the woman's family some closure. He heard a light tap on the door.

"Two visitors for you, sarge."

"Send them in."

Locklear looked up to find Ling Ling and Letitia Grant standing in the doorway.

He stood and offered the women seats at the table in the centre of the room.

"We were here earlier but you weren't around so we delayed our flight back to New York until later. Letitia has something for you that she didn't want to hand over to anyone else."

Letitia moved forward and reluctantly placed a package on the desk at the centre of the room. She sat down and looked to Ling for direction.

"I lied to you about the box," she began.

"I know," Locklear replied.

"I didn't want to hand it over because it is the only thing I have that belonged to my

grandma."

Locklear unravelled the thick brown paper from the front and sides, revealing a discoloured silver box about ten inches long and six inches wide. It was plain except for a silver crucifix on the lid. He lifted it and found it was unexpectedly heavy. He tried to unlock the fragile clasp at the front of the box and found it would not open.

"Did you ever look in it?" he asked.

"Yes."

"And?"

"There ain't nothing in it."

Locklear looked up in surprise.

"Nothing?"

"Except …"

"Except what?"

"See for yourself."

Locklear tried again to open the clasp but his large hands were too awkward.

Letitia took it from him. She placed it on the table and pushed two tiny levers upward.

The hinged lid sprang open.

"There's a knack to it."

Locklear stared into the box, speechless.

He placed his hands inside and pushed his fingers around the inside of the empty container.

Letitia reached forward again and pressed hard inside the gable ends of the box. Locklear heard a click as the young woman lifted the base to reveal a false bottom.

Locklear ran his hands into the dry, grey material.

"It's … it's soil," he finally said.

"I told you there was nothing in it. It's just dirt."

She took a letter from her pocket and handed it to Locklear.

"Only I found this on top of the dirt."

Locklear opened the letter as carefully as he could. He thumbed ancient paper and felt its velvety, shiny surface.

"It's in German," he said.

Letitia sighed and lifted the box again. "Sure is heavy."

Ling touched her shoulder. "We better be getting to the airport."

Locklear followed the women to the station door.

"Thank you," he said to Letitia. He held her hand. "I

hope you make it, Letitia. I hope someday I see your paintings in some fancy New York art gallery."

Grant blushed and pulled her hand away but the smile remained on her lips as the pair walked down the station steps to a waiting taxi.

Locklear looked at his watch. He returned to the incident room and locked the box in the station safe at the far end of the room. He took the letter and checked the home address for Anabel Schumer's parents and drove the eight blocks to her house. When he rang the bell, Albert Schumer opened the door swiftly.

"I saw you coming," he said.

Schumer had the look of a man hoping for good news but his eyes told a different story. He waited for Locklear to speak.

"There's no news on Anabel," Locklear said.

Locklear had to decide if he would tell the girl's father that they had news on other murder victims or not. He decided on the latter and followed Schumer down the hallway to a back lounge room where Anabel's mother sat in her wheelchair watching TV.

"This is my wife, Heidi," Albert said.

"Mrs Schumer," Locklear said with a nod.

Heidi Schumer turned off the TV and gazed at Locklear. She obviously, like her husband, thought the sergeant was there to either return joy to their home or tell them the devastating news that their hearts already knew but their minds refused to accept.

"He has no news, Heidi," her husband said.

He sat beside his wife and gestured to Locklear to take a seat.

Locklear sat and fixed his eyes on an old man sitting under a radio at the other end of the room, humming to himself.

"This is my father, Hans," Schumer offered. "He came to

this country when he was only nineteen and spoke perfect English but he has dementia and he mostly only speaks German now. He doesn't seem to remember English now apart from constantly asking where my daughter is. It's a strange thing."

Locklear took the letter from his pocket.

"I'm really sorry that we have no news on Anabel's whereabouts but we are doing everything we can," he said, glancing awkwardly at the girl's mother. "But I received this letter today as evidence in the case." He handed the letter to Schumer. "I heard you were German and I thought you might translate it for me. I am sorry to have to ask you. I can see this is a terrible time for you both but ... it might help. It might help us figure out Anabel's whereabouts."

"How?" Schumer asked.

Locklear had no answer. "Will you help me?"

"Sergeant, I was born here in Virginia and my wife was too. I speak German but I can't read it."

Locklear fixed his eyes on the old man again. "What about your father?"

Schumer sat beside the old man and spoke to him in low, hushed tones. He handed him the letter.

The old man gazed at the letter then looked up at Locklear and seemed suddenly alert and aware of his surroundings.

"Read it aloud, Papa," Schumer said.

The old man laughed and spoke in German to his son.

"What?" Locklear asked.

"He said it's like a fairy tale – you know, written in language used in fairy tales."

"Does he mean, old language?"

Schumer spoke again to his father.

"Yes. He said exactly like that. Papa said these words aren't used anymore."

Schumer began to laugh at something his father said.

"You know, he means like 'thus forth' in English – 'ye olde' – that sort of language.

Locklear walked over and pointed at the words on the top righthand corner of the letter.

"What is this?" he asked.

Hans provided an answer. Schumer translated.

"It's a date – May 9th, 1861."

"A month after the Civil War began," Locklear replied. "What else does it say?"

Locklear waited while the two men conversed.

"Papa can't understand some of the words. He never saw them before. It might be a rural dialect. But he says that it's a letter from a mother to her son named Eli and she is asking for a promise to return and is trusting him to ..."

Schumer stopped and asked his father to repeat the last part of the sentence.

"To return the treasure ... to bring it safely back."

"Does it say what the treasure is?"

"No."

The elder Schumer suddenly became animated and started flailing his arms around.

"OK, Papa, relax!" said Schumer. "Papa says I'm wrong. I translated the word *treasure* wrongly. The word in German has many meanings but in this case Papa thinks it means something treasured instead of something valuable."

"Like an heirloom?"

Papa Schumer nodded. "Heirloom," he repeated, smiling. Then he turned to his son. "Where is Anabel?"

"She'll be back soon, Papa."

Schumer stood and, beckoning to Locklear, left the room.

Locklear collected the letter from the old man, thanked him, said goodbye to Mrs Schumer and followed Albert out and down the hall.

"Those few minutes are the longest we've got him off the subject of Anabel," Schumer said. "He dotes on her."

He opened the door and Locklear stepped out onto the doorstep.

"We don't know that she's dead, Mr Schumer. There is hope yet," he said although he didn't really believe it.

"Anabel would never leave us wondering if she is alive or dead. She wouldn't do that to us. I know my daughter is gone. I just want to bring her home here and say goodbye."

Locklear did not respond. Every inch of him knew Schumer was right but he didn't want to confirm it. Not yet and not without a body.

He drove south to his motel and, exhausted by the events of the day, lay on his bed fully clothed. When he had woken in that same bed that morning Jacob Shank and Peter Wyss were alive, Samuel Shank was still an eighty-three-year-old man well enough to sit at his company's head. In those few short hours so much had changed, including the fact that he had allowed his emotions to bring him to the brink of losing his battle for sobriety.

There was nothing else he could do but lie down and ruminate over his disappointment that the box which had been missing for more than one hundred and fifty years held nothing but dried-out soil and a mother's letter to her son.

Chapter 27

The 6am call from Jerome Stein raised Locklear from a dreamless night. He woke refreshed and pressed the button to answer the call from the IRS man who seemed determined to talk to him. Stein was still in town and arranged to meet Locklear at the station at 7am. Locklear rose, changed from the clothes he had slept in and stuck a note under Mendoza's door telling her he'd meet her at the station later. He bought a coffee en route and was sitting in the station by 6.45am.

When Stein entered the incident room, Locklear noticed the shiny new briefcase tucked under the taxman's arm.

"You didn't like the one with ventilation in it?" Locklear quipped.

Stein sat without invitation. "I was worried that a briefcase with two bullet-holes would give other defaulters ideas," he said with a grin.

"Wise."

Stein placed his briefcase on the ground and clasped his hands together. "Sergeant Locklear, I wanted to talk to you that day at the creamery but I couldn't risk it."

"Do I take it that Samuel Shank wasn't paying his taxes?"

"There were … irregularities," Stein replied curtly.

"Mr Stein, *you* wanted to talk to *me*. Are you going to tell me what those irregularities were, or do I have to guess?"

"I wanted to talk to you, but it was to find out what you knew. I knew you were a cop as soon as I laid eyes on you. We've been trying to get Shank for years but he kept pulling the noose off his neck at the last minute."

Locklear thought about the tax inspector's unfortunate choice of metaphor.

"Our investigation has nothing to do with money," Locklear replied.

"In my experience everything that happens in this world begins and ends with money, Sergeant Locklear."

"Our investigation is sensitive. It's highly confidential. What I will say is that it involves murder ... several of them."

Stein did not look shocked. He pushed his thick-rimmed glasses back. "OK. In confidence?" he asked.

Locklear nodded.

"Shank has been claiming tax breaks on expensive medical benefits he'd supposedly been paying for his staff for years. When we looked into his wage system, he'd been overtaxing his staff and in each case it was around ten percent over and above what he was paying for them in insurance."

"So ... he claimed to be paying for their medical plan but in reality...they were paying it without knowing and he was adding more on?" Locklear asked.

"Exactly. We checked with the insurer and Shank wasn't buying the plans he was claiming for. He purchased lower plans so when his workers got sick ..."

"Shank paid the shortfall and they were indebted to him ... to the point of silence," Locklear said, finishing Stein's sentence.

"What did you do?"

"We served him with tax bills which he ignored. He took him to court for that and several other breaches of tax law. Each time – he walked."

"If those cases are closed, why were you at Shank Creamery the other day?"

"He hasn't paid his taxes for the past year. Shank Creamery filed for bankruptcy two months ago."

"They're broke?" Locklear asked, astounded.

"B.R.O.K.E. It seems Jacob Shank and Beth Stoll have a passion for the finer things in life. They've bled the company dry. There's nothing left. I'm telling you this in the hope that you can help me. I hadn't lost an investigation in my whole career until I came up against Shank and he beat me over and over again."

"Well," Locklear said, leaning back on his chair and stretching his arms upwards, "I don't think you'll have to worry about Shank much longer. Shot twice yesterday, once in the shoulder and then a bullet to his chest. There's no way he'll survive that at his age."

"It's who will come after him that I worry about. That granddaughter – believe me – she's more ruthless, more evil than Shank and his son were put together."

"She's missing," Locklear replied.

"For now. A few seconds after that man opened fire in the lobby, I saw her escape out a door behind the reception area. Looked like she'd been in a fight – there were scratch marks across her face."

Locklear's attention heightened. He hoped the gentle Helena Wyss had been smart enough to inflict those wounds on Stoll and, with it, provide evidence that Stoll was a murderer.

Stein stood and moved to the door.

"Did you see what type of car she was driving?" Locklear asked.

"Yes. A blacked-out SUV."

"Registration?"

"Do you have something for me or not?" Stein asked.

Locklear mulled over the situation.

"I do have something for you. A book recording Shank's financial transactions."

"And you'll give it to me?"

Locklear nodded.

"Virginia plates – 186121. It's registered to the company. I had planned on confiscating it."

Locklear visualised the numbers in his head. If the digits were designed to commemorate the start of the Civil War and the age at which the Fehrs were driven to suicide by the Shanks, it was in poor taste. Stein was right. Beth Stoll was evil and she was also crazy. A dangerous combination.

"I can't give it to you yet but I will. Soon as I figure out what was driving Shank to do the things he did."

Stein placed his hat on his head. "I wouldn't work too hard at it, Locklear. I meant what I said. Everything is about money, in the end."

Locklear saw Stein out and charged Lennox with finding Stoll's SUV. He returned to the safe and took out the box.

When he arrived at Harrisonburg Hospital, he went directly to the intensive care section. Maguire had been posted outside Shank's private room all night in the hope that Beth Stoll would go there.

"Sarge, Doc says no one's allowed to interview him yet," he said.

"OK. Do you want to go for a coffee?"

"I'm desperate."

"OK. I'll stay for a while. Go wake yourself up."

As soon as Maguire disappeared, Locklear stepped into Shank's room.

He stood at the door for a few minutes before he approached the bed. The bullet to the man's shoulder had only caused a flesh wound but the shot to his chest had damaged an artery. Even with the removal of both bullets, the surgeon did not think the old man would make it. The blood loss had been too great.

Locklear surveyed the white-painted room which was almost as void of interest as the room Sara Fehr lay in except the young woman's room was sparser, more dismal and did not have the air conditioning that whirred in this ice-cold room.

A slight flicker of an eyelid told him the old man was not unconscious.

"Open your eyes, Shank. I have something you want to see before you take your last sorry breath."

Locklear waited as Shank slowly raised his eyelids to a half-open position.

"What do you want?" he panted.

Locklear unfurled the brown paper and held the box out for Shank to see.

The old man's eyes shot open. He coughed and grimaced in pain as his eyes filled with tears. Locklear wasn't sure if his weeping was due to pain or emotion. If it was due to the pain of a gunshot wound, it was a feeling he was familiar with.

"Hurts, doesn't it?" he asked.

Shank reached forward and touched the edge of the lid gently as the tears continued to flow. He tried to sit up but pain gripped him. He fell back, panting.

"Where? Where?" Shank coughed and, unable to finish his sentence, gasped for air.

"A penniless ex-heroin addict named Letitia Grant had it."

"Who's she?" Shank whispered.

"A descendant of John Grant."

Shank fixed his eyes on the box and raised his hands up to Locklear.

"Please, please, let me hold it."

"This was never buried on the Fehr farm. John Grant took it with him when he escaped to New York. He gave it to his wife and it was passed on from generation to generation of Grants, all thinking it was a family heirloom when it was something he stole from Eli Shank exactly one hundred and fifty years ago. Now, Shank, you will be dead in the next couple of days if not hours – so why don't you try to redeem yourself before you die. Why don't you do one decent thing in your life and tell me why the hell this box is so important?"

"Have you looked inside?" Shank whispered.

"Yes. There's nothing in it but dirt."

"You had no right."

"Every right. I have it now."

"I want Beth to have it."

"Beth, when we find her, won't have much use for this in prison."

Samuel Shank broke down. "Please!" he gasped. "Don't send her to prison. Please ... not my Beth."

"You should have thought of that before you led her into a life of crime."

"It wasn't crime!" he gasped. "Please let me hold it before I die."

Locklear handed the box to Shank, hoping to elicit more information.

Unable to bear its weight, the old man dropped it onto his chest. He screamed in pain.

Maguire rushed inside and stood open-mouthed at the sight of the box on top of the old man's wounded chest.

"I told you Doc said no interviews, sarge!"

"It's OK, Maguire. I'm just showing him something."

"What's that?"

"Something of great value to our friend here but he won't say why. Go wait outside, Maguire."

Maguire reluctantly left as ordered and Locklear pulled a seat over to the bed.

He leaned forward, opened the box and tipped its

contents forward for Shank to see.

"See – it's just soil."

Shank dug his fingers into the soil and cried.

"Now, are you going to tell me what this is?"

"*Pain!*" Shank gasped.

Locklear closed the box and returned it to its brown-paper covering. He rang the bell and waited while a nurse administered an injection into the drip and left.

"Now, tell me. Tell me everything."

Shank's eyes closed slowly as the pain medication rushed into his bloodstream.

"What will do you for Beth?"

"I'll see that she gets a nice cellmate."

He was not going to lie to Shank. It was not in his nature despite it sometimes being a requirement of the job. He had Mendoza for that.

Shank's breathing became more laboured. He raised his hand, asking Locklear to wait until his breathing slowed. Locklear wondered how much of the scene in front of him an act, an attempt to stall for time.

"Talk or I'll renege on my promise to make sure Beth gets a nice cellmate. Might make sure she gets a roommate with a gripe against you. I'd say there are a few ..."

"OK," Shank replied with a clear voice. His breathlessness seemed to have suddenly disappeared. "The first Mennonites arrived in this country in the late 1680s to escape war and persecution. My ancestor, Jan Shank, did not want to give in to this and held on until he could no longer remain in his home. In the year 1711, he had no choice but to follow his brethren to America. Our homeland was ravaged by war. Our people were persecuted for their beliefs."

"So they made a new life in America."

"Yes, with heavy hearts they took a ship to this country. Many died on the way. Women, old men ... children."

"I need to hear about the box."

"I'm getting to it. But you need first to understand those first Mennonites and what was sacred to them."

Locklear waited.

"My ancestors settled here in Virginia and began to farm once more. They grew their own food and raised cattle and attended church. Jan became the pastor and the Shanks have been pastors ever since."

"Until Bishop Rahn demoted you."

Shank ignored this. "I am telling you this for Beth. So you will understand her."

Locklear doubted her would ever understand Beth Stoll or her grandfather. Nothing was worth the pain they had put people though.

"They were welcome in America and free to practise their ways. But deep in the heart of Jan Shank was a regret that he had to leave his farm.

"*The box!*" Locklear said.

Shank grimaced. "Before my ancestor walked away from his farm in Germany with his wife and children, he knelt on the ground and filled that box with soil from around his parents' graves and so took with him a small piece of the earth he had loved and that they and those that went before them had toiled for. He handed the box down to his eldest son who passed it down through the generations for one hundred and fifty years."

"Until the Civil War?"

"Yes," Shank said quietly. He pulled the covers up around himself.

Locklear pulled them back down. He needed Shank awake, cold, and uncomfortable.

"Tell me about Eli Shank."

"Eli was an unhappy man. He was restless. The war started and of course, as Mennonites, my ancestors were not permitted to take part. But some of the young men in the community were restless. They wanted to do their part. But in Eli's case it was to get away ... for adventure ..."

Locklear hazarded a guess. "And, perhaps, a licence to commit murder?"

Shank lowered his head. He did not answer. He continued, "He pleaded with his father for permission but this was denied. Then, soon after the war started, Eli's mother relented and helped him steal away in the night. Before he left she gave him the box as a promise from him that he would return. She knew he understood the importance of the box and what it meant to the family and believed that, by giving it to him, he would survive the war and return to her to take his place as pastor of the community."

"So Grant stealing the box from him would have prevented Eli from being able to go home?"

Shank nodded. "Eli knew that the Fehrs were hiding Grant on their farm. They were stupid, idealistic fools."

"They were heroes."

"Grant was a criminal."

"They didn't know that. They offered Christian refuge to someone in need. Isn't that something your Bible advocates?" Locklear said.

"Daniel and Joshua Fehr shamed Eli and shamed the Shanks. They shamed my family."

"Eli shamed himself," Locklear retorted.

"Each generation of Shanks has been charged with a responsibility to get the box back. Some tried harder than others. My father, Samuel, put a curse on the Fehr farm. He said nothing would grow there as long as they refused to give us back what was rightfully ours."

"They never had the box, Shank. Grant fooled them. He never buried it on the farm. I doubt they even believed that he stole it – at least not at first. I believe that the brothers thought Eli had lost his mind and they were protecting an innocent black man from certain death."

"You can believe what you like. You did not know them.

You do not know the Fehrs. Luke Fehr – he is a dangerous man.

"Because he stood up to you? Because he didn't embody the Mennonite passivity that enabled you to terrorise the community?"

Shank did not reply.

"I want to know *how*," Locklear demanded, "and *why* your family managed to force the Fehrs to hang themselves for generations."

"My ancestors were the pastors here always. They made the rules and the community followed. The Fehrs knew they had to do what was right. They had to make retribution to my family and to the community. Eli's father was a very old man. Eli should have become pastor on the day he turned twenty-one but when the Fehrs protected Grant they blocked Eli's route home. He could not go home without the box so they effectively ended the life that he had been destined to follow."

Locklear thought about Eric Stoll's story that Eli's father and younger brother were found dead which paved the way for Eli to return home to his doting mother but he did not know which happened first and he would never know.

"All of this for a box full of soil? Your family ruined the lives of generations of Fehrs for dirt from a farm thousands of miles away from America – the country that gave your family refuge? How in your God's name does that fit in with your beliefs?"

"It is a pact," Shank replied quietly.

"What?"

"A pact. Eli decided the terms and Daniel Fehr agreed to it. When John Grant disappeared off the farm, Daniel realised that he and Joshua had been deceived. Joshua had died by then. Daniel agreed that it was the responsibility of the Fehrs that the box be returned to the Shanks

And, until it was, the eldest male of the Fehr family would take their own lives on their 21st birthday in compensation for the life they took from Eli."

"So, Eli killed Adam Fehr?"

"He killed himself."

"That's not the way Grant told the story. Even before he was shot, he said he didn't kill Adam Fehr. He said Eli did."

"That's a lie."

"Shank, do you have any idea how ridiculous this is? How insane it was for your ancestor to force this family to kill themselves for a piece of dirt? This was over one hundred and fifty years ago. You could have stopped it. Your grandfather or his father could have stopped it. You must have known in this modern world that this was absurd, that what your family were doing was illegal, was a crime."

"I've told you, they shamed us. They took away our good name in the community. Everyone knew Eli had been shunned. They had to be punished, they had to feel the pain of what they did to us and, until they compensated, they were shunned from the community. We do not live by your rules, by your law. We never have and we never will."

"What about the rules of your God? Your commandments? Thou Shalt Not Kill?"

"They killed themselves!" Shank spat.

"What about the Yoders, the Ropps and Mrs Whieler? They had nothing to do with this pact and yet you and your family terrorised them until they signed over their farms to you. Most of those people are dead by your hands."

Shank said nothing. He had already confessed to his involvement in their fates in front of Locklear. Peter Wyss had achieved that much and had given his life for the truth.

Locklear paced up and down and shook his head, trying to make sense of Shank's tale.

"I just can't believe that this was all for a piece of dirt. I don't buy it. I just don't."

"Then you don't understand us. It is a pact. It cannot be broken."

"It *was* a pact," Locklear replied. "But it's over now."

He walked to the door and opened it.

"It *is* over, Shank, because look at you! You're dying and your granddaughter is going to prison. There's no one left to do your dirty work."

Shank looked away to face the window.

"I know you're broke Samuel. The IRS has frozen all of your accounts. Beth can't run with no money."

Shank did not move his eyes from the window but Locklear could see the nervous swallow, the clench of his jaw.

"Will you give her the box, please? It's been in my family for three hundred years, missing for the last one hundred and fifty of those. I just want to die knowing I did not shame my family. Please ... please promise me you'll give her the box. I ask nothing more."

Locklear followed the old man's eyes out of the window. He visualised Stoll staring out of her prison cell with the box as a reminder of how she threw her life away for a piece of dirt.

"Giving her the box does not absolve the shame you brought on your family but, OK, I will give her the box."

Shank returned his eyes to the sergeant. There was a slight smile on his face.

"She's still going to prison, Shank."

"You haven't caught her yet. I still have eyes everywhere."

It was time for Locklear to clench his jaw, to express his frustration. Even in the face of death and defeat, even when Locklear had granted him his last wish, Shank was still defiant.

"No, but we will catch her and the eyes you have everywhere will close as soon as you take your last breath. The power you are addicted to and the hold you have over this community will die with you. It's over."

Locklear did not look back at the man as he opened the door. Outside, Maguire was nowhere to be seen.

Chapter 28

In Harrisonburg station, Mendoza had not arrived into work and no one could account for Maguire's whereabouts. Carter, as far as Locklear had heard, was sitting with Sara Fehr, watching the woman slowly lose her battle with pneumonia.

Locklear returned the silver box to the safe and lifted the phone to ring Mendoza's mobile. It rang out. He tried twice more. No answer. The last time he had seen the trooper was when he drove by the diner where she was having dinner with Maguire and some other cops he did not know well. He tried Maguire's cell again as he drove to the diner.

Marilyn Monroe was not on duty but a young Rock Hudson told him Mendoza had left with the cops around 9pm. Locklear wondered if Mendoza had hooked up with one of them and the thought of this aroused feelings of both jealousy and paternity in him – feelings of concern he did not want or need.

He went to her motel room. When there was no answer, he peered through the window and noticed that the bed had been overturned and that Mendoza's suitcase had been emptied onto the floor. With one swift boot, he kicked the door in and ran to the side of the bed, expecting to see her on the floor. A sharp pain cut into his foot, his injury not quite healed yet. He removed his piece and crept to the bathroom which was empty. Locklear sat on a chair and thought about who he would call for help. He did not want to take Carter away from Sara's bedside. With her family in hiding, Carter and Maria Whieler, who sat by her side all night while Carter sat by day, were the only two people Sara had. With no other option, he dialled the number but hung up after two rings. There was no way he could let Sara die alone. The sound of a muffled engine slowly broke into his thoughts. He stood and walked to the door where Mendoza was parking her car.

"*Where the hell have you been?*" he barked.

Mendoza locked her car and walked into her room.

"Jesus, sarge, if you wanted to look through my underwear, you didn't have to kick my door in. I'd just have showed it to you!"

"That's not funny, Mendoza. Someone wrecked your room – obviously looking for the box –must somehow know we have it ..."

"You have the box!" she interrupted.

Locklear stared at the woman. Black mascara was caked on her eyelashes and she had dark lines under her eyes. His trooper had obviously had a long, hard night.

"Yes, while you were enjoying yourself, Letitia Grant showed up with the box. There's nothing in it but some German soil. And this morning I spoke to the IRS guy who wanted to talk to me. Turns out Shank is broke."

Mendoza's tongue moved in her mouth as though she was trying to figure out what to ask about first.

"German soil?"

"Yep."

"How is that treasure?"

"Beats me. Come on- we have to find ourselves a hotel. If they know where you are, they know where I am. Things are heating up, Mendoza. Things are about to get even more nasty around here – so, until it's over, that means you don't leave my sight."

On the phone, Irene argued with Locklear as he fought for more expensive accommodation – a hotel where people's comings and goings could be seen from the reception area. When Locklear's voice rose to an unhealthy level, Mendoza took the phone off him.

"Hi, Irene – sorry about that. He hasn't taken his happy pills today. Look, we only need one room but make it two single beds. He's just told me he doesn't want to take his eyes off me, but I don't want to tire him out entirely. He's getting on in years. Yes, yes, that hotel would be fine. You're so good. Much appreciated. I owe you."

Mendoza ended the call and smiled at her boss.

"Now – that's how you get what you want, sarge."

"And did you get what you wanted last night, Mendoza?"

"Yep ... and then some!" she chuckled.

There was something about her laugh that stopped Locklear staying mad for long.

"I'm glad you're OK," he said.

The cell rang and Locklear lifted it. It was Carter.

"Samuel Shank went into cardiac arrest a few minutes after you left. They resuscitated him until he stabilised but he had another arrest and he died half an hour ago."

Locklear could sense a change in Carter's voice. He sounded sad.

"Are you OK?"

"Sara Fehr passed away nine minutes ago. Exactly twenty-one minutes after Shank. Seems like she wanted to make a statement. He took her life the day she was twenty-one years of age and she held on for twenty-one minutes after he took his last breath."

"I'm sorry, Lee."

"Thanks, sarge. Is there any progress on the case?"

"Stoll is on the loose and she's dangerous. And someone thrashed Mendoza's room."

"Are you OK?" Carter asked her anxiously.

"She's fine – she stinks of beer but she's fine."

Mendoza frowned at him.

"We're moving to a hotel – more security," Locklear said. "Lee, do you have anywhere else for you and your family to stay until this blows over?"

Carter was silent for a moment. "Sir, my wife's here in the hospital. Looks like she's going to have the baby early. Dad is still in hospital and I dropped Seth to my aunt's house."

"OK – leave him there and don't let anyone else know where he is, OK?"

"OK," Carter replied weakly.

"Find somewhere to stay yourself too."

Locklear lifted the phone and asked Lennox for an update. There was still no sign of Maguire and no car had rung in to report a sighting of Stoll's SUV.

He made one last call. Albert Schumer answered immediately. Locklear asked if he would do one more thing for him, if he would offer Maria Whieler refuge in his home and keep her there until Stoll was apprehended. Maria did not fully understand how much of a threat she was to the Shanks or the value of what she knew. Now that Sara was dead, the Shanks no longer needed the vulnerable young woman to report on the comings and goings at Sara Fehr's bedside and would make sure that she was not in a position to cause them any harm. Albert agreed.

Happy that Whieler would be looked after, Locklear ended the call and threw the phone at Mendoza.

"Here – call your son – tell him you'll be home by Saturday."

"Sarge!"

"Tell him."

"That's three days away!"

"If what happens next is what I think will happen, Stoll is on her way here – if she is not already in town. She knows she's going to prison so she's got nothing to lose. I think she plans to kill anyone she needs to – to tidy up loose ends."

"She'll never get away with that, sarge."

"That's the problem with Stoll, Mendoza. Her family have got away with murder for so long that she thinks they are invincible. She thinks she can do what she likes and that she'll drive away from this carnage and start afresh."

"But with what, sarge? You said it yourself. The Shanks are broke."

Locklear inhaled deeply as he turned the car towards the station. "I don't know yet," he answered.

It was one of the last few pieces of the puzzle that did not fit, that was absent in fact.

There was something that did not fit about the silver box. Shank was a ruthless man yet he was brought to tears at the sight of something so worthless, so sentimental. It didn't fit. He could feel it itch at his brain.

At the station, Locklear grouped several cops in the incident room and updated them. Maguire was missing – no one seems to know his whereabouts. His partner Jones suggested Locklear check the hot-dog stands before jumping to conclusions.

Locklear banged on the table to bring the group to order and sat on the table in the centre of the room.

"Stoll is *dangerous*. She is travelling with two armed men who will think nothing of putting a bullet in your chest. Wear a vest. Keep your attention up. Don't phone anyone. Don't warn anyone. Don't tell your husbands or wives or your kids that you love them. I don't want Stoll getting any notice that we are expecting her. She's smart so she's not going to barge in here in broad daylight. She'll bide her time and when she gets what she wants she'll –"

"What does she want?" another rookie interrupted.

Locklear went to the safe and took out the silver box. He held it up.

"This – this is what she wants. Now, I've made a promise to her grandfather that I'll give it to her but not before I bring her in and not before she's safely behind bars for life. Jones and Braun – I want you to take turns guarding Schumer's house but be discreet. Mendoza and Jenkins – I want you to stay on patrol around Dayton. If you see Stoll, don't approach her. Ring for back-up. If you see any of the Fehrs – any of them at all – bring them in for safety. I need two more patrolling Shank Creamery – no one gets in or out. I don't care who they are or what they want – they don't get in."

"What about Shank's wife, sir? You want us to bring her in?"

Locklear remembered the old woman in the lace bonnet on the first morning he had arrived in Dayton. Carter had said she was a sweet lady.

"No, leave her be, but one of you swing by her house on your patrol. Stoll might have a soft spot and might want to see her grandma before she goes to prison."

Locklear looked around the room for the cop who was due to be on desk duty that night.

"Williams – you're here tonight, right?"

Williams nodded.

"Don't take your eyes off this safe and no one goes near it, right?"

"OK, sarge."

"OK, everyone get to your posts and keep in radio contact. Slightest sign of anything interesting – and I don't care how minute it is – you call it in."

"Call it in? Sarge, Williams is as deaf as a post. He couldn't hear the radio if you put a siren on it!" Jones quipped.

"Huh?" Williams said.

"*That's enough!*" Locklear shouted. He looked pityingly at Williams and then searched the room for an alternative. His eyes rested on Mendoza. "*OK – Williams!*" he said, raising his voice. "You man the reception area. Any person of interest comes in, you call me immediately. *Do you understand?*"

Williams nodded. "Yes, no need to shout, sarge."

"You – stay here," he said, looking at Mendoza. He deliberately avoided using her name. He did not want to be accused of favouritism even though that's exactly what it was. "Answer the phones."

"Answer the phones! Sarge – do I look like a secretary to you?"

Locklear ignored her. "Your priority is to answer the phones and guard the safe."

"No, sarge!" Mendoza pleaded.

"That's an order, trooper. OK – everyone out. Let's get to it."

Locklear waited a while longer after the cops in their patrol cars left. He stood in the incident room thinking about what he would do if he were Bethany Stoll. Stoll was, he reasoned, a pragmatic woman whose main aim would be to secure any funds she could to finance her new life. Once she had secured this, she might not bother with settling scores. Money was what the woman needed. There was no point in her trying to access the accounts at Shank Creamery. Stein had frozen them all by court order that very day – something she would realise very soon. Hard cash, and lots of it, was what she needed and the only place he believed she would get this was by raiding the safe at Shank Creamery – if, indeed, there was a safe there at all.

As he left the station, Mendoza was still smarting at being left behind and did not say goodbye. First, he drove by Shank Creamery to see if there was any sign of Stoll and checked in with Collins and Gonzalez who were patrolling the creamery. Then he drove past Shank's house. Every blind was pulled and the house was in darkness.

Trooper Jones walked up to the car. "She's not here, sarge."

Locklear's phone rang. It was Mendoza.

"I'm still mad."

"I know."

"But I thought you should know – we just got a call from Stein to say that a woman just tried to use a credit card belonging to Shank Creamery to book into a hotel in New York. The woman registered under the name of Beth Stoll."

Locklear did not reply.

"Sarge?"

"Yes, I'm still here. It's a trick. She wants us to think she's there. She wants us to let our guard down." Locklear ran his hands through his thick hair. "Ask the hotel to fax the image to the station. They probably have security cameras behind the desk. If it's her, phone me back."

Locklear put down the phone. He started the car up again and made his way towards the Fehr farm. He parked and stood out on the land with only the moonlight and the distant lights of Harrisonburg to light his way.

He walked up to the barn and soaked in the silence. When his eyes adjusted to the blackness, he pushed on through the dried earth beyond the barn and climbed the steep hill on the northern face of the farm. He climbed further, stopping only when his foot stood on something hard. Locklear removed his cell from his pocket and used the light from the screen to illuminate the earth beneath him. A long-handled shovel lay on the ground about a foot from a freshly dug hole. He sighed and sat down on the dirt and looked up into the brilliant night sky.

"I guess I always knew you were still around. There's nowhere better for someone like you to hide but here. You know the woods better than anyone else. I need you to come out and talk to me. I need to tell you about Sara."

Locklear waited but the only reply he received was the screech of an owl on the distant farm. He shivered and rubbed his tender foot, the memory of the trap resurfaced and of the vision of his mother's face when he was in danger.

"Luke, there's no need for you to dig anymore. The Shanks are dead – father and son. The box is not here. That's what the Shanks have been looking for – their treasure. Turns out its nothing but a silver box full of soil from their homeland. It never was here. Grant lied to your ancestors."

A twig snapped in the distance. Locklear turned his head and tried to follow the small echo that followed. A bird squawked, breaking his concentration. Silence followed.

"I know you didn't kill Helena Wyss. I know you are innocent."

Another sound, smaller, lighter, a pebble perhaps dashing its way across the ground. It landed at Locklear's feet. He bent down and ran his hands around the earth looking for it until his fingers found the item – flat, hard, round. He stood and rubbed the smooth coin between his fingers.

"My sister is free," the voice said.

Locklear remained silent. Somehow Luke Fehr knew that his sister had passed away. Whether this was because Maria Whieler had somehow got word to him or if Fehr knew by instinct that his twin had taken her last breath, Locklear didn't know.

When he reached the roadway, Locklear sat in his car and ran the dollar coin between his fingers. He inhaled deeply and wondered what the coin meant and what Luke Fehr was trying to say.

Chapter 29

The coffee house on the highway between Harrisonburg and Dayton became Locklear's new office for the long hard night that lay ahead. He sat in the back booth of the brightly lit house and drank two strong black coffees while taking calls from his troopers stationed along the route and from stakeouts in both towns. Not one trooper had anything to report. All quiet on the western front, as Jones put it. He made a mental note to sit the young rookie down and give him some useful advice. Humour had no place in the middle of an investigation. It lightened the mood and made troopers lose their edge. Jones would have to accept that and adjust – or find another way to earn a living.

The call from Williams to say Carter's wife had had a baby girl and that all was fine was not the news he meant Williams to keep him up to date with, but he was happy for the trooper and knew the birth would give the man a lift on the day he had lost the love of his life.

The call from Mendoza caused him to leave his third coffee untouched and drive out of the lot like a man possessed. The security photo from the New York hotel had been faxed into the station and, according to Mendoza, was definitely Beth Stoll.

Locklear parked urgently in the station lot, blocking several cars from exiting. He looked at Williams who appeared to be sleeping at the reception desk.

"*Williams!*" he shouted as he passed the dozing man.

Williams opened his eyes and tried his best to pretend he had not been asleep.

"There's no sign of anyone, sarge," he said.

"*Williams – for fuck sake stay awake! Do you understand how crucial it is that we find this woman?*"

"I do, sarge. I've been drinking coffee all night. I don't know how I fell asleep. Honest, sarge, it's not like me."

Locklear noticed William's slurred speech. "*Have you been drinking?*"

"No, sarge! I don't drink. Never have. I'm just tired."

Locklear lifted his cell.

"Jones – come back to the station and man the desk."

Locklear put the phone down before Jones had a chance to offer any witticism.

"Williams – when Jones gets here – go home."

"Sir. I don't need –"

"I said go home. You live alone?"

"With my wife."

"Well, tell her to keep an eye on you. You feel any worse, go to the hospital. Do you hear me?"

Williams nodded.

Locklear raced to the back room where Mendoza was sitting staring at the phone. She glared at Locklear.

She stood and faced him.

"Look, sarge, I became a cop because I wanted to be out there. Out where the real work is. I didn't sign up to sit behind a desk waiting for the phone to ring."

"I know. I just don't want to see your kid grow up not knowing you."

"Fair enough, sarge, but you sent Collins and Gonzalez out and they're female. You've got to stop trying to protect me. I can handle myself. I wouldn't be in this job if I was scared."

Locklear placed his hands on the trooper's shoulders.

"That's what worries me, Mendoza. The fact that you aren't afraid. I didn't leave you behind because you're a woman. Your need to prove yourself is dangerous. Fear is good. Fear will stop you getting killed."

"You're not afraid."

"Yes, but I'm an asshole, Mendoza."

The trooper grinned.

"I've been shot twice in my career. First bullet nearly killed me. Landed me in hospital for two months followed by six months on disability. I was careful and still I got shot. It only takes one bullet to end your life. You need to be more careful, Mendoza."

"Did they get the perp?"

"I didn't see him – not up close anyway but I know who it was."

"Who?"

"A guy named Nick Lombardi."

"The guy Andrew Fehr worked for?"

"One and the same."

"Well, then why ... I mean how do you bring yourself to speak to him?"

"Water under the bridge, Mendoza. I couldn't prove it and I had more important business to settle with him."

"Like?"

"Trying to crack his heroin business. It was killing hundreds and ruining the lives of thousands more. I was one man. Do the math."

"Did you succeed?"

"No, and that gets me more than the fact that he shot me."

"Does he know you know it was him?"

"I doubt it."

"Are you ever going to tell him?"

Locklear thought about this for a moment. "No. Now, are we good? Can we get back to what we should be talking about?"

"Sure."

Locklear lifted the photo faxed over from the hotel and shook his head.

"It's her all right, sarge."

Locklear studied the photo which captured a side view of the woman as she stood at the hotel's reception desk. Beth Stoll was dressed in a short business skirt. Her light-brown hair hung loose around her shoulders. Stoll appeared much paler than when he had seen her at her grandfather's offices only days before. Locklear could see the marks on the left side of her face. The marks had probably been sustained when Helena Wyss fought for her life and were much worse than the injuries Jerome Stein had reported.

"Do you have the number of the hotel?"

Mendoza dialled the number and handed the receiver to Locklear.

"Ask for Jesús. He's a friend of mine. We grew up together in Virginia. I didn't know he worked there until I phoned looking for the photo."

Locklear spoke with Jesús who seemed to have a crush on Mendoza and told Locklear how fond he was of the trooper at least three times in the fifteen-minute conversation. Stoll had tried to check in with a man and, when her card was rejected, she paid cash for the room for two nights. She had not checked in and then absconded to provide herself with an alibi as Locklear had expected her to, but was sitting in full view in the foyer with the man, looking scared. After securing Jesús's promise to ring Locklear if the woman as much as moved a muscle, Locklear placed the receiver down and began to pace the room.

He lifted the phone and did something he wished he didn't

need to. He prided himself on sticking to the rules one hundred per cent of the time, but he had no choice. He was dealing with a ruthless person and he needed to stop her. He called Robbins who was luckily on duty and who reluctantly agreed to arrest her and put a tail on the man to see where he went. He ended the call by reminding Locklear that the hotel was out of his East Harlem jurisdiction and he would do it as a favour he expected to be remembered.

"What's happening?" Mendoza asked.

"First off, Jesús wants to be your next husband."

Mendoza laughed. "He's not my type."

"I hope your type, Mendoza, isn't another cop. I'd have thought one cop husband would be enough for you."

"Your right, sarge. One cop husband was enough," she replied.

Locklear sat down and tapped his fingers off the table.

"Why would a woman wanted for suspected murder and tax fraud sit in open view in the lobby of a popular hotel?"

"She's waiting for someone," Mendoza offered.

"Or she's waiting for something to happen somewhere else while she can be seen on camera. A perfect alibi. Her second goon is missing but I'm not worried about him. These hired guns don't do anything without the boss's say-so. As long as Stoll is in custody, he'll sit on his hands and wait it out."

Another half hour passed before Robbins phoned back.

Locklear smiled as the call ended and snapped his cell shut.

"OK, she's in custody. Robbins has her in lock-up at the station. He said he got a lot of sour looks from cops for locking up an innocent, crying woman. And your friend Jesús might not be so fond of you now. When the goon saw the cops arrive, he took out his piece and tried to take them down. Shot a few holes into the marble pillars. They have him in custody now."

"All airports have been alerted. If Stoll or her goon gets

out, they won't be able to board a flight to Virginia or anywhere else. I told Robbins to make sure he drags out processing her for as long as he can."

Mendoza blew out and stretched her arms upwards. "What now?"

"We'll fly there tomorrow morning and bring Stoll back here for interview. We'll have to get an order first though. From here on in I want this all done right. There's no way I'm letting Stoll get off the hook on any minor legal loophole."

"Well, I'd suggest a beer but I think it'd be better if I got you to bed – your bed, that is!"

Locklear laughed and radioed for everyone who wasn't due to be on tonight to go home. When he got to the reception area, Jones was in place and Williams had gone home.

"Jones – you and I need to talk," he said as he opened the door to the station.

"What about, sarge?"

"I'll tell you tomorrow!"

The Hampton Inn on University Boulevard was almost as good a hotel as Locklear needed. The wood-panelled reception area was manned twenty-four hours a day and had three security cameras stationed around the large, open lobby. A heavy-set security man stood inside the door, successfully protecting the plush hotel from undesirable patrons, one of which had been Locklear until he flashed his badge.

"You do need a shave!" Mendoza teased.

Locklear slipped the man a note and asked him to call the room if anyone of Stoll's description entered the hotel.

"Aren't you going overboard?" Mendoza asked. "She's locked up in New York and she doesn't have wings."

"Just taking out insurance. Always have plan A B, C – all the way to Z if you can."

"That's pretty sad."

"No – it's practical. Always be ready. Always expect the unexpected."

"Sounds exhausting, sarge," she said as lifted the phone to order room service. "I'm starved. What do you say to getting up Irene's nose by ordering steak?"

"Sounds good."

"Would you'd mind if I ordered a beer? I mean, if it'd be hard on you I won't."

Locklear waved from his bed where he sat and rubbed his toe which was still smarting from kicking in Mendoza's door earlier. Now he had two damaged feet.

When their delicious steak dinner was finished and Mendoza had polished off not one, but four bottles of beer, she joined Locklear on the sofa facing the TV in the luxurious room.

"You going to finally tell me what O stands for?"

"What?"

"Your first name. What is it?"

"Mendoza, if I wanted you to know my first name, I'd have told it to you."

"Why the secrecy? It's just a name!"

Locklear ignored her.

"What if I tell you something about myself and you then tell me your name?"

Locklear laughed. "Mendoza, I'm trying to watch the news."

"OK, but you're missing out."

Locklear continued to watch TV while the trooper stumbled into bed, anxious to give her privacy while she changed. He did not turn when she stumbled in the bathroom or when she stubbed her toe on the wardrobe door. He did not want to look at her in that white nightdress again. He did not want to arouse feelings that he could do nothing with. Feelings that would lead to nothing and to nowhere, except trouble.

"Em ... I'm alright, by the way!"

"You're drunk, Mendoza. Go to bed."

Within minutes, he could hear his trooper snoring behind him. He turned off the TV and changed in the bathroom before climbing into the next bed.

He lay back on the pillow and prayed for sleep to come to him but there were too many loose ends rolling around in his mind. He was fairly sure Luke had dug his last hole on the farm and that the treasure hunt that had spanned one hundred and fifty years was now over for the Fehr family. But the itch he felt every time he was missing something scratched at his consciousness and hindered his quest for sleep. The faces of all the people he had met in the course of the investigation raced across his field of vision, The Fehr siblings, Helena and Peter Wyss, the dysfunctional Shank family, Maria Whieler, Anabel Schumer, Letitia Grant, Jerome Stein – they had all played a part in a case that still had too many unanswered questions.

More puzzling right now was the missing cop Maguire. Locklear was the last person to have seen him when he showed up at the hospital and Mendoza had said that the cop left the company they were in and headed home alone the night before. Maguire's new partner, Jones, had been in that company but he had not shown any real concern that his buddy was missing. In fact, hardly any of the company seemed worried about Maguire's sudden disappearance. He decided he needed an answer to that particular question now and went to the bathroom to phone someone who might be able to shed some light on the subject. He waited while the phone rang five times and was about to hang up when a sleepy voice answered.

"Kowalski?"

"Locklear? Are you OK? I heard ..."

"No, I didn't drink, Alex. I'm fine. Really."

"It's 1am. When I saw your number, I was sure ..."

"No. I won."

"I'm glad but you should have called me. We had a deal, remember? You call me if you are in trouble and I call you."

Locklear remembered the deal but in the years since he'd quit Alex Kowalski had not phoned him even once. There was no need. He had not been tempted. Kowalski had a choice. Drink or family. He chose the latter.

"What do you know about Maguire?"

"Frank?"

Locklear remained silent. He didn't know Maguire's first name. He rarely knew anyone's first name unless he had a reason to.

"He's a good cop. Long service. I think his old man was a cop too."

"Is he clean?"

"If you're asking me if he's corrupt, then no. Definitely not. But he has had some problems."

"Like?"

"Maguire is a gambler. Got himself into a lot of trouble a few years back."

"Trouble how?"

"He spent a lot of time in casinos. Lost everything, wife, kids, house, the lot. It still didn't make him stop. She left town. Took the kids with her."

"Did his habit mean he ever went missing from duty?"

"Too frequently, I'm afraid, but I thought he'd managed to turn things around. Last I heard he was still spending most of his off-duty time in casinos but his work was OK."

"Was it severe enough to warrant people not thinking too much of him disappearing?"

"Guess so."

Locklear put the phone down and got back into bed. Maguire was an addict of a different sort but Locklear still understood its power, even if the object of their addiction

The Pact

was different. No doubt the man was sitting in some rundown poker house right at this moment spending his meagre cop salary on a bet he couldn't win.

Sleep still evaded him but he tried to will himself to relax and rest. The niggling feeling that he was missing something returned and tormented him as he twisted and turned in the bed. The concern he felt for Maguire would not leave his mind. Even if Maguire was a gambler, it did not explain him walking off his post in the middle of an investigation. Kowalski had said that his work was OK so the feeling that something was wrong continued to irritate his nerves. He rose again and brought his phone with him to the bathroom.

He rang Lennox who he felt was an upright, honest type of cop.

Lennox, however, was not too happy about the 1.30am call. Locklear could hear a baby crying in the background and the sound of a very irate wife, complaining.

"Just tell me about the last time you saw Maguire. Was he his usual self or did you notice anything different?"

Lennox yawned and blew out. "I was in the diner with him and a few other cops."

"Who else was there?"

"Jones – by the way, that rookie is an ass, sarge. Don't know how he graduated."

"I know, I'll deal with him tomorrow."

"Em, Mendoza was there, Jenkins and Gonzalez."

"Did Maguire leave with you?"

"No, he split earlier. He was his usual self. Nothing unusual."

"And he didn't seem worried about anything?"

"No – look, sarge, everyone likes Frank but he's hooked on those casinos. No one likes to say anything bad about him, especially with his wife splitting with the kids. He's a good guy so guess that's why no one told you."

"What did you do after that?"

"Em ... Mendoza and Gonzalez hooked up and left so I went for a beer with Jenkins."

"Did you say Mendoza and Gonzalez hooked up?"

"Yes."

"Gonzalez is a woman."

"Yeah. I noticed that."

Locklear laughed at what a fool he had been.

"You didn't know?" Lennox asked.

"No. But I think Mendoza tried to tell me. I just wasn't listening."

Locklear put the phone down and walked back to his bed. He walked to Mendoza's bed and moved the hair back off her face. She stirred. He eased himself into bed and lay as still as he could while he waited for sleep to come. When he did finally drift off it was the face of Jerome Stein that was foremost in his vision. In his dreams, the balding man with the thick dark glasses and ever-present briefcase stood over his bed and repeated the same phrase over and over.

"Everything is about money, in the end."

On the other side Luke Fehr threw thirty pieces of silver onto the bed. Locklear could feel the weight of the metal on his chest and in his dreams gasped for breath. He reached out and tried to catch one coin as it rolled off the bed and spun on the ground until it crash-landed on the wooden hotel room floor. Locklear jumped when the sound suddenly appeared real and seemed to be coming from the other side of the large bedroom. He reached for his gun and listened as the noise lessened until it came to an abrupt stop. He turned on the light to find that the dollar coin Luke Fehr had thrown at him had slipped from the pocket of his jeans which hung loosely from a chair in the room. He rose and lifted the coin from the floor. It was a regular dollar coin but it was a message. He was missing something. Something Stein had said. It was all about the money. That was what Luke had also tried to tell him earlier on the farm. It was not about revenge or saving face. It was not the pact the gullible Fehrs had thought it to be.

It was about money and now he knew where it was. The money was in the box.

Chapter 30

It took Locklear only six minutes to drive at speed from the hotel to Dayton station where he knew what to expect before he even got there.

En route he had taken a call from Robbins who said the badly beat-up Stoll was demanding to talk to him and was insisting that she was not Bethany Stoll but a missing person named Anabel Schumer. When he told Robbins to hold onto her for at least another hour, he had to hang up on the cop to drown out the expletives coming down the phone.

Locklear rubbed his throbbing head and inhaled deeply and braced himself for the carnage he was expecting to find inside the station.

Trooper Jones was lying across the reception desk. Locklear pulled his gun and crept inside. He placed his fingers on the man's carotid artery. The bullet-hole at the centre of his head told the sergeant that the newly graduated rookie had died instantly. On the desk was an open comic book which the trooper had probably been reading, and possible even laughing at, in the seconds before he died. It didn't look like Locklear was going to have to talk to Jones about his inappropriate sense of humour after all.

He pushed his back against the wall and listened for

sounds coming from the incident room but all he could hear were muffled voices. Two, maybe three. The muffled voice was male but there was one female voice and he already knew who it was. He listened to the heavy Germanic accent, the sharp tones and curt language of Bethany Stoll.

Locklear walked back down to the reception area and did something he should have done before he arrived there. He pressed the emergency switch under the main desk, something Jones had obviously not had a chance to do. Within minutes, patrol cars would come screaming onto the lot and provide him with the back-up he needed. But he needed Stoll alive. He wanted the woman to pay for everything she had done. He wanted her to suffer. He opened the door to the station and crept down the side of the building until he reached the incident room which spanned the entire back section of the structure. He reached the window which was slightly open and peeped with one eye to scan the room.

Beth Stoll had her back to him. Maguire was sitting on a chair, trying to open the safe with the combination Locklear had changed yesterday and which only he, Carter and Mendoza knew. Maguire's hands were loosely bound but his legs were taped around the front legs of the chair. The cop's eyes were wild. He tried to speak through the tape bound across his face – trying, Locklear reasoned, to tell the woman that he did not have the code.

Stoll walked forward and slapped him.

"*I said open it.*"

The goon standing to her right glanced towards the window. Locklear pulled back swiftly and flattened himself against the wall, hoping he had not been seen. He would have to wait here for the back-up to arrive. It would be suicide to go in there alone. The odds were against him. He knew the woman would not go down without a fight and that her hired killer would show him no mercy. Maguire began to whimper.

Locklear risked peering in again.

The goon walked slowly over and punched the cop in the face.

"Take it off," Stoll finally said.

The goon pulled the tape off in one clean move.

Maguire roared.

Stoll approached him and brushed her gun against his face.

"Now, Francis," she teased. "You know you owe my grandfather's casino a lot of money and this is the way you will clean your slate. Now, you either open that safe or Manny here will put a bullet in your brain. It's your choice."

"I swear I don't have it. It's been changed. I swear it."

"I'm going to count to three," Stoll said as she pulled the trigger.

"You lied to me. You said if I kept an eye on Anabel you'd clear my debts. I told you when I saw her at the station but you came back for more and you – you killed that girl. Why did you have to kill her?"

"Oh, hush now, Francis, I didn't kill her. She was too useful for me. Same height, weight, even the same colour hair. We could have been sisters. In fact, right now, she *is* me."

Locklear went against all of his rules and lifted his phone to turn on the recording device. He knew the recording would probably be inadmissible in court but it was worth a try. He also knew now who had told Stoll that Esther Fehr had been arrested and brought to Dayton station. Maguire was the rat but Locklear still felt sorry for the man. He had had no choice and would now lose the only thing he had left in the world: his job. Or his life.

"You are an evil woman, Stoll. Did you kill Helena Wyss? Did you kill Peter's wife? He was my friend. Why did you have to do that? They were good people!"

"Yes, I'm afraid that I did have to put an end to Helena.

She wouldn't tell me what I wanted to know."

"She didn't know anything. She was a farmer. A simple woman."

"She knew where exactly Luke Fehr was hiding. If she'd told me, she'd be alive now living her miserable existence."

"It's you who has a miserable existence. Nothing is ever enough for you. After I told you about Anabel you came back for more. You said if I told you if Locklear got the box, you'd free me, that I've have paid my debts. I did what you asked. I ruined my career. My reputation. I did it so I could be finally free from you and from your grandfather."

Stoll laughed. "You should never trust what people say, Francis. Always get it in writing. You should know the law. It's your job. "And," she rubbed the nuzzle of her gun against his temple, "as soon as I get the IRS off my back, the casino will be mine so you won't be dealing with an old fool like my grandfather or even with Uncle Jacob. You'll be dealing with me."

"I'd rather die!" Maguire spat.

"Well, you might have your wish very shortly. *Open it.*"

"I can't."

Maguire closed his eyes and waited for the bullet to enter the chamber, the bullet which would end his life.

Locklear did the only thing he could do, something that would blow his cover and maybe get himself *and* Maguire killed. He moved his gun through the slight opening.

Maguire spotted him.

"*I can't do it! I can't do it!*" he screamed.

Locklear knew the increased loudness of Maguire's voice was designed to mask the sound of him readying his gun for fire. He pulled the trigger and waited for the sound that told him the bullet was in the chamber.

"*Shut up!*" Stoll said.

Maguire begged for mercy. Locklear knew the gambler was making enough noise for him to take the woman and her assassin down. He took aim and in one shot brought the goon to his knees. It was a shot designed to disable him. A shot through the right shoulder. An old favourite. He took another aim and shot the man in the left knee. Perfect. The goon would be no trouble now but he would live and would hopefully give evidence against Stoll in exchange for a lighter sentence. Stoll spun around and raised her gun to fire but she did not need to. A click at the back of Locklear's head told him he was not alone. He looked behind him to find goon number two with a gun pointed at him.

"*Throw the gun down.*"

Locklear threw his weapon down and stared through the window at the defeated face of Maguire. Stoll moved to the window and smiled her catlike smile at him.

"*Put your hands behind your back.*"

Locklear obeyed the goon. He had no choice. His only hope would be for the back-up he called for to arrive. Back-up that should have been here by now.

"*Turn around.*"

He turned and, with no other option, walked in front of the goon around the side of the station.

"*In!*" the goon said as he opened the station door.

They walked to the incident room.

"*Sit!*" the man said as he banged a chair down beside Maguire.

"I'm sorry, sarge," Maguire said.

Locklear ignored him as the goon taped his legs and arms to the chair.

He knew that Stoll intended to shoot him after he opened the safe and wondered if this, the third time he would be shot in his life, would be the bullet that would kill him. He wasn't afraid to die. He just wished he had succeeded in putting Beth Stoll behind bars before it happened. That way he would die knowing that the Fehrs could go home and live in peace.

The Pact

When he was tied up and could pose no risk to Stoll, she approached him and pointed the gun into his face.

"You're kind of cute, you know. You have lovely hair and you have the saddest eyes. You remind me of a teddy I had as a girl."

"You're crazy!" Locklear spat.

"It was a compliment, Locklear. Don't you know how to take a compliment when you receive one?"

Locklear turned away from her and rested his eyes on Maguire.

"Don't look to him. He's can't help you. He'll be dead in a few minutes."

Maguire began to sob.

"Shut up, Maguire!" Locklear snapped.

Locklear had to think quickly. He had to find a way to knock the woman off course. He had to buy himself some time, enough hopefully for back-up to arrive.

"Didn't your mother teach you anything?" he said. "Oh wait – that's right. She died on you and left you and your brother to the mercy of your uncle and grandfather."

"*Shut up!*" she screamed.

Locklear knew he was on the right course. The cool, controlled woman's anger level had gone from zero to ten in a matter of seconds at the mention of her family.

"Locklear, what are you doing?" Maguire asked.

"I saw your brother. He's a good man. But he's disappointed in you. He said you are lost."

"*I said shut up!*"

"*Shut up!*" Maguire echoed.

Stoll moved closer and raised her gun to Locklear's head.

"I wonder if your uncle had your parents killed? Did you ever find out what happened to them? Did you ever really know how they died? I'd be willing to wager that your childless uncle needed an heir. The problem was your parents were raising you both as Old Order Mennonites. I guess

Jacob knew that if he allowed that to continue, you'd be no use to him – he had a different life in mind for you both. With your parents out of the way, your brother was right there for the taking. He only took you as back-up."

"*Shut up!*" Stoll screamed.

Locklear listened to her voice and the high-pitched scream told him Stoll would soon lose control of her anger. He knew he had better take it down a notch or two.

"Did you miss your mother?"

"It was a car accident," she replied. Locklear could see the slight downturn of her mouth, the glistening of her eyes.

"Well, sure, a death cert has to say something but you always wondered, didn't you? You spent time awake at night wondering. Especially when your brother left you to return to the farm. He left you there while your uncle turned you into a monster."

"*Stop it! Stop it!*" Stoll screamed.

"For fuck sake, Locklear, stop it!" said Maguire. "She has a gun pointed in your face."

"Don't sweat it, Maguire. She's going to kill us whether she gets the box or not. Aren't you?"

"Yes," Stoll replied. She straightened her spine and moved closer to Locklear. "After I get the box."

"Now, see, I'm curious about the box, Beth. Can I call you Beth?"

"*Open the fucking safe!*" the goon said.

Stoll began to smile. "You're brave, Locklear, I'll give you that. But bravery won't save you. It'll only slow down the time it takes you kill you."

"That's what he wants. He's probably waiting for back-up," the goon said.

"Oh, well," Stoll said, moving even closer to Locklear's face. "You'll be waiting a long time because Francis here disabled the panic button after he put sleeping pills into the desk cop's coffee. Nobody is coming to save you."

Locklear's head snapped around to stare at Maguire.

"I'm sorry, sarge. I didn't want anyone else getting killed. This way she gets what she wants and leaves."

"*You stupid – fucking – moron!*"

"Now, now, Locklear. There's no need for profanity. Francis was only doing what I told him to do. He didn't think anyone would get hurt."

"I didn't, sarge. Honest. I just thought she'd take the box and go."

"Your partner is lying dead outside, Maguire. You got him killed and now you're going to get us both killed."

Locklear decided on a new tactic. He called it his Laurel and Hardy routine. He inched forward and lunged his chair at Maguire.

"You stupid goddamn fucking –"

Locklear fell head first into Maguire's lap and bit the cop on the leg. Maguire screamed and tried to push the sergeant off him. Locklear unleashed his teeth from the cop's meaty leg and tried to headbutt him.

"*Stop him!*" Stoll screamed.

The goon rushed forward, punching Locklear in the jaw and sending his chair flying across the room.

"*Lift him up*," Stoll ordered.

The goon moved behind the chair and shoved Locklear into an upright position under the window.

"I'm going to enjoy this more than I thought I would," Stoll said.

She spread her legs and straddled Locklear. He tensed and moved his face away.

"Give me the code."

"No," Locklear replied.

She turned and pointed her gun at Maguire.

"Give it to me or I'll shoot him."

"Shoot him," Locklear replied.

"*No!*" Maguire pleaded. "Give her the code, sarge. Please."

Stoll pulled the trigger and sent a bullet into Maguire's knee. His chair fell over and he lay on his back as blood seeped through his trousers.

Maguire screamed. "Sarge, for God's sake give it to her!"

Stoll turned to face Locklear again. He met her gaze and held it fixed there. He had looked into the face of evil before but never at this close range.

"*Code.*"

"*No.*"

"I'll kill him."

"Do it. He's finished anyway. If he lives until tomorrow, he'll lose his job and his reputation in the town. His life is over. Do it."

"You're bluffing."

"No, I'm not, Stoll. I'm really not."

Stoll leaned into his face and licked Locklear. She moved her lips to his mouth and kissed him before biting painfully down on his lower lip.

"You know, I think you and I might have made a good couple. I didn't know you had such a dark side."

Locklear smiled. "Maybe we would."

"*Code.*"

Locklear laughed. "Beth, now you know I'm not giving you that code."

Stoll turned around and pulled the trigger. A second bullet hit Maguire. This one silenced him. Locklear tried to see where the bullet had struck but Stoll blocked his view.

"*Code.*"

"I'm still not giving it to you."

"I'll kill you."

"You're going to kill me anyway."

Stoll smiled and kissed Locklear one more time. She bit down harder on his lip. He struggled as blood oozed down his mouth.

Stoll moved back to survey her captive and smiled,

The Pact

revealing Locklear's blood smeared on her white teeth. Locklear stared as the woman's expression changed from perverse pleasure to surprise. The expression lasted only a moment, a fleeting second, before one shot rang out. A bullet to the shoulder. Point blank. Stoll fell backwards onto the floor. A second bullet fired. This time to the woman's thigh. The shooter intended to keep Stoll alive but impotent. The goon raised his gun to fire back at the shooter outside the window. Locklear managed to throw himself at the man, knocking him to the ground.

The sash lifted and the shooter climbed inside. Mendoza. She raised her gun and tried to shoot as the pair tussled on the floor. A shot rang out, deafening Locklear. The goon's grip loosened. He was dead.

"You OK, sarge?"

"Mendoza, you could have killed me."

"You're welcome, sarge," she replied as she untied him.

Locklear stumbled over to Maguire who had not moved since Stoll had shot him for a second time. He checked the cop's vitals. Maguire was alive. He checked the first goon. He was alive.

"What took you so long, Mendoza?"

"Well, I waited outside the window for a while because I figured you were enjoying yourself ... so ..."

Locklear laughed.

He stood over Stoll with Mendoza at his side. The woman was alive but dazed.

"I guess we better call an ambulance."

Locklear turned to face the trooper.

"You saved my life."

"It was worth saving."

He placed his arms around her and embraced her in way he had not held another human being in a very long time.

"Come on," he said then. "Let's wrap this case up and go home."

Chapter 31

Mendoza and Locklear waited patiently for Carter before they opened the box that countless people had lost their lives for. When the young trooper arrived, all three sat quietly at the table in the incident room, looking at the silver container in the middle of the table. Stoll would survive the bullet wounds Mendoza had inflicted on her as would one of her goons. Maguire would also survive but he wouldn't be coming back to his job and it remained up to Kowalski to determine what charges would be brought against the man once he'd recovered.

"How we are going to do this?" Mendoza asked.

Locklear lifted the box and turned it every way. There didn't seem to be any other clasps.

"Should we break it?" Carter asked.

Locklear exhaled. "I'd rather not, least not unless I have to."

He put the box back on the table.

"What about taking it for some sort of scan – like at the airport?" Mendoza suggested.

"I don't want anyone else knowing about the box. Not until I know what's in it," Locklear replied.

"We have to open it. You have no choice. Just break it" Carter said.

Locklear retrieved a hammer from the janitor's cupboard

The Pact

in the station and returned to the incident room. He lifted the hammer over the box.

"OK, here goes ..."

"*Wait!*" Mendoza shouted. "I saw this thing on TV. A movie. The box had treasure in it and it had a false bottom."

"This is not a movie, Mendoza" Locklear replied.

"I know but it's worth a try."

Locklear put the hammer down and lifted the box again. He opened the top section where the letter from Eli's mother had been stored. There was nothing there.

"Turn the soil out," Carter suggested.

"I already did that. There's nothing there!" Locklear snapped.

"Well, look again," Mendoza said.

Locklear turned the box upside down and emptied the box of its sentimental contents. He put the box back on the table and ran his fingers into each corner, looking for a false bottom.

"There's nothing here," he sighed.

Carter lifted the box awkwardly, wincing as he used his left arm in its sling.

"It's really heavy and the weight from the silver can't account for it all."

"OK, college genius," said Locklear. "Tell us what you think."

Carter rummaged around the inside of the box with his fingers.

"I just did that!" Locklear snapped.

Carter began to press inside the thick hinged lid of the box. There was a loud click.

Locklear's heart quickened.

Carter ran his hands down to the other end of the lid and pressed hard until he heard another click.

He prised the interior panel of the lid down and revealed a small opening into a third chamber inside it.

He looked at his boss. "Do you want to do the honours, sarge?"

Locklear moved into Carter's place as Mendoza drew a breath and held it.

Locklear pushed his fingers through the small opening and tried to grip something cold inside. He withdrew his fingers.

"Mendoza – would you try?"

"Why me?"

"Because your tiny fingers will be able to grab it."

"Grab what?"

"Something ice-cold and smooth."

"OK, sarge, but I hope it's nothing creepy."

Mendoza swapped places with her boss and pushed two fingers through the opening.

"I have it. It's really heavy," she said as her tongue twisted around her mouth.

She pulled and pulled but the item was too big to retrieve from the small space it rested in.

"Just break it," Carter said again.

"No. If someone got it in there then we must be able to get it out. We have to think about this," Locklear replied. "Put your fingers in again, Mendoza, and try figure out how long it is."

The trooper put her fingers back into the space and ran them along the length of it.

"It feels like a ..."

"*Like a what?*" Locklear asked.

"Never mind," she said. She did not want to disappoint her boss. The contents of the box would do that in the next few minutes.

Mendoza pushed the item around as she tried to move it into a position that would enable her to pull it through the opening in the box.

Locklear curled his fists into a ball in frustration as he waited for her to reveal the treasure.

"OK," she finally said. "I have a hold of a narrow section. I'll pull it through."

The Pact

Slowly and with great care she gripped the shaft of what she now knew was a long and very heavy, metal key.

She lifted it out and glanced briefly at her boss who was speechless.

"There's paper as well," she said as she returned her narrow fingers into the hollowed-out space.

She pulled the paper out and handed it to Locklear who held the key in his hand.

"What is it?" Carter asked.

Locklear unfolded the paper and studied the document.

"It's a map and, look, someone's written on it," Mendoza said.

Her boss had still not uttered one word.

"Sarge?"

"Carter – get me the book Jefferson's wife gave me in New York. Open the section where there's a letter written by Grant."

Carter went to Locklear's desk and retrieved the book. He opened it to the relevant page and laid it on the table.

Locklear looked from the writing on the map to the letter in Hennessy's book.

"It's the same writing – look."

Carter and Mendoza studied the handwriting.

"So, Grant drew this map?"

Locklear nodded. He ran his hands over his unshaven face.

"I reckon Grant saw Eli with this box and thought it was valuable. He took it and found a double use for the box by hiding his map and key in it for safe keeping. I'd say that chamber was where Mennonites hid valuables they were trying to smuggle out of Germany so that they had something to barter with when they arrived in America. Grant must have cottoned onto it and when he found there was nothing in it, he at least found a good place to hide his map and the key to whatever it opens."

"So, when Eli found out Grant had stolen the box from him, Grant wouldn't admit to it because he had hidden his own treasure in it?" Carter asked.

"Exactly," Locklear replied.

"I gather at some point Eli figured out that there was something far more valuable in the box?" Mendoza suggested.

Locklear took a deep breath. He lifted the book written by Hennessy. It was dated 1867. Two years after the war had ended.

"I do believe now that at first Eli simply wanted the box so he could go home. He was a despicable man but he just wanted to be accepted back into the community. When Grant was apprehended in New York, the newspapers were full of his arrest for treason, murder and there were references to missing valuables which he had admitted to stealing. Eli would have heard about it, if not from this book, then from the newspapers. Something like that would have been printed all over this country. Even back then. Maybe he assumed that there was something more valuable in the box now?"

"Probably – and every generation of the Shanks knew the dirty secret too. More recently, the desperation to find the box increased when the Shanks realised they were bankrupt."

"Hence the reason to go after Andrew?"

"Yeah, I guess they thought Luke was lying about not having found it. Maybe they thought he knew where it was and, while he wouldn't cash it in himself, he'd get at them by not handing it over. Unless, of course, his brother was in danger."

"But, what does this mean? What could Grant have stolen back then that could possibly be so valuable?" Mendoza asked.

Carter lifted the map and turned it sideways. A broad smile washed over his face.

The Pact

"Well, Mr Historian, do you want to tell her or will I?" Locklear asked.

Carter laughed. "It's Confederate gold. Stolen Confederate gold that has been missing since the end of the Civil War!"

"But, sarge," said Mendoza. "We have no idea what the code means and we have no idea where to find it."

Locklear examined the map. It contained neither a townland reference nor landmarks and consisted only of a simple, child-like drawing of a small forested area with badly drawn miniature trees dotted around the page. In the front line of the wood, the fifth tree was marked with an X with a coin drawn beside it.

On the side of the map Grant had written *IF1861*.

"I know what it means," he said. "IF is the initials of Isacc Falk. He was Helena Wyss's ancestor and he died in the Civil War. 1861 refers to the year he died."

"So, it's a grave?" Carter asked.

Locklear looked at Lee. "No. His body was never returned to the family. I guess the man was buried where he fell. Helena told me that Isaac's wife carved his initials into the tree in the woods at the back of the Wyss farm. It's in the exact spot I got caught in that trap and it's the tree we found Helena Wyss hanging from."

"Sir, how would Grant have come into possession of the gold?" Carter asked. "I mean, there are lots of myths surrounding the treasure – it wasn't gold as in gold bars or nuggets. I remember studying it in college. It was actually what's known as 'specie' so it was a mix of silver and gold coins and they're actually worthless now – in monetary terms anyhow. I'd say if the coins exist they'd only be considered valuable to a museum."

"But the Shanks obviously didn't know that."

"Obviously not," Carter replied.

Locklear sighed. "All that murder, and deceit. All for nothing."

"There may even be some truth in the rumour that the gold never really existed, that the 'missing' gold was actually used to pay Confederate soldiers at the end of the Civil War. The story that many historians think is correct is that only some of the gold was stolen but the amount taken only really accounted for about $70,000. It happened when the coins were moved from Richmond by train to Danville and from there it was moved on horseback and by wagon train. It was heavily guarded by Confederate soldiers but the wagons were hijacked in Wilkes County in Georgia. That's a long, long way from where Grant was hiding. Some of it has been found over the years but a lot of the coins were never found."

"Remember Grant said that he met up with 'others in the same situation'?" said Mendoza. "I think he meant thieves, outlaws. It's possible that he met up with thieves who had been in Wilkes County and had been involved in the heist."

"Bushwackers, Mendoza," Locklear interrupted.

Carter looked at his boss.

"I read," he said in response to the look of surprise on his trooper's face. "He also had a horse by the time he met up with the Fehrs. I think it's very likely that he met up with one or some of the thieves and in turn stole the gold and a horse from them."

"Sounds likely."

Carter looked upwards as though a light had been switched on over his head. His mouth opened.

"Sir, I wrote my thesis on the history of Harrisonburg in the 1800s. When I was doing my research I read a piece somewhere about three bushwhackers who were imprisoned for stealing Confederate gold. A Confederate soldier who they'd bayoneted during the theft in Wilke's county ID'd them and said they had made off with a locked ammunition trunk full of coins. They were apprehended a few miles from Harrisonburg but they had nothing on them. They swore that a black Union soldier had stolen it from them and had taken their horses. Of course, no one believed them and they were imprisoned in Richmond. Two of them escaped together and were never heard from again and the third made a later escape and made it all the way to Canada."

Locklear tapped the map and grinned. From his grave somewhere in New York, Grant had led them on a merry dance. He figured the man had run from Dayton when it was clear that Eli Shank was going insane but he intended to return swiftly to dig up the treasure he had hidden in the woods at the back of Wyss's farm. His capture and subsequent death by firing squad prevented the man from ever collecting his prize. The treasure had been here all along.

"Well, let's get digging."

The pouring rain in the woods the following morning did nothing to dampen Locklear's mood. The investigation was coming to the end. He had solved the more recent part of the case and the testimony of Stoll's surviving goon, who admitted to carrying out the attempted murder of Andrew Fehr at the behest of Stoll and her Uncle Jacob, would mean that the angry woman would spend the rest of her natural life in jail. The goon's description of the last moments of Helena Wyss's life had brought him to tears which he had shed in the privacy of his hotel room. Helena Wyss, he said, had fought Stoll bravely and it was their employer who had taken the woman's life and taken it, he reported, with pleasure. He also admitted to the killing of Aaron Fehr in his cabin at the pinnacle of Fehr farm on the orders of Jacob Shank. Locklear wondered if the old man had chosen the site so that, as the second son of his family, he could see the Shanks when they eventually came for him. The hired killer insisted that Samuel Shank knew nothing of the murders and that the uncle and niece had kept much of the more sinister side of the business from him. Locklear wasn't sure if this was true but it didn't matter now anyway. Shank was dead, Jacob was dead.

Carter stood to one side as Locklear and Lennox dug the

land beneath the tree where only days before Helena Wyss had been strung up and where Locklear himself had been saved by the kindness of Luke Fehr.

He glanced around himself and knew the man was watching from the distance. He could feel his eyes, his brooding presence and wondered how a man like Luke Fehr could go back to living a normal life after so many years living in the shadows.

A loud clink rang out as Lennox's shovel met with hard metal. With renewed energy Locklear and he shovelled off the sodden earth until a large box was revealed. They freed the earth from around its sides and then, with great difficulty, hauled the leaden box from its ancient grave.

They laid it on the ground and sat back panting from its weight.

Locklear knelt on the cold wet ground and ran his hands over the top of the box. He looked upwards into the tree and tried to visualise Helena Wyss alive, watching him uncover the secrets that in all that time had been so close, but it was his mother's eyes he saw and he realised then what Wachiwi had been trying to tell him that day he climbed the tree – the day that he saw her image surrounded by pearls – that it was here in this spot that the secrets to his case lay. It was not something he would ever tell his troopers, or even Kowalski. No one would ever understand or believe him. It was something he hardly believed himself or understood.

"Should we open it here?" Carter said.

Mendoza produced the huge, ancient key and slid it into the lock. Surely it would have rusted over the years? But with one swift click it turned. She pulled back the clasp and opened the box, hoping her boss would not be disappointed.

All four stood and stared down at its contents.

"No wonder he needed a horse," Mendoza breathed. She knelt and ran her hands through the heavy coins. "There are hundreds of them. Carter, are you sure these coins are worth nothing?"

Carter smiled. "Well, let's put it this way, you won't be exchanging any of them for dollars at Wells Fargo!"

Locklear dug his hands deep into the box and rummaged around.

"What are you looking for, sarge?"

"Pearls."

Mendoza laughed. "Now – *those* I could use."

Locklear stopped when he felt something different between his fingers. He pulled it from under the heavy coins. A string of pearls.

"Sarge! How did you know there were pearls in there?"

Locklear sat back and thought about what answer he'd give. Some of the response he decided to give was true, so he wasn't lying. Not altogether anyhow.

"Just a hunch. I figured the Shanks must have suspected that the coins were worthless and even if they weren't they're stolen goods. They couldn't offload them even if they wanted to. They always knew there was something else in the box."

Locklear dug his hands in again and pulled out another necklace, then another followed by two gem-stoned rings.

"Looks like Grant had a sideline going as he made his way through the south. I bet much of this belongs to that old lady who put him up."

Locklear stood and looked down at his filthy trousers.

He wiped the rain from his face and glanced up higher into the tree line where he thought, for just a moment, that he saw Luke Fehr standing in a clearing that did not exist. He blinked. When he opened his eyes the man was gone.

The rain began to beat down hard on the group. Locklear leaned back and let the rain pour down his face. It was over. He had solved the case. Past and Present. It was time to go home.

Chapter 32

The short drive to the Schumer household one week later was a task Locklear was happy to be charged with. He glanced at Anabel Schumer, recently released from a New York hospital and escorted by plane by the recently promoted Robbins, as she sat in the passenger seat beside him. The marks on the woman's face would heal and in time, he hoped, the mental scars of her days in the captivity of Beth Stoll's men and their threats to hurt her family if she didn't comply with them would fade and the woman would get on with life back in her home town.

As he pulled over to the kerb Anabel wrapped her arms around his neck and kissed him. He patted her arm as it crossed his chest but did not turn to look at her.

"Thank you," she said.

He waited kerbside and watched for only a moment as she hugged her father and grandfather at the door but drove off before the girl's father had a chance to thank him.

Anabel had only made it as far as her first bus changeover and the five-hour stopover gave the goons ample time to catch up where they laid in wait for the vulnerable woman. She never made it onto her final bus to Minnesota and remained captive until Stoll came up with a good use for her lookalike – to impersonate her in New York and provide her with an alibi while she committed murder in Harrisonburg.

Peter and Helena Wyss had left their farm to the Fehr siblings; the will had been written in a solicitor's office in Richmond seven years before when the Wysses had first fostered three of the Fehr children. The gift would, Locklear hoped, provide Luke Fehr with a means to make a living from farming. Locklear wondered if the man now slept in a bed, in a house, with his siblings, knowing that he and his family were safe. The transition from nomadic to settled living was a difficult one, a transition Locklear himself was familiar with.

At Dayton police station, he watched from the periphery as Carter and his wife proudly showed off their new baby girl on a brief visit to the station. Carter had handed in his notice as soon as the treasure was lifted from the ground and Lennox had gladly accepted it. He walked over to Locklear who stood alone at the window and handed the baby to him.

"Oh no, Carter, don't do that. I don't know how …"

"It's fine. I wanted to introduce you to Sara – Sara Carter."

Locklear looked down at the sleeping baby.

"Your wife doesn't mind?"

Carter glanced over at his wife who was talking to cops in the corner.

"No. She thinks the name is fitting. To celebrate new beginnings and acknowledge what is past," he replied.

"What are you going to do now?"

Carter smiled and the boyish man who had met Locklear on his first day on the case returned.

"I've accepted a research position at Virginia's Commonwealth University in the fall. I'll be getting back to what I always wanted to do. It'll mean moving the family to Richmond. My dad's going to follow when he's well enough."

"I'm glad for you," Locklear replied.

"We'll be neighbours. I was hoping you'd come and visit. Mendoza too. We'll all be living in the same city. It'll be nice."

Locklear looked over at Mendoza who was in deep conversation with Gonzalez. He nodded but did not answer.

"Say maybe," Carter insisted.

"Maybe," Locklear replied.

He handed the sleeping infant back to her father.

"She's beautiful," he said. "Congratulations."

Locklear watched the crowd mingle in the room he would no longer now call his incident room and listened as they easily conversed with each other.

He smiled as Mendoza approached him and poured herself a coffee.

Locklear smiled. "Gonzalez, eh?"

Mendoza laughed and looked across the room at the cop.

"I'm hurt, Mendoza. All the time I thought you had eyes only for me."

The cop laughed again. "I'm going back to Richmond, Sarge. That's where I belong. I hear there's a sergeant there who has trouble keeping troopers on. Seems like they all get fed up with his idiosyncrasies and his moods. I heard he has an opening. I was thinking of applying."

Locklear laughed. "I'll keep that in mind."

"Hug?"

Locklear moved forward and pulled the woman to him. She patted his back. When he stood back there were tears in her eyes.

"Thank you," she said.

"For what?"

Mendoza wiped her eyes. "For getting over the fact that I wasn't a man," she joked.

"You're going to have to cut down on the whinging though if you're to work under me," he said.

The Pact

"See you in Richmond."

Locklear watched as she left the station and started up her busted-up car. He listened as it noisily made its way out of the lot and onto the highway which would lead her to Richmond. To home.

He took one final look around and slipped quietly out the station door. Only Carter saw him exit but said nothing. He knew the man well enough by now to know that this was the way he lived his life. Alone, aloof and in the shadows.

Locklear took one last drive around the town before starting out on the long drive to Wallens Ridge maximum security prison. Tomorrow he would see Beth Stoll and keep the promise he had made to her grandfather. He drove past the Baptist church which Carter would no doubt miss and the diner where he would miss Marilyn Monroe who he had become quite fond of. He swung a left and glanced briefly at Jack's Hideaway bar where he had almost succumbed to his disease, to his desire to quell his emotions.

Before he headed out onto the highway for the four-hour journey, he drove by Lombardi's car yard. Nicky Junior was washing cars in the lot and singing along to rap music blaring from the lot's speakers. Locklear slowed and pulled up at the kerb.

He grinned as Nicky threw the hose down to give him the finger and was about to pull away when the kid's expression changed slowly. Nicky Lombardi raised his hand and waved – an acknowledgement to the man who brought his father into his life. Locklear turned the key as Nick Lombardi Senior came to the entrance and raised his hands up. He could see the trademark cigar in the reformed criminal's left hand.

"*Stop!*" he shouted.

Locklear took his foot off the gas but kept the motor running.

"*What?*"

Nick came up to the car. "I just wanted to say thank you. What you did, I just wanted to say thanks … thanks for bringing my boy to me. I thought I was alone now. I didn't even know he existed … not until you did what you did for me."

Locklear stared straight ahead. He didn't know what to say to a man like Lombardi.

"I'm sorry for what I did … I'm sorry I …"

Locklear swung his head around.

"Don't say any more, Lombardi. Don't utter one more goddamn word."

A confession, even after all of this time, would have to be reported and Lombardi needed to be around to look after the kid.

"You knew it was me. What I never figured out was why you didn't rat me out. You could still turn me in."

Locklear wanted to tell the crook that it was because he was determined that he didn't go down for shooting him but would face trial for the manslaughter of so many others – vulnerable addicts whose lives he turned into a never-ending nightmare. He wanted this for the families whose lives would never be the same again, for the children left behind, the husbands, mothers, everyone. And to achieve that, he had needed Lombardi on the streets. But Locklear knew that there was another reason and that reason was Rosa.

"I did it for your wife. As lousy a husband as you were, she needed you. Anyway, I had no proof. I didn't get a good enough look at you. I was busy dying."

Lombardi stood back and took a deep pull on his cigar.

"You always liked my Rosa."

Locklear didn't answer. He had always been a sucker for pent-up, repressed women, especially beautiful ones.

"Anyway, I wanted to get a chance to tell you – you never owed me nothing yet you did something like this for me. Never knew people could be that way."

"Shut up, Lombardi, and just get on with your life."

Lombardi smiled. "Thank you."

Locklear pulled slowly from the kerb and headed out on the highway as the sun set in the sky. As he drove southwest on Route 81 he watched the sun as it lowered on the horizon. Purple and pink hues danced across the magnificent sky and as he drove westward would slowly turn to midnight blue before a new day dawned across the beautiful Virginian land.

Chapter 33

At eleven the following morning Locklear was already sitting in the visitor's section of Wallens Ridge prison with Lennox for their pre-arranged meeting with Beth Stoll. In the reception area, Lennox pointed to a familiar man with weary eyes sitting in the corner of a waiting area. Eric Stoll, dressed in traditional Mennonite clothes, had lost weight since Locklear had last seen him.

"He's been sleeping in his car outside of the compound grounds. Security have tried to move him on but he won't go. He comes inside every day hoping to see his sister but she refuses to see him."

Locklear passed the newly appointed pastor who, deep in thought or prayer, did not look up at the policemen.

Before they entered the area where they would meet with Stoll, Lennox put his arm forward, blocking Locklear's path.

"There's something you should know. She's appealing her incarceration on the grounds of insanity."

Locklear exhaled loudly. Stoll certainly was insane but he did not doubt that she fully understood that her actions were wrong and he believed that she had the capacity to face trial.

"Well, let's hope a jury see through it."

Locklear and Lennox chose the middle partition of the

The Pact

meeting room which at this time of the morning held no other visitors. A glass panel divided the cops from prisoners and armed guards stood on both sides of the dividing panel. Ten minutes passed before the door opened and Stoll, dressed in a prison-issue orange jumpsuit, shuffled in with a guard who had NIELSEN embroidered onto her uniform. Her legs were chained as were her hands. Her hair hung loose and appeared dirty but her face appeared as defiant, as sneering, as angry, as it did on every occasion Locklear had seen the woman. The guard pushed her hand down roughly on Stoll's shoulder and shoved her onto the waiting chair. She cried out in pain.

"Are they giving you pain medication?" he asked.

He had not intended to begin his interview with the evil woman in this way although how exactly he intended to conduct the meeting he did not know.

"That's what you came all this way for? To see if I'm getting enough aspirin?"

"We had to stop giving the medication to her, sir," Nielsen said. "She was collecting morphine pills and sleeping pills and when we insisted on supervising her swallowing them in front of us, she wouldn't take them. We were worried she'd try commit suicide."

Locklear smiled. The concern he had felt only moments before for the woman vanished in a second. Beth Stoll was still calculating, still scheming.

"Oh, Beth won't commit suicide. She loves herself too much for that. But what she will do is try to drug someone with them to assist in escape."

Nielsen smiled. "She'd need to be Houdini to get out of those chains."

"Well, you just make sure they stay on," Locklear replied.

Stoll glared at him.

Locklear lifted the box towards the window. Stoll's face remained impassive. Stone-like.

"I promised your grandfather I'd give this to you."

Stoll did not speak.

"Do you want it?"

Stoll's lips parted briefly. She licked her lips. Catlike.

She raised her hands up to the glass and touched its grimy surface.

She turned to look at Nielsen. "Can I have it, please?"

Nielsen looked to the armed guard standing on Locklear's side of the partition. He came forward and searched the box. Without speaking he emptied the dirt onto a table and searched to ensure the box was empty. He piled the dirt back in. He nodded to Nielsen.

A door at the end of the partition opened and the box was placed inside.

The armed guard on the opposite side rechecked Stoll's handcuffs which allowed for no movement. Locklear knew what the guard was doing. He was ensuring that Stoll would be unable to pick up the box to use it as a weapon.

"It's clear."

Nielsen pulled Stoll from the seat and rechecked her cuffs. The staff at Wallens Ridge were taking no chances with Stoll.

"Clear."

Stoll sat down and waited while the silver box was placed in front of her. Neilsen stood back. Locklear and Lennox watched from the other side of the partition. Stoll looked up and for a moment she did not move. She ignored Lennox and fixed her stunning eyes on Locklear.

"Look away," she ordered.

"Not a chance," Locklear replied.

"I'm entitled to privacy," Stoll growled.

Neilsen took one step forward. Stoll tensed.

"You lost all privileges the day you came here," Nielsen said. "Now, you either open that box or you go back to your cell right now. I'm sure Mary will be glad to see you back so soon."

Locklear looked at Lennox.

"The prison is overcrowded. She's been put in the same cell as Mary Gunderson."

Locklear tried to remember where he had heard that name before. His mind raced as Stoll continued her standoff. Then he remembered. Gunderson was the woman whose husband committed suicide after their daughter had been raped and murdered by the man Stoll defended and she was serving life for shooting the rapist in court. Jeb Carter had told him that Mary Gunderson had learnt fast about life in the maximum-security prison and had become as violent as the other inmates in the years she had been here.

Locklear understood Stoll's urgent need to be declared insane. She wasn't going to last the week.

Stoll reached forward and opened the upper section of the box slowly.

"It's empty but there's a section below," Locklear offered.

Lennox, thinking Locklear had gone soft, looked at the sergeant.

Locklear knew what he was doing. He wanted to see Stoll's face when she realised the lower chamber of the box was also empty.

Stoll held the lid upwards to block the cop's view of the box.

"Did you look in it?" she asked.

"Funny, your grandfather asked me the same question."

Stoll knew she was not going to get an answer. She looked behind to Neilsen.

"Don't think you're taking that to your cell," Neilsen said. "It'll be held for you until your rel ... it'll be passed on to your next of kin."

Neilsen had been about to say *'until your release'* but stopped herself in time. Everyone there, everyone except perhaps Stoll, knew she was never getting out of there alive.

She held the lid up as high as she could and rummaged

around the base of the box. Locklear watched as the frantic woman began to push the base. When nothing moved, she began to pull, grip, tear.

"Are you looking for something, Beth?" he asked.

Stoll slammed the lid shut and stared at Locklear. Hot, angry tears welled in her eyes.

"It's empty, Beth. We got everything – the coins – they're worthless by the way but you already knew that. It was the jewellery you were after. We had someone value it. Turns out some of those gems are very valuable. You would have got enough money to start a new life anywhere you wanted. If you had gotten away with it."

Stoll tried to lift the box, presumably to throw it at the glass panel protecting Locklear. Nielsen moved forward and in one swoop lifted the box and pushed Stoll's head onto the table. She squirmed and tried to push back. The armed guard made ready. Stoll could see him on the periphery. She relaxed and did not move until Nielsen moved back. Neilsen moved to give the box to the armed guard at the end of the room who would put it in storage for the woman until her fate was decided.

"Don't bother. I don't want it," she said.

Locklear stood. "Your grandfather asked me to ensure you got the box."

Stoll curled up her lips and sneered at him. "So that I could use what he knew was inside to get away. I was never interested in a piece of dirt from the old country and neither was he. You should give it to my brother. It's the kind of thing he would cherish."

"If you survive this place, Stoll, and I doubt you will, you might get out in about fifty years. I'll be long dead by then and you'll be an old woman. It's 2016 now and that box has been in your family for three hundred years and was missing for the last one hundred and fifty of those. Your ancestors had to leave their homeland because they were persecuted for

The Pact

their beliefs. They carried anything of value they could sell in that box so they could start a new life in America, to give you the life you have today. A life that you threw away."

Locklear stopped talking to see if his words had any impact on the woman. They didn't.

"But you were only interested in what was inside it, what good it could do you. I feel sorry for you, Beth. I really do."

Stoll looked at Neilsen and stood slowly.

"Take me back."

Neilsen pulled the woman backwards and twisted her until she faced the door.

"Stoll?"

She turned her head to take one last look at Locklear.

"It's a good year to put things right."

The door buzzed open and Stoll disappeared from view.

Locklear waited until the armed guard retrieved the box and gave it back to him.

In the reception area he approached Eric Stoll and sat down beside him.

"Eric?"

Eric Stoll looked up. Locklear could see the utter grief, the despair, the hopelessness etched on the kind man's face. Locklear held the box and placed it into Eric's hands. He opened his pocket and lifted the letter written by Eli Shank's mother and placed it on top of the box.

"This is the box that caused the rift between you and the Fehr family. It was carried by your ancestor Jan Shank in 1711 as he left to come to America. You and your daughters are the last of the family now. I hope you treasure it."

"My sister!" he wept.

"Your sister is gone, Eric. The woman behind these walls is not her. I think it's best you remember her as the little girl she was. You can't help her."

"I can pray for her."

"Yes, you can but that's all you can do. Go home, Pastor.

Go home to your family and try to build a bridge over the rift in your community. Forgive the Fehrs. They were innocent victims just like Beth once was."

Eric nodded but did not move. Locklear left the pastor sitting there, staring at the box, wondering what might have been and what would happen now.

He left the prison and made his way to his car. It was still only 1pm and there was one last thing he needed to do before he travelled that last piece of road to Richmond.

Chapter 34

The entrance to the Fehr farm in Dayton somehow looked different to Locklear as he approached the holding from the south. The summer was almost over and the sun was already setting in the red sky as he parked his car and walked towards the barn. The house, he noticed, no longer looked abandoned. The screen door had been repaired and no longer emitted the banshee-like screech which had unnerved Mendoza in the first days of the extraordinary investigation. The front door, which had been absent, was replaced and the wood porch looked freshly swept and scrubbed. The windows, once dusty and neglected, were freshly washed and gleamed in the light of the setting sun. A warm wind blew around the yard and seemed to whisper to Locklear. A breath of hope, of fresh possibilities, a new future.

He pushed on and glanced briefly down the valley to the home the Wysses had tried hard to defend. Their farm now belonged to Luke Fehr and he hoped that the man would finally be able to live the life he had wanted and had executed a long hard battle to protect. Locklear inhaled the fresh warm air and knew this would be the last time he would stand on this soil. He loved these places, the open air, the sun, the green. It spoke to his heart in a way cities never could. He knelt down and rubbed the dry, lifeless earth between his fingers just as he had done on the first day the investigation began. The eyes which had followed him as soon as he set foot on the farm were behind him now, stunning grey eyes speckled with the last rays of sun, of hope, that there could be better times. Locklear did not move.

"You always knew there was no curse on this farm, didn't you? That's why you read all those books on geology, books you shared with Andrew. You realised that the dry soil and absent grass was due to natural causes. Didn't you?"

"Yes," a voice responded.

Locklear tried not to react. He gently returned the soil to the ground. He stood to his full height but did not turn around.

"And the night your brother was strung up here. You were here, waiting. You knew it was going to happen. I guess Plett told you or perhaps it was you who told him. One way or the other, you were both here to save him and you did."

Locklear received no answer but could hear footsteps moving closer.

Locklear pointed to his left but kept his back to the man.

"And that outhouse there – that's the one Sara locked you in the morning you were going to hang yourself. You still believed in the pact then but you were only twenty-one years old. I guess you've learnt a lot since then. I guess you began to see through it the day Maria Whieler gave you her mother's journal and when the Ropps and the Yoders disappeared. You knew then that this was nothing but a farce, that greed and not honour was at the centre of the pact."

"I knew even before then. My father Isaiah knew it too. He fought Shank until he took his last breath. There was no way he was going to take his life and leave us motherless children to his mercy."

Locklear breathed in the melodious sounds of the voice of

Luke Fehr. The man did not have the harsh accent of Beth Stoll or the sharp tones of Samuel or Jacob. His voice was soft, quiet, gentle.

Another step crunched on the dry earth.

"What I don't understand is why *you* nearly took that step, to kill yourself when your siblings depended on you. Why you didn't go to the police for help?"

Locklear heard the man take a deep intake of breath and exhale. He could feel the breath leaving Luke Fehr's lungs and knew the man was standing right behind him.

"There was no one I could trust. I had no what you English called *leverage*. Not until Maria gave me the journal. Then I had something that the Shanks wanted. I had some control. I had advantage. I could finally protect my family."

"So you fought the battle alone, living out there in the woods, digging for something that did not exist."

"I did not know that it did not exist. I believed the story handed down from one Fehr to another."

"There are pieces of that story missing, pieces that I still don't understand. Will you tell me now? Now that you are all safe."

Luke Fehr exhaled. Locklear could feel his cool breath on the back of his neck. He turned slowly and saw the face of the man up close for the first time with the sun in his eyes. Luke Fehr was dressed in Mennonite clothing. Gone was the casual clothing, the brown boots and the cowboy hat. Dark black trousers and a white collarless shirt had replaced the jeans and check shirt. The plain clothes only served to accentuate the man's unique looks, his chiselled jaw, the light brown hair flecked with gold, and the iridescent eyes.

Luke retold the story of how Grant, threatened with death by Eli, promised the insane Mennonite a treasure more valuable than the worthless box he had taken from him. Grant assured Eli that he would give him a bounty of pearls, diamonds and valuable gems that could offer a new life to the man that had been shunned from his family at the loss of the silver box. He convinced Eli that the treasure had been buried on the Fehr farm but that he was no longer sure of its exact position. Eli believed Grant and, desperate for the box to regain his father's approval and the treasure of the jewels if his favour was not forthcoming, he forced the Fehr brothers to dig with Grant all day and into the night until the bounty was found.

"He was crazy," Locklear offered.

"He had darkness of the heart," Luke responded.

"But the Fehrs knew the real reason he wanted the treasure. Your ancestors knew it contained stolen treasure and that Eli was lying. Yet your ancestors remained quiet. They did not tell the community, the elders."

"My ancestor had made a commitment and we had to honour it. We were now outsiders. We had no right to come to church, to worship, to dress in plain clothes. We were stripped of everything we knew. The elders would not have listened to my ancestors. Daniel hoped that when he found the box everything would go back to normal, everything would be OK, and we could be Mennonite again."

"But the box was never here on the farm," Locklear said.

"No."

"And you knew this?"

"I felt it."

"Why did you keep digging?"

"Because I had to keep hope. They came here. Shank's son and his men. They told me I was running out of time to save what was left of my family."

"Why did you not leave?"

"This is our home."

Fehr followed the sergeant's eyes along the old clapboard, along the roof and gutters which had been replaced by the community who came out of their fields to help the Fehrs. Men came carrying wood, saws, nails and set to work alongside the eldest Fehr wordlessly. Others repaired the barn door, chopped wood, painted, washed, scrubbed. Eric Stoll arrived with a cow in calf. The new pastor set the animal down in the barn and left without speaking but it was a start. It was an offering, a sign that there might now be peace between the two families. As the sun set on the farm at the end of the long day, more women arrived and set down food on tables carried by the men from nearby farms. When the work was done and the house finally ready to offer rest to the returning family, the community sat and ate with the Fehr orphans. Their fear of the wrath of Shank was gone.

Locklear turned to look once more at Luke Fehr.

"What will you do now?"

Luke Fehr looked to the heavens and took a deep breath from the cooling evening air. The sun had set behind the wood at the back of the Wysses' farm and the trees appeared to glow in pinky misty rays.

"I will work this farm and Helena's also. I will care for my siblings and live a good life. That's all I ask. That's all I need."

"Where are they?"

Luke Fehr looked up at the window and signalled. The door opened and Esther Fehr, dressed in a plain grey dress and white lace bonnet walked out followed by Abigail. Last to exit was Andrew dressed in the same black suit and white shirt as his older brother. Locklear looked at the vulnerable boy and smiled at him. The marks on his neck had paled but would be a lifelong reminder of the pact that had raged for one hundred and fifty years and was now, hopefully, and finally, over.

Locklear put out his hand.

Luke took it. "Thank you," he said.

Locklear did not speak. He waved and walked down to where his car waited to take him on the three-hour journey home.

As he neared Richmond, his mood lowered as the green fields

and small farming villages gave way to the high-rise blocks and straight lines of planned suburbs of the city he called home. He crossed the river and drove by his precinct on the corner of Greyland and South Meadow. Locklear turned down South Meadow and passed the turn-off for Rosewood Avenue where he now knew Mendoza lived with her widowed mother and her son. At the end of South Meadow he took a sharp left into Dakota Avenue where his apartment building faced the city's cemetery.

He collected his mail in the empty foyer of the quiet block, which consisted of three utility bills, and climbed the stairs to his apartment on the third floor. He opened the door and was met with stuffy smell of an airless space. Locklear glanced around the quiet apartment. On the windowsill over the kitchen sink he checked his cactus and was surprised by his disappointment that the plant was fine and did not need his immediate care. He sat down on his worn armchair in the lounge and listened to the clock ticking from the kitchen wall behind him. Locklear looked at his watch. It was barely after 11pm. He turned on the TV and waited for Kowalski to call.

The End